TEEN : D

妖怪伝

悪魔気活地

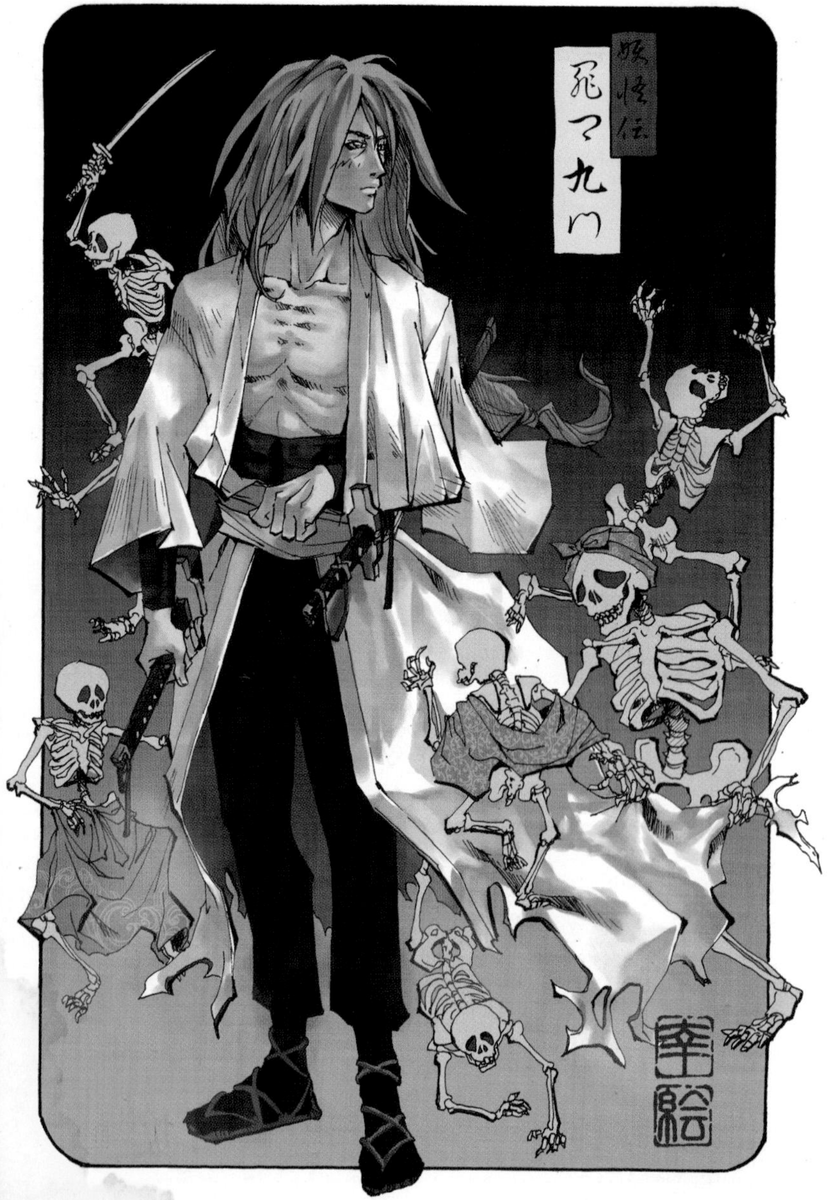
妖怪伝

Yōkaiden

1

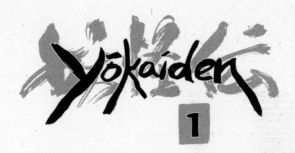

Yōkaiden

1

NINA MATSUMOTO

BALLANTINE BOOKS · NEW YORK

Yōkaiden volume 1 is a work of fiction. Names, places, and incidents are either a product of the author's imagination or are used fictitiously. Any resemblance to actual events, locales, or persons, living or dead, is entirely coincidental.

A Del Rey Trade Paperback Original

Published in the United States by Del Rey Books, an imprint of The Random House Publishing Group, a division of Random House, Inc., New York.

DEL REY is a registered trademark and the Del Rey colophon is a registered trademark of Random House, Inc.

ISBN 978-0-345-50327-5

Printed in the United States of America

www.delreymanga.com

9 8 7 6 5 4 3 2 1

CONTENTS

Yōkaiden

1

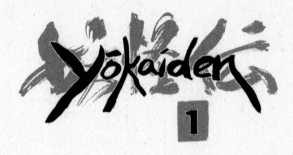

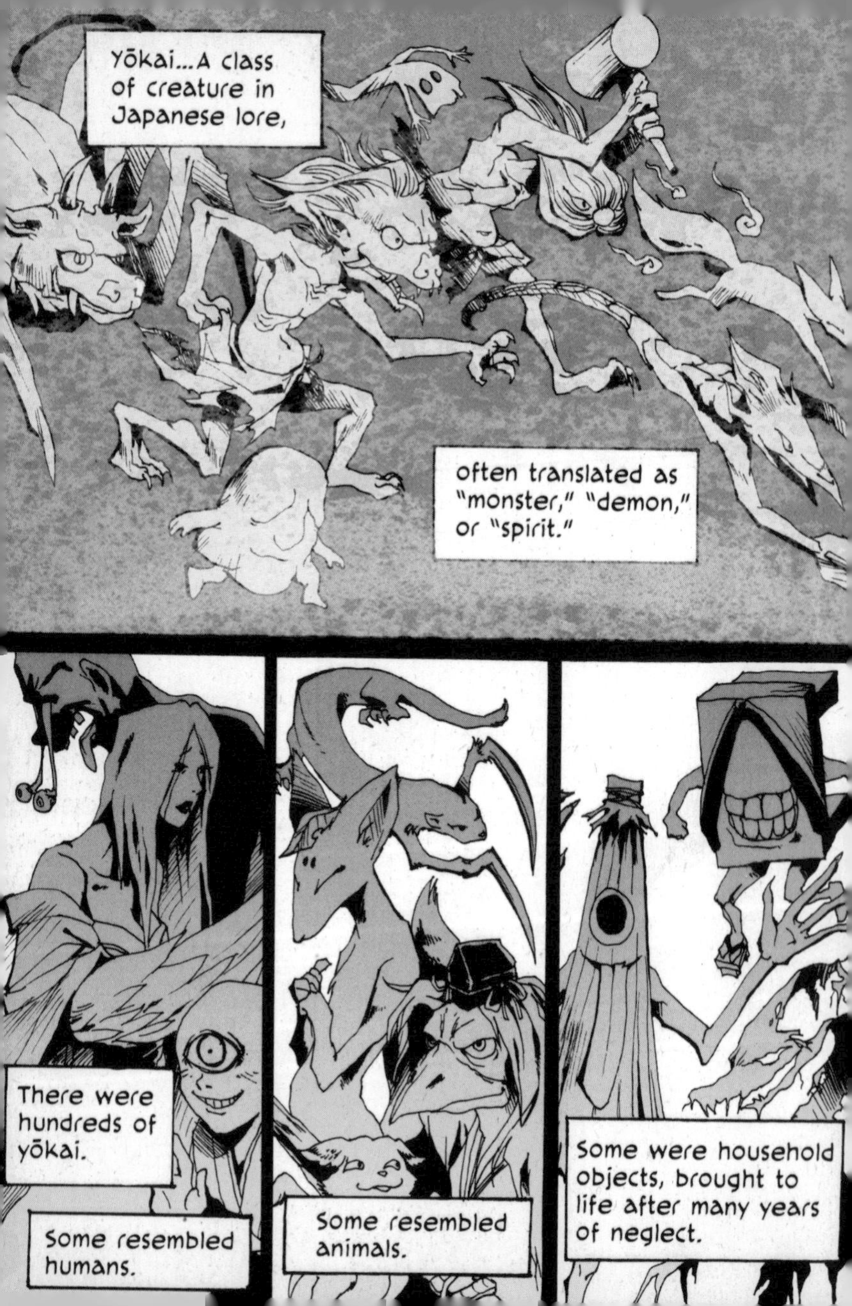
Yōkai...A class of creature in Japanese lore,
often translated as "monster," "demon," or "spirit."
There were hundreds of yōkai.
Some resembled humans.
Some resembled animals.
Some were household objects, brought to life after many years of neglect.

Born from fear, they were the source of the strange, unearthly noises at night.

They were what led people to believe they were being followed.

They were what caused the mysterious disappearances of objects and people.

Many sought out humans to play harmless pranks on them...

But some wanted blood.

As technology advanced, they vanished.

They are gone, but are not forgotten.

The world of yōkai lives on in tales, such as this one...

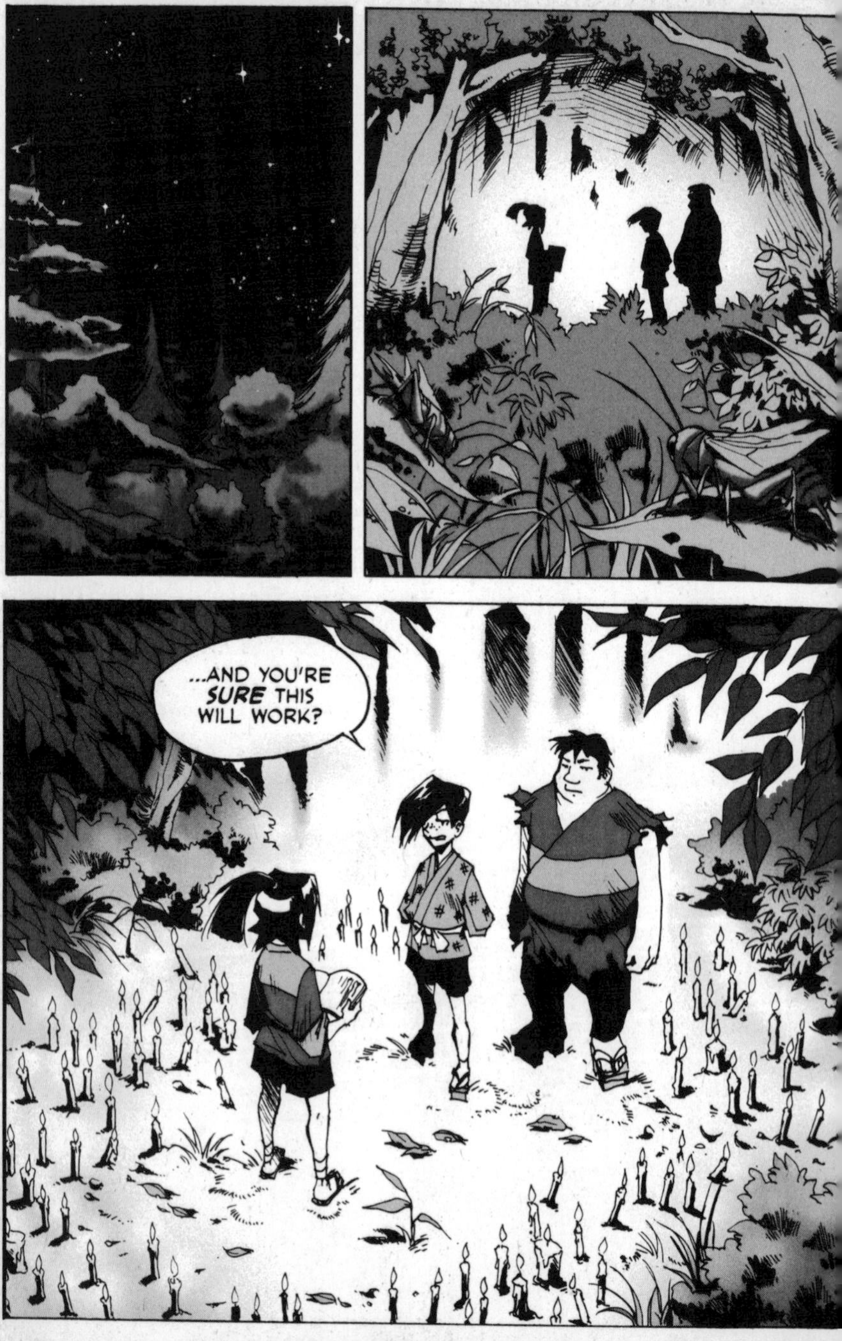
...AND YOU'RE *SURE* THIS WILL WORK?

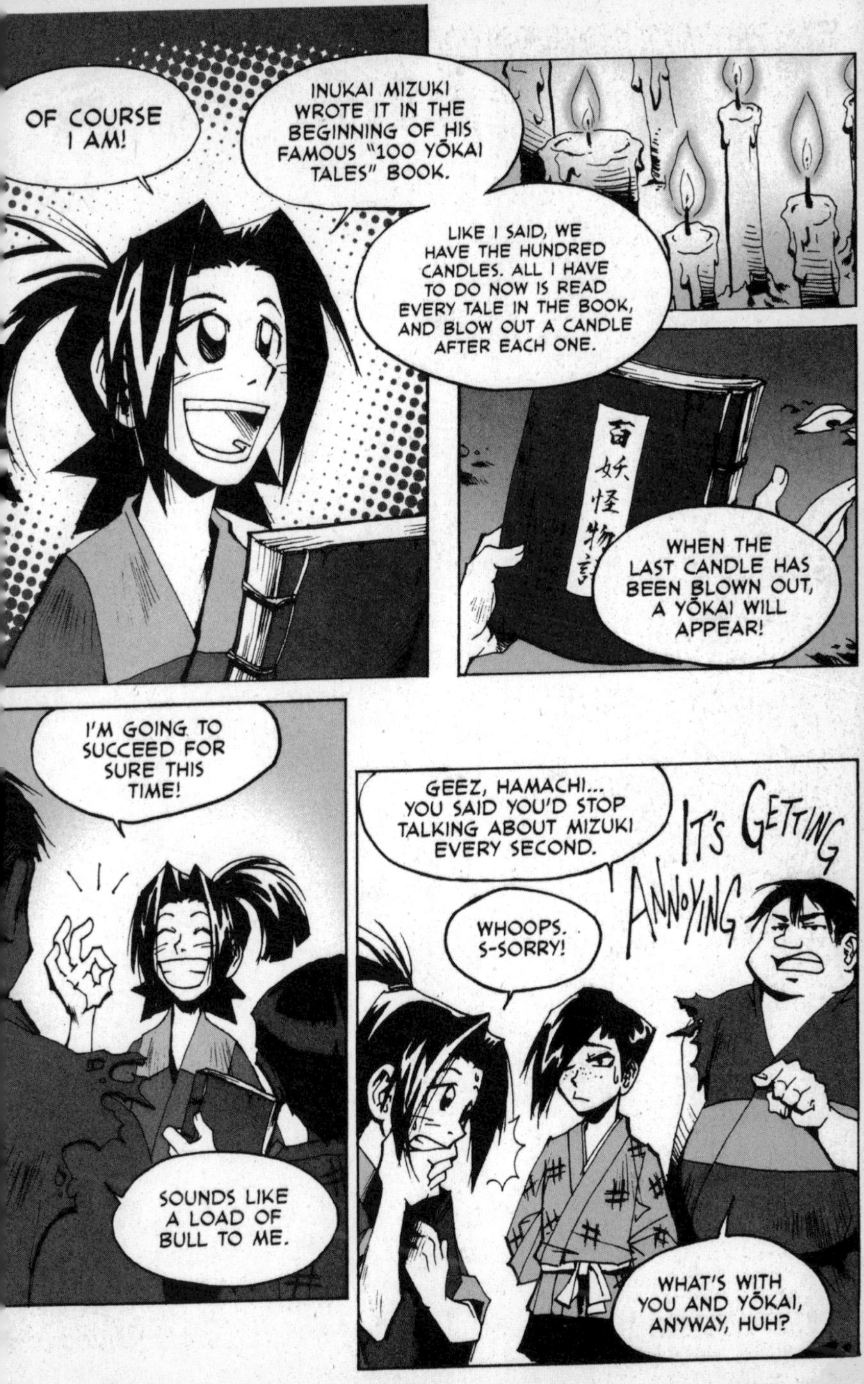
OF COURSE I AM!
INUKAI MIZUKI WROTE IT IN THE BEGINNING OF HIS FAMOUS "100 YŌKAI TALES" BOOK.
LIKE I SAID, WE HAVE THE HUNDRED CANDLES. ALL I HAVE TO DO NOW IS READ EVERY TALE IN THE BOOK, AND BLOW OUT A CANDLE AFTER EACH ONE.
WHEN THE LAST CANDLE HAS BEEN BLOWN OUT, A YŌKAI WILL APPEAR!
I'M GOING TO SUCCEED FOR SURE THIS TIME!
SOUNDS LIKE A LOAD OF BULL TO ME.
GEEZ, HAMACHI... YOU SAID YOU'D STOP TALKING ABOUT MIZUKI EVERY SECOND.
IT'S GETTING ANNOYING
WHOOPS. S-SORRY!
WHAT'S WITH YOU AND YŌKAI, ANYWAY, HUH?

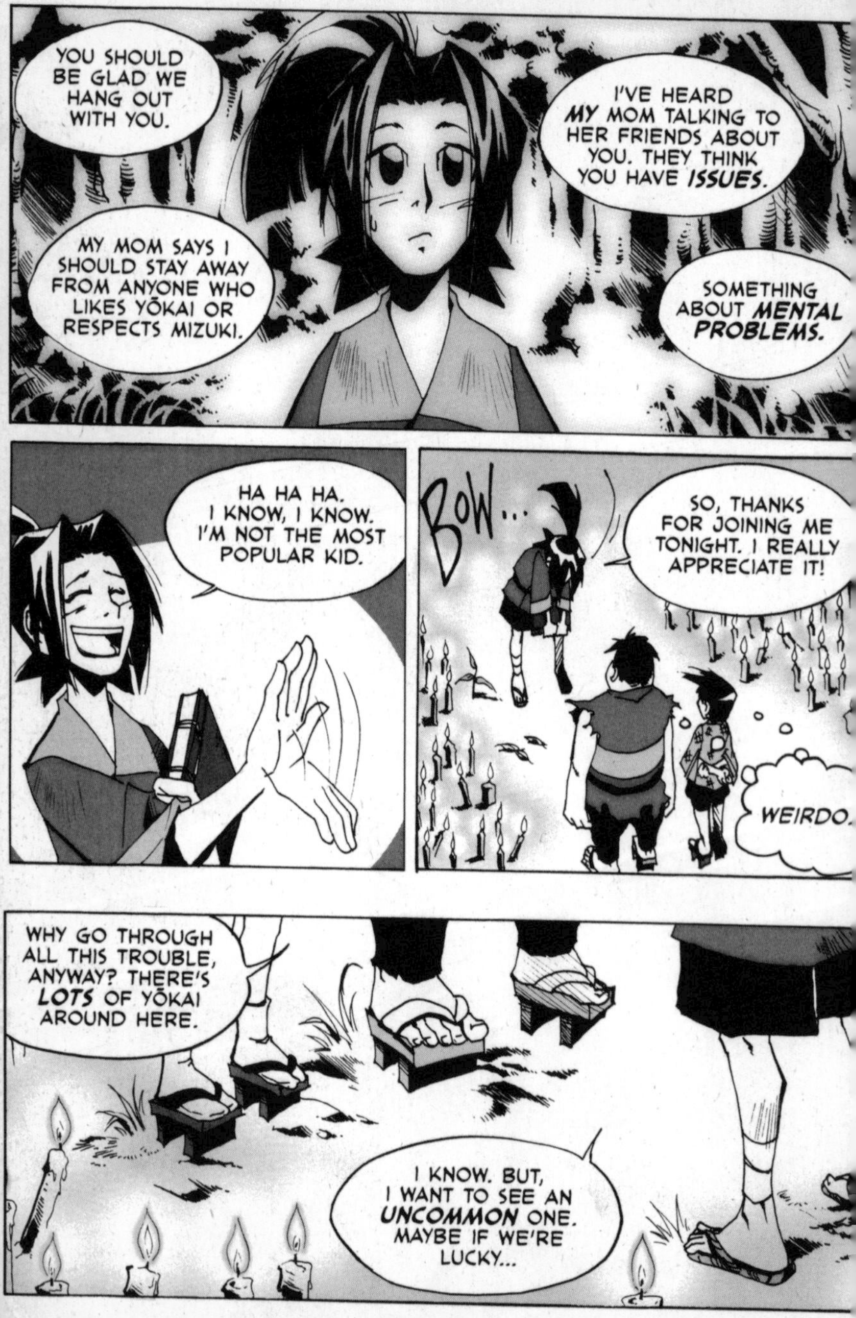
YOU SHOULD BE GLAD WE HANG OUT WITH YOU.
I'VE HEARD MY MOM TALKING TO HER FRIENDS ABOUT YOU. THEY THINK YOU HAVE ISSUES.
MY MOM SAYS I SHOULD STAY AWAY FROM ANYONE WHO LIKES YŌKAI OR RESPECTS MIZUKI.
SOMETHING ABOUT MENTAL PROBLEMS.
HA HA HA. I KNOW, I KNOW. I'M NOT THE MOST POPULAR KID.
BOW...
SO, THANKS FOR JOINING ME TONIGHT. I REALLY APPRECIATE IT!
WEIRDO.
WHY GO THROUGH ALL THIS TROUBLE, ANYWAY? THERE'S LOTS OF YŌKAI AROUND HERE.
I KNOW. BUT, I WANT TO SEE AN UNCOMMON ONE. MAYBE IF WE'RE LUCKY...

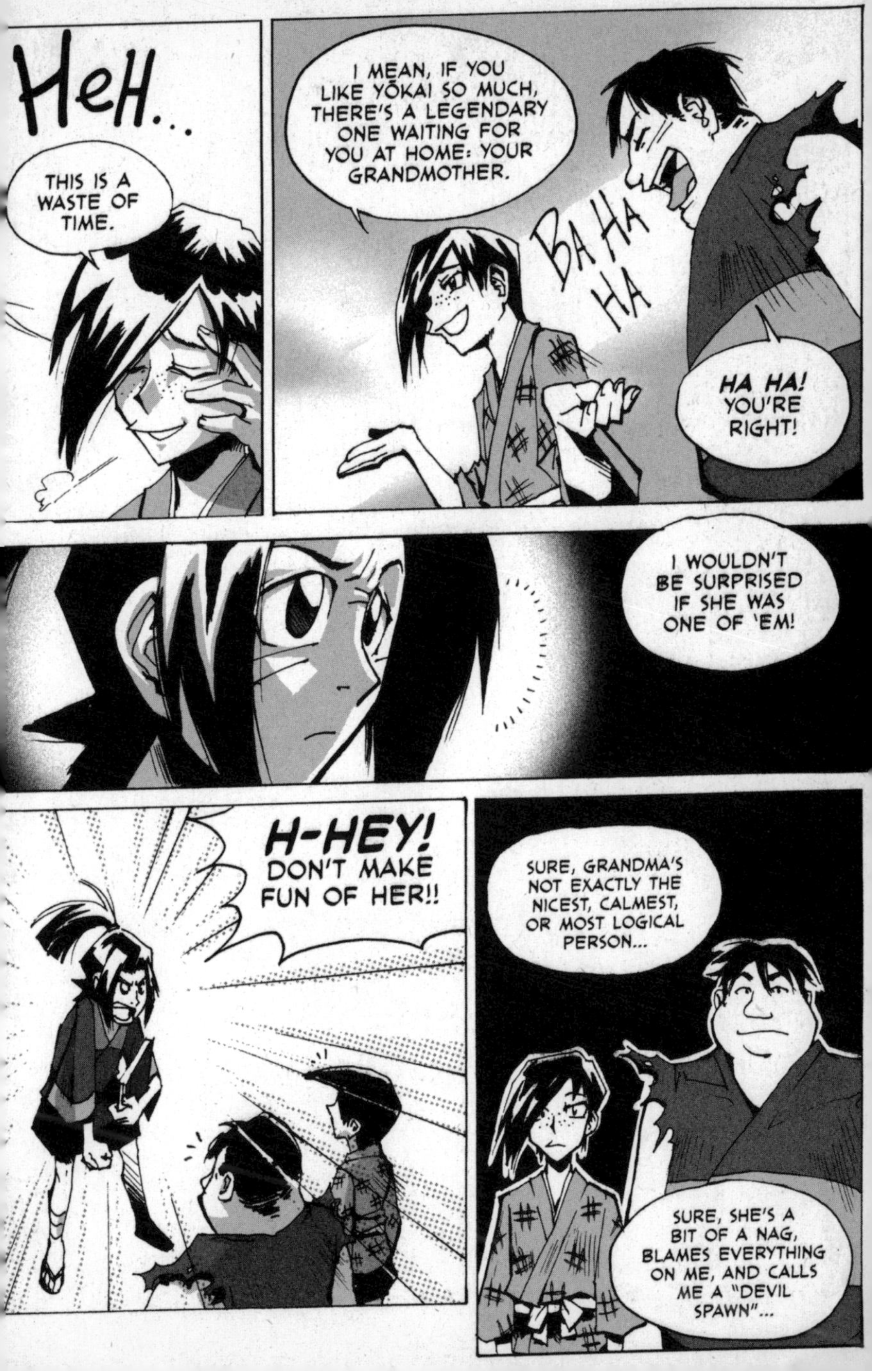
HEH...
THIS IS A WASTE OF TIME.
I MEAN, IF YOU LIKE YŌKAI SO MUCH, THERE'S A LEGENDARY ONE WAITING FOR YOU AT HOME: YOUR GRANDMOTHER.
BA HA HA
HA HA! YOU'RE RIGHT!
I WOULDN'T BE SURPRISED IF SHE WAS ONE OF 'EM!
H-HEY! DON'T MAKE FUN OF HER!!
SURE, GRANDMA'S NOT EXACTLY THE NICEST, CALMEST, OR MOST LOGICAL PERSON...
SURE, SHE'S A BIT OF A NAG, BLAMES EVERYTHING ON ME, AND CALLS ME A "DEVIL SPAWN"...

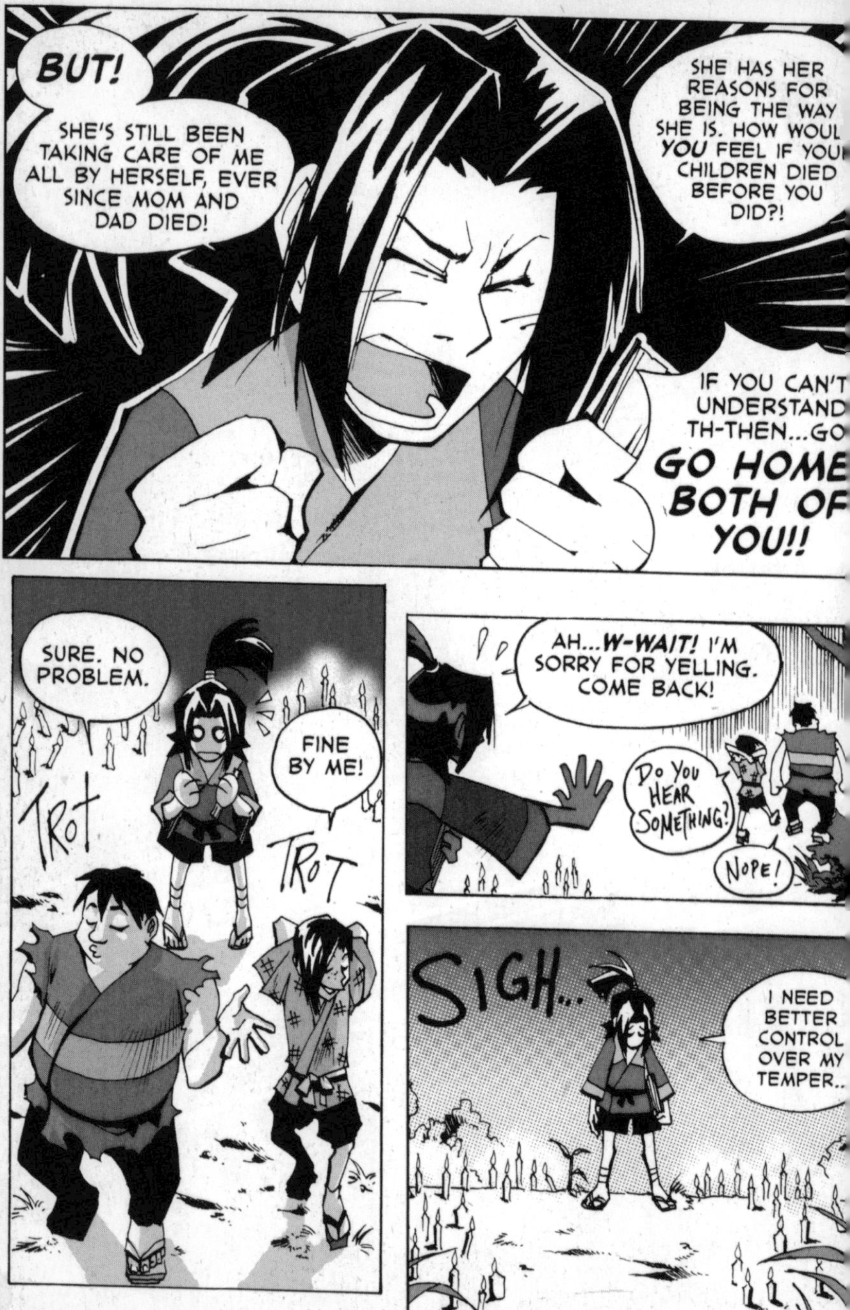
BUT!
SHE'S STILL BEEN TAKING CARE OF ME ALL BY HERSELF, EVER SINCE MOM AND DAD DIED!
SHE HAS HER REASONS FOR BEING THE WAY SHE IS. HOW WOUL YOU FEEL IF YOU CHILDREN DIED BEFORE YOU DID?!
IF YOU CAN'T UNDERSTAND TH-THEN...GO GO HOME BOTH OF YOU!!
SURE. NO PROBLEM.
FINE BY ME!
TROT
TROT
AH...W-WAIT! I'M SORRY FOR YELLING. COME BACK!
DO YOU HEAR SOMETHING?
NOPE!
SIGH...
I NEED BETTER CONTROL OVER MY TEMPER...

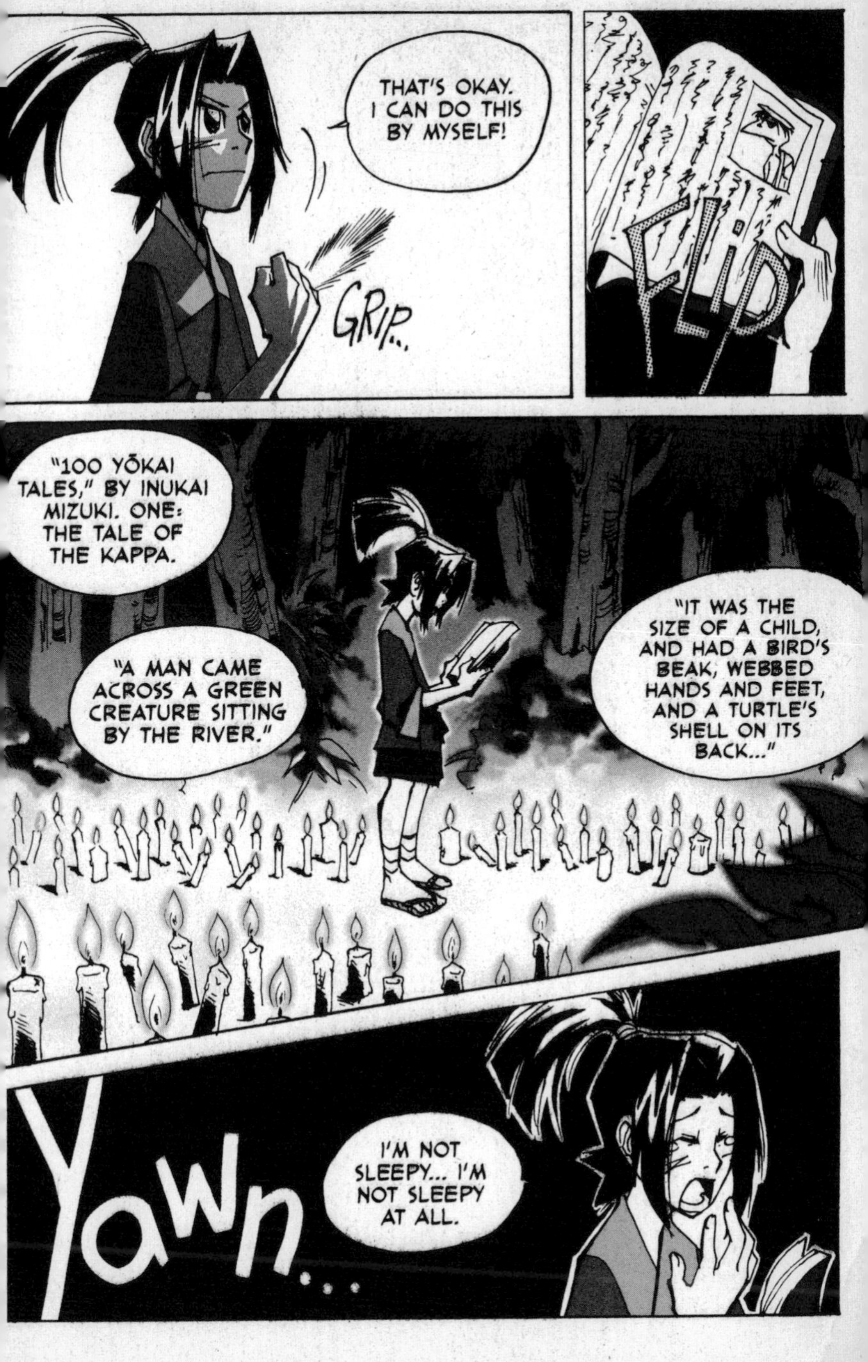
THAT'S OKAY. I CAN DO THIS BY MYSELF!
GRIP...
FLIP
"100 YŌKAI TALES," BY INUKAI MIZUKI. ONE: THE TALE OF THE KAPPA.
"A MAN CAME ACROSS A GREEN CREATURE SITTING BY THE RIVER."
"IT WAS THE SIZE OF A CHILD, AND HAD A BIRD'S BEAK, WEBBED HANDS AND FEET, AND A TURTLE'S SHELL ON ITS BACK..."
Yawn...
I'M NOT SLEEPY... I'M NOT SLEEPY AT ALL.

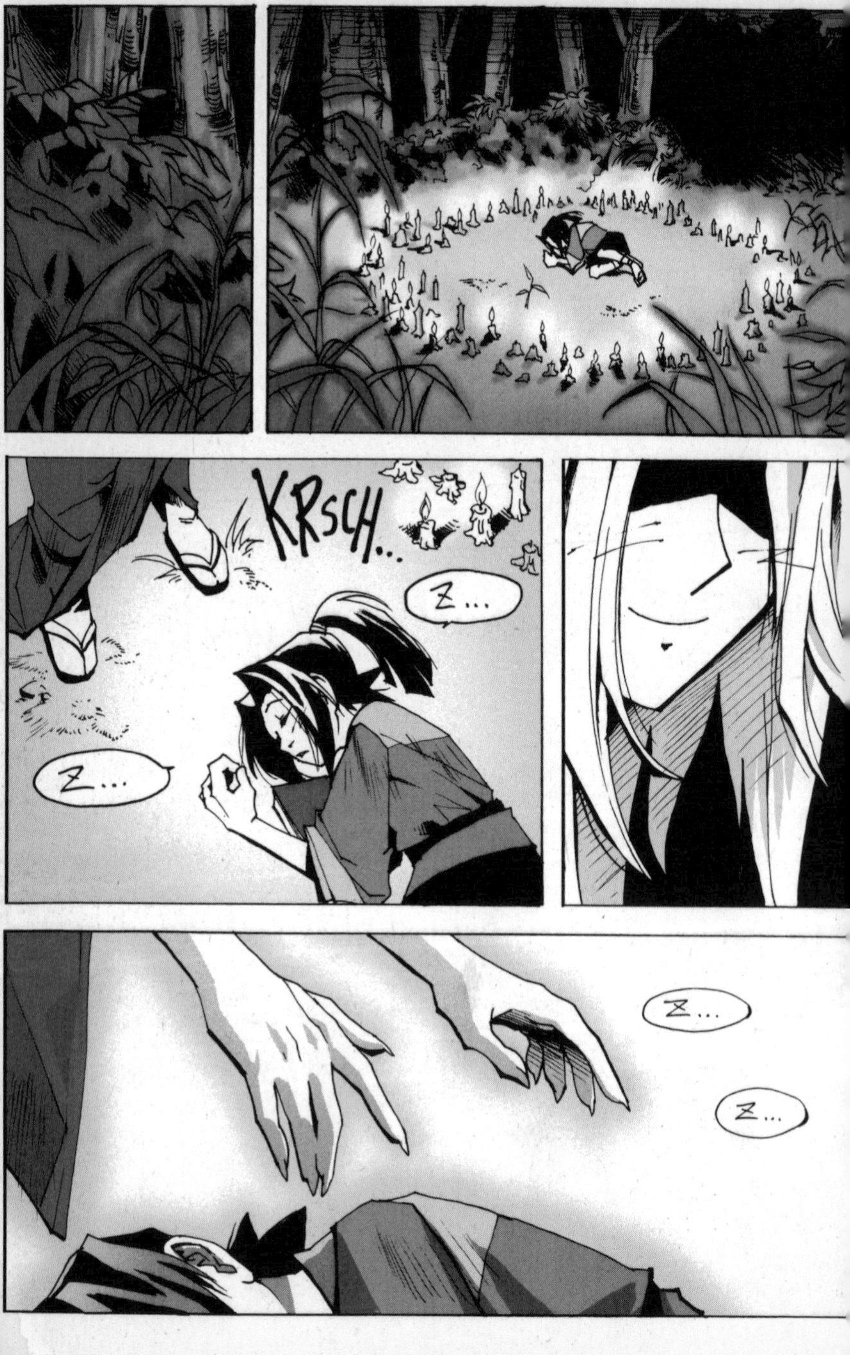
KRSCH...
Z...
Z...
Z...
Z...

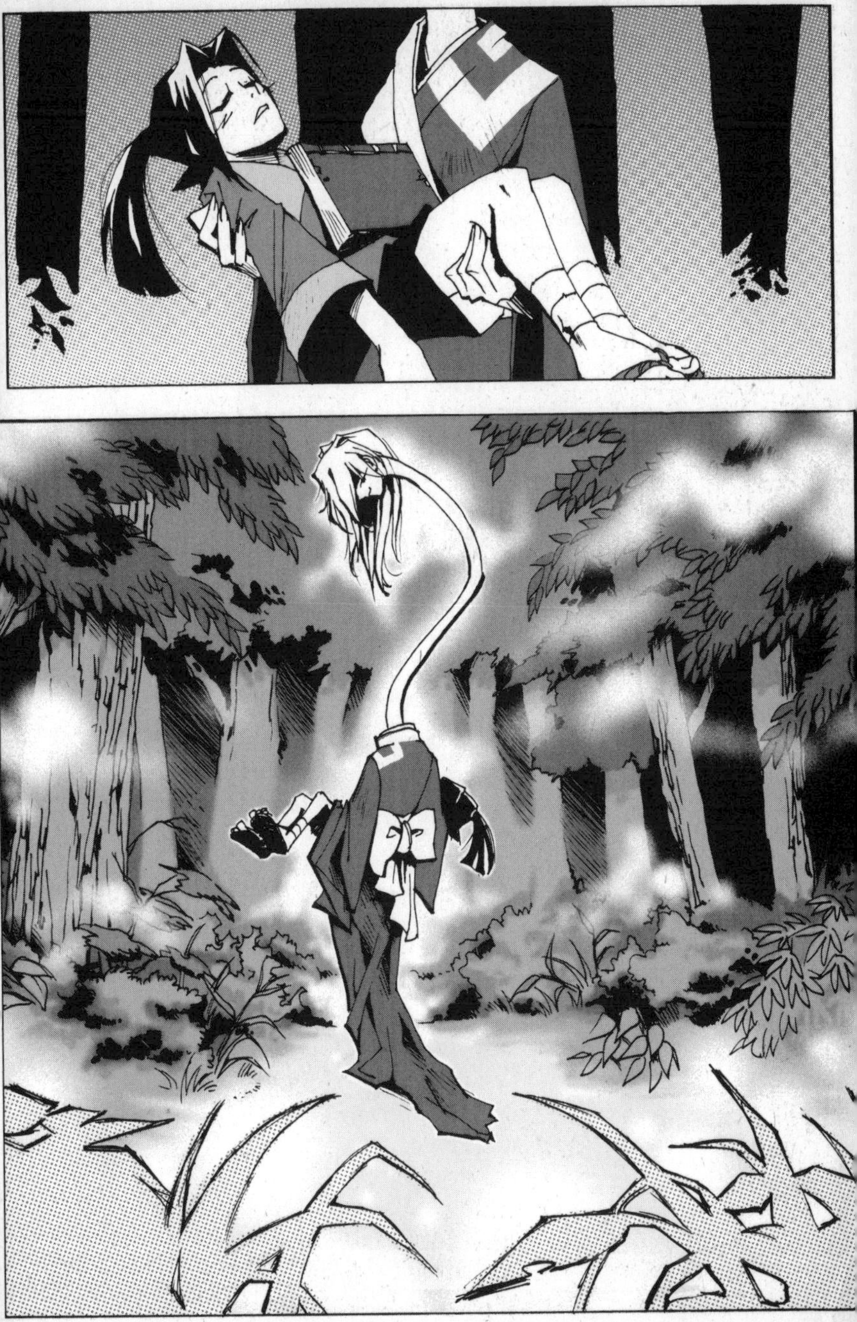

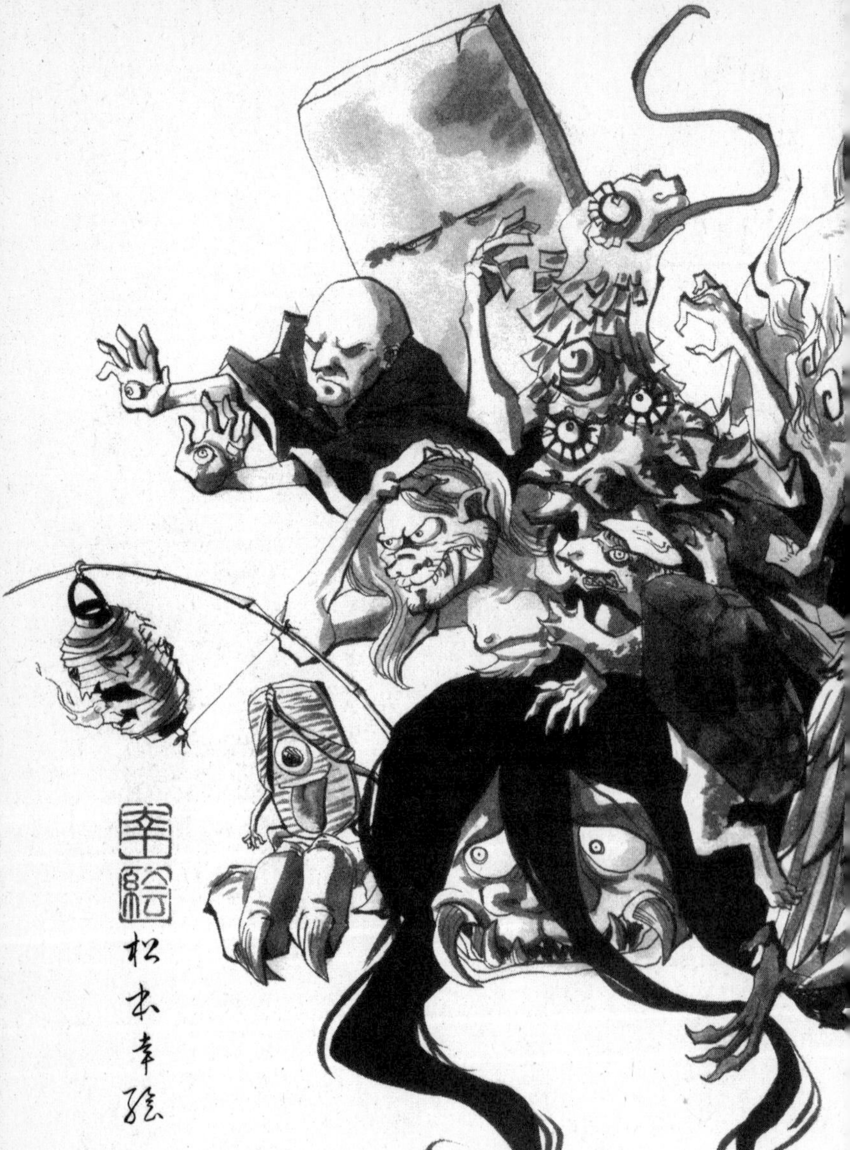
幸絵
松本幸絵

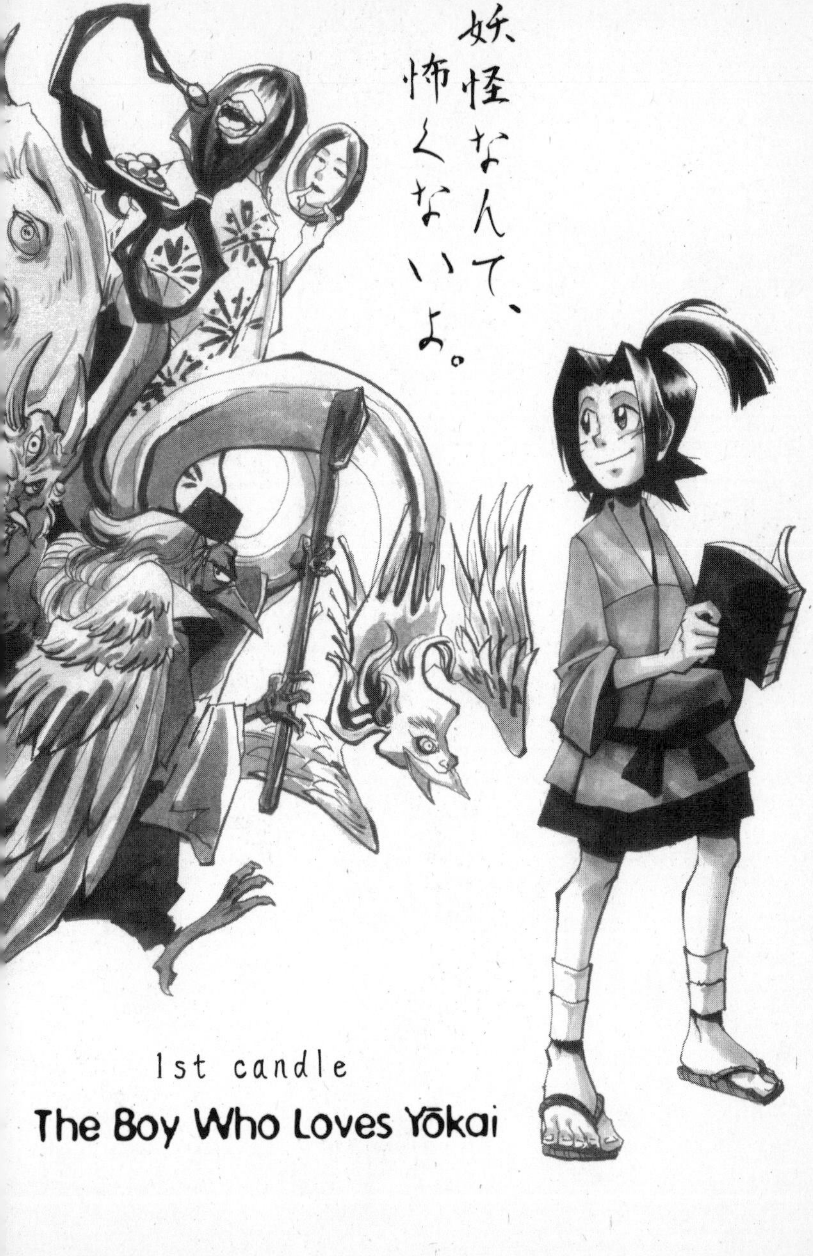
妖怪なんて、
怖くないよ。

1st candle

The Boy Who Loves Yōkai

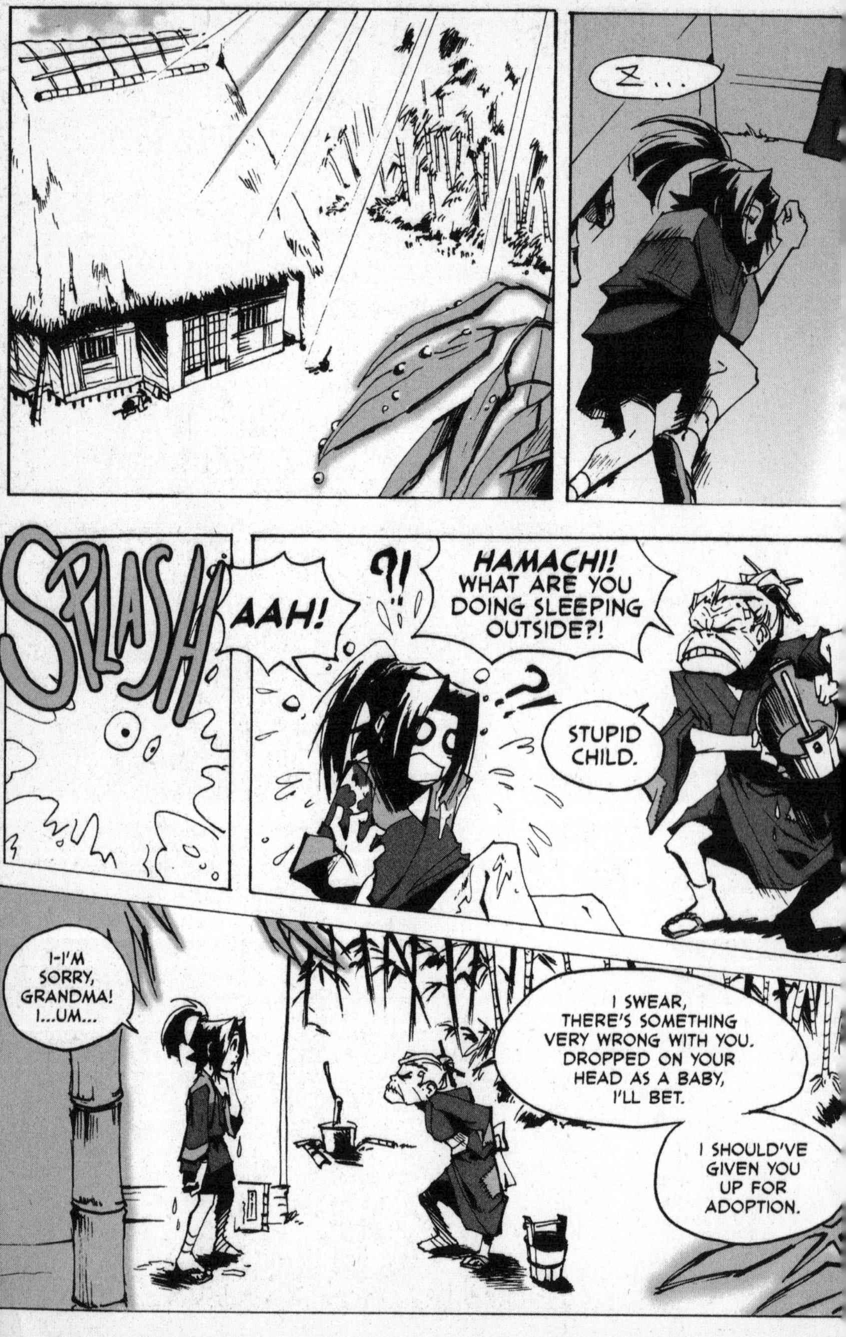
Z...
SPLASH
AAH!
?!
HAMACHI! WHAT ARE YOU DOING SLEEPING OUTSIDE?!
?!
STUPID CHILD.
I-I'M SORRY, GRANDMA! I...UM...
I SWEAR, THERE'S SOMETHING VERY WRONG WITH YOU. DROPPED ON YOUR HEAD AS A BABY, I'LL BET.
I SHOULD'VE GIVEN YOU UP FOR ADOPTION.

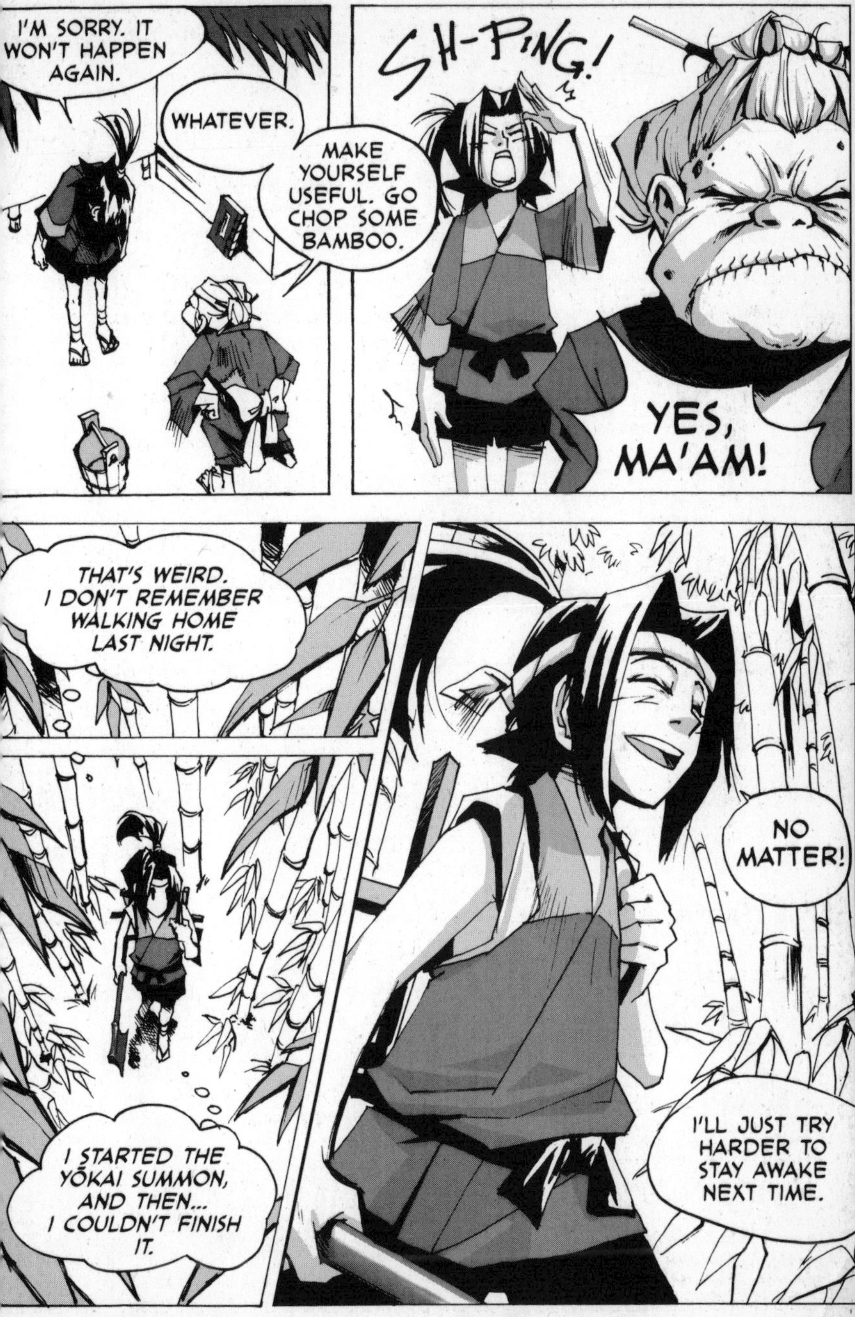
I'M SORRY. IT WON'T HAPPEN AGAIN.
WHATEVER.
MAKE YOURSELF USEFUL. GO CHOP SOME BAMBOO.
SH-PING!
YES, MA'AM!
THAT'S WEIRD. I DON'T REMEMBER WALKING HOME LAST NIGHT.
I STARTED THE YŌKAI SUMMON, AND THEN... I COULDN'T FINISH IT.
NO MATTER!
I'LL JUST TRY HARDER TO STAY AWAKE NEXT TIME.

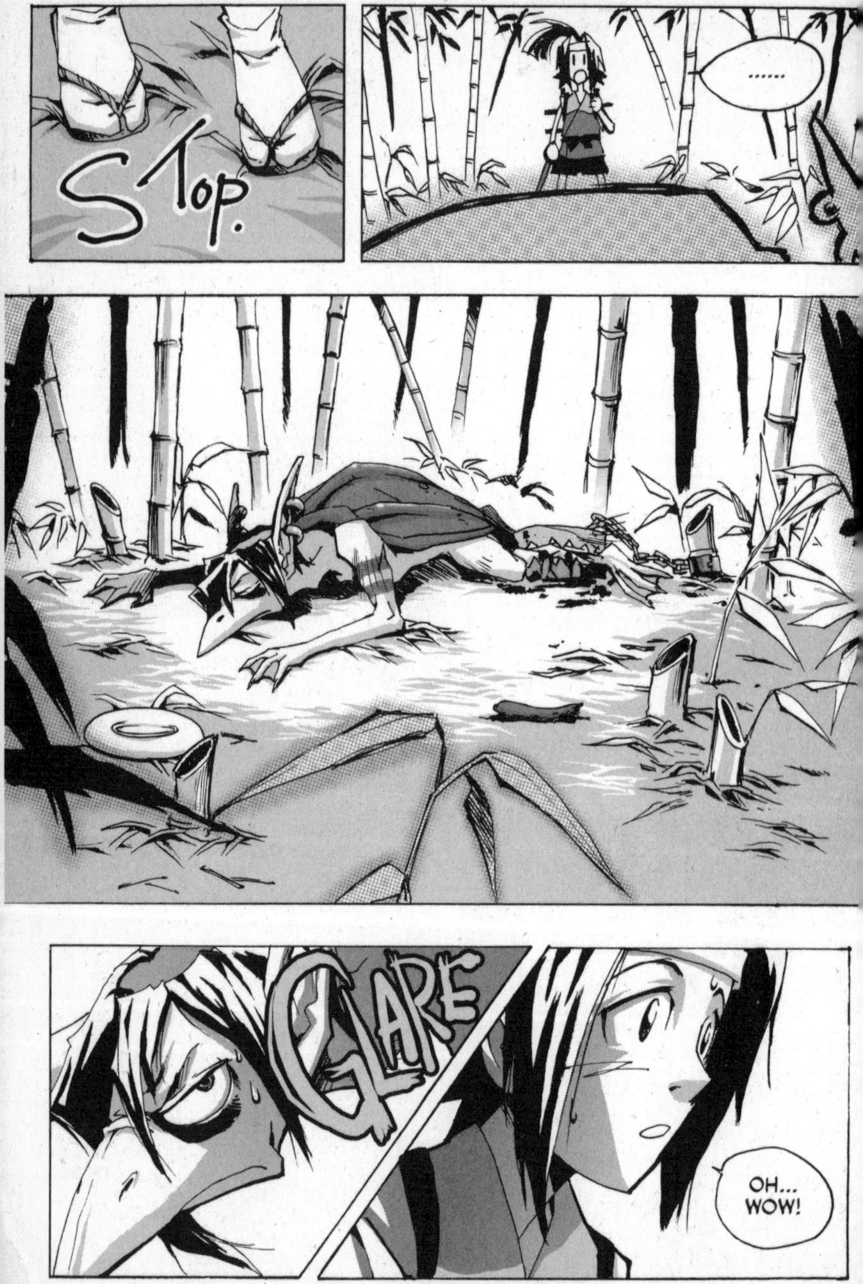
......
STOP.
OH... WOW!
GLARE

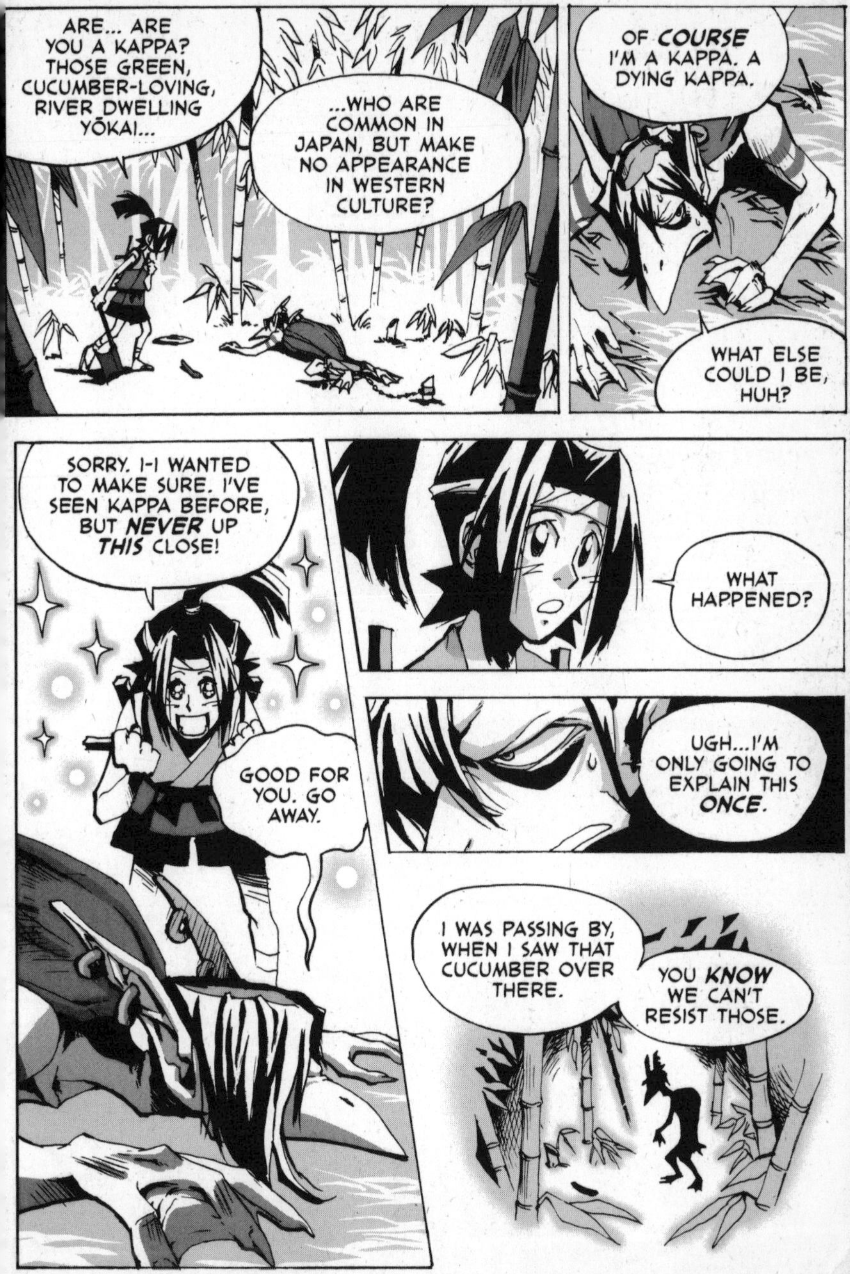
ARE... ARE YOU A KAPPA? THOSE GREEN, CUCUMBER-LOVING, RIVER DWELLING YŌKAI...
...WHO ARE COMMON IN JAPAN, BUT MAKE NO APPEARANCE IN WESTERN CULTURE?
OF COURSE I'M A KAPPA. A DYING KAPPA.
WHAT ELSE COULD I BE, HUH?
SORRY. I-I WANTED TO MAKE SURE. I'VE SEEN KAPPA BEFORE, BUT NEVER UP THIS CLOSE!
GOOD FOR YOU. GO AWAY.
WHAT HAPPENED?
UGH...I'M ONLY GOING TO EXPLAIN THIS ONCE.
I WAS PASSING BY, WHEN I SAW THAT CUCUMBER OVER THERE.
YOU KNOW WE CAN'T RESIST THOSE.

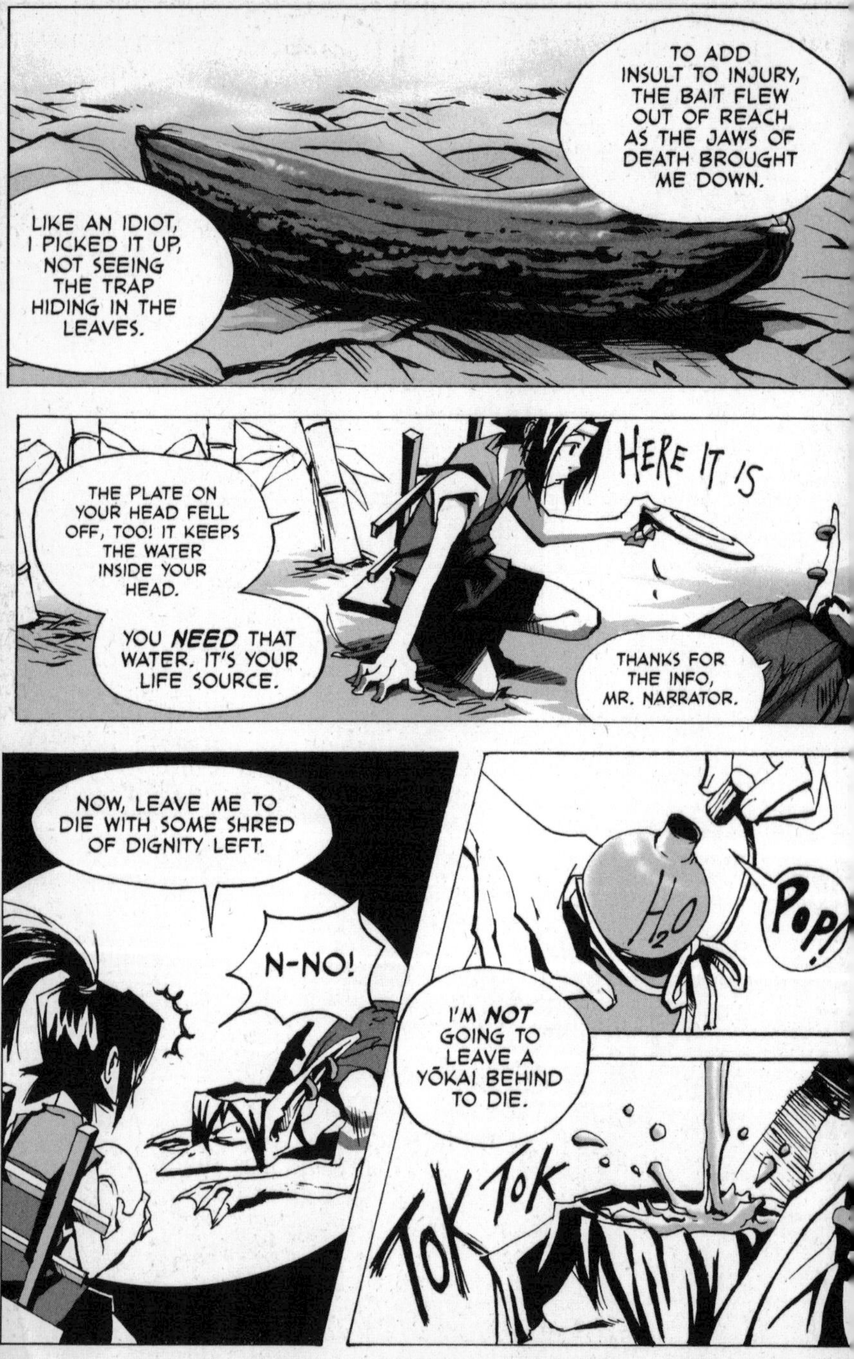
LIKE AN IDIOT, I PICKED IT UP, NOT SEEING THE TRAP HIDING IN THE LEAVES.
TO ADD INSULT TO INJURY, THE BAIT FLEW OUT OF REACH AS THE JAWS OF DEATH BROUGHT ME DOWN.
THE PLATE ON YOUR HEAD FELL OFF, TOO! IT KEEPS THE WATER INSIDE YOUR HEAD.
YOU NEED THAT WATER. IT'S YOUR LIFE SOURCE.
HERE IT IS
THANKS FOR THE INFO, MR. NARRATOR.
NOW, LEAVE ME TO DIE WITH SOME SHRED OF DIGNITY LEFT.
N-NO!
POP!
I'M NOT GOING TO LEAVE A YŌKAI BEHIND TO DIE.
TOK TOK

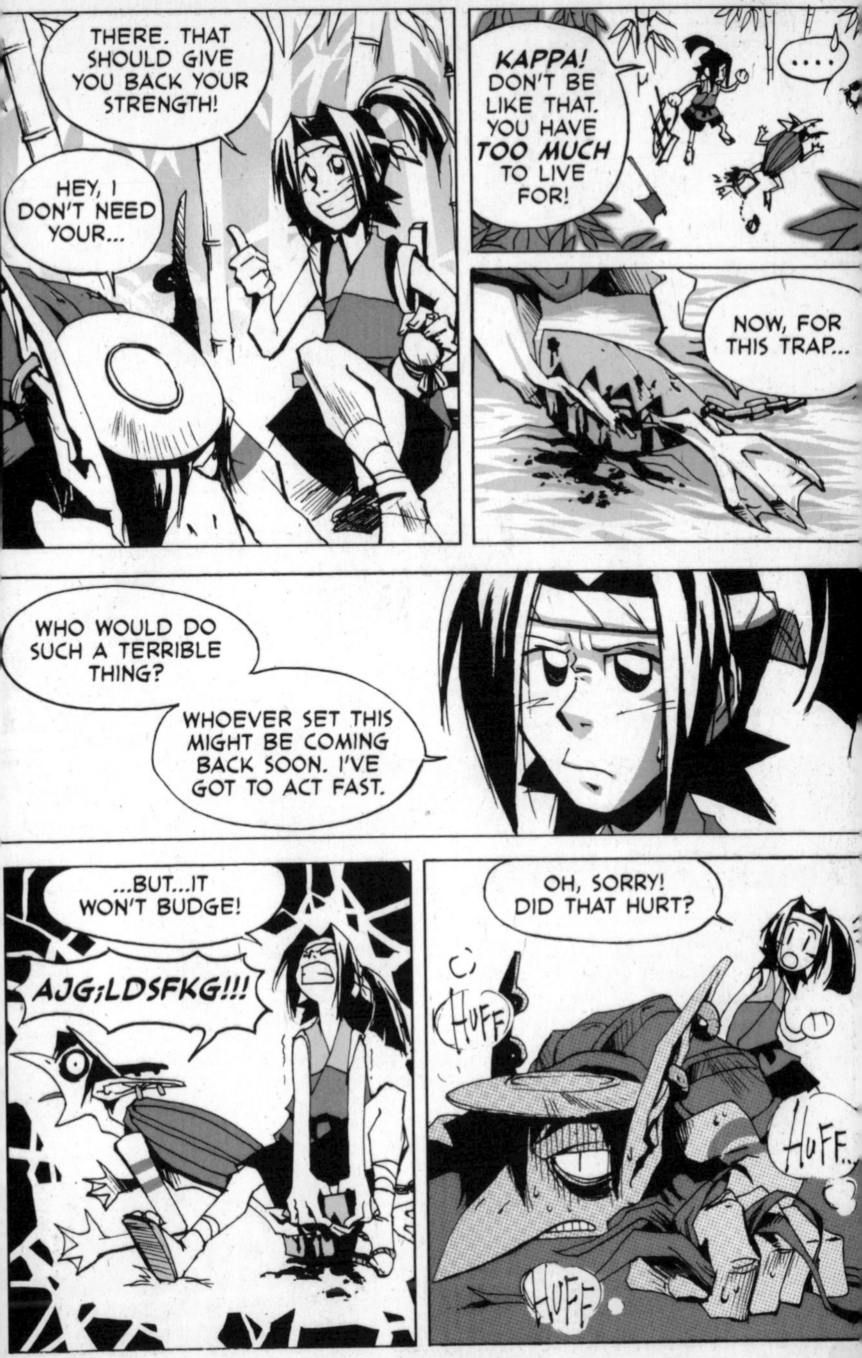
THERE. THAT SHOULD GIVE YOU BACK YOUR STRENGTH!
HEY, I DON'T NEED YOUR...
KAPPA! DON'T BE LIKE THAT. YOU HAVE ***TOO MUCH*** TO LIVE FOR!
....
NOW, FOR THIS TRAP...
WHO WOULD DO SUCH A TERRIBLE THING?
WHOEVER SET THIS MIGHT BE COMING BACK SOON. I'VE GOT TO ACT FAST.
...BUT...IT WON'T BUDGE!
AJG;LDSFKG!!!
OH, SORRY! DID THAT HURT?
HUFF
HUFF...
HUFF

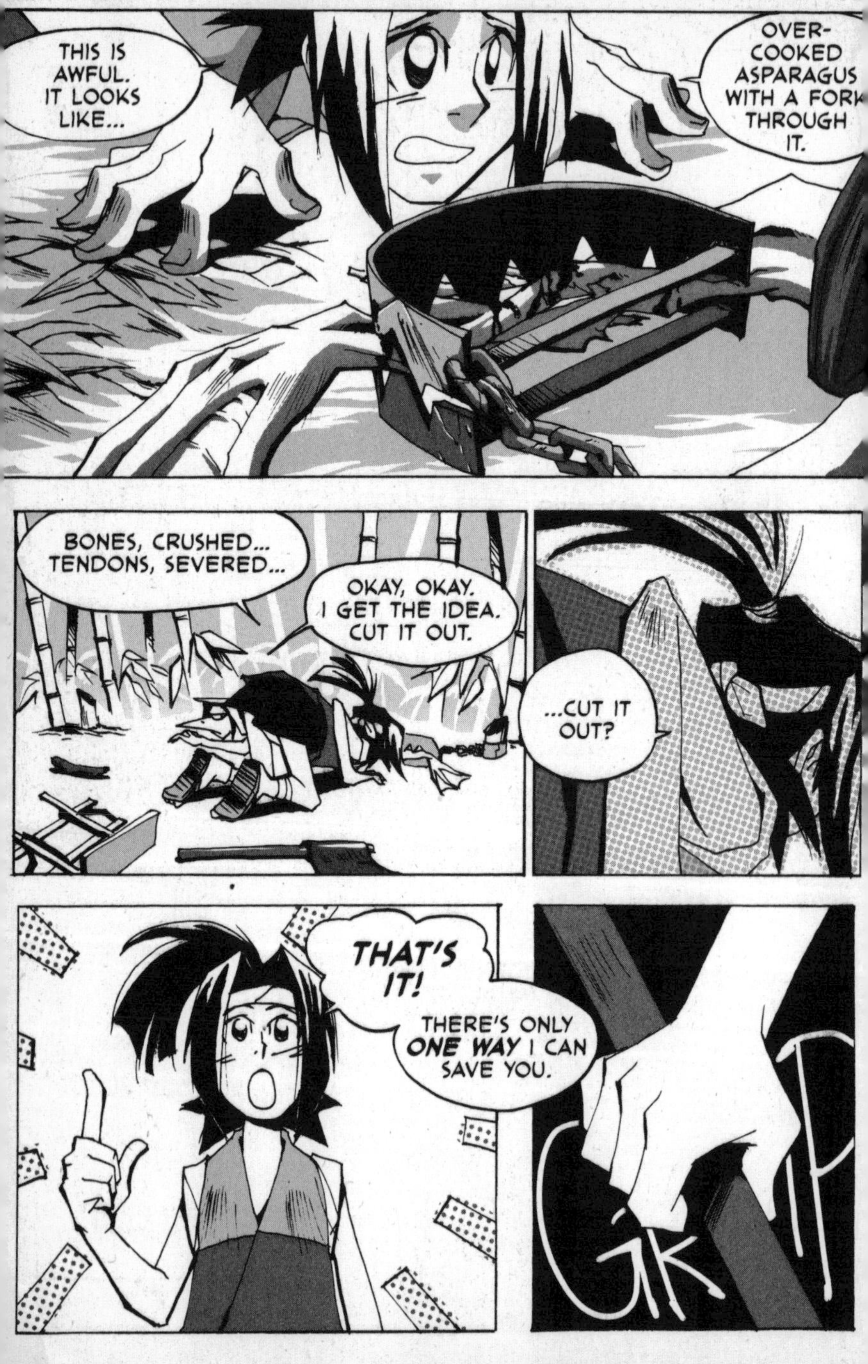
THIS IS AWFUL. IT LOOKS LIKE...
OVER-COOKED ASPARAGUS WITH A FORK THROUGH IT.
BONES, CRUSHED... TENDONS, SEVERED...
OKAY, OKAY. I GET THE IDEA. CUT IT OUT.
...CUT IT OUT?
THAT'S IT!
THERE'S ONLY ONE WAY I CAN SAVE YOU.
GRIP

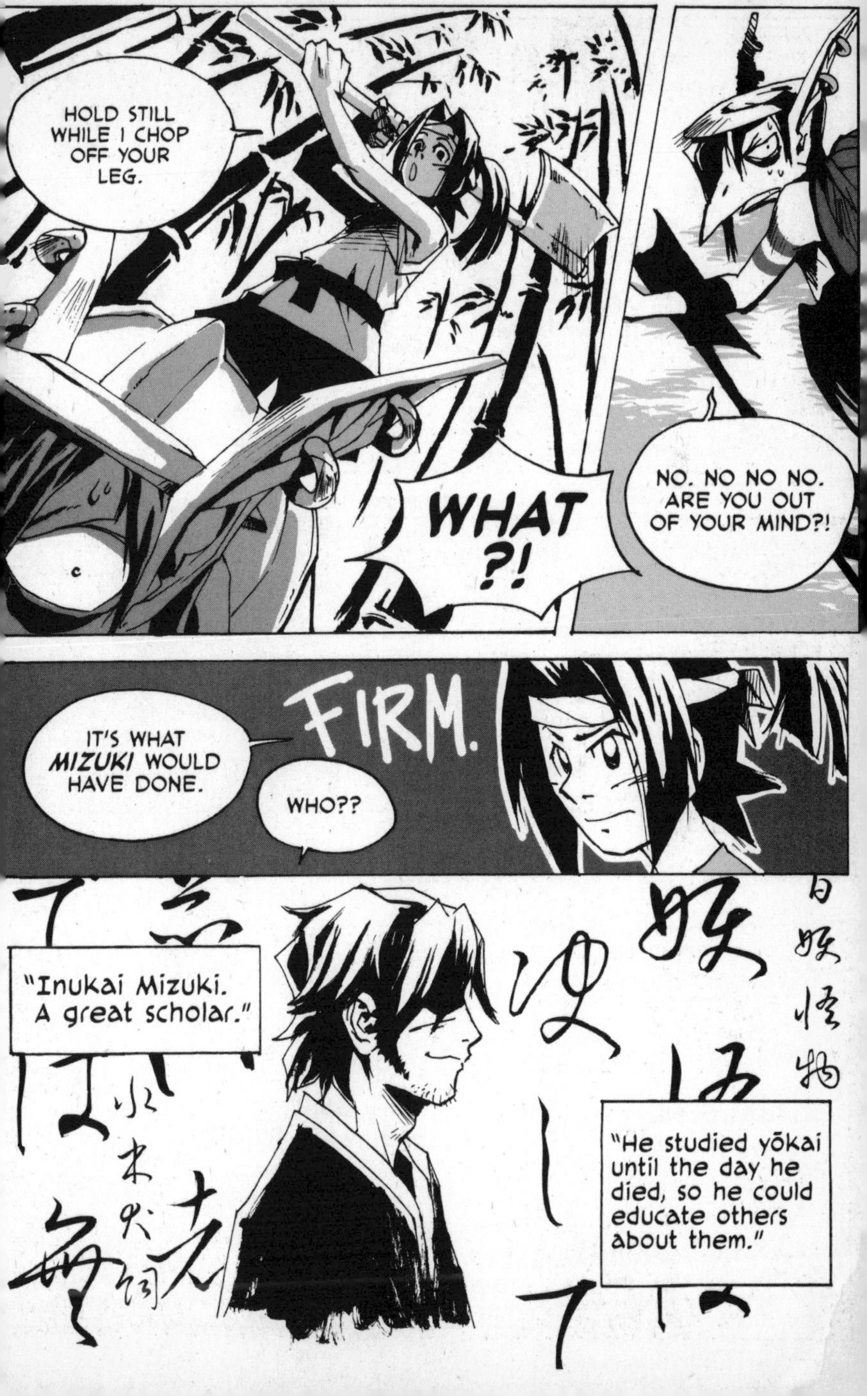
HOLD STILL WHILE I CHOP OFF YOUR LEG.
WHAT ?!
NO. NO NO NO. ARE YOU OUT OF YOUR MIND?!
FIRM.
IT'S WHAT *MIZUKI* WOULD HAVE DONE.
WHO??
"Inukai Mizuki. A great scholar."
"He studied yōkai until the day he died, so he could educate others about them."

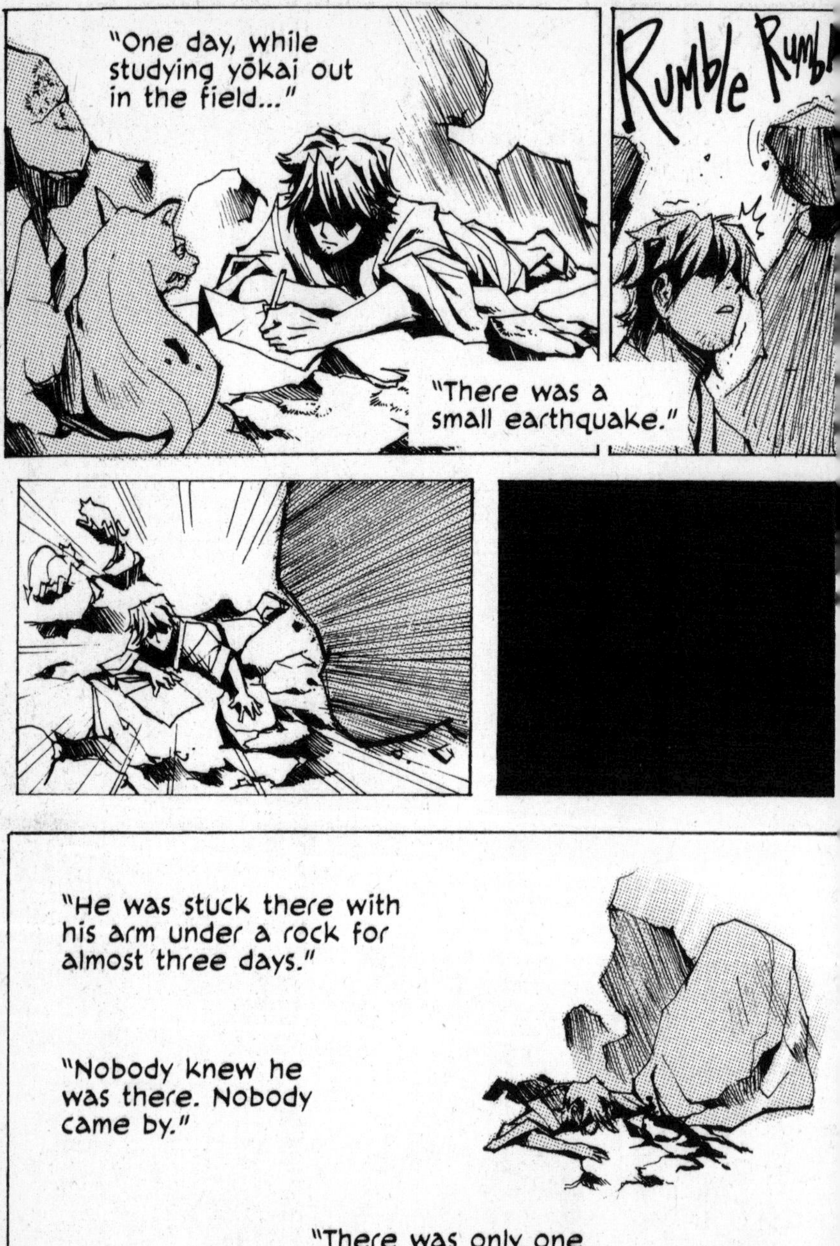
"One day, while studying yōkai out in the field..."
Rumble
"There was a small earthquake."
"He was stuck there with his arm under a rock for almost three days."
"Nobody knew he was there. Nobody came by."
"There was only one way to save himself..."

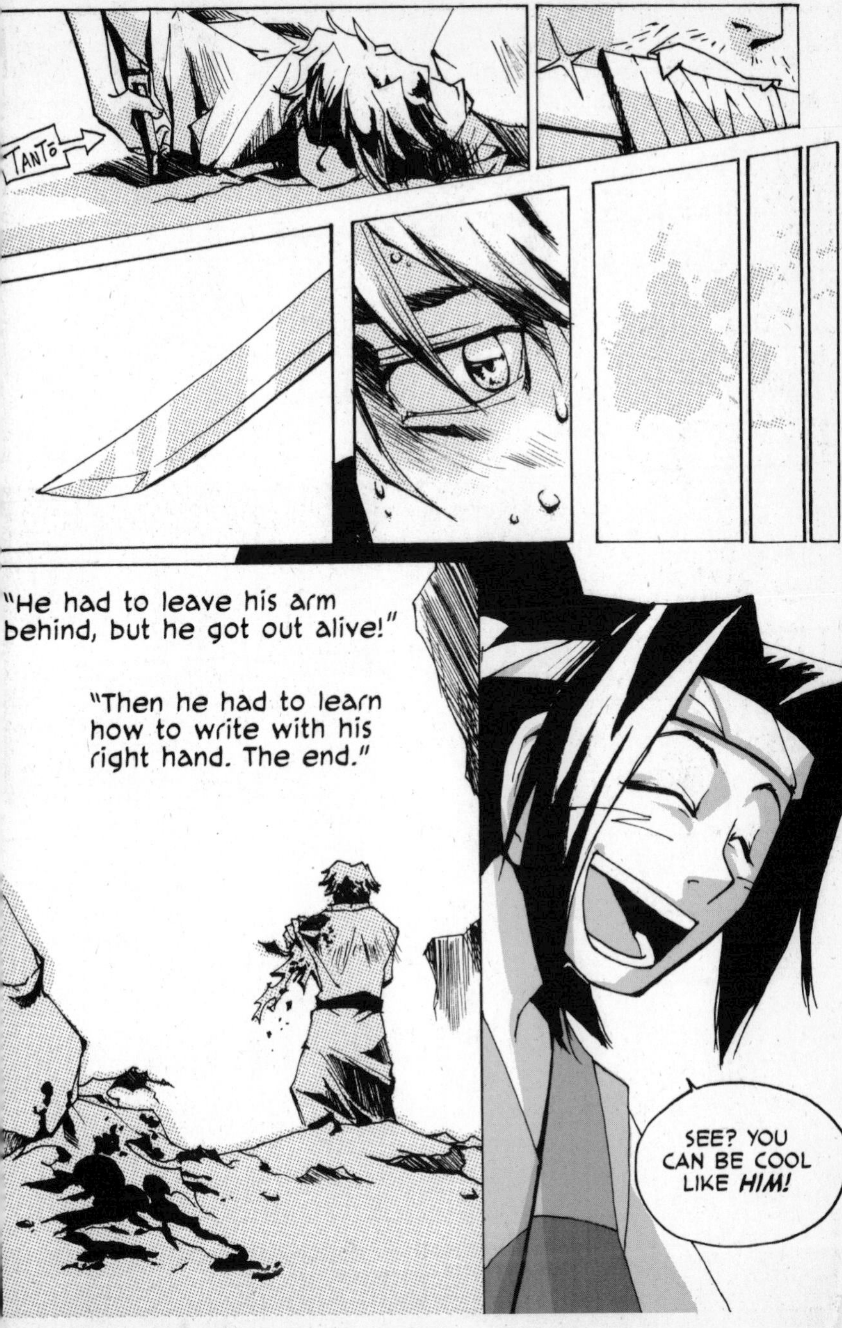
TANTŌ
"He had to leave his arm behind, but he got out alive!"
"Then he had to learn how to write with his right hand. The end."
SEE? YOU CAN BE COOL LIKE *HIM!*

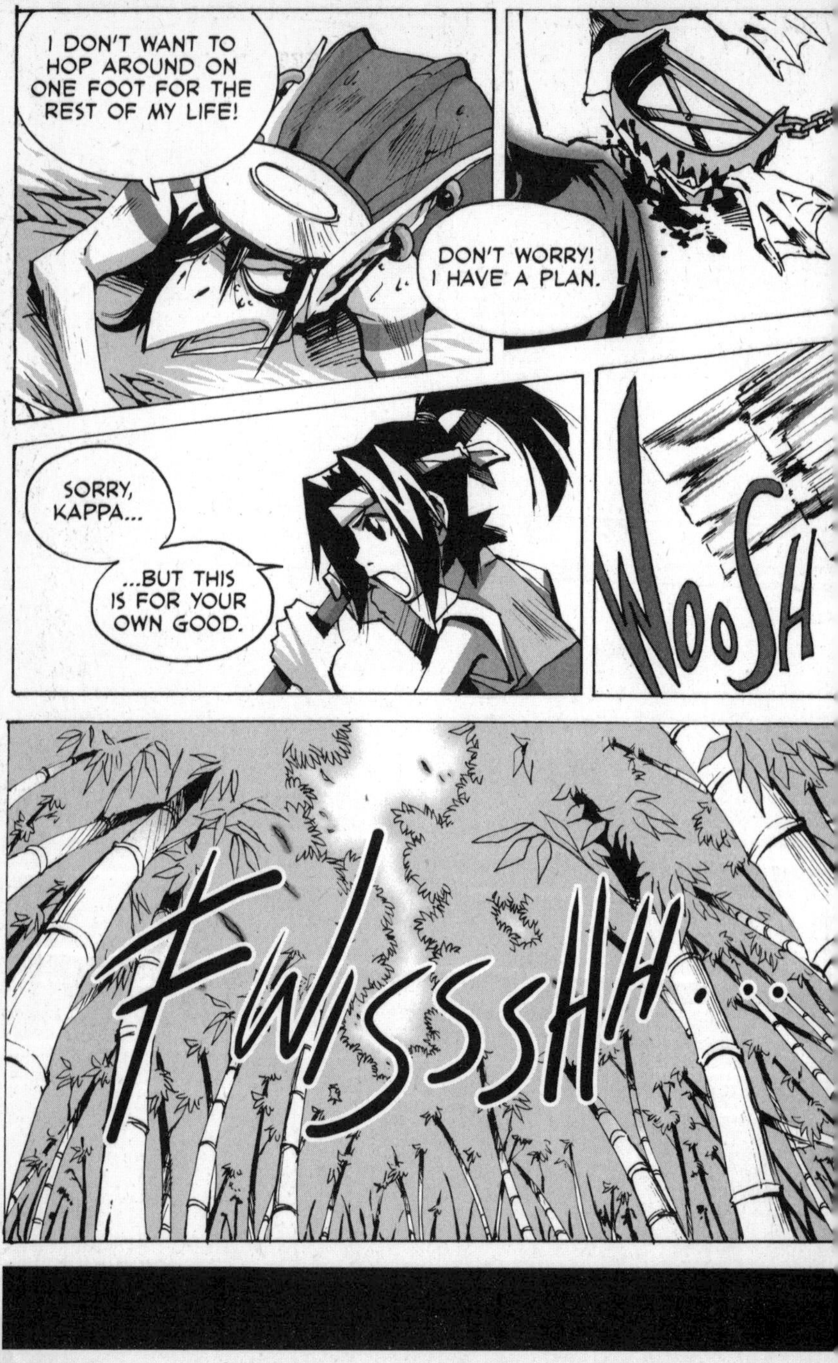
I DON'T WANT TO HOP AROUND ON ONE FOOT FOR THE REST OF MY LIFE!
DON'T WORRY! I HAVE A PLAN.
SORRY, KAPPA...
...BUT THIS IS FOR YOUR OWN GOOD.
WOOSH
FWISSSHH...

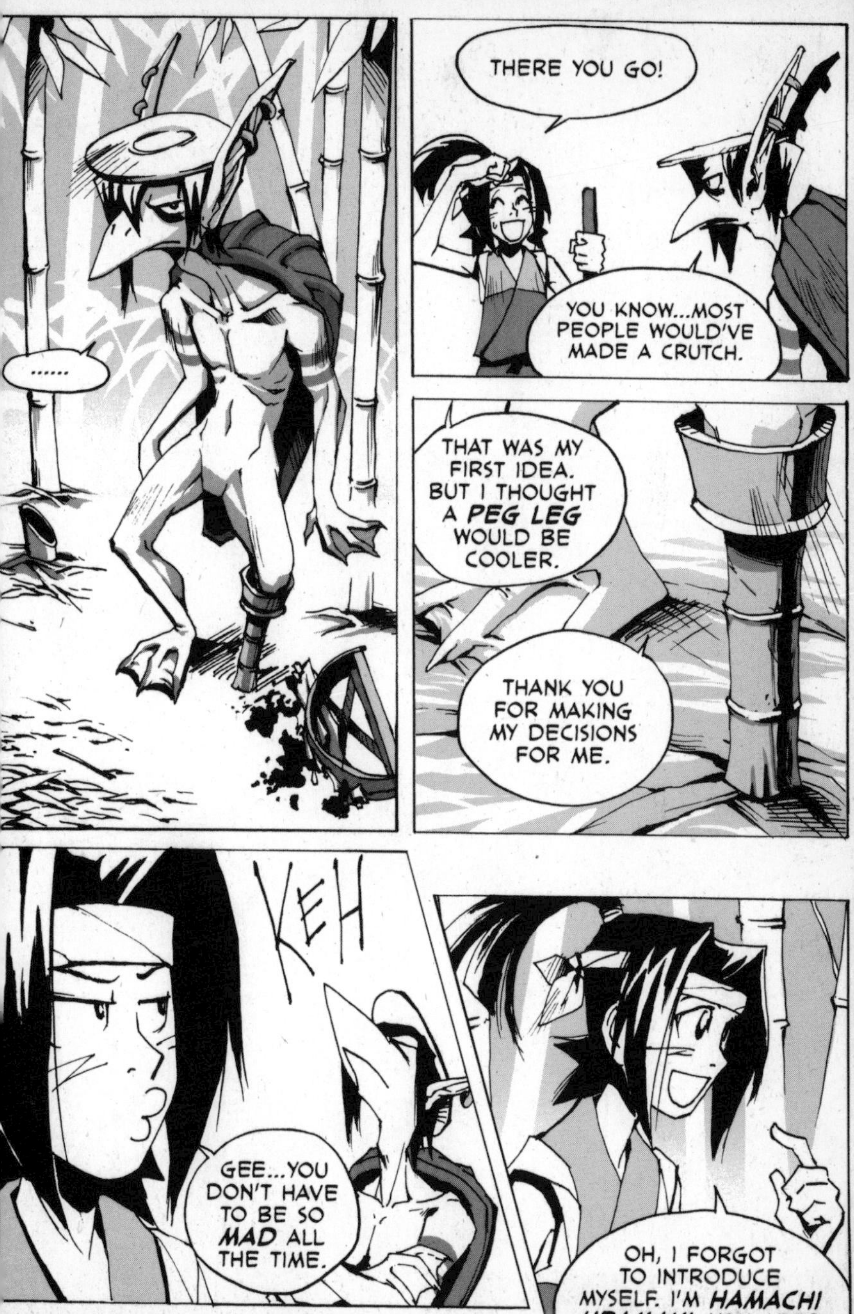

....
THERE YOU GO!
YOU KNOW...MOST PEOPLE WOULD'VE MADE A CRUTCH.
THAT WAS MY FIRST IDEA. BUT I THOUGHT A PEG LEG WOULD BE COOLER.
THANK YOU FOR MAKING MY DECISIONS FOR ME.
KEH
GEE...YOU DON'T HAVE TO BE SO MAD ALL THE TIME.
OH, I FORGOT TO INTRODUCE MYSELF. I'M HAMACHI URAMAKI. YOU ARE?

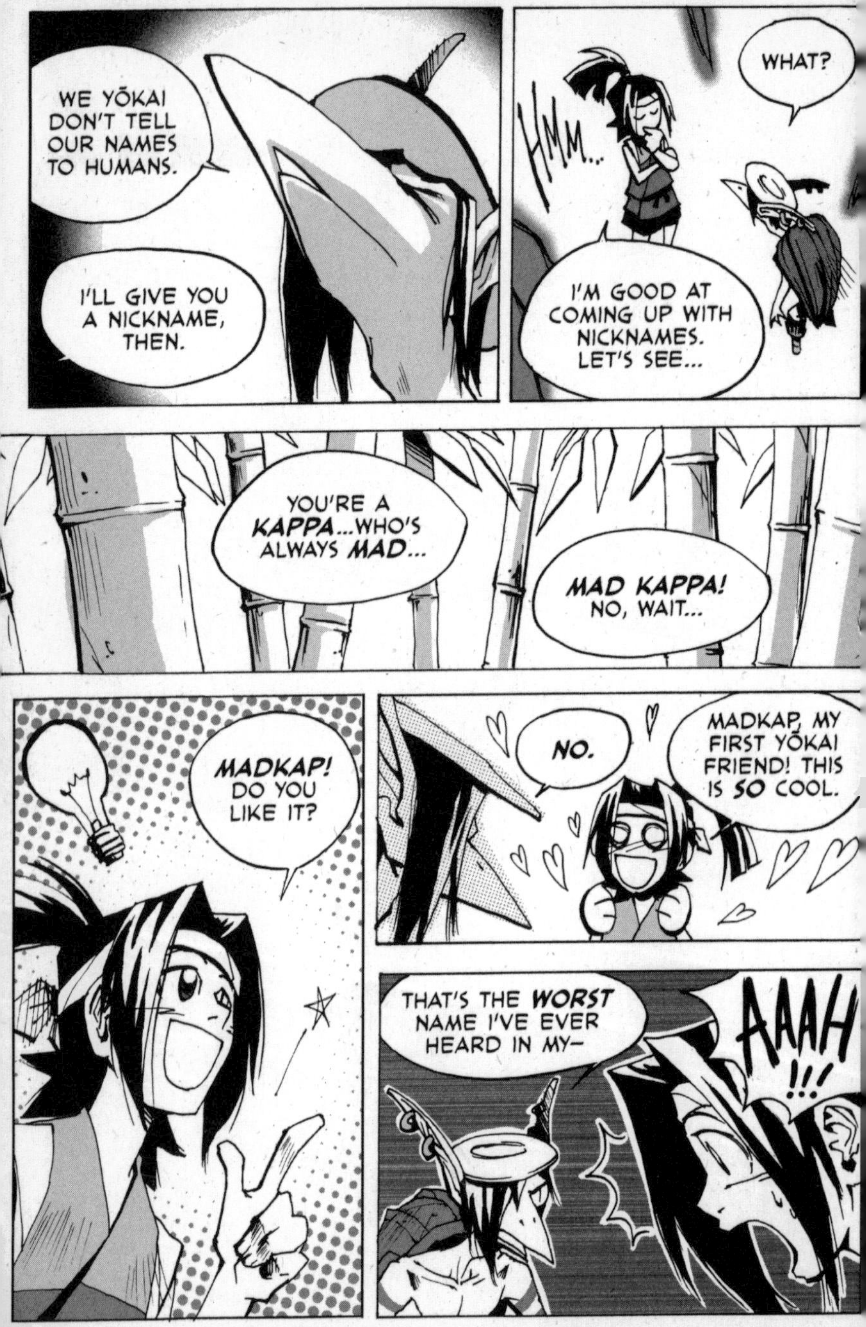
WE YŌKAI DON'T TELL OUR NAMES TO HUMANS.
I'LL GIVE YOU A NICKNAME, THEN.
HMM...
WHAT?
I'M GOOD AT COMING UP WITH NICKNAMES. LET'S SEE...
YOU'RE A KAPPA...WHO'S ALWAYS MAD...
MAD KAPPA! NO, WAIT...
MADKAP! DO YOU LIKE IT?
NO.
MADKAP, MY FIRST YŌKAI FRIEND! THIS IS SO COOL.
THAT'S THE WORST NAME I'VE EVER HEARD IN MY–
AAAH !!!

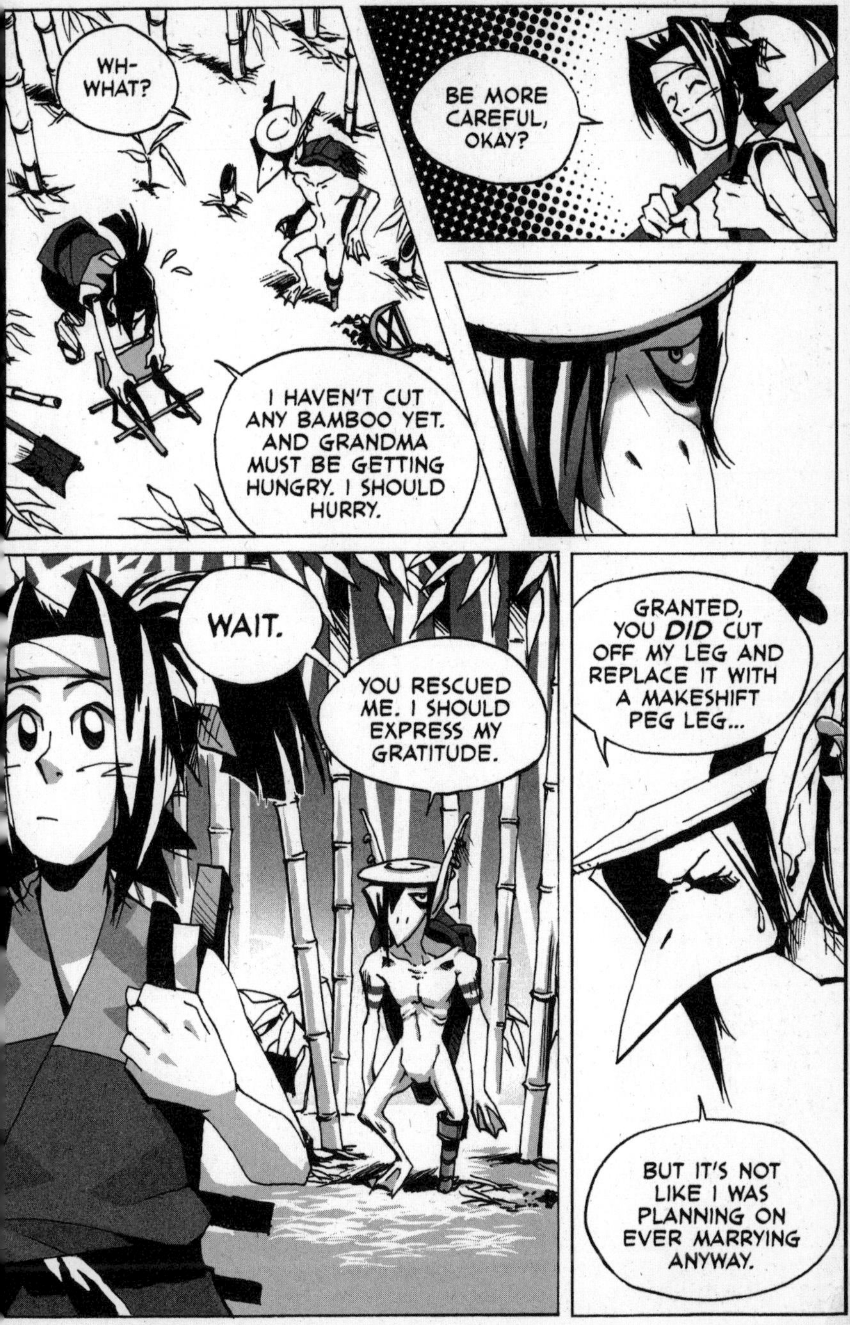
WH-WHAT?
BE MORE CAREFUL, OKAY?
I HAVEN'T CUT ANY BAMBOO YET. AND GRANDMA MUST BE GETTING HUNGRY. I SHOULD HURRY.
WAIT.
YOU RESCUED ME. I SHOULD EXPRESS MY GRATITUDE.
GRANTED, YOU *DID* CUT OFF MY LEG AND REPLACE IT WITH A MAKESHIFT PEG LEG...
BUT IT'S NOT LIKE I WAS PLANNING ON EVER MARRYING ANYWAY.

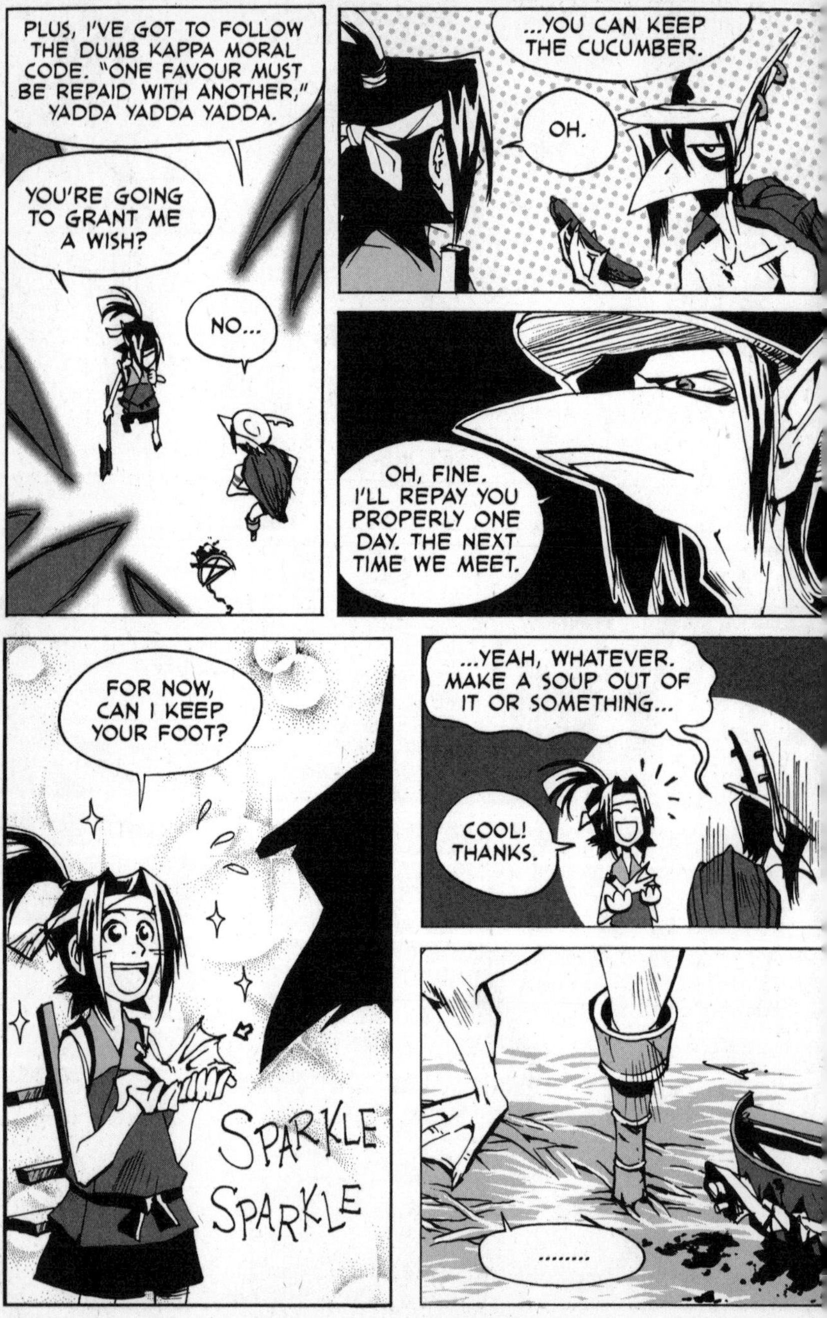
PLUS, I'VE GOT TO FOLLOW THE DUMB KAPPA MORAL CODE. "ONE FAVOUR MUST BE REPAID WITH ANOTHER," YADDA YADDA YADDA.
YOU'RE GOING TO GRANT ME A WISH?
NO...
...YOU CAN KEEP THE CUCUMBER.
OH.
OH, FINE. I'LL REPAY YOU PROPERLY ONE DAY. THE NEXT TIME WE MEET.
FOR NOW, CAN I KEEP YOUR FOOT?
SPARKLE
SPARKLE
...YEAH, WHATEVER. MAKE A SOUP OUT OF IT OR SOMETHING...
COOL! THANKS.
....

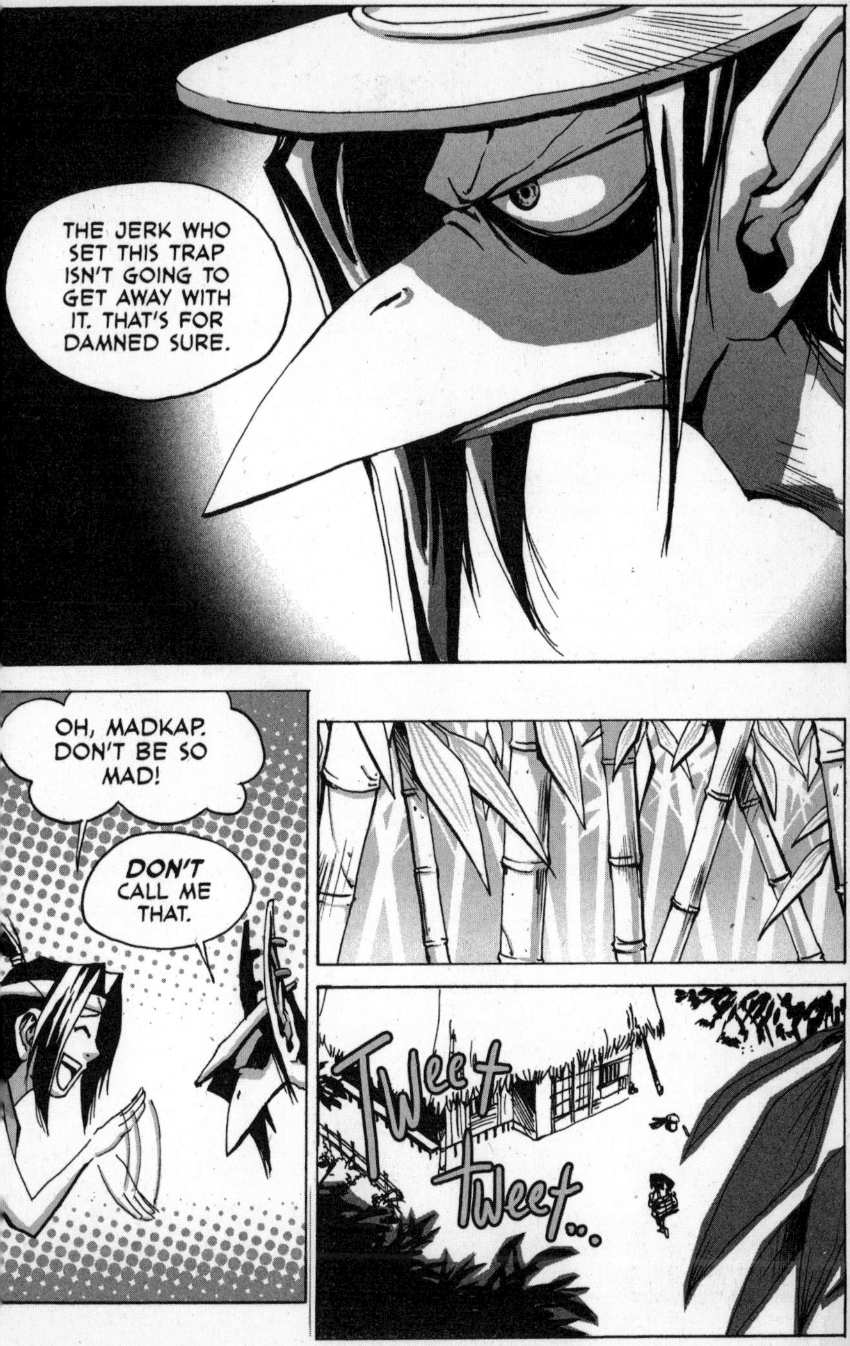
THE JERK WHO SET THIS TRAP ISN'T GOING TO GET AWAY WITH IT. THAT'S FOR DAMNED SURE.
OH, MADKAP. DON'T BE SO MAD!
DON'T CALL ME THAT.
Tweet tweet...

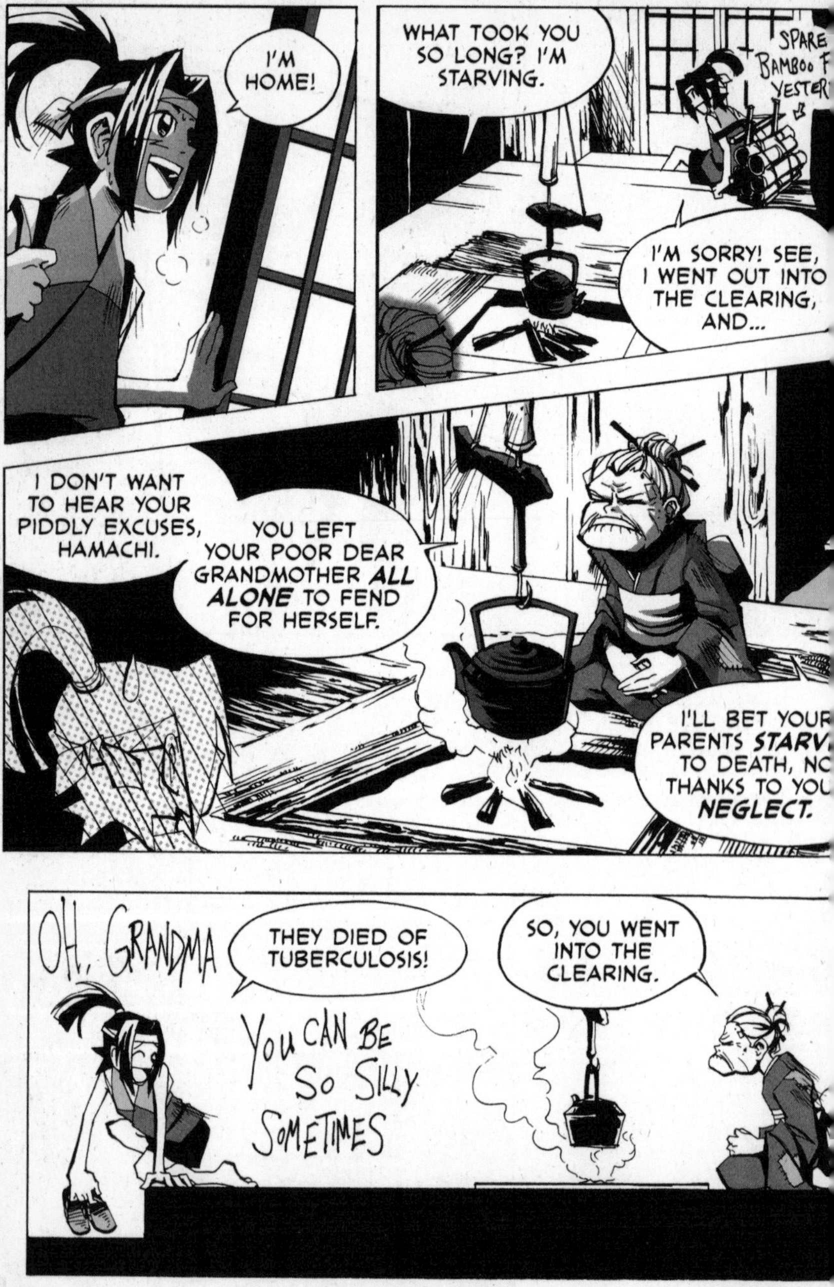
I'M HOME!
WHAT TOOK YOU SO LONG? I'M STARVING.
SPARE BAMBOO F YESTER
I'M SORRY! SEE, I WENT OUT INTO THE CLEARING, AND...
I DON'T WANT TO HEAR YOUR PIDDLY EXCUSES, HAMACHI.
YOU LEFT YOUR POOR DEAR GRANDMOTHER ALL ALONE TO FEND FOR HERSELF.
I'LL BET YOUR PARENTS STARV TO DEATH, NO THANKS TO YOU NEGLECT.
OH, GRANDMA
THEY DIED OF TUBERCULOSIS!
YOU CAN BE SO SILLY SOMETIMES
SO, YOU WENT INTO THE CLEARING.

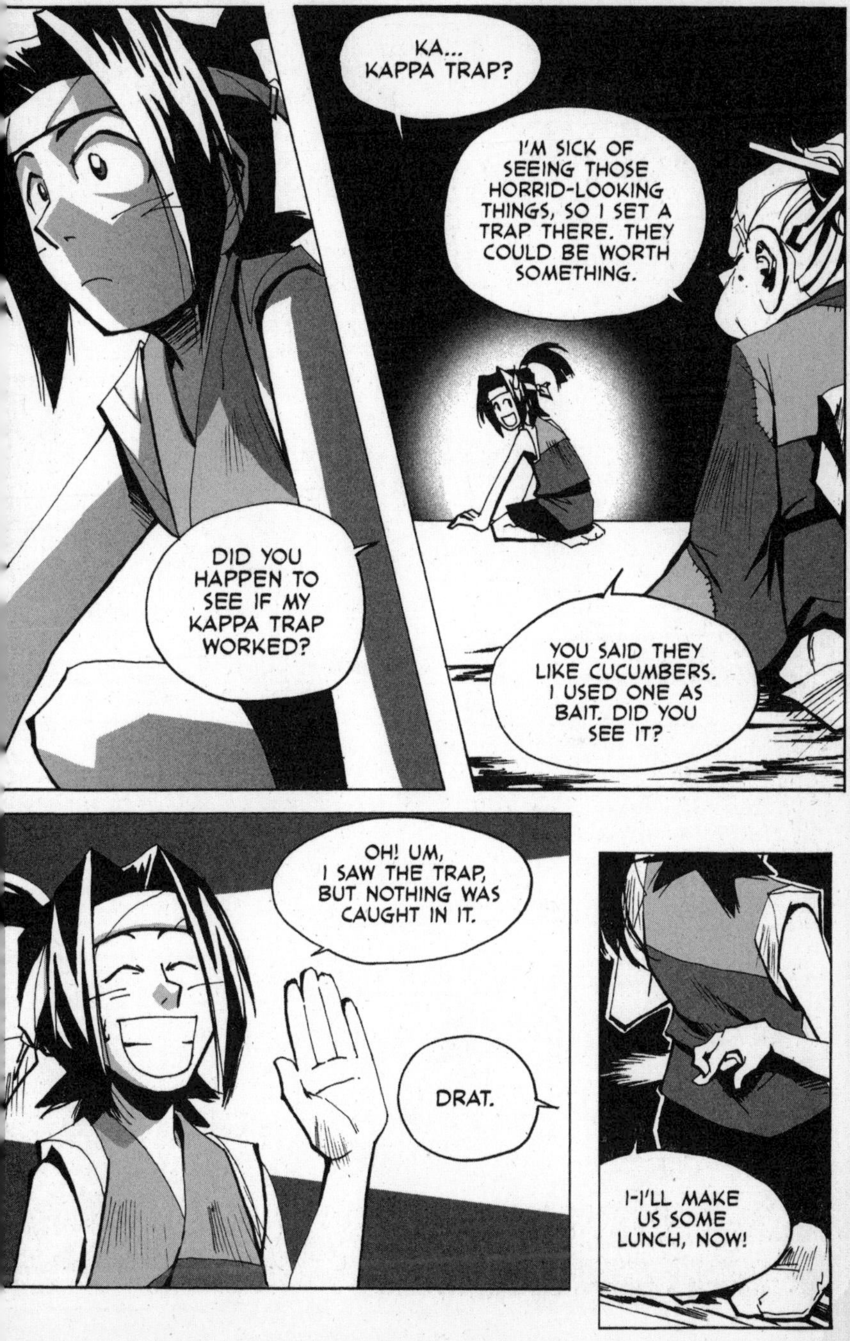
KA... KAPPA TRAP?
I'M SICK OF SEEING THOSE HORRID-LOOKING THINGS, SO I SET A TRAP THERE. THEY COULD BE WORTH SOMETHING.
DID YOU HAPPEN TO SEE IF MY KAPPA TRAP WORKED?
YOU SAID THEY LIKE CUCUMBERS. I USED ONE AS BAIT. DID YOU SEE IT?
OH! UM, I SAW THE TRAP, BUT NOTHING WAS CAUGHT IN IT.
DRAT.
I-I'LL MAKE US SOME LUNCH, NOW!

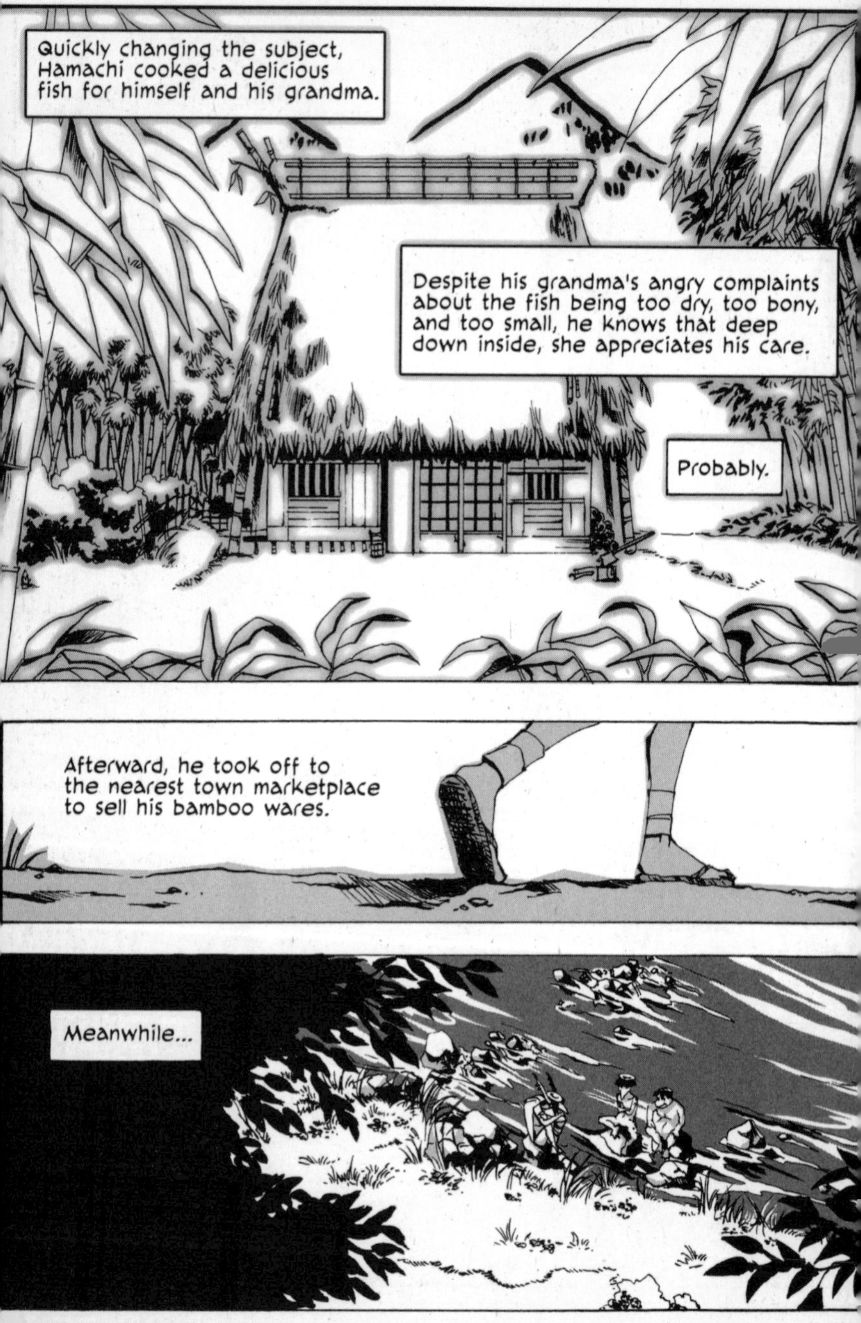
Quickly changing the subject, Hamachi cooked a delicious fish for himself and his grandma.
Despite his grandma's angry complaints about the fish being too dry, too bony, and too small, he knows that deep down inside, she appreciates his care.
Probably.
Afterward, he took off to the nearest town marketplace to sell his bamboo wares.
Meanwhile...

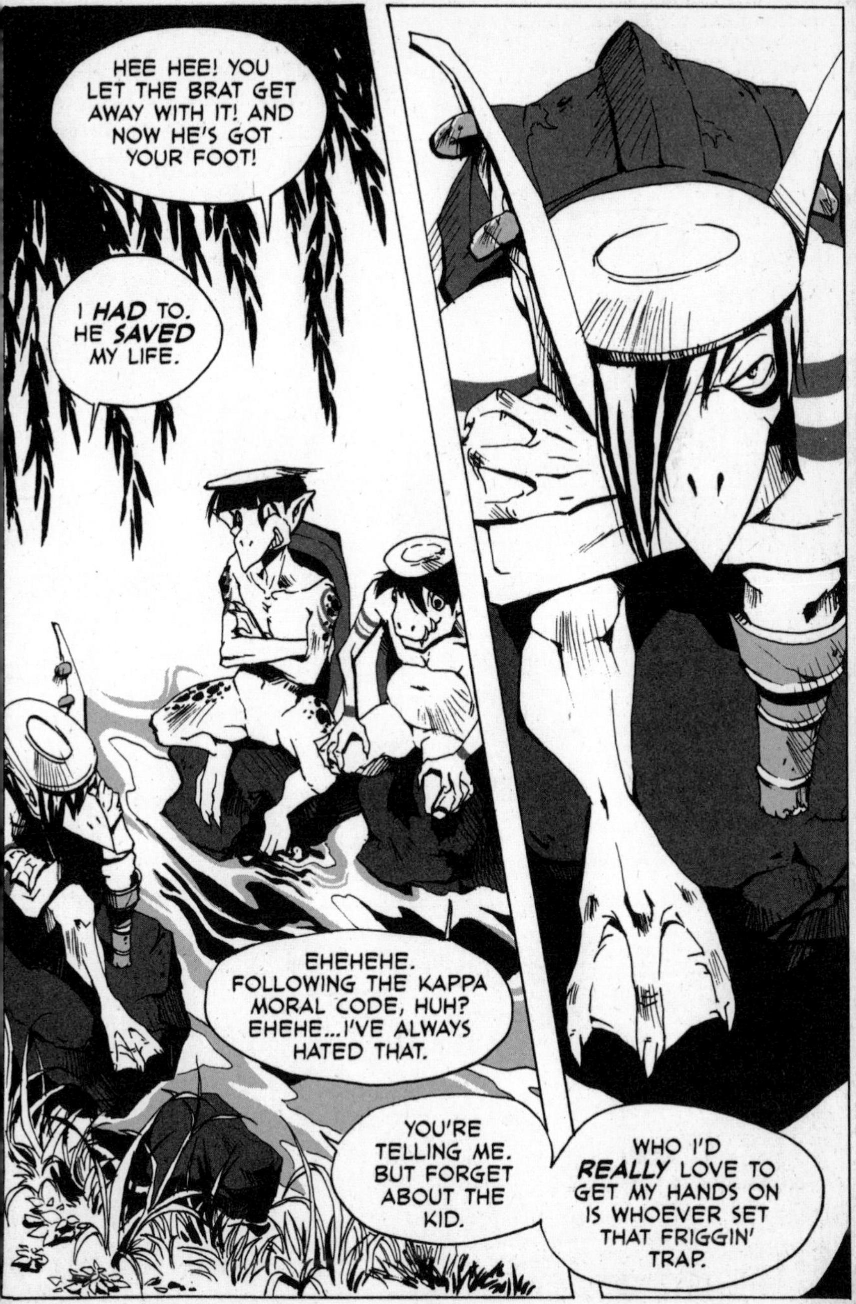
HEE HEE! YOU LET THE BRAT GET AWAY WITH IT! AND NOW HE'S GOT YOUR FOOT!
I *HAD* TO. HE *SAVED* MY LIFE.
EHEHEHE. FOLLOWING THE KAPPA MORAL CODE, HUH? EHEHE...I'VE ALWAYS HATED THAT.
YOU'RE TELLING ME. BUT FORGET ABOUT THE KID.
WHO I'D *REALLY* LOVE TO GET MY HANDS ON IS WHOEVER SET THAT FRIGGIN' TRAP.

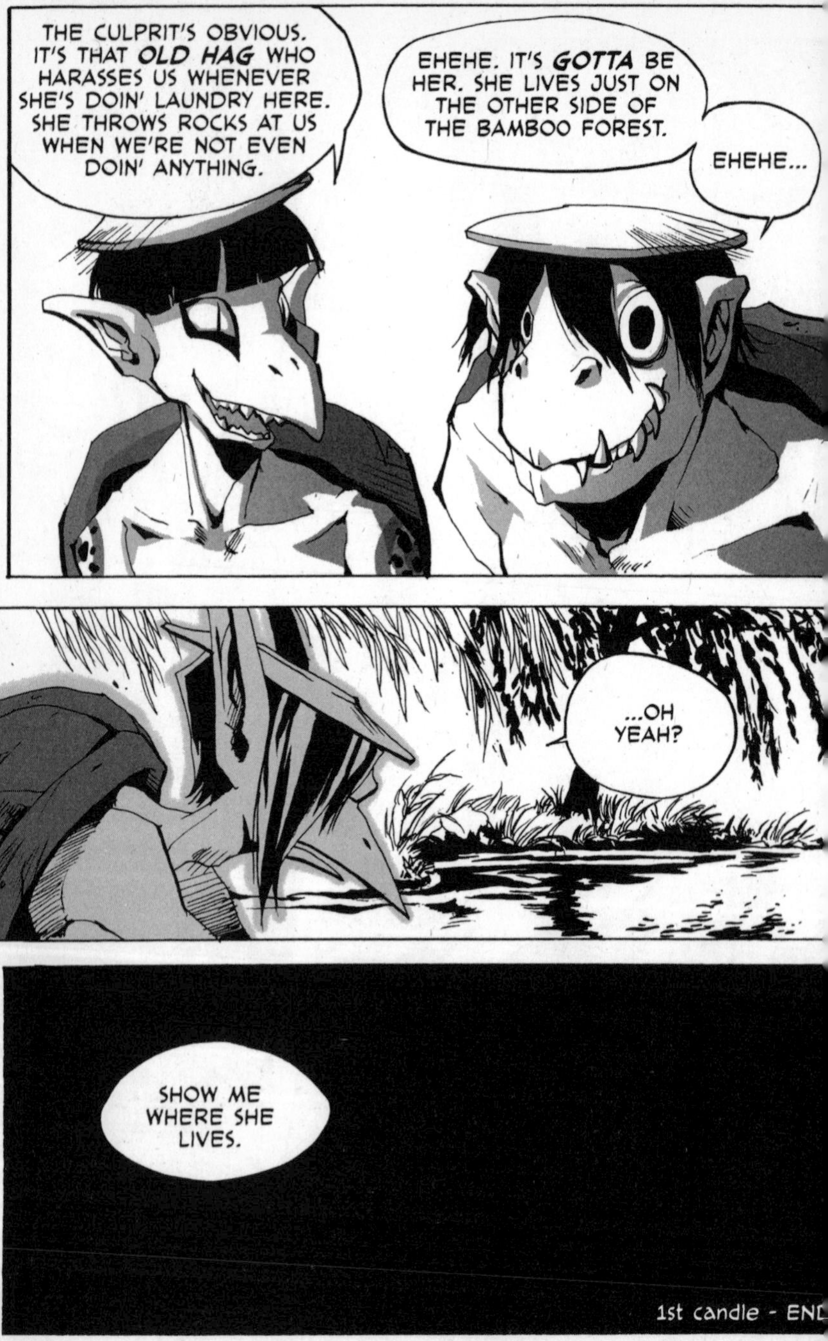
THE CULPRIT'S OBVIOUS. IT'S THAT *OLD HAG* WHO HARASSES US WHENEVER SHE'S DOIN' LAUNDRY HERE. SHE THROWS ROCKS AT US WHEN WE'RE NOT EVEN DOIN' ANYTHING.
EHEHE. IT'S *GOTTA* BE HER. SHE LIVES JUST ON THE OTHER SIDE OF THE BAMBOO FOREST.
EHEHE...
...OH YEAH?
SHOW ME WHERE SHE LIVES.
1st candle - END

Inukai Mizuki's FIELD GUIDE to YŌKAI

KAPPA 河童

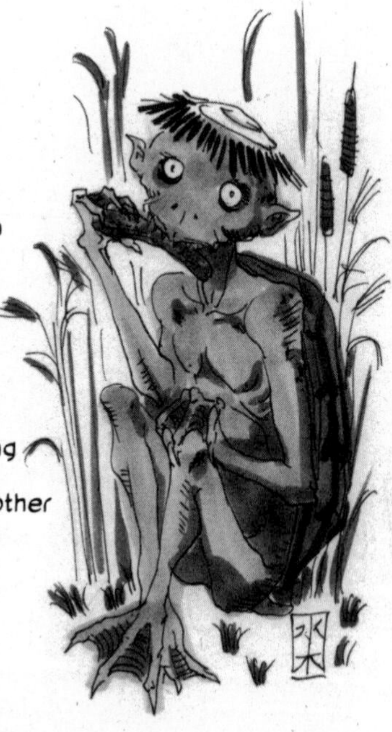

Kappa pride themselves on being some of the more civilized, intelligent yōkai. They have built their society within the rivers of our land and adhere to a strict moral code.

One should take care to never insult a kappa; doing so has proven to make them extremely hostile. As such, great caution should be taken when dealing with a kappa face-to-face. When treated with courtesy and respect, kappa are harmless.

Mischievous tricks are something they may partake in from time to time but, in general, they do not bother humans. A common misconception is that they kidnap any children who come too close to the river. This is, in fact, an urban myth spread by parents attempting to scare their children away from open waters.

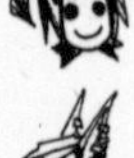

"IF YOU CAN, TRY FLIPPING ONE ONTO ITS BACK TO SEE IF IT CAN GET BACK UP ON ITS OWN."

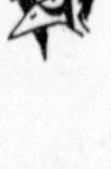

"...YOU'RE THINKING OF TURTLES."

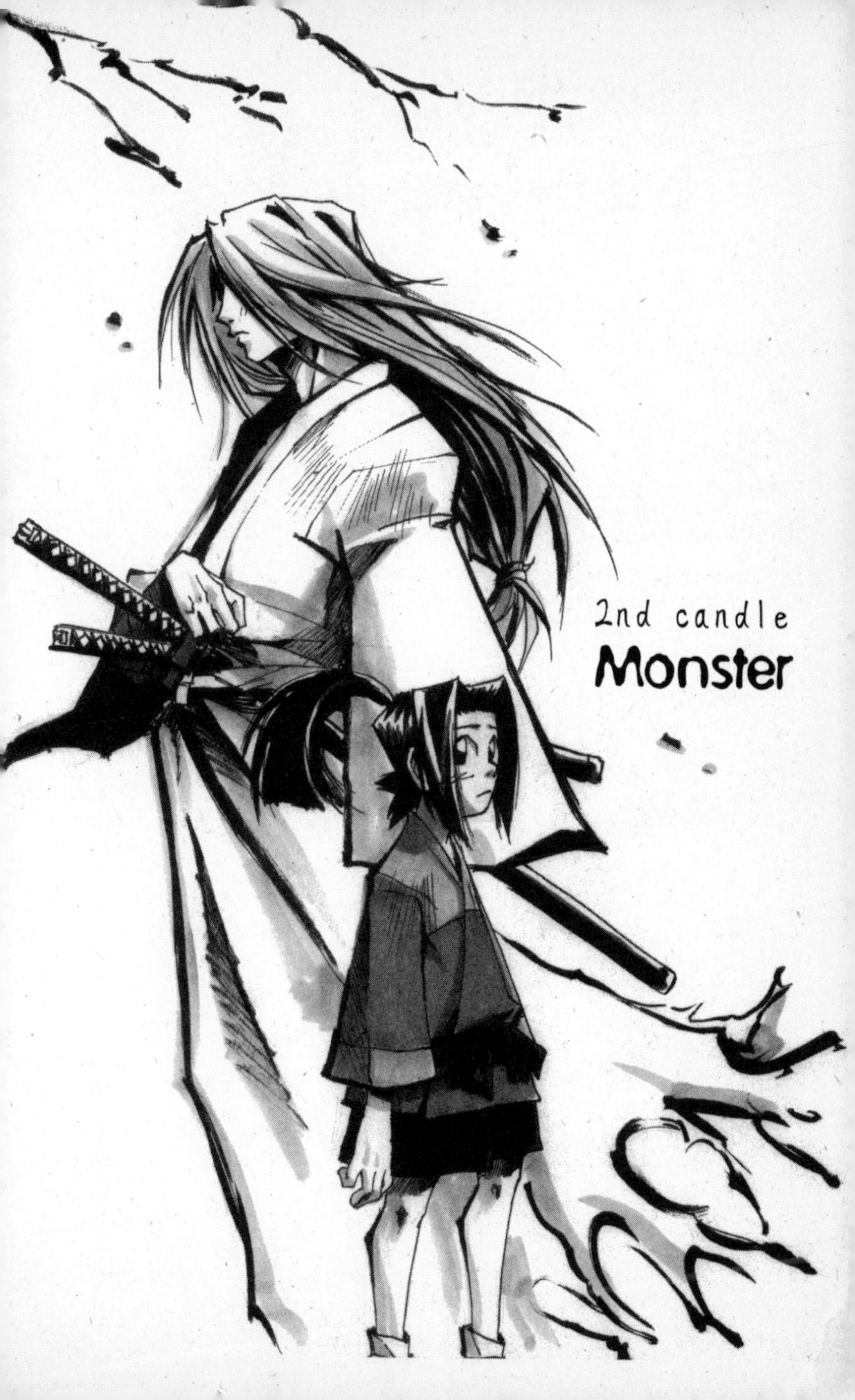
2nd candle
Monster

SHAMOJI VILLAGE
MARKETPLACE

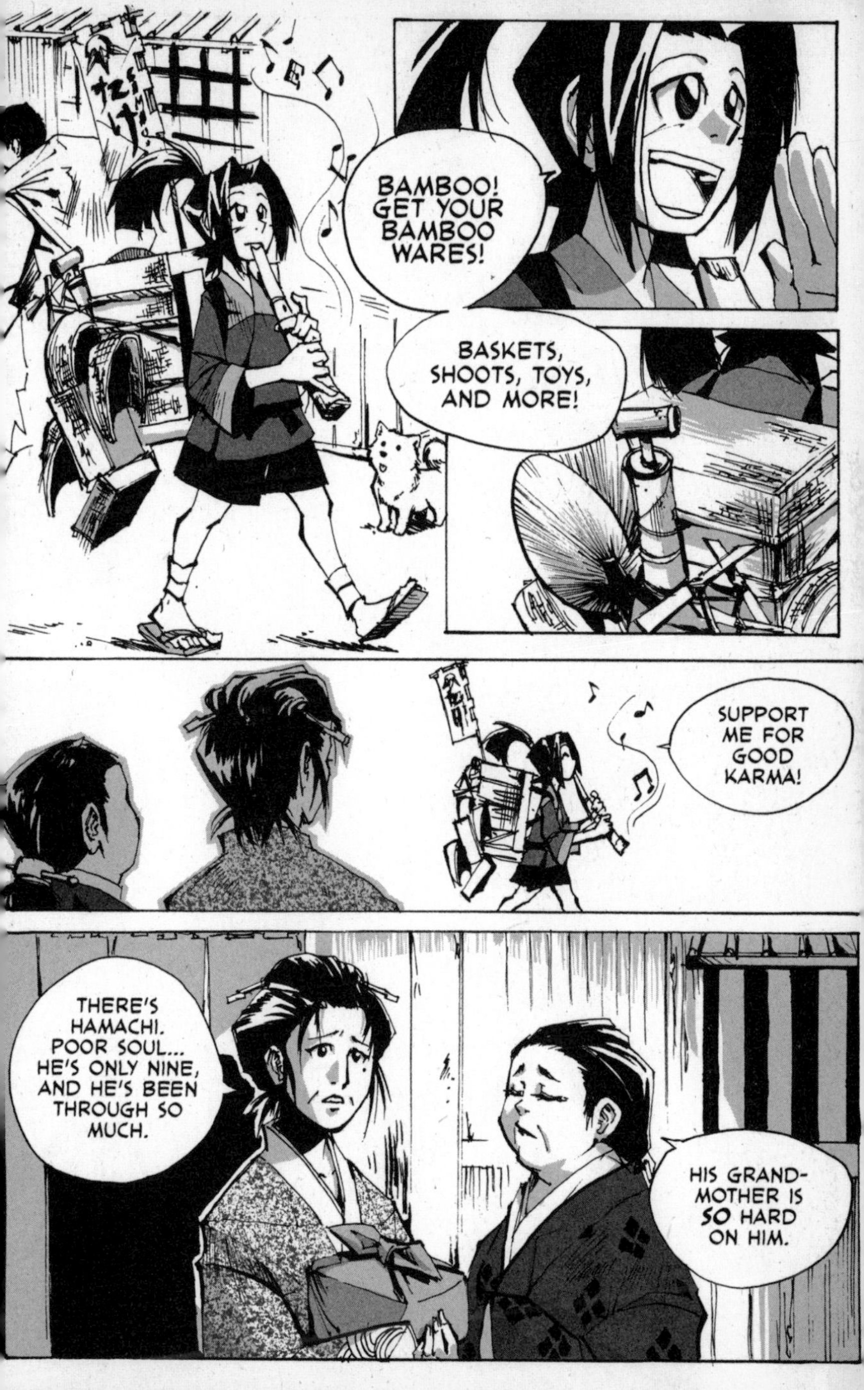
BAMBOO! GET YOUR BAMBOO WARES!
BASKETS, SHOOTS, TOYS, AND MORE!
SUPPORT ME FOR GOOD KARMA!
THERE'S HAMACHI. POOR SOUL... HE'S ONLY NINE, AND HE'S BEEN THROUGH SO MUCH.
HIS GRAND-MOTHER IS **SO** HARD ON HIM.

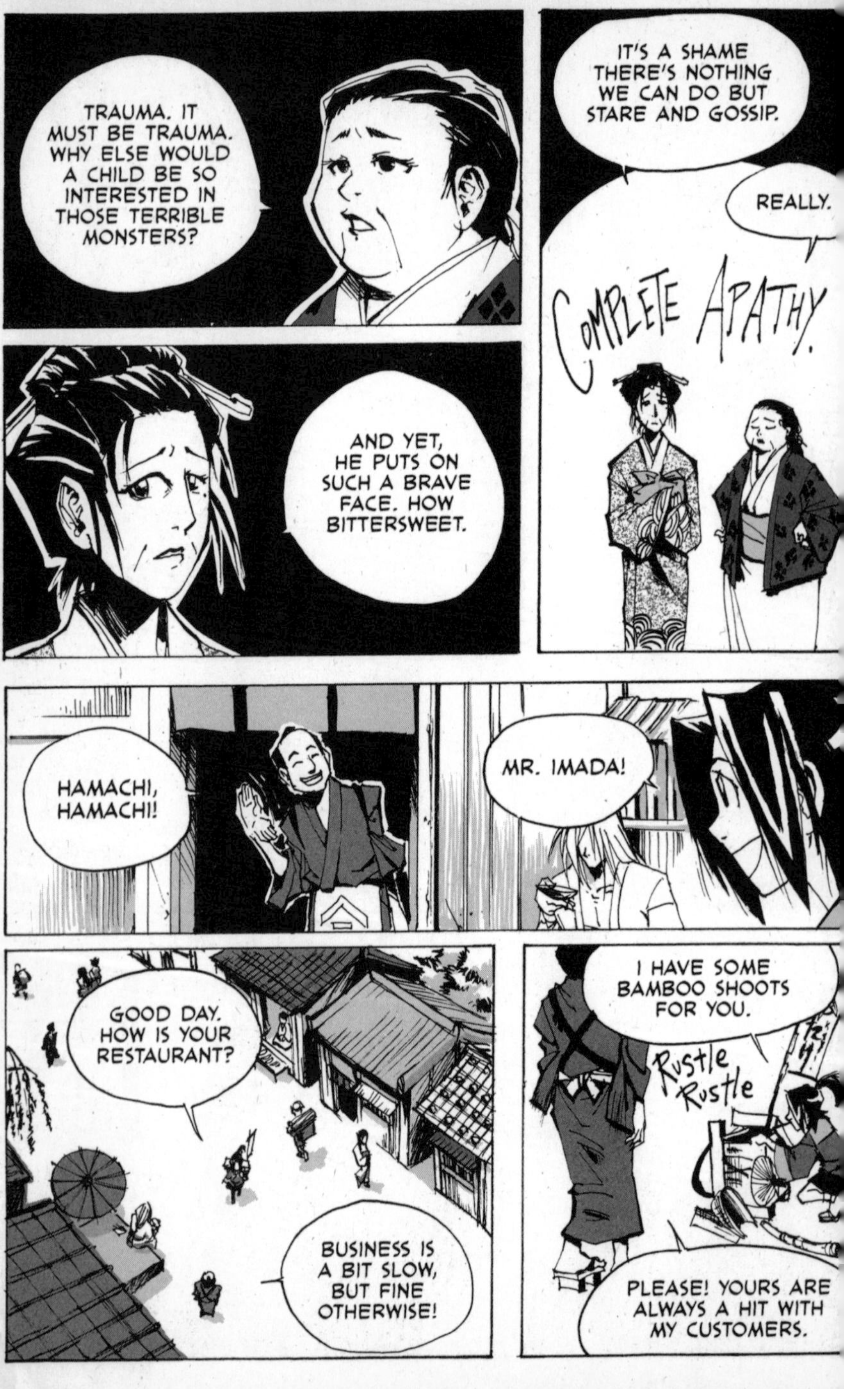
TRAUMA. IT MUST BE TRAUMA. WHY ELSE WOULD A CHILD BE SO INTERESTED IN THOSE TERRIBLE MONSTERS?
IT'S A SHAME THERE'S NOTHING WE CAN DO BUT STARE AND GOSSIP.
REALLY.
AND YET, HE PUTS ON SUCH A BRAVE FACE. HOW BITTERSWEET.
COMPLETE APATHY.
HAMACHI, HAMACHI!
MR. IMADA!
GOOD DAY. HOW IS YOUR RESTAURANT?
BUSINESS IS A BIT SLOW, BUT FINE OTHERWISE!
I HAVE SOME BAMBOO SHOOTS FOR YOU.
Rustle Rustle
PLEASE! YOURS ARE ALWAYS A HIT WITH MY CUSTOMERS.

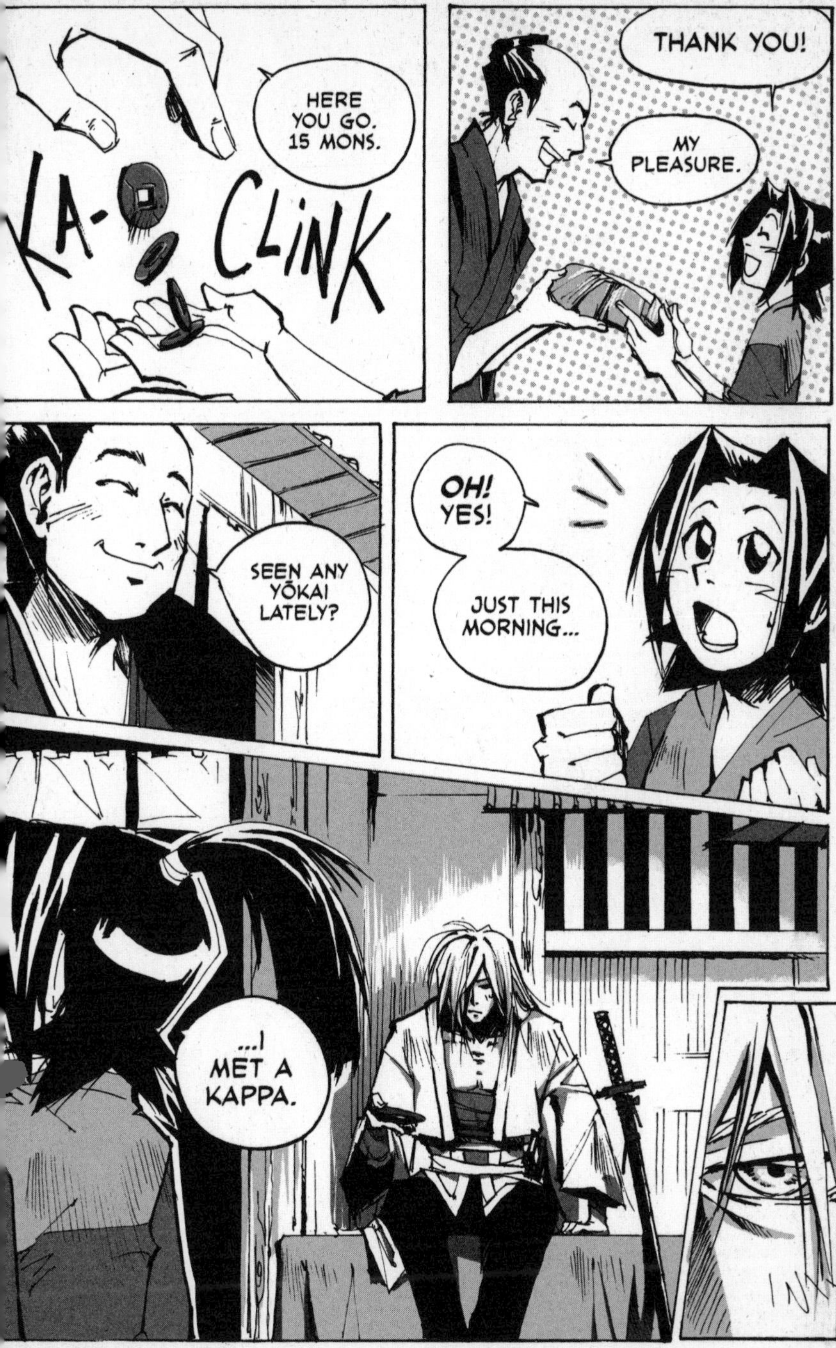
HERE YOU GO. 15 MONS.
KA-CLINK
THANK YOU!
MY PLEASURE.
SEEN ANY YŌKAI LATELY?
OH! YES!
JUST THIS MORNING...
...I MET A KAPPA.

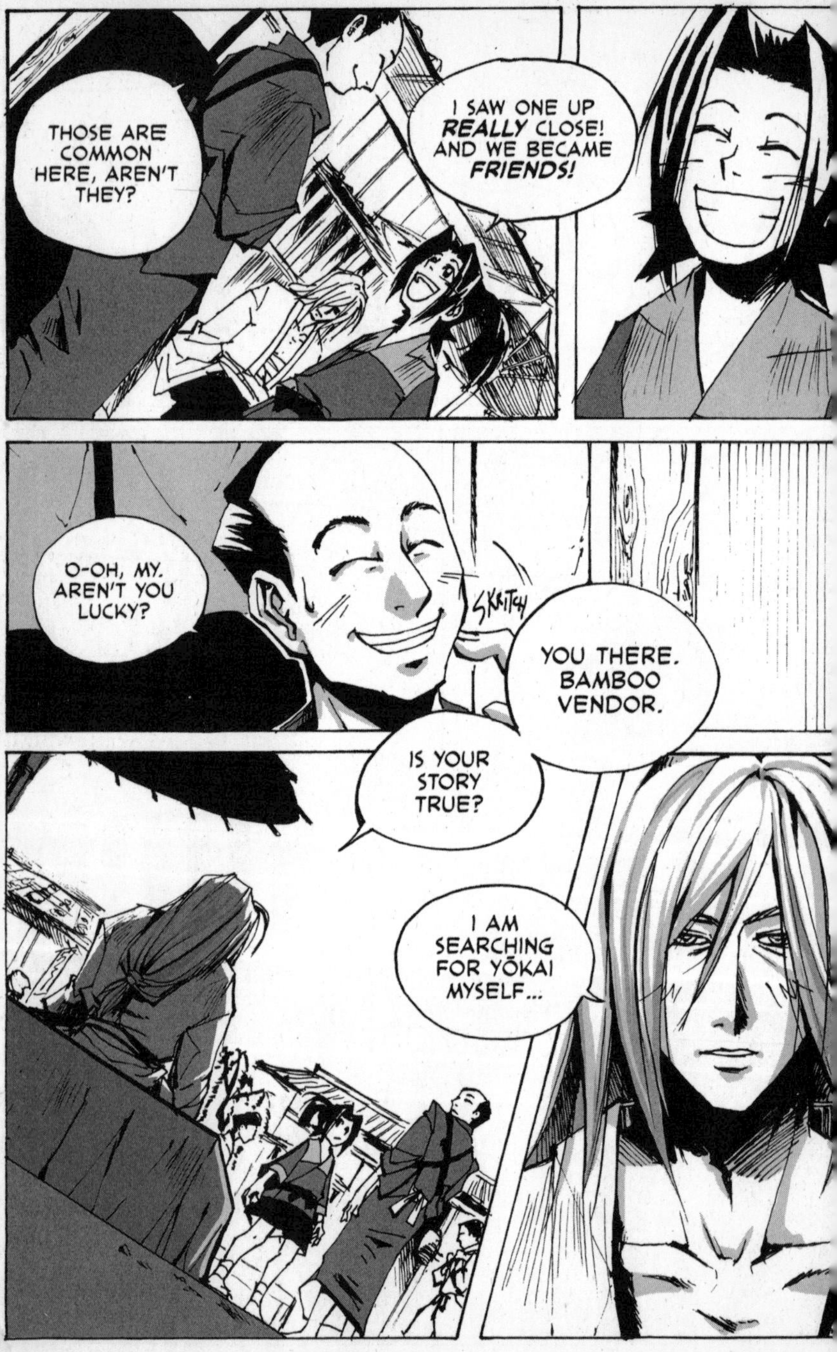
THOSE ARE COMMON HERE, AREN'T THEY?
I SAW ONE UP *REALLY* CLOSE! AND WE BECAME *FRIENDS!*
O-OH, MY. AREN'T YOU LUCKY?
SKRITCH
YOU THERE. BAMBOO VENDOR.
IS YOUR STORY TRUE?
I AM SEARCHING FOR YŌKAI MYSELF...

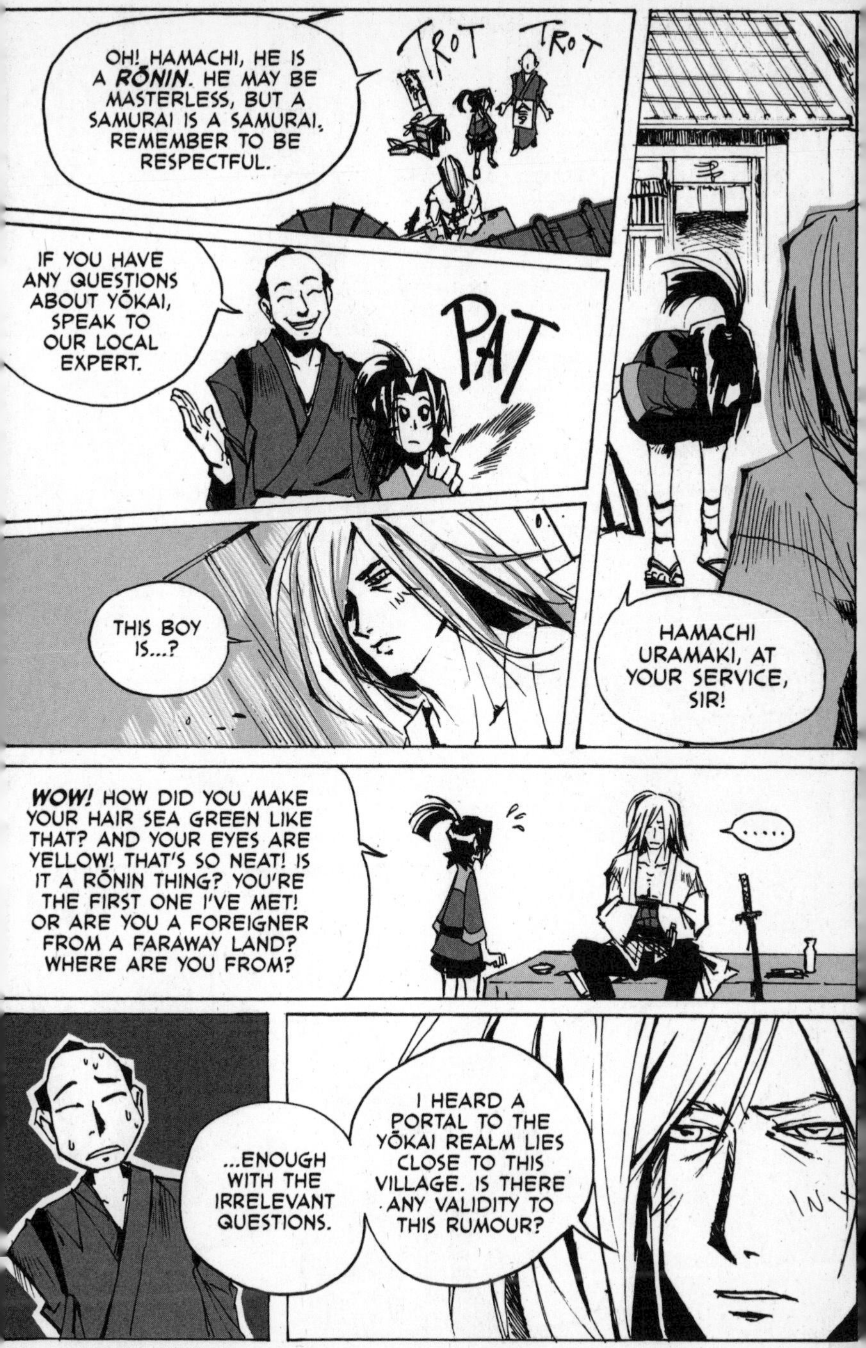
OH! HAMACHI, HE IS A ***RŌNIN***. HE MAY BE MASTERLESS, BUT A SAMURAI IS A SAMURAI. REMEMBER TO BE RESPECTFUL.
TROT TROT
IF YOU HAVE ANY QUESTIONS ABOUT YŌKAI, SPEAK TO OUR LOCAL EXPERT.
PAT
THIS BOY IS...?
HAMACHI URAMAKI, AT YOUR SERVICE, SIR!
WOW! HOW DID YOU MAKE YOUR HAIR SEA GREEN LIKE THAT? AND YOUR EYES ARE YELLOW! THAT'S SO NEAT! IS IT A RŌNIN THING? YOU'RE THE FIRST ONE I'VE MET! OR ARE YOU A FOREIGNER FROM A FARAWAY LAND? WHERE ARE YOU FROM?
......
I HEARD A PORTAL TO THE YŌKAI REALM LIES CLOSE TO THIS VILLAGE. IS THERE ANY VALIDITY TO THIS RUMOUR?
...ENOUGH WITH THE IRRELEVANT QUESTIONS.

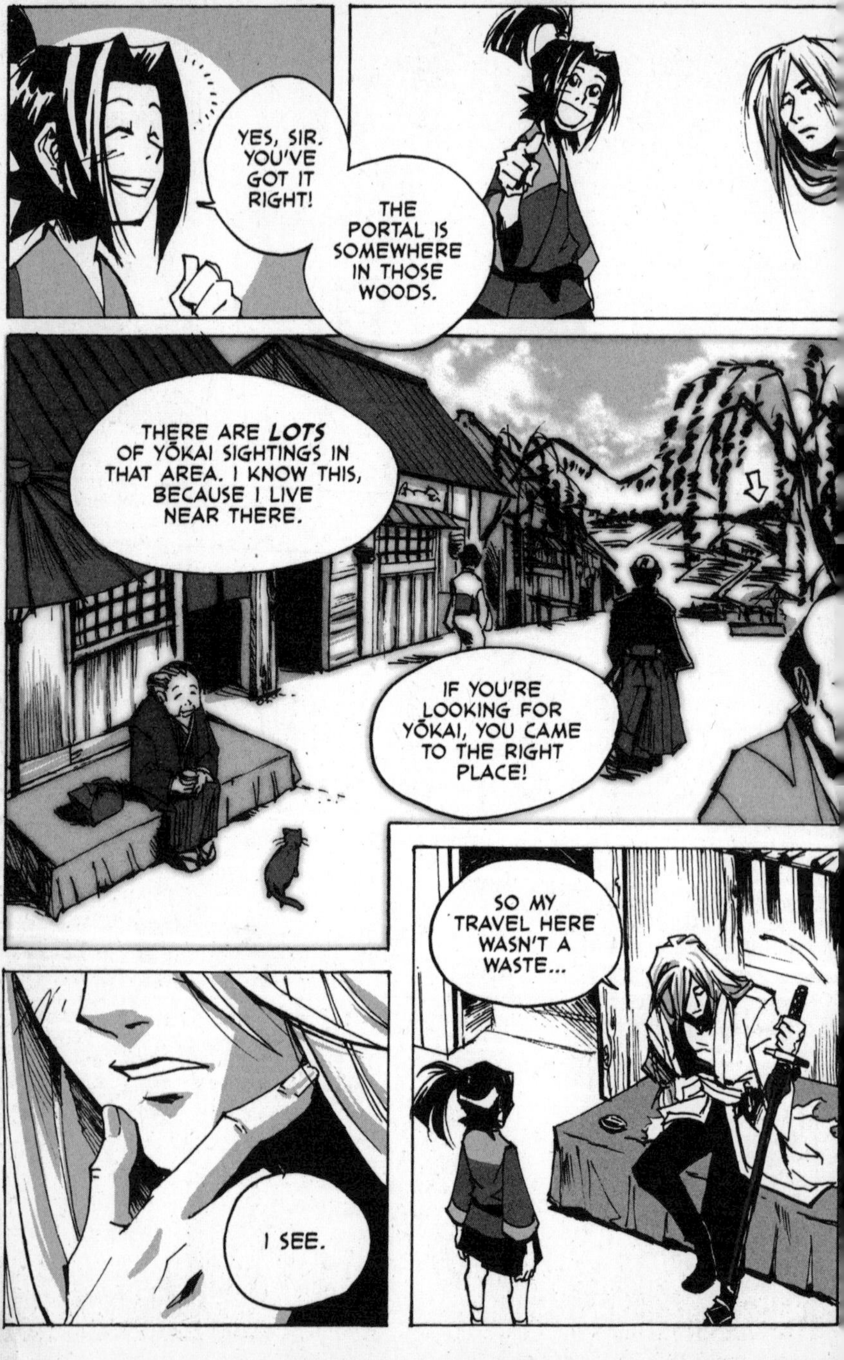
YES, SIR. YOU'VE GOT IT RIGHT!
THE PORTAL IS SOMEWHERE IN THOSE WOODS.
THERE ARE *LOTS* OF YŌKAI SIGHTINGS IN THAT AREA. I KNOW THIS, BECAUSE I LIVE NEAR THERE.
IF YOU'RE LOOKING FOR YŌKAI, YOU CAME TO THE RIGHT PLACE!
SO MY TRAVEL HERE WASN'T A WASTE...
I SEE.

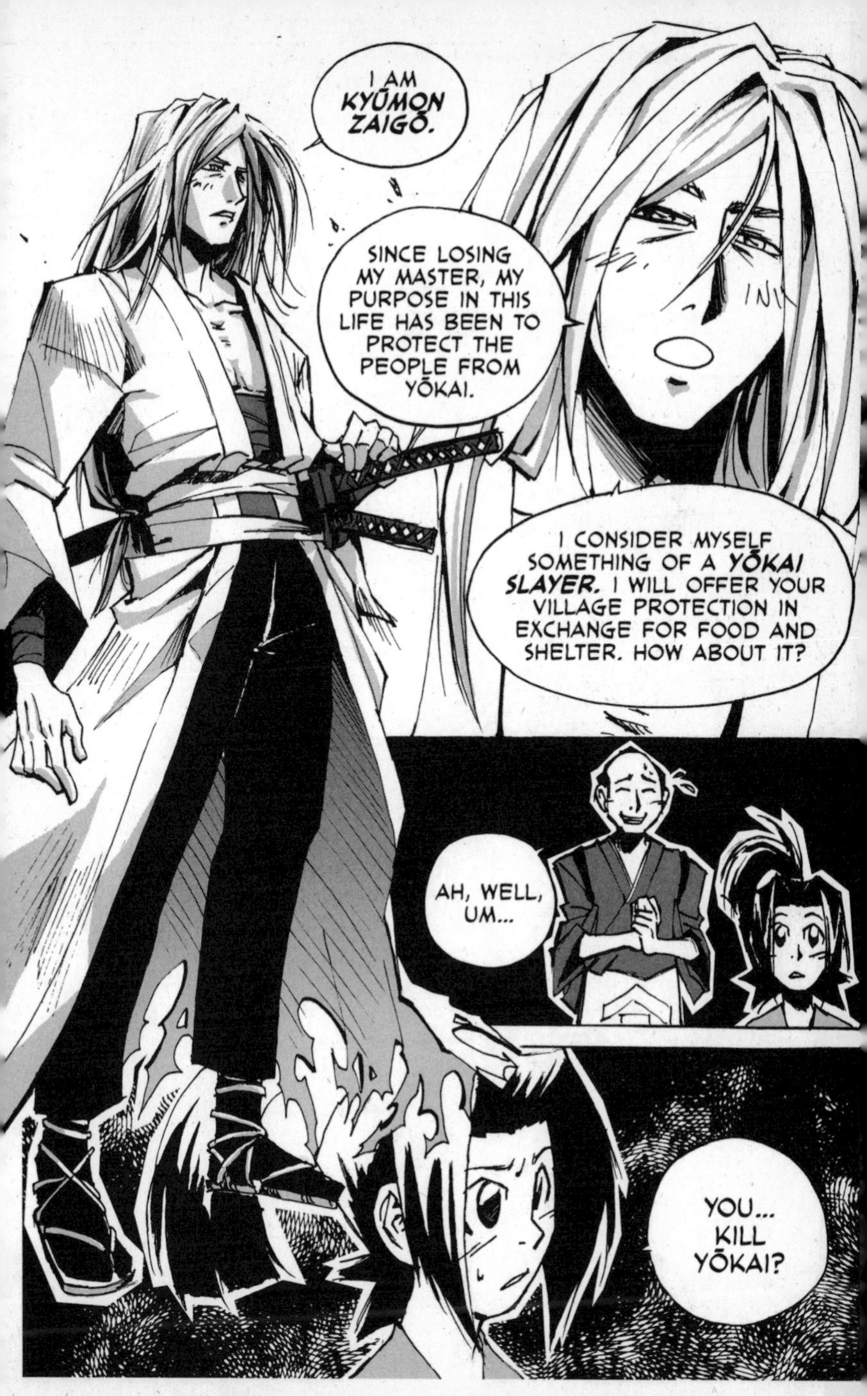
I AM KYŪMON ZAIGŌ.
SINCE LOSING MY MASTER, MY PURPOSE IN THIS LIFE HAS BEEN TO PROTECT THE PEOPLE FROM YŌKAI.
I CONSIDER MYSELF SOMETHING OF A YŌKAI SLAYER. I WILL OFFER YOUR VILLAGE PROTECTION IN EXCHANGE FOR FOOD AND SHELTER. HOW ABOUT IT?
AH, WELL, UM...
YOU... KILL YŌKAI?

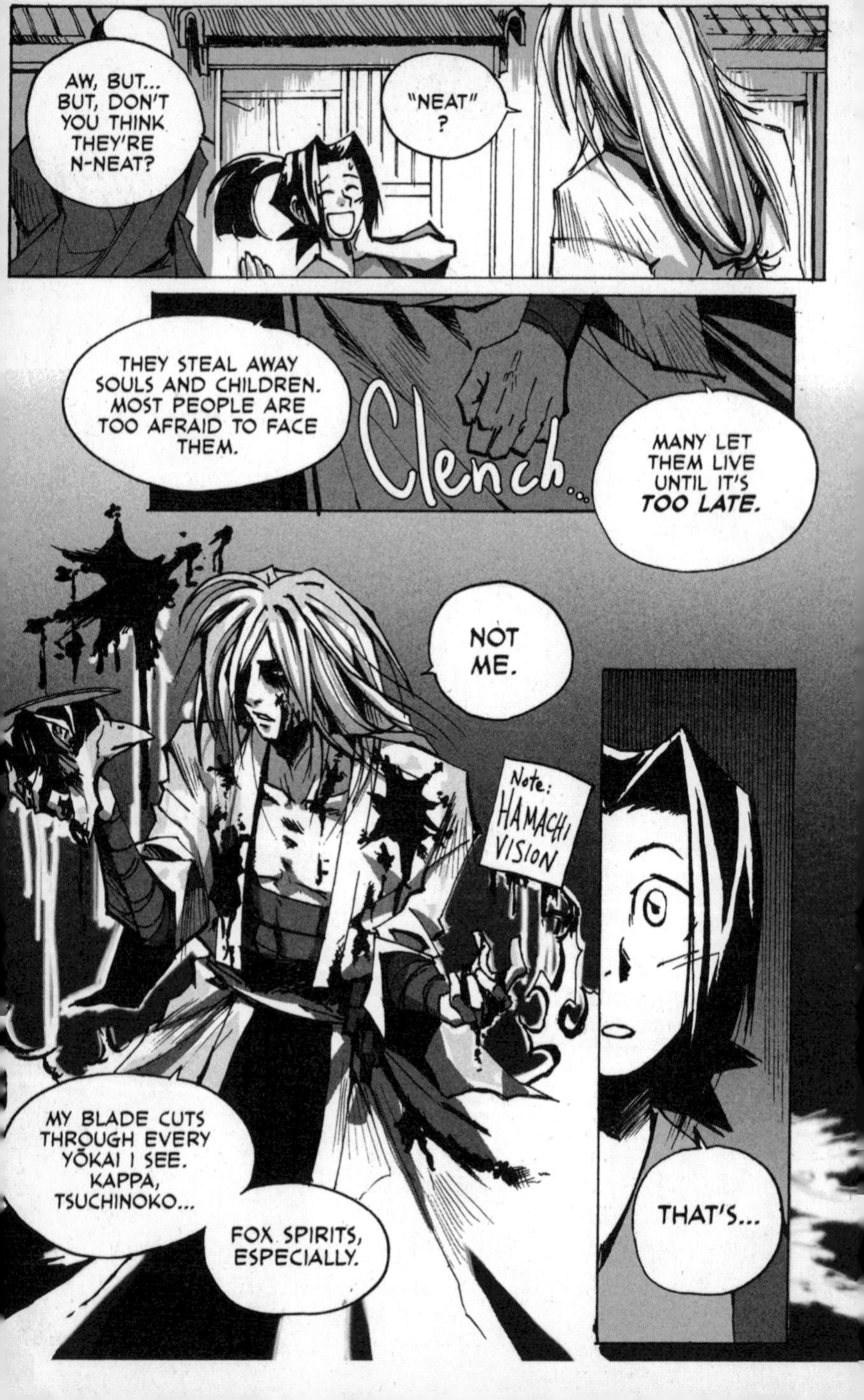
AW, BUT... BUT, DON'T YOU THINK THEY'RE N-NEAT?
"NEAT" ?
THEY STEAL AWAY SOULS AND CHILDREN. MOST PEOPLE ARE TOO AFRAID TO FACE THEM.
Clench...
MANY LET THEM LIVE UNTIL IT'S TOO LATE.
NOT ME.
Note: HAMACHI VISION
MY BLADE CUTS THROUGH EVERY YŌKAI I SEE. KAPPA, TSUCHINOKO...
FOX SPIRITS, ESPECIALLY.
THAT'S...

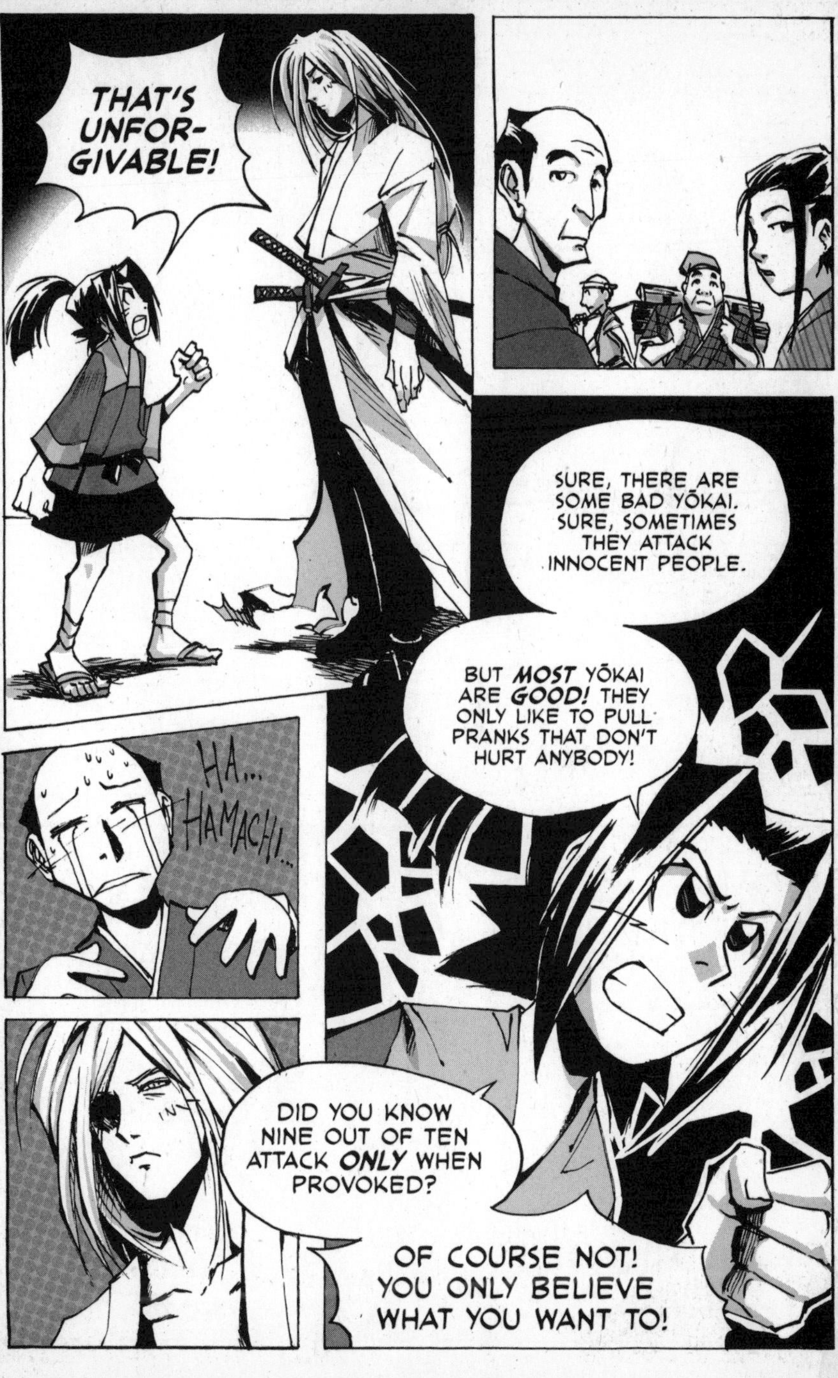
THAT'S UNFOR- GIVABLE!
SURE, THERE ARE SOME BAD YŌKAI. SURE, SOMETIMES THEY ATTACK INNOCENT PEOPLE.
BUT MOST YŌKAI ARE GOOD! THEY ONLY LIKE TO PULL PRANKS THAT DON'T HURT ANYBODY!
HA... HAMACHI...
DID YOU KNOW NINE OUT OF TEN ATTACK ONLY WHEN PROVOKED?
OF COURSE NOT! YOU ONLY BELIEVE WHAT YOU WANT TO!

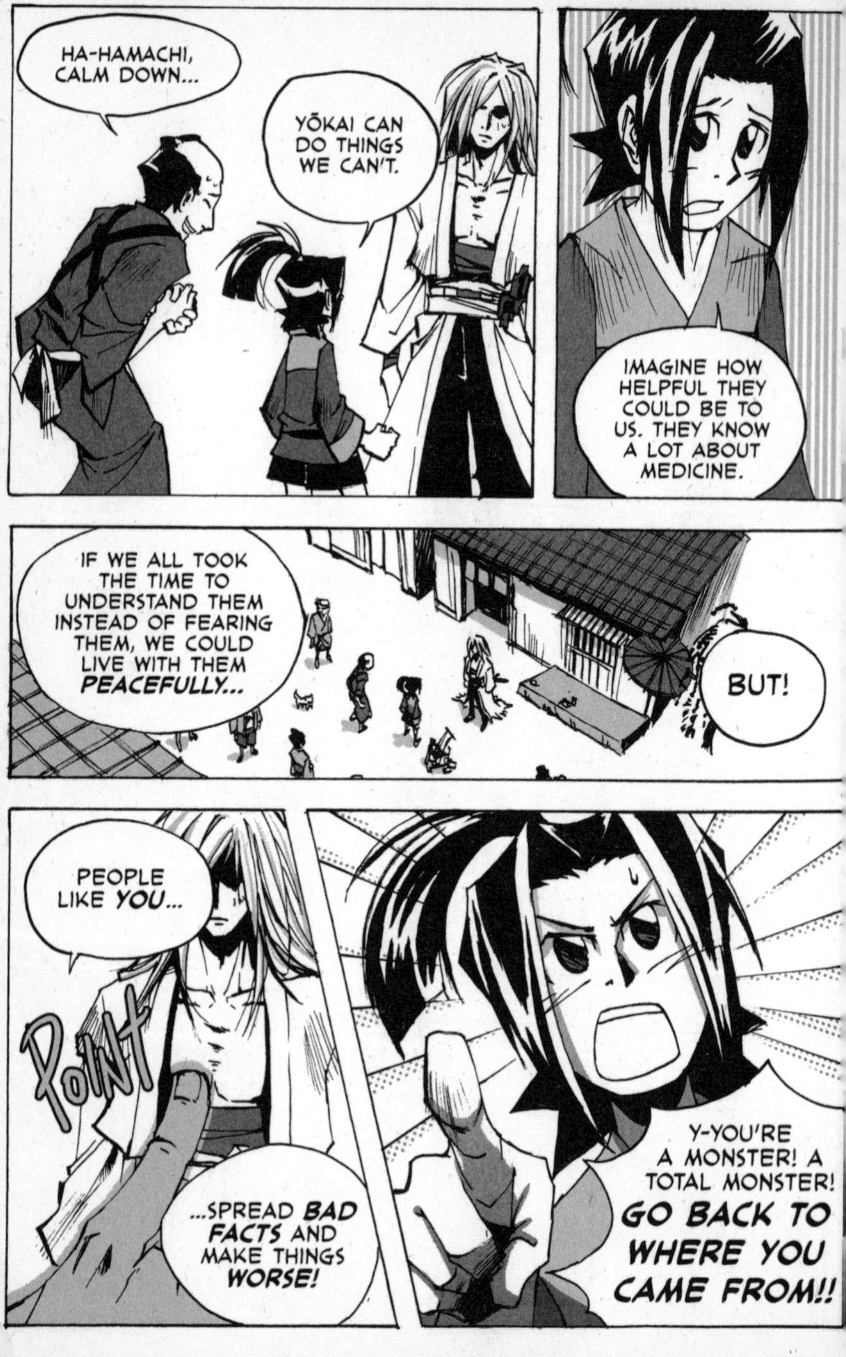
HA-HAMACHI, CALM DOWN...
YŌKAI CAN DO THINGS WE CAN'T.
IMAGINE HOW HELPFUL THEY COULD BE TO US. THEY KNOW A LOT ABOUT MEDICINE.
IF WE ALL TOOK THE TIME TO UNDERSTAND THEM INSTEAD OF FEARING THEM, WE COULD LIVE WITH THEM PEACEFULLY...
BUT!
PEOPLE LIKE YOU...
POINT
...SPREAD BAD FACTS AND MAKE THINGS WORSE!
Y-YOU'RE A MONSTER! A TOTAL MONSTER!
GO BACK TO WHERE YOU CAME FROM!!

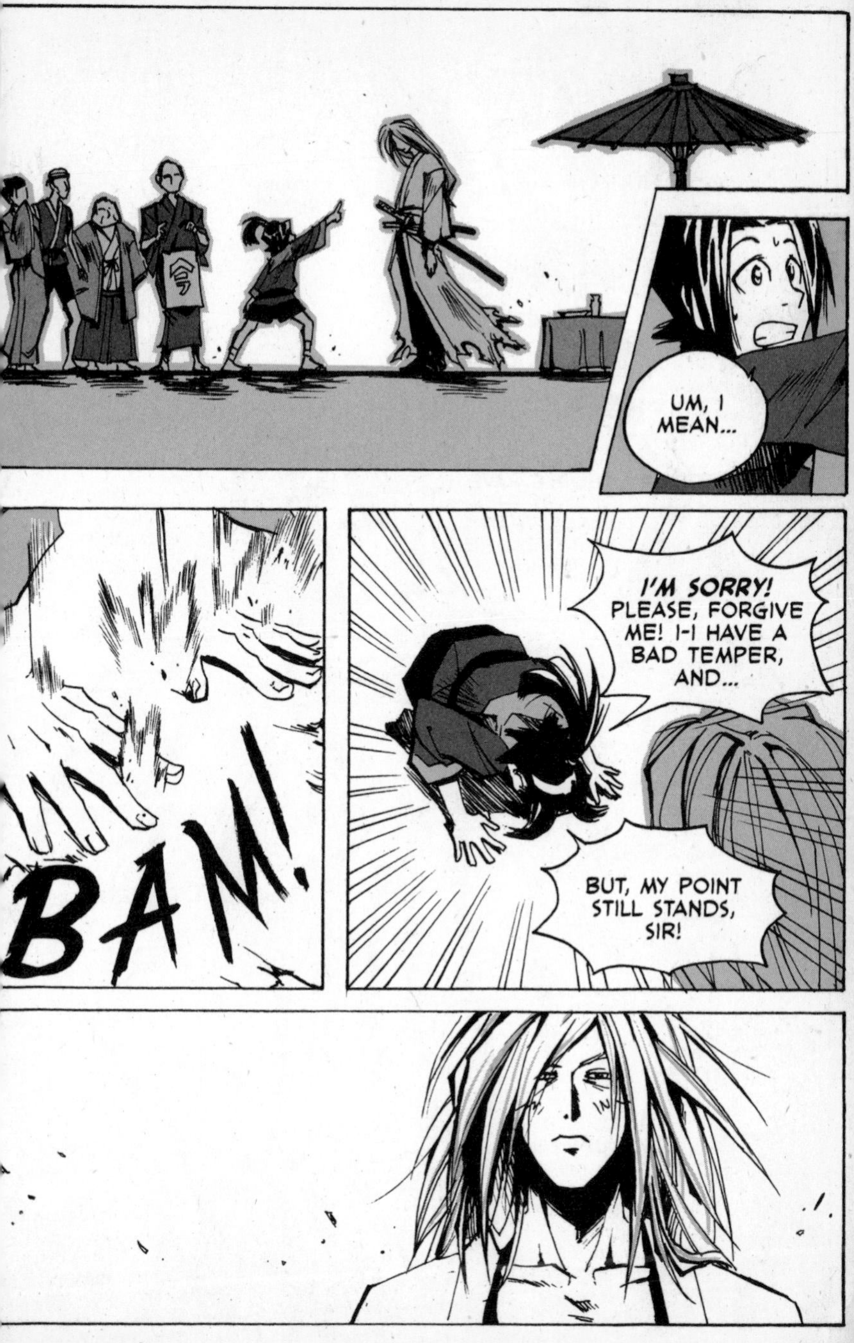
UM, I MEAN...
BAM!
I'M SORRY! PLEASE, FORGIVE ME! I-I HAVE A BAD TEMPER, AND...
BUT, MY POINT STILL STANDS, SIR!

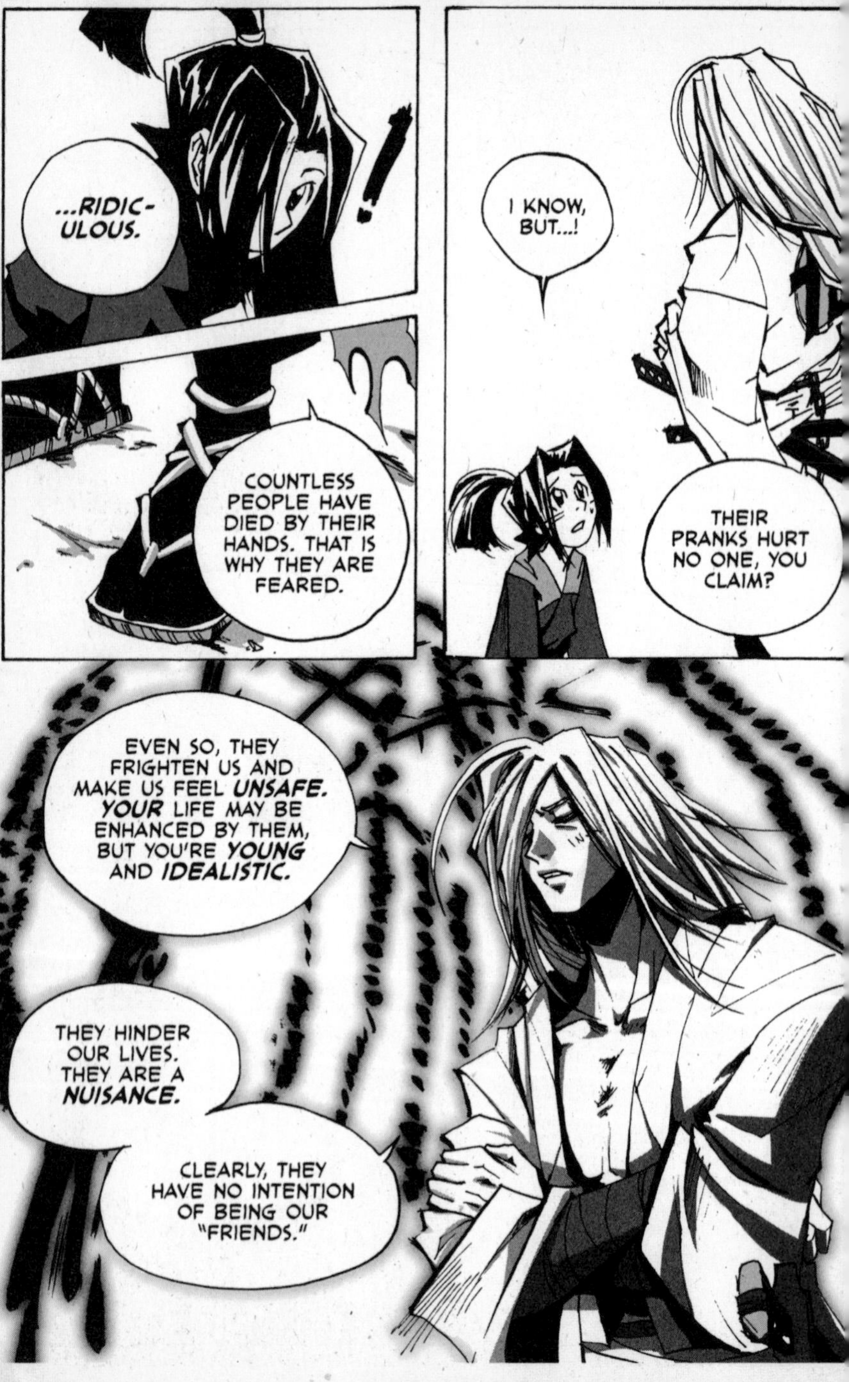
...RIDIC-ULOUS.
COUNTLESS PEOPLE HAVE DIED BY THEIR HANDS. THAT IS WHY THEY ARE FEARED.
I KNOW, BUT...!
THEIR PRANKS HURT NO ONE, YOU CLAIM?
EVEN SO, THEY FRIGHTEN US AND MAKE US FEEL UNSAFE. YOUR LIFE MAY BE ENHANCED BY THEM, BUT YOU'RE YOUNG AND IDEALISTIC.
THEY HINDER OUR LIVES. THEY ARE A NUISANCE.
CLEARLY, THEY HAVE NO INTENTION OF BEING OUR "FRIENDS."

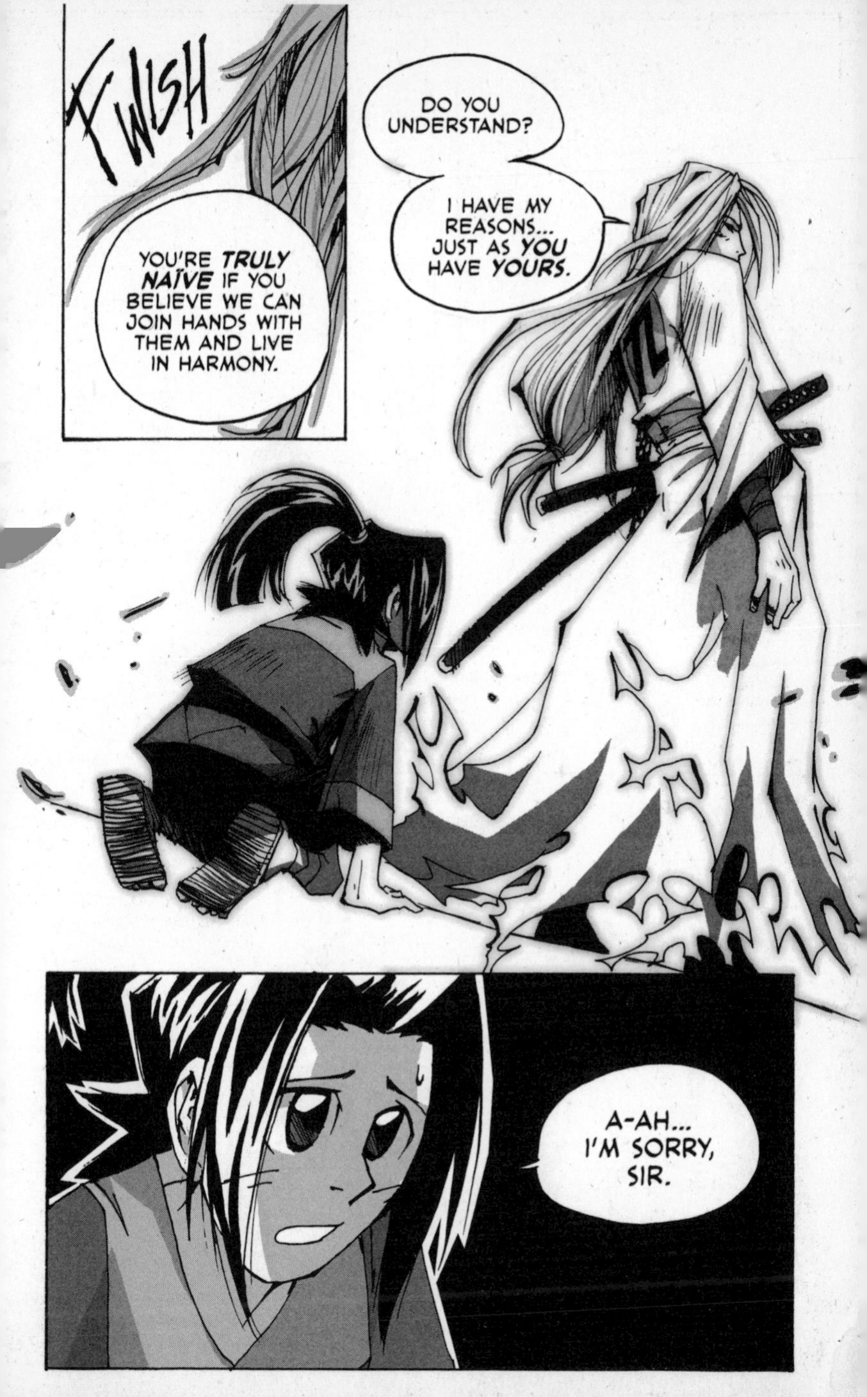
FWISH
YOU'RE TRULY NAÏVE IF YOU BELIEVE WE CAN JOIN HANDS WITH THEM AND LIVE IN HARMONY.
DO YOU UNDERSTAND?
I HAVE MY REASONS... JUST AS YOU HAVE YOURS.
A-AH... I'M SORRY, SIR.

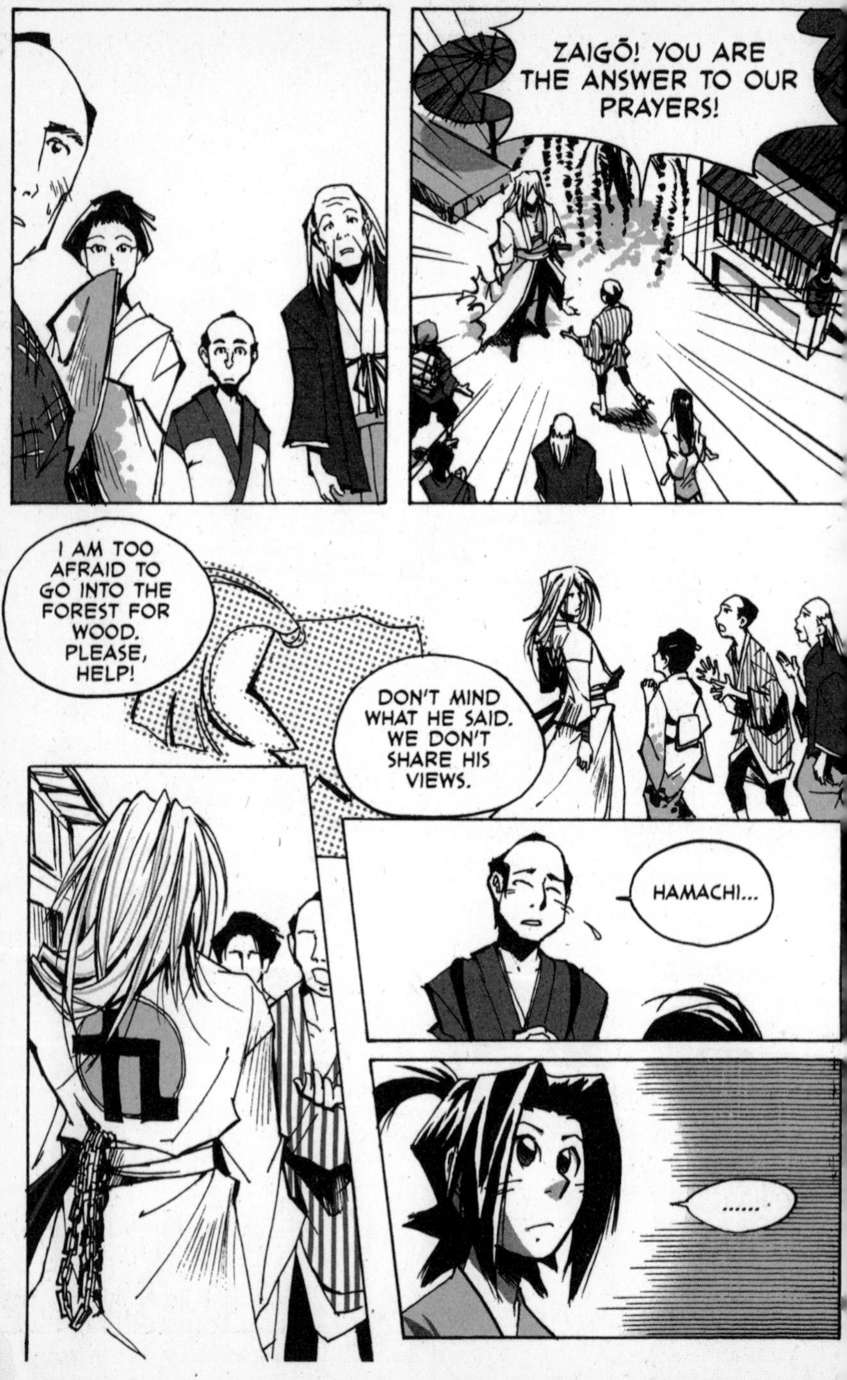
ZAIGŌ! YOU ARE THE ANSWER TO OUR PRAYERS!
I AM TOO AFRAID TO GO INTO THE FOREST FOR WOOD. PLEASE, HELP!
DON'T MIND WHAT HE SAID. WE DON'T SHARE HIS VIEWS.
HAMACHI...
......

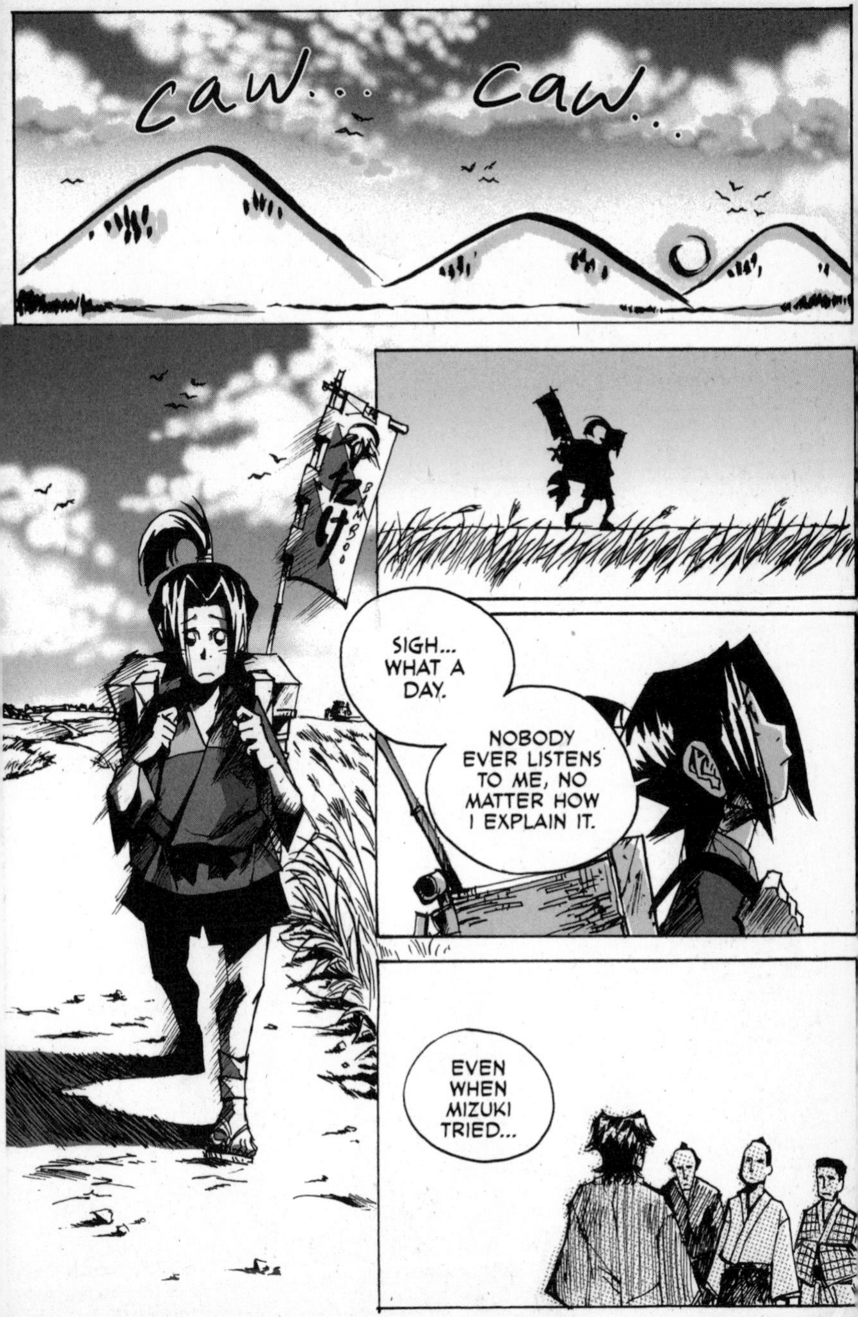

CAW... CAW...
BAMBOO
SIGH... WHAT A DAY.
NOBODY EVER LISTENS TO ME, NO MATTER HOW I EXPLAIN IT.
EVEN WHEN MIZUKI TRIED...

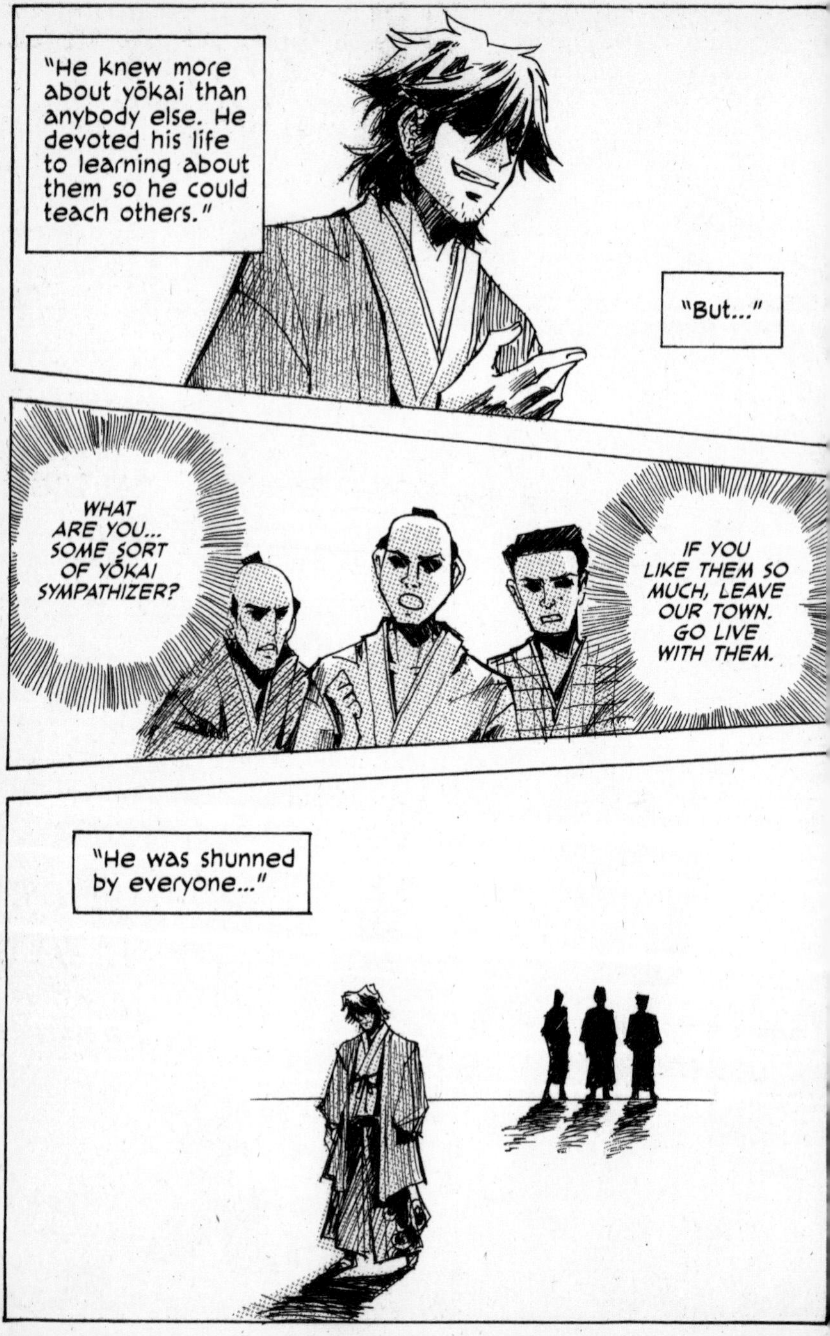
"He knew more about yōkai than anybody else. He devoted his life to learning about them so he could teach others."
"But..."
WHAT ARE YOU... SOME SORT OF YŌKAI SYMPATHIZER?
IF YOU LIKE THEM SO MUCH, LEAVE OUR TOWN. GO LIVE WITH THEM.
"He was shunned by everyone..."

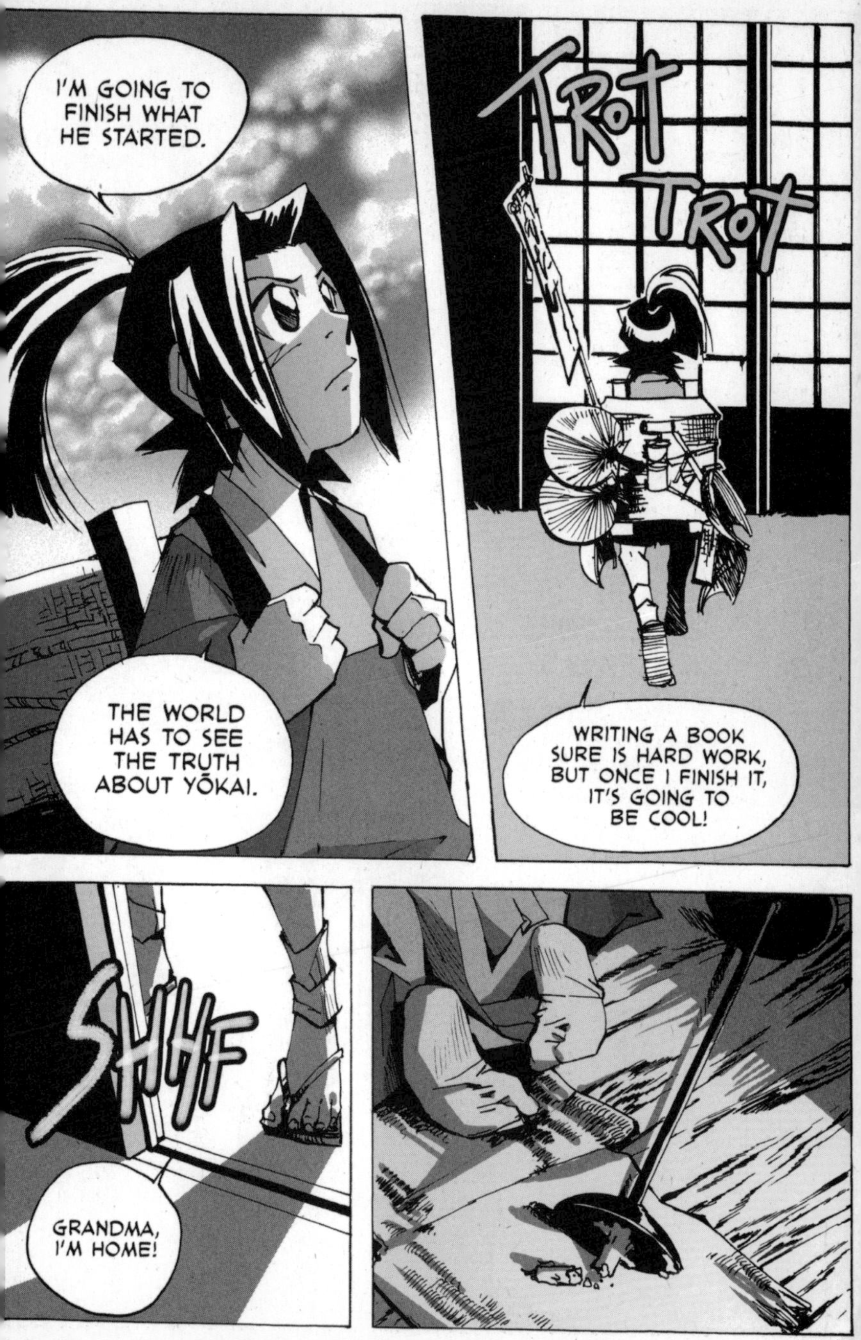
I'M GOING TO FINISH WHAT HE STARTED.
THE WORLD HAS TO SEE THE TRUTH ABOUT YŌKAI.
TROT TROT
WRITING A BOOK SURE IS HARD WORK, BUT ONCE I FINISH IT, IT'S GOING TO BE COOL!
SHHF
GRANDMA, I'M HOME!

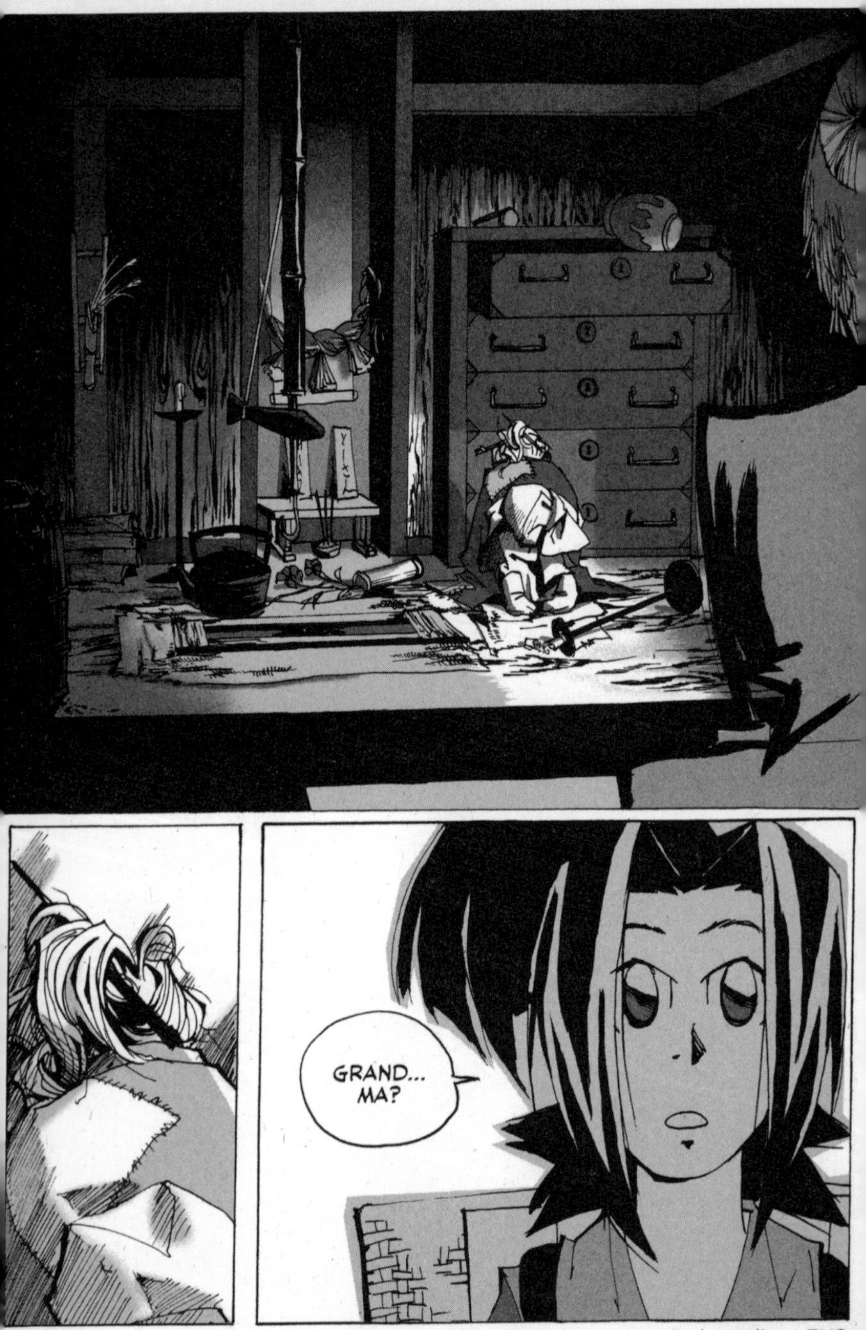
GRAND... MA?

2nd candle - END

HAMACHI'S JOURNAL

SHAKUHACHI

blow here

root

"IT'S AN END-BLOWN FLUTE MADE OF BAMBOO! THE NAME MEANS '1.8 FOOT.' HAVE YOU EVER SEEN THOSE WEIRD MONKS WHO WALK AROUND WEARING BASKETS OVER THEIR HEADS, PLAYING SOME INSTRUMENT? THEY'RE PLAYING THE SHAKUHACHI. SEE HOW IT'S ALL BIG AND CLUBBY AT THE END? THAT'S THE BAMBOO ROOT. YOU CAN REALLY HURT SOMEONE BAD BY HITTING THEM WITH IT."

long sword

← long hair

short sword

RŌNIN

"THEY'RE MASTERLESS SAMURAI, RIGHT? SORRY. I DON'T KNOW TOO MUCH ABOUT THEM. THEY'RE REALLY NOT COMMON WHERE I LIVE. WE DON'T GET TOO MANY TRAVELLERS. ACTUALLY, I HEARD THAT WHEN A SAMURAI BECOMES MASTERLESS, HE'S SUPPOSED TO KILL HIMSELF. IT'S PART OF THE SAMURAI CODE. WHY ARE THERE RŌNIN, THEN? AREN'T THEY SUPPOSED TO BE DEAD?"

 "I'D SUGGEST TAKING ART LESSONS BEFORE ATTEMPTING TO CAPTURE MY LIKENESS."

 "I'M SORRY. I'VE NEVER BEEN GOOD AT DRAWING HANDS."

3rd candle

An Eye for an Eye

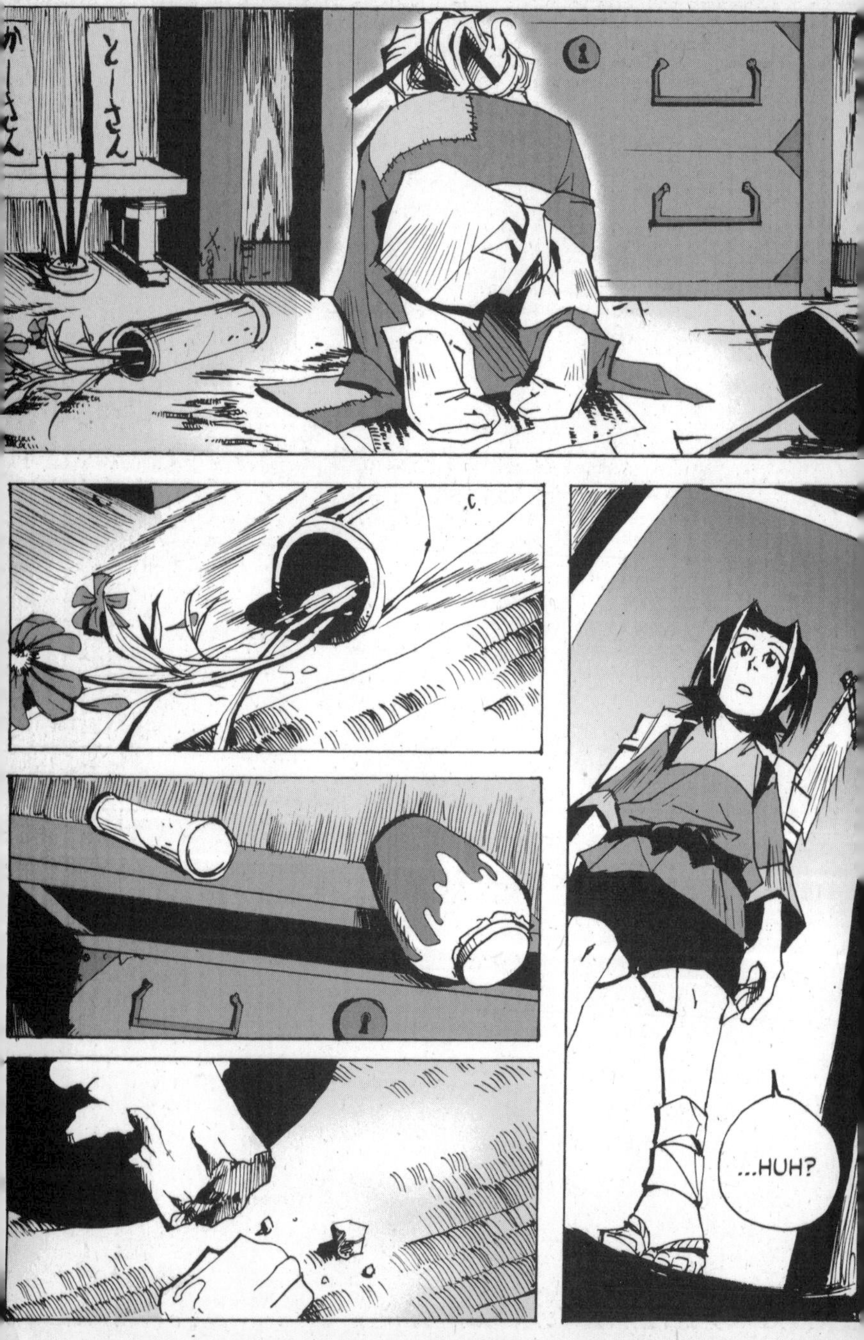
とーさん
かーさん
...HUH?

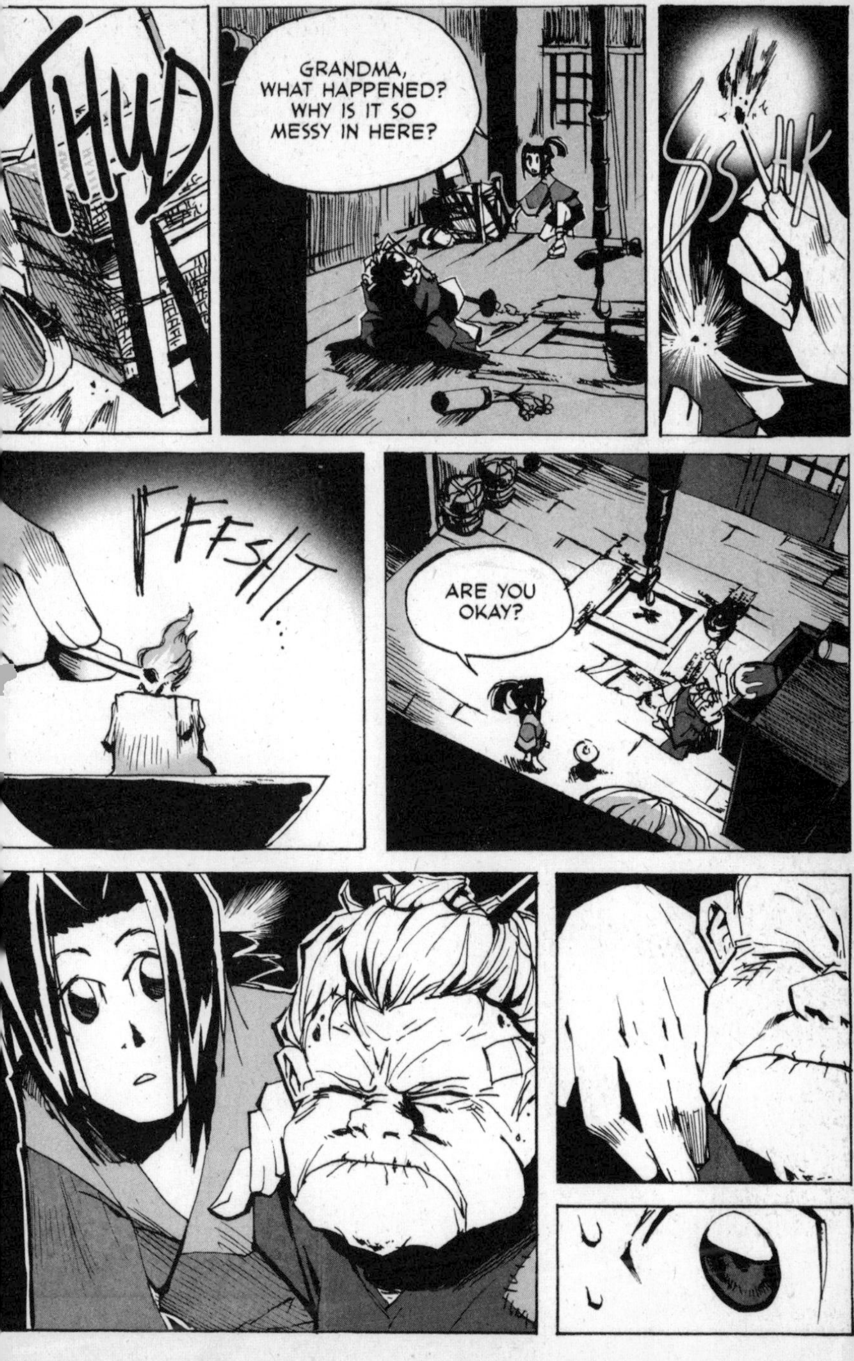
THUD
GRANDMA, WHAT HAPPENED? WHY IS IT SO MESSY IN HERE?
SSHK
FFFSHT
ARE YOU OKAY?

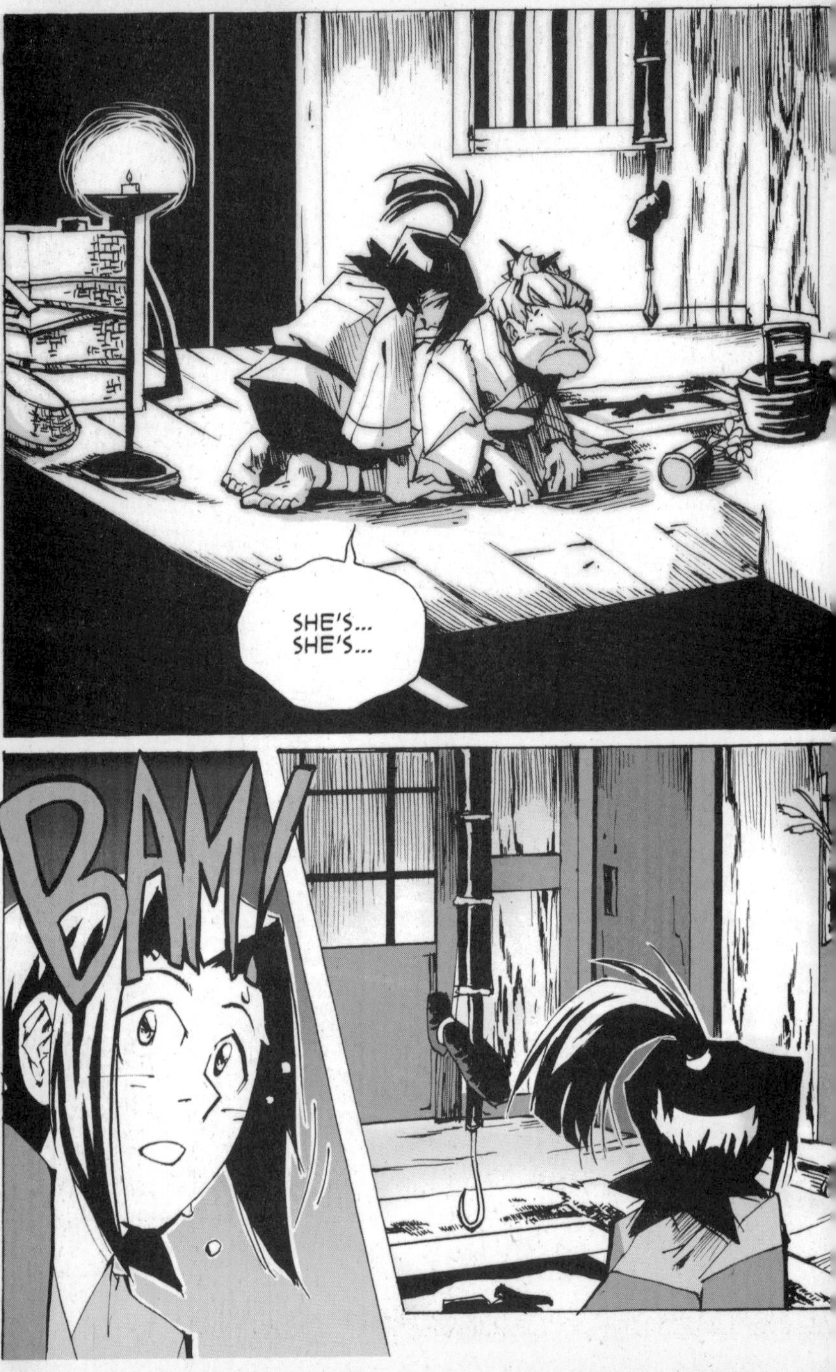
SHE'S... SHE'S...
BAM!

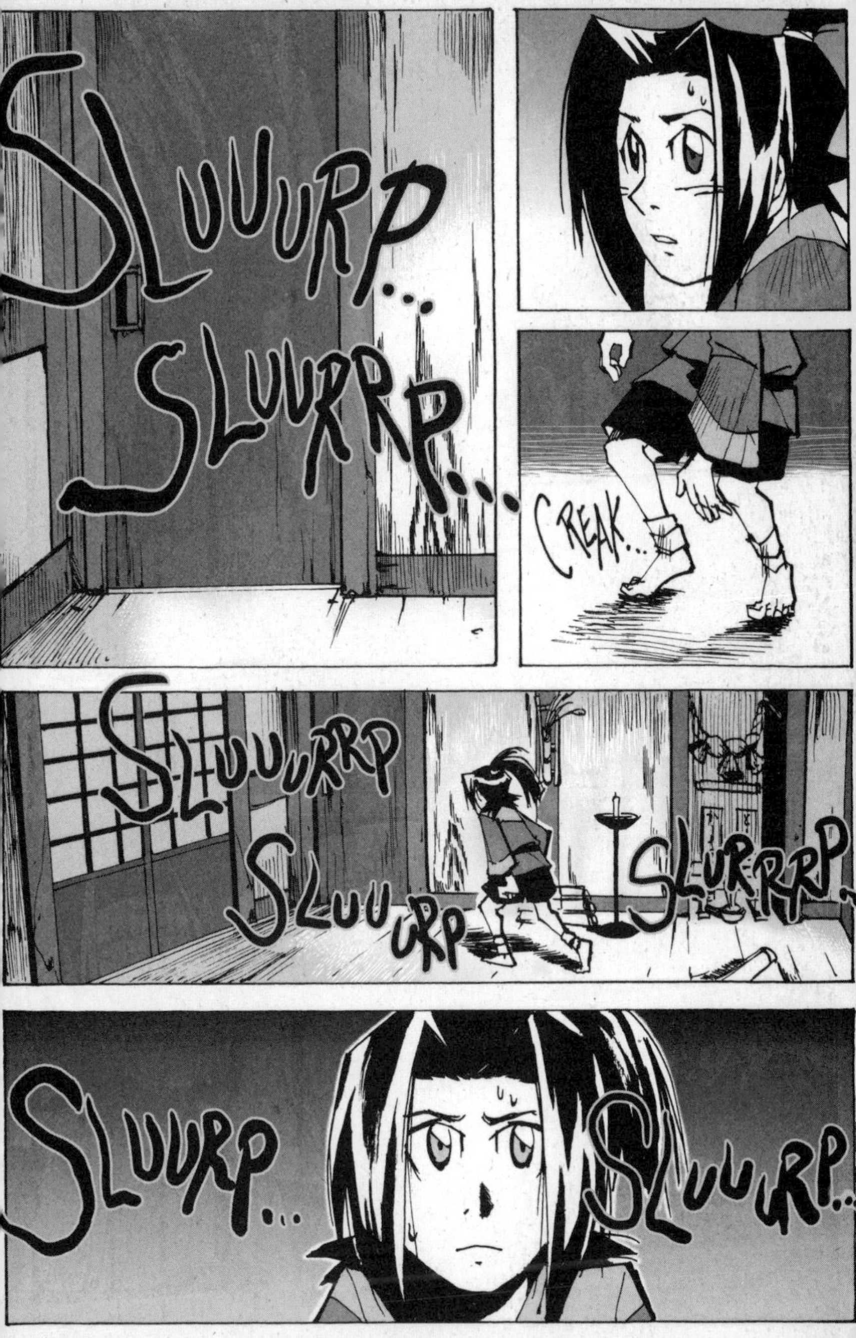
SLUUURP...
SLUURRP...
CREAK...
SLUUURRP
SLUUURP
SLURRRP...
SLUURP...
SLUUURP...

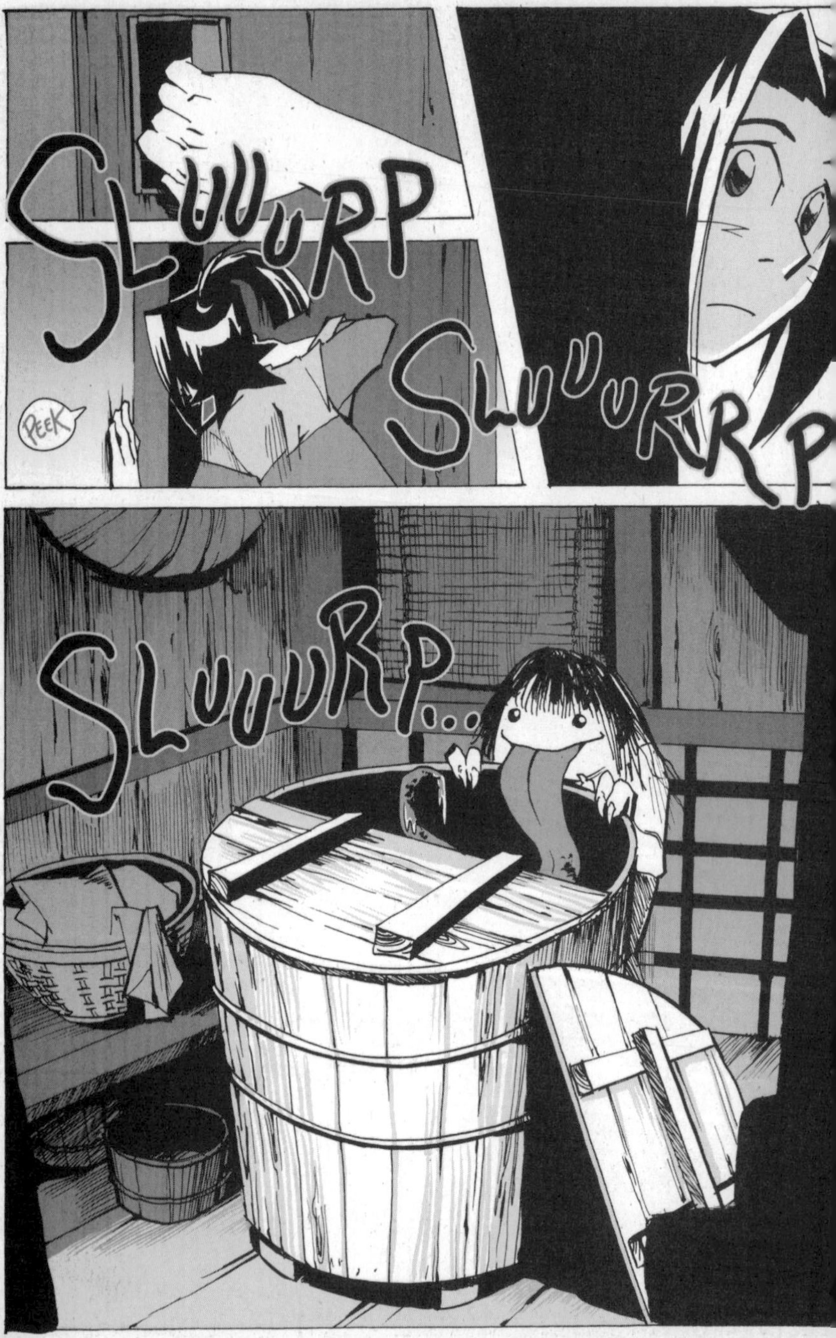
SLUUURRP
SLUUURP
PEEK
SLUUURP...

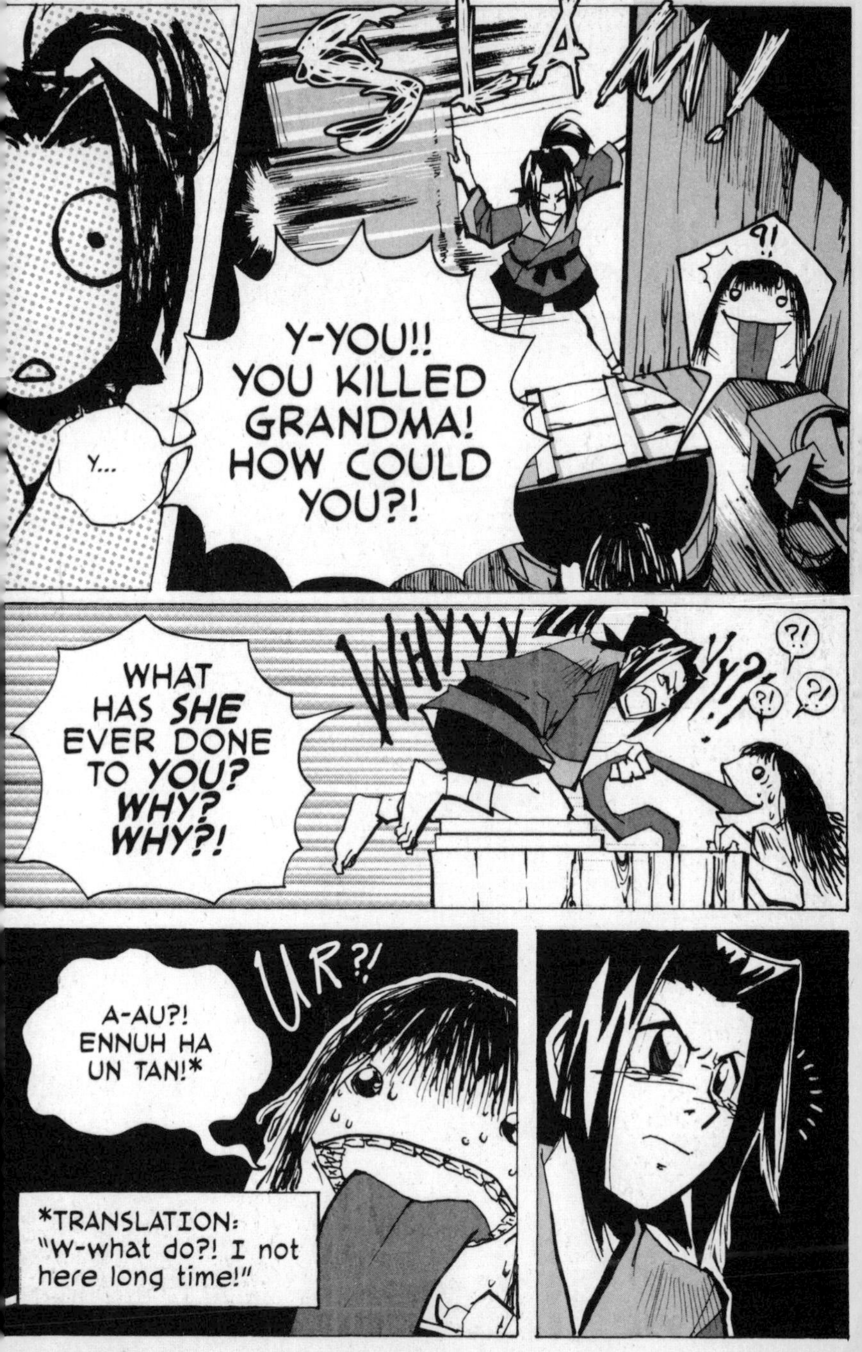
SLAM!
?!
Y-YOU!! YOU KILLED GRANDMA! HOW COULD YOU?!
Y...
WHAT HAS SHE EVER DONE TO YOU? WHY? WHY?!
WHYYYYYY?!
?!
?!
?!
UR?!
A-AU?! ENNUH HA UN TAN!*
*TRANSLATION: "W-what do?! I not here long time!"

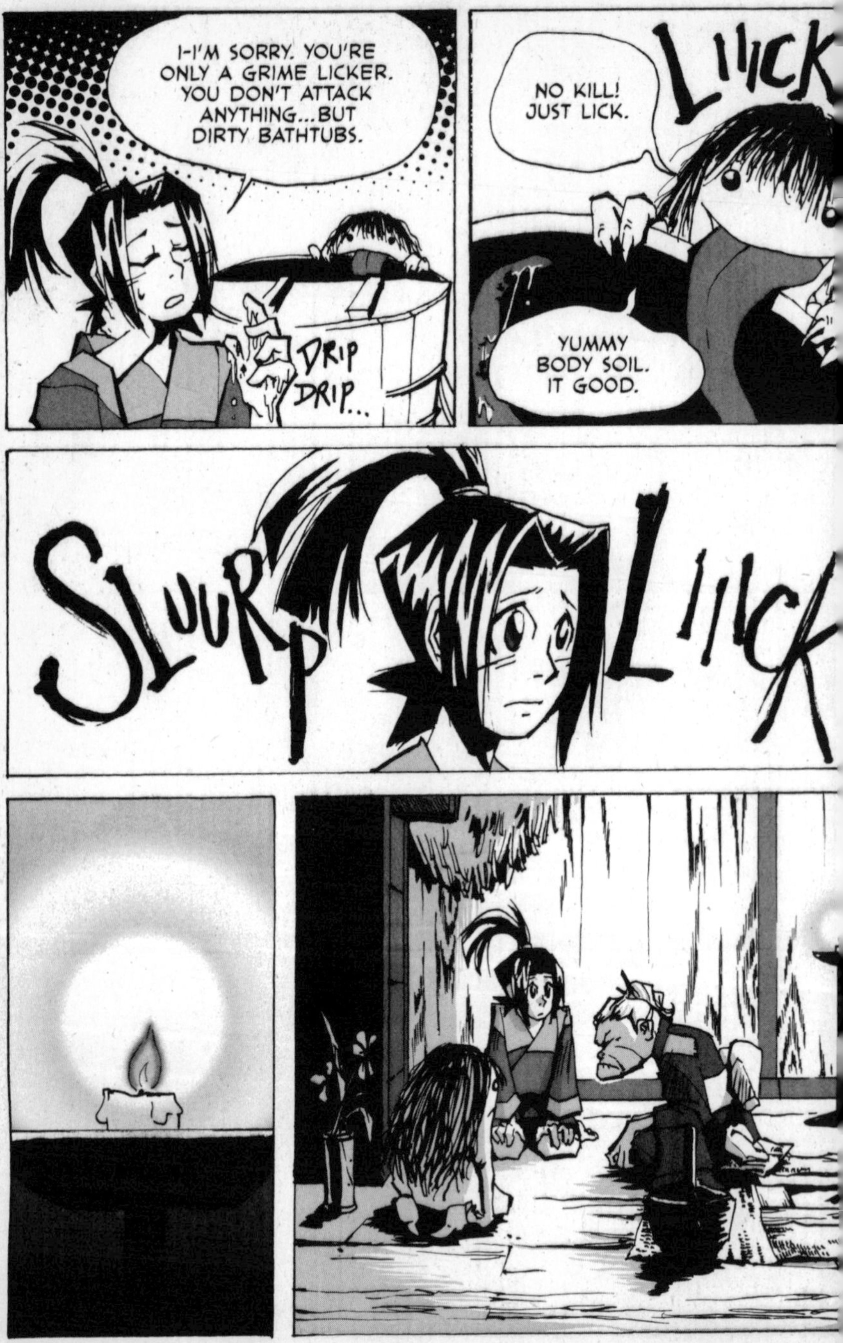

I-I'M SORRY. YOU'RE ONLY A GRIME LICKER. YOU DON'T ATTACK ANYTHING...BUT DIRTY BATHTUBS.
DRIP DRIP...
NO KILL! JUST LICK.
LIICK
YUMMY BODY SOIL. IT GOOD.
SLUURP
LIICK

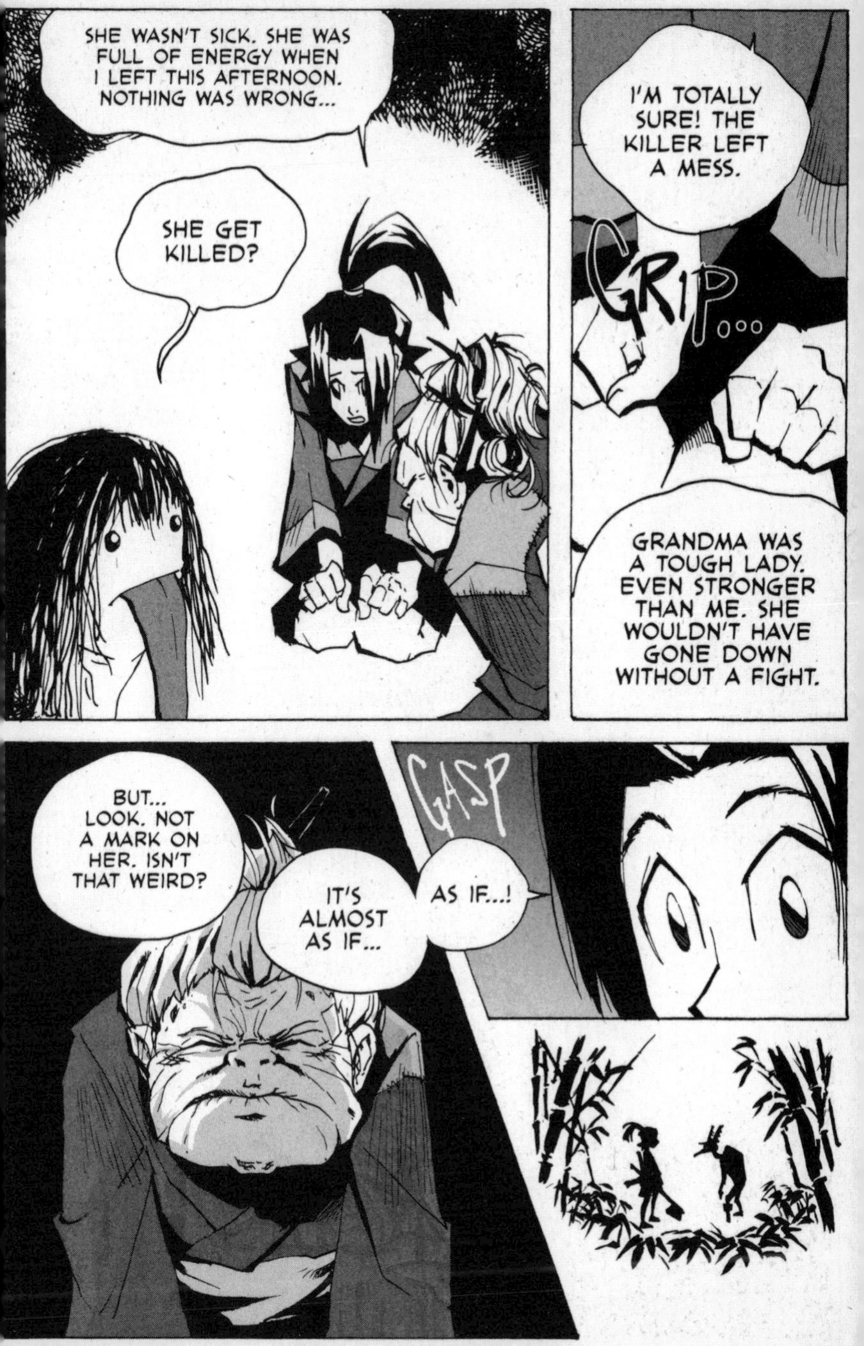
SHE WASN'T SICK. SHE WAS FULL OF ENERGY WHEN I LEFT THIS AFTERNOON. NOTHING WAS WRONG...
SHE GET KILLED?
I'M TOTALLY SURE! THE KILLER LEFT A MESS.
GRIP...
GRANDMA WAS A TOUGH LADY. EVEN STRONGER THAN ME. SHE WOULDN'T HAVE GONE DOWN WITHOUT A FIGHT.
BUT... LOOK. NOT A MARK ON HER. ISN'T THAT WEIRD?
IT'S ALMOST AS IF...
GASP
AS IF...!

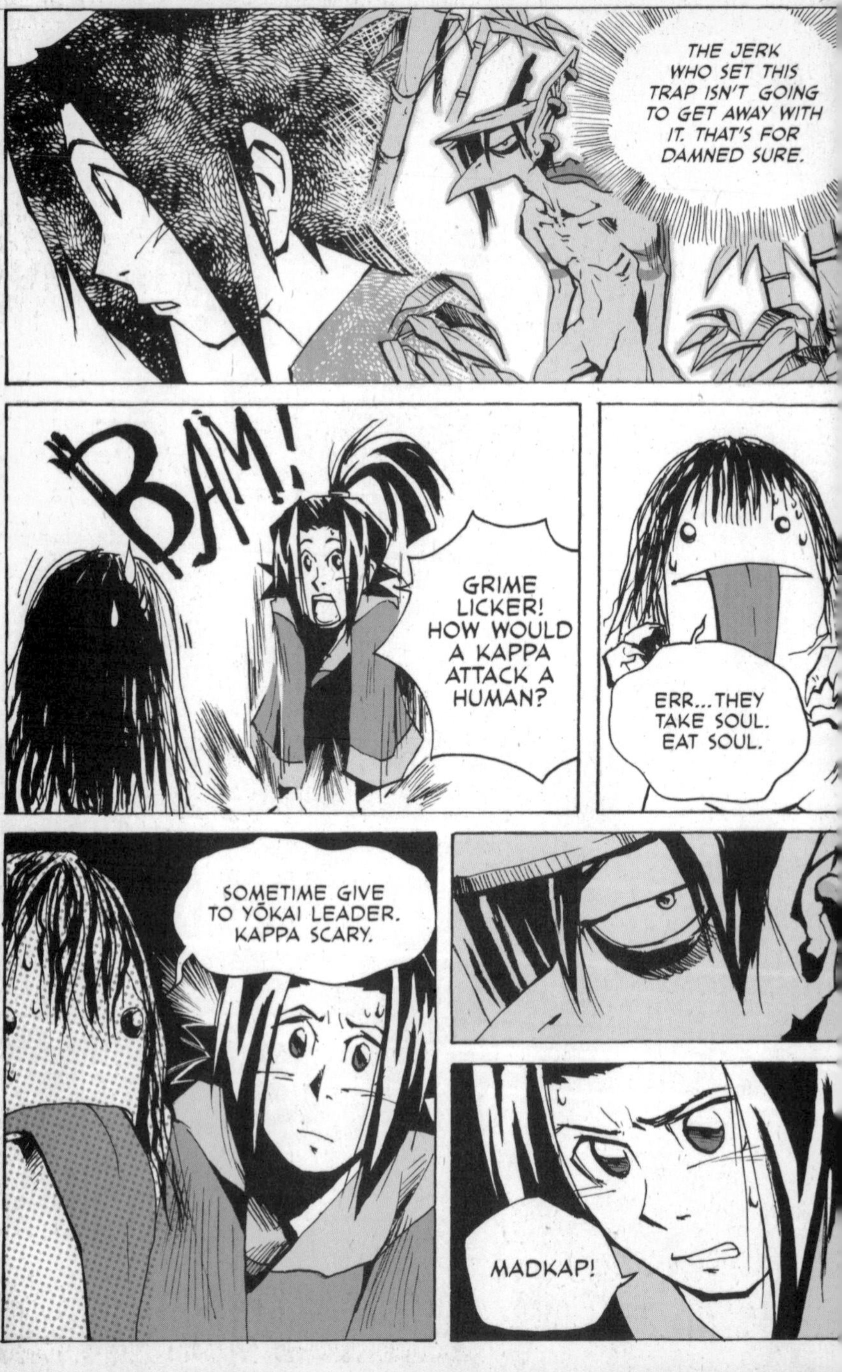
THE JERK WHO SET THIS TRAP ISN'T GOING TO GET AWAY WITH IT. THAT'S FOR DAMNED SURE.
BAM!
GRIME LICKER! HOW WOULD A KAPPA ATTACK A HUMAN?
ERR...THEY TAKE SOUL. EAT SOUL.
SOMETIME GIVE TO YŌKAI LEADER. KAPPA SCARY.
MADKAP!

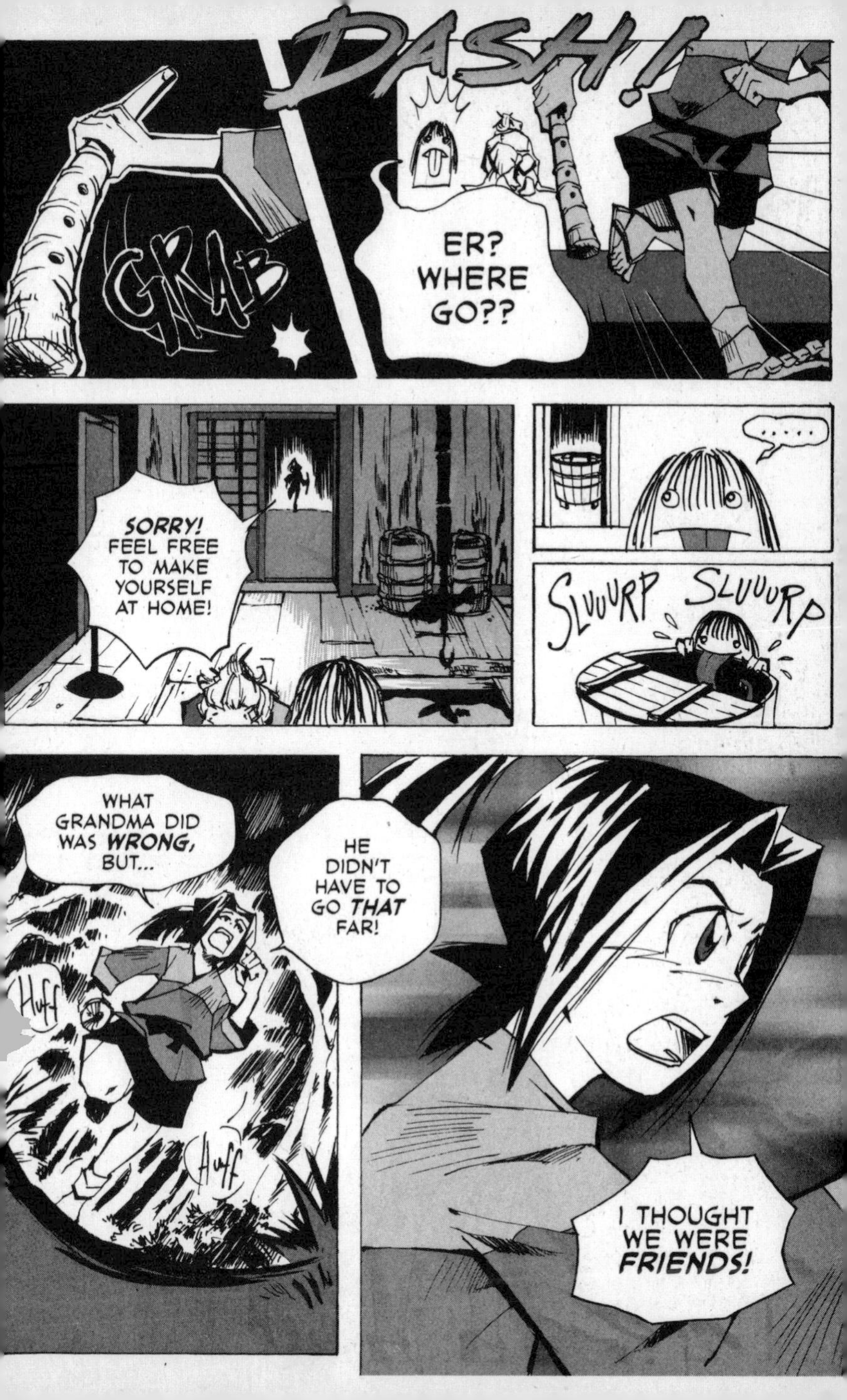
DASH!
GRAB
ER? WHERE GO??
SORRY! FEEL FREE TO MAKE YOURSELF AT HOME!
.....
SLUUURP SLUUURP
WHAT GRANDMA DID WAS WRONG, BUT...
HE DIDN'T HAVE TO GO THAT FAR!
Huff
Huff
I THOUGHT WE WERE FRIENDS!

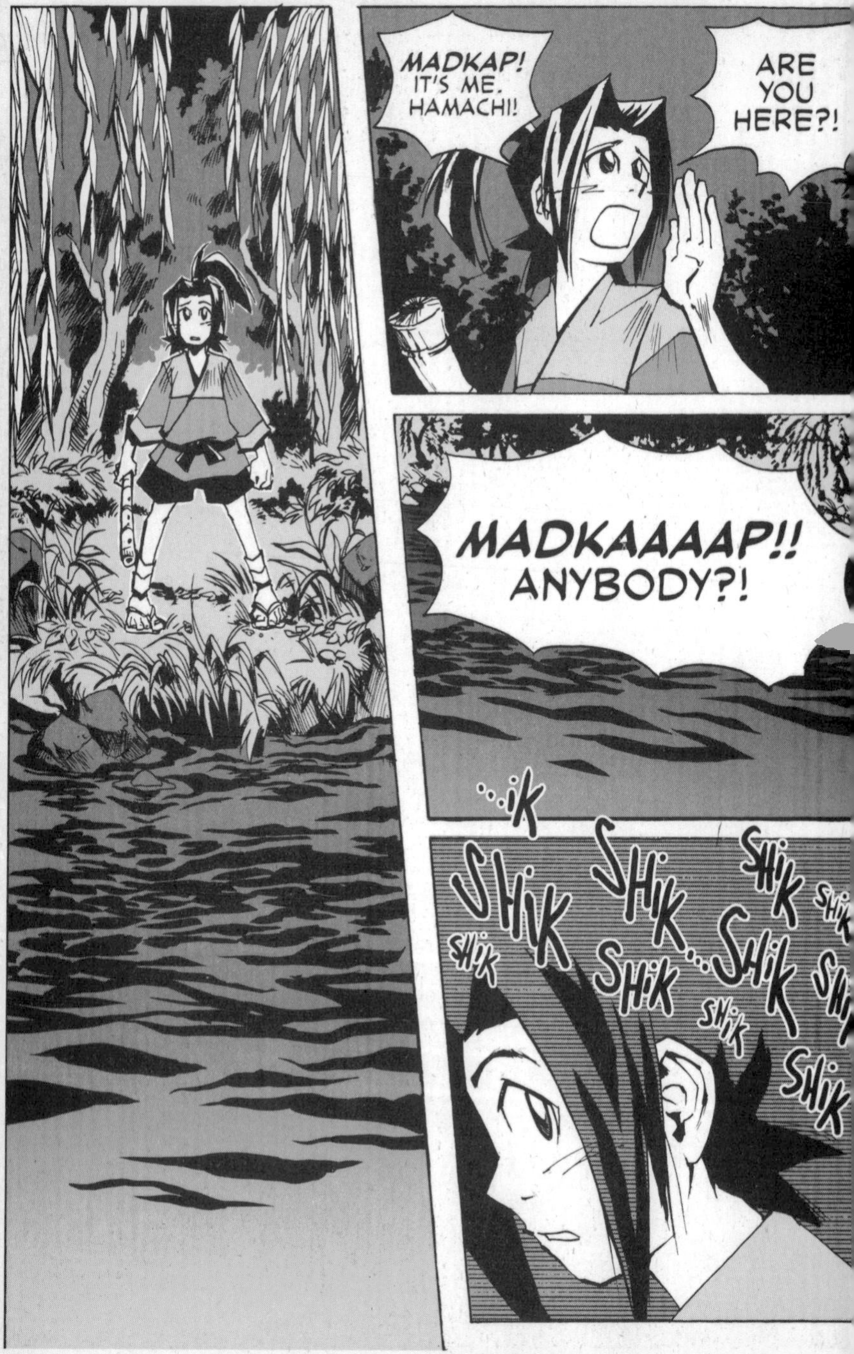
MADKAP! IT'S ME. HAMACHI!
ARE YOU HERE?!
MADKAAAAP!! ANYBODY?!
...ik
SHIK SHIK SHIK SHIK... SHIK SHIK SHIK SHIK SHIK SHIK SHIK

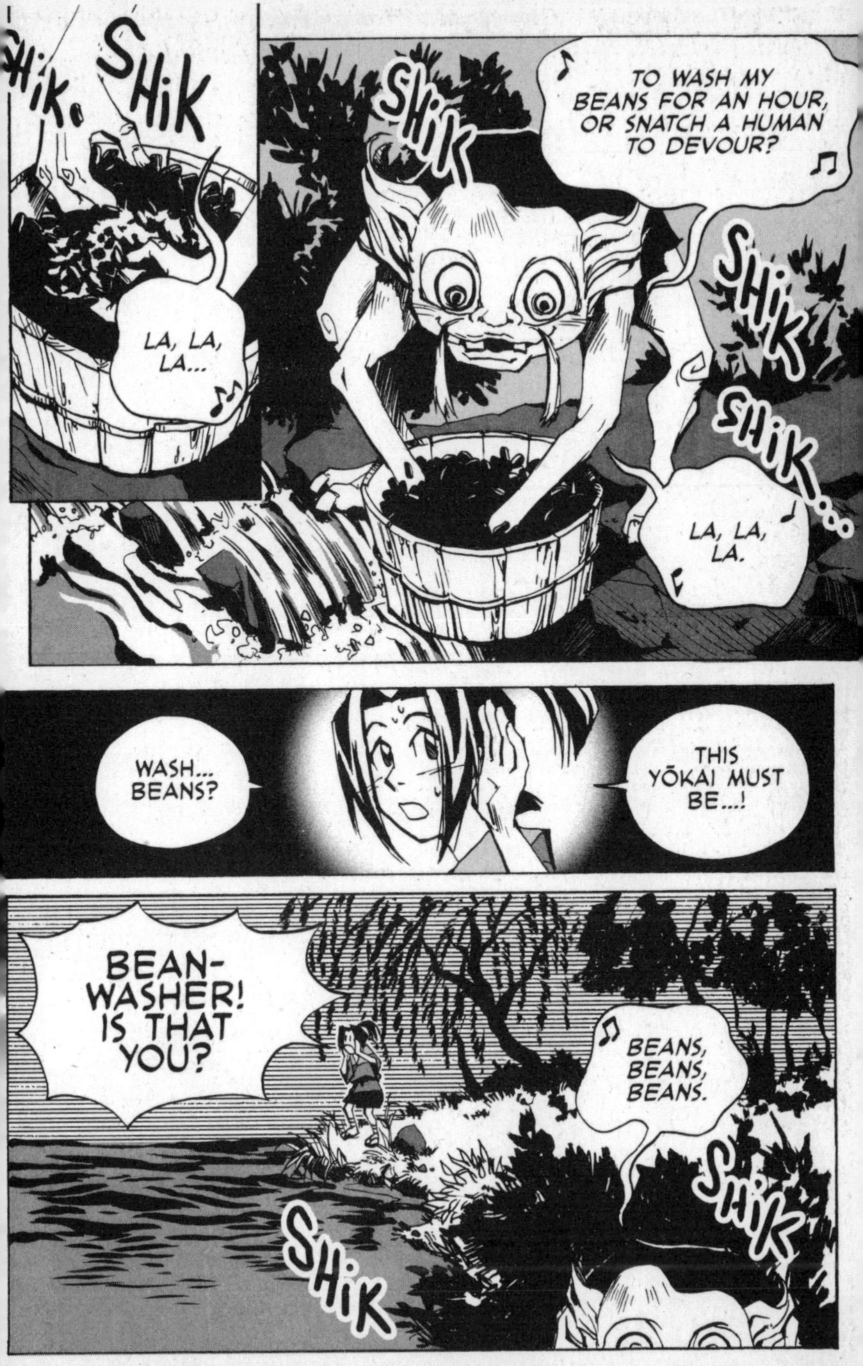
SHIK.
SHIK
LA, LA, LA...
SHIK
TO WASH MY BEANS FOR AN HOUR, OR SNATCH A HUMAN TO DEVOUR?
SHIK
SHIK...
LA, LA, LA.
WASH... BEANS?
THIS YŌKAI MUST BE...!
BEAN-WASHER! IS THAT YOU?
BEANS, BEANS, BEANS.
SHIK
SHIK

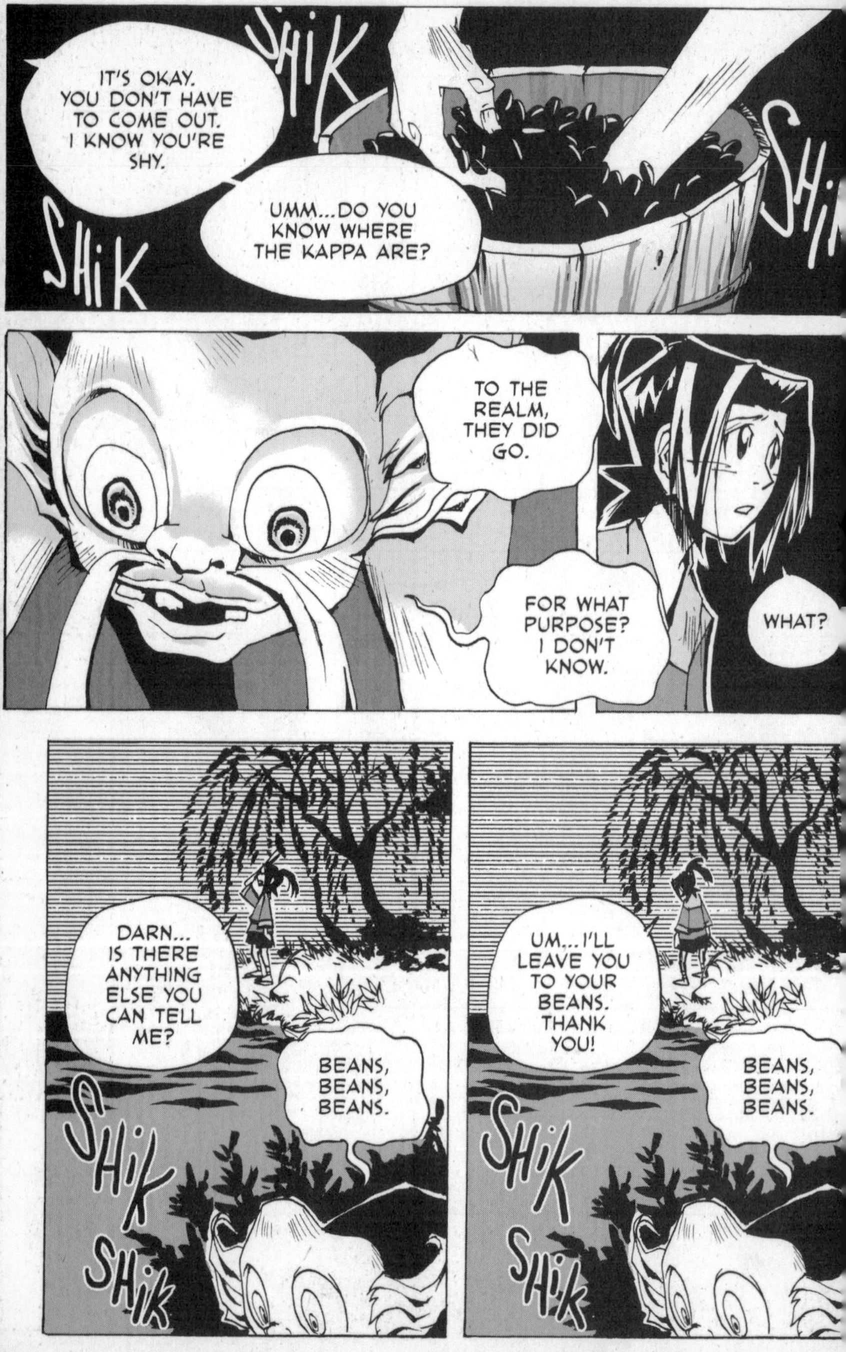
SHIK
IT'S OKAY. YOU DON'T HAVE TO COME OUT. I KNOW YOU'RE SHY.
SHIK
UMM...DO YOU KNOW WHERE THE KAPPA ARE?
SHI
TO THE REALM, THEY DID GO.
FOR WHAT PURPOSE? I DON'T KNOW.
WHAT?
DARN... IS THERE ANYTHING ELSE YOU CAN TELL ME?
BEANS, BEANS, BEANS.
SHIK SHIK
UM... I'LL LEAVE YOU TO YOUR BEANS. THANK YOU!
BEANS, BEANS, BEANS.
SHIK SHIK

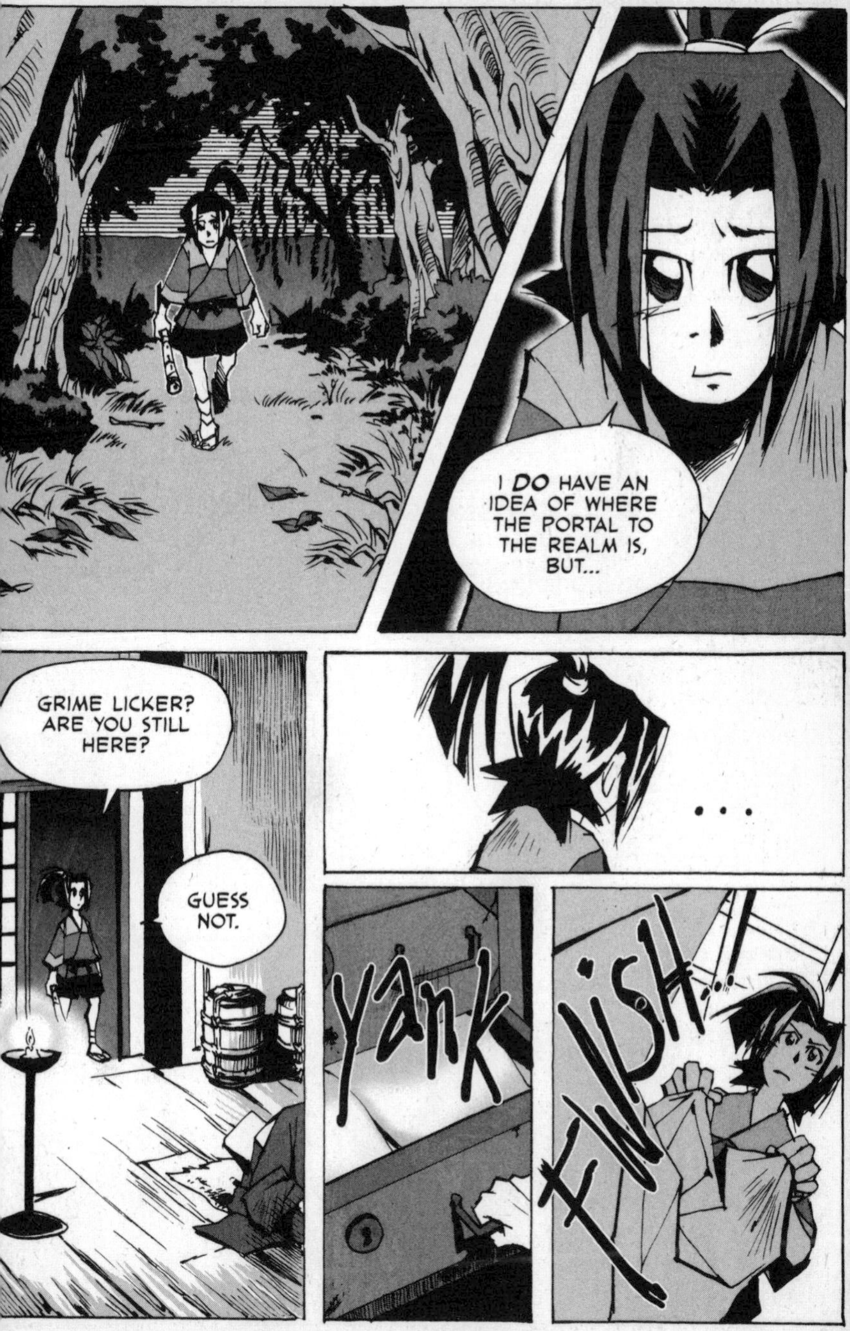
I DO HAVE AN IDEA OF WHERE THE PORTAL TO THE REALM IS, BUT...
GRIME LICKER? ARE YOU STILL HERE?
GUESS NOT.
...
yank
FWISH!

SHAKUHACHI.

YŌKAI GUIDEBOOK.

FOOD.

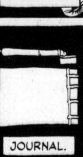

JOURNAL.

WATER.

AND MY MITTS.

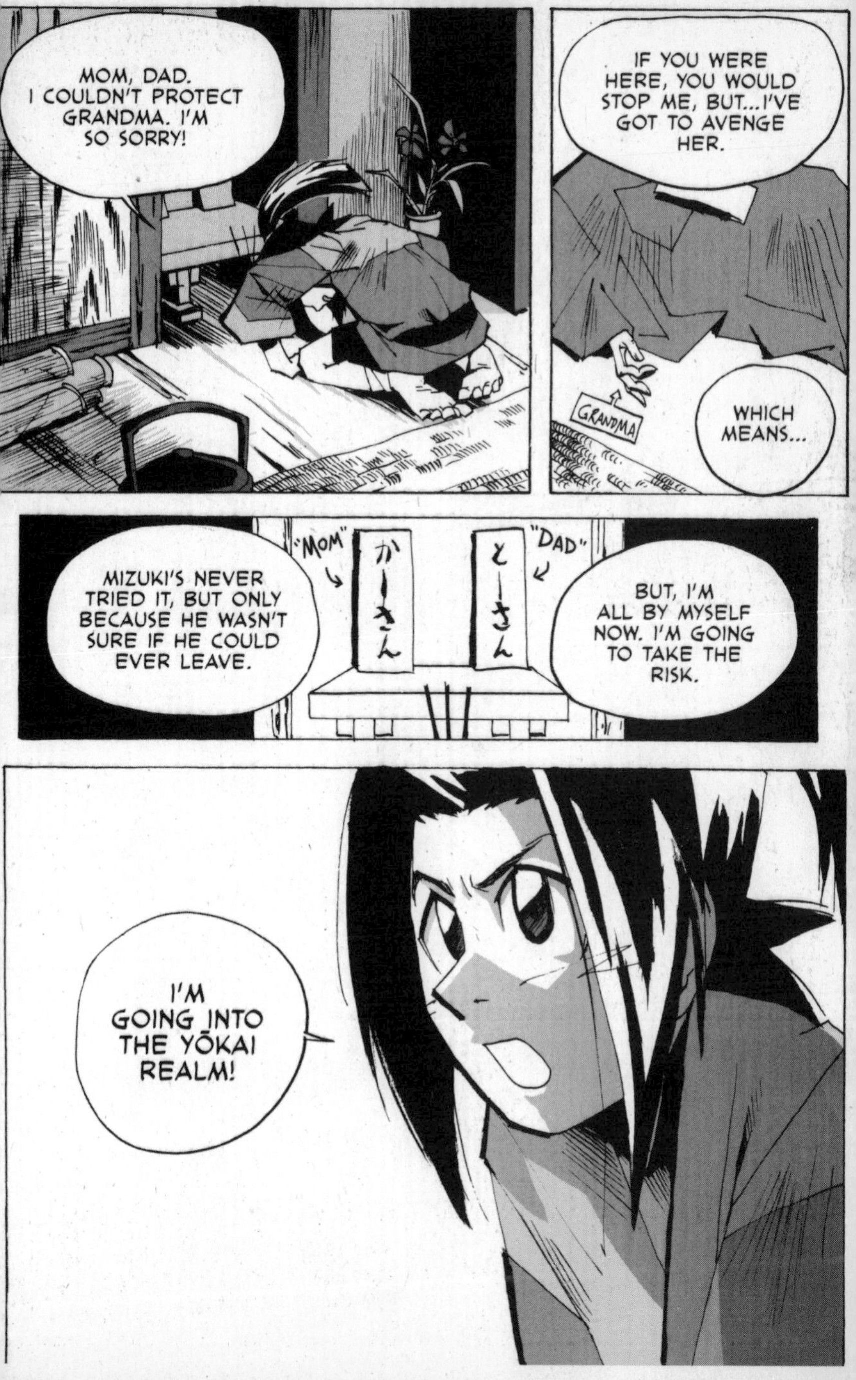
MOM, DAD. I COULDN'T PROTECT GRANDMA. I'M SO SORRY!
IF YOU WERE HERE, YOU WOULD STOP ME, BUT...I'VE GOT TO AVENGE HER.
GRANDMA
WHICH MEANS...
"MOM"
"DAD"
かーさん
とーさん
MIZUKI'S NEVER TRIED IT, BUT ONLY BECAUSE HE WASN'T SURE IF HE COULD EVER LEAVE.
BUT, I'M ALL BY MYSELF NOW. I'M GOING TO TAKE THE RISK.
I'M GOING INTO THE YŌKAI REALM!

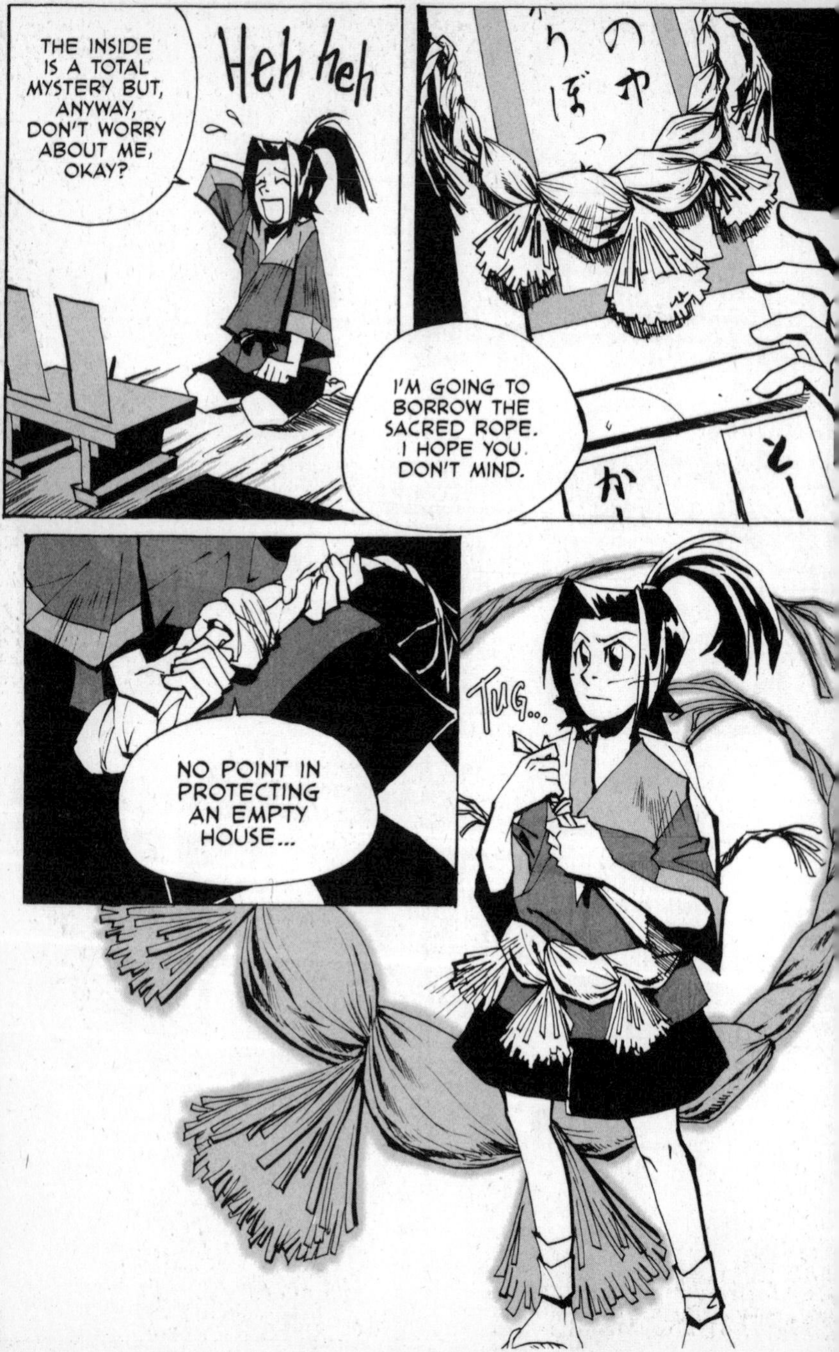
THE INSIDE IS A TOTAL MYSTERY BUT, ANYWAY, DON'T WORRY ABOUT ME, OKAY?
Heh heh
I'M GOING TO BORROW THE SACRED ROPE. I HOPE YOU DON'T MIND.
NO POINT IN PROTECTING AN EMPTY HOUSE...
TUG...

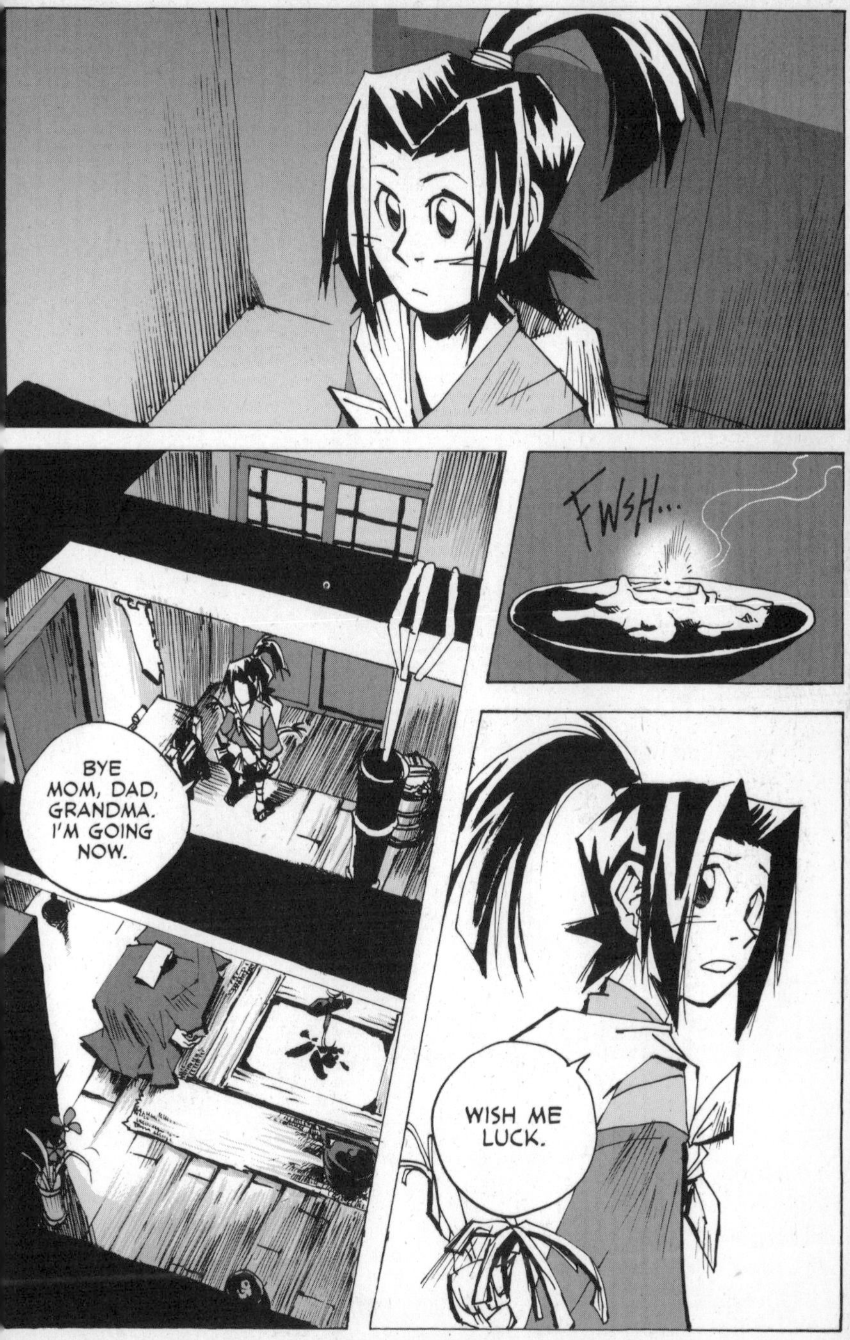
BYE MOM, DAD, GRANDMA. I'M GOING NOW.
FWSH...
WISH ME LUCK.

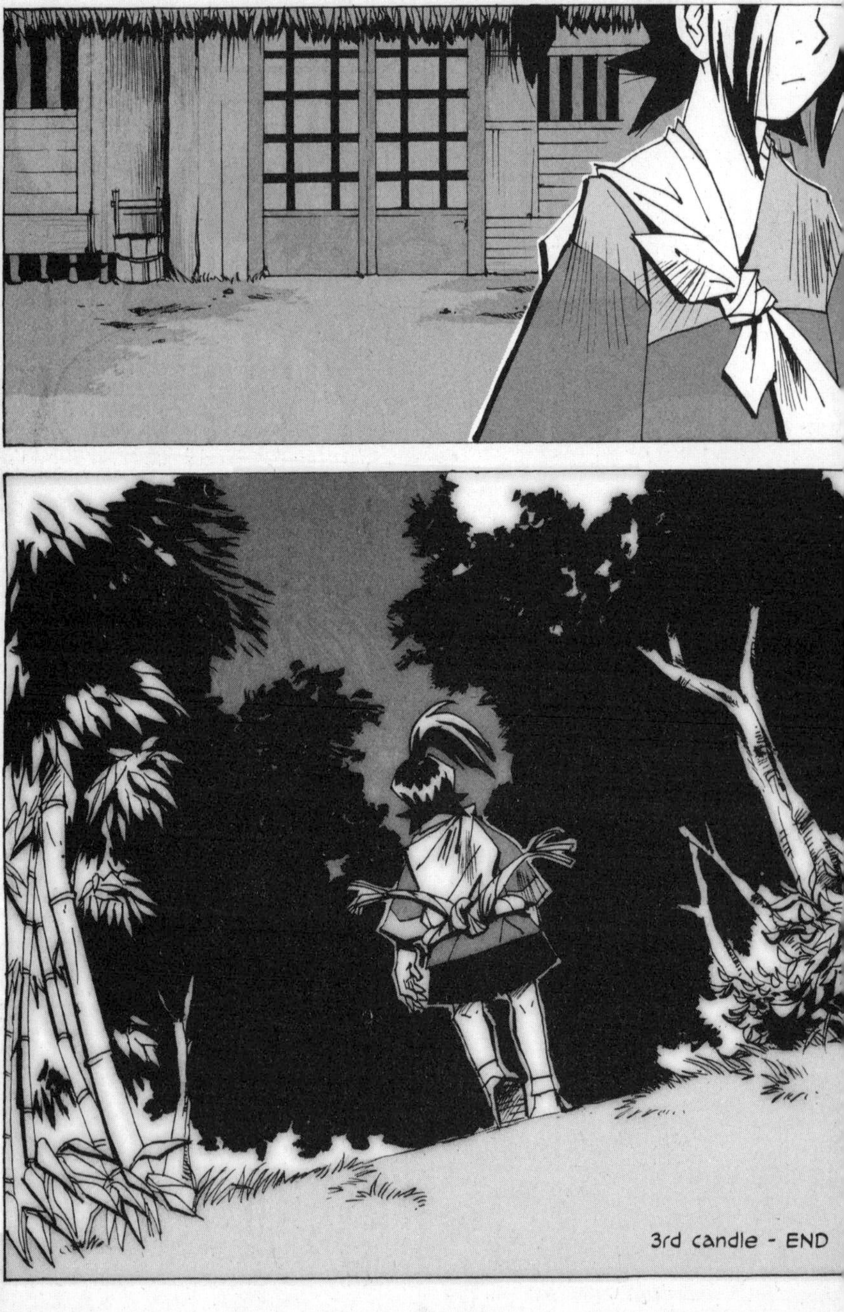
3rd candle - END

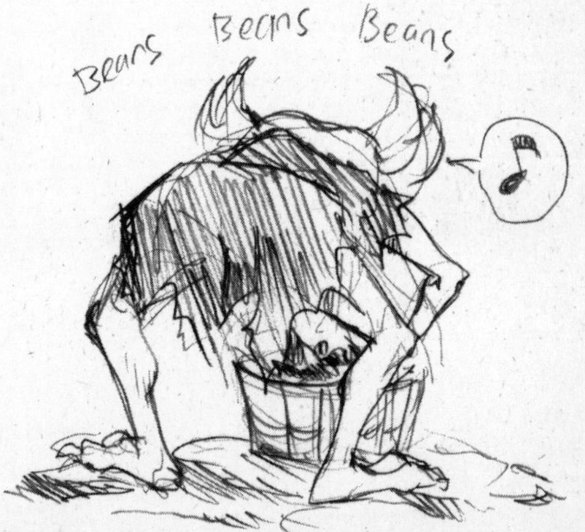

Beans
Beans
Beans

Inukai Mizuki's FIELD GUIDE to YŌKAI

GRIME LICKER
(a.k.a. akaname) 垢嘗め

When your bathtub is not cleaned properly and human body residue builds up within it, the grime licker will enter your house during the night and lick it clean for you. The only downside is that when you bathe in that bathtub afterward, the grime licker's saliva will cause you to fall ill.

BEANWASHER
(a.k.a. azuki-arai) 小豆洗い

The beanwasher lives for azuki beans. He can be heard (but never seen) gingerly washing his azuki beans by the river. He can instantly determine the number of beans in the tub by feeling around inside it with his hands. If even a single bean falls out, he will hunt it down, and resume washing.

 "OBSESSIVE-COMPULSIVE DISORDER IS A SERIOUS PROBLEM."

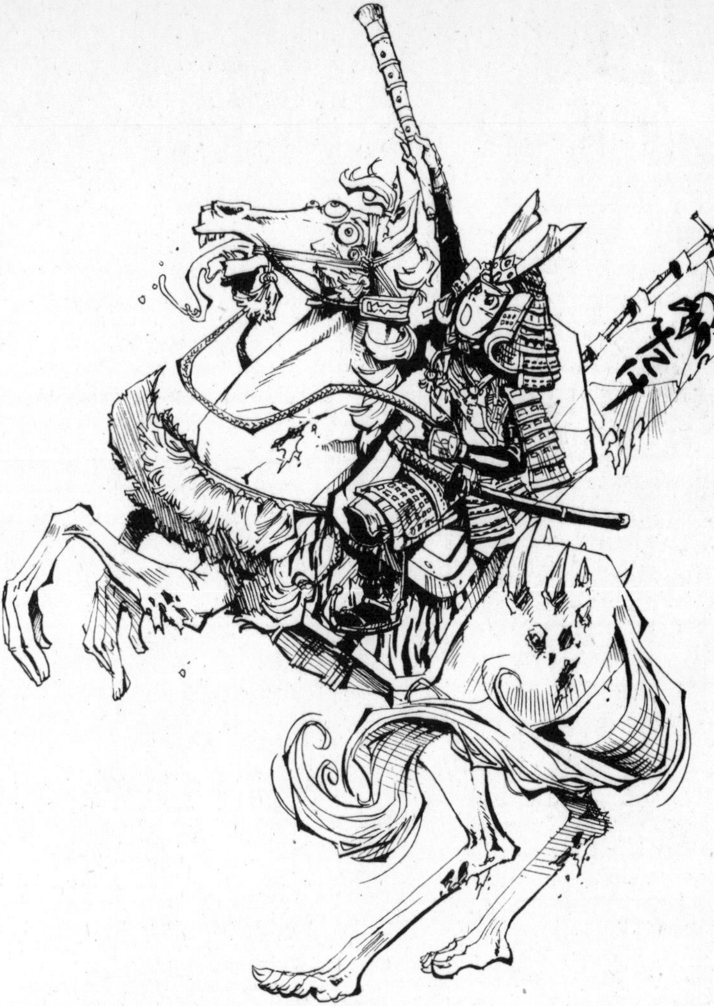

4th candle

Portal

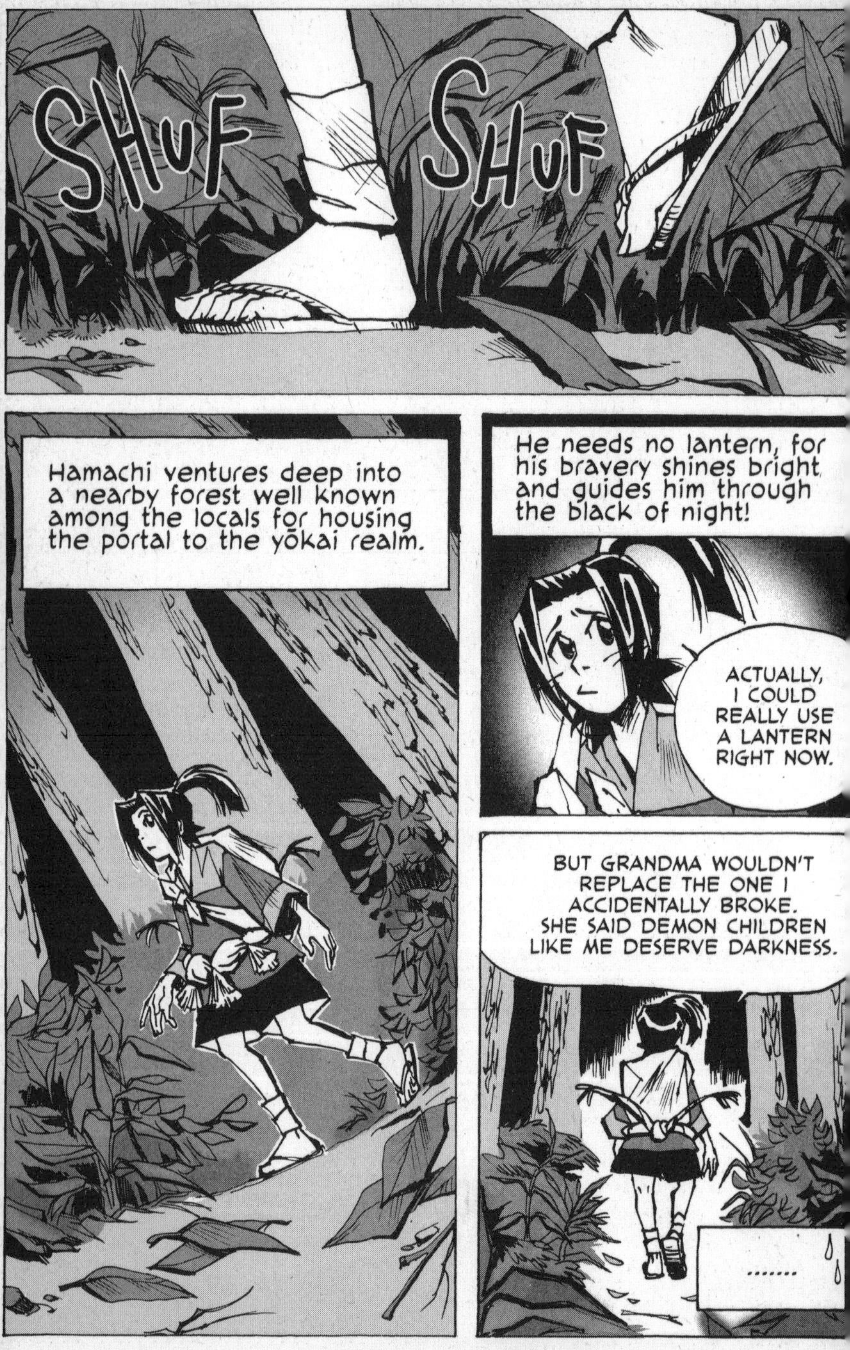
SHUF SHUF
Hamachi ventures deep into a nearby forest well known among the locals for housing the portal to the yōkai realm.
He needs no lantern, for his bravery shines bright and guides him through the black of night!
ACTUALLY, I COULD REALLY USE A LANTERN RIGHT NOW.
BUT GRANDMA WOULDN'T REPLACE THE ONE I ACCIDENTALLY BROKE. SHE SAID DEMON CHILDREN LIKE ME DESERVE DARKNESS.
....

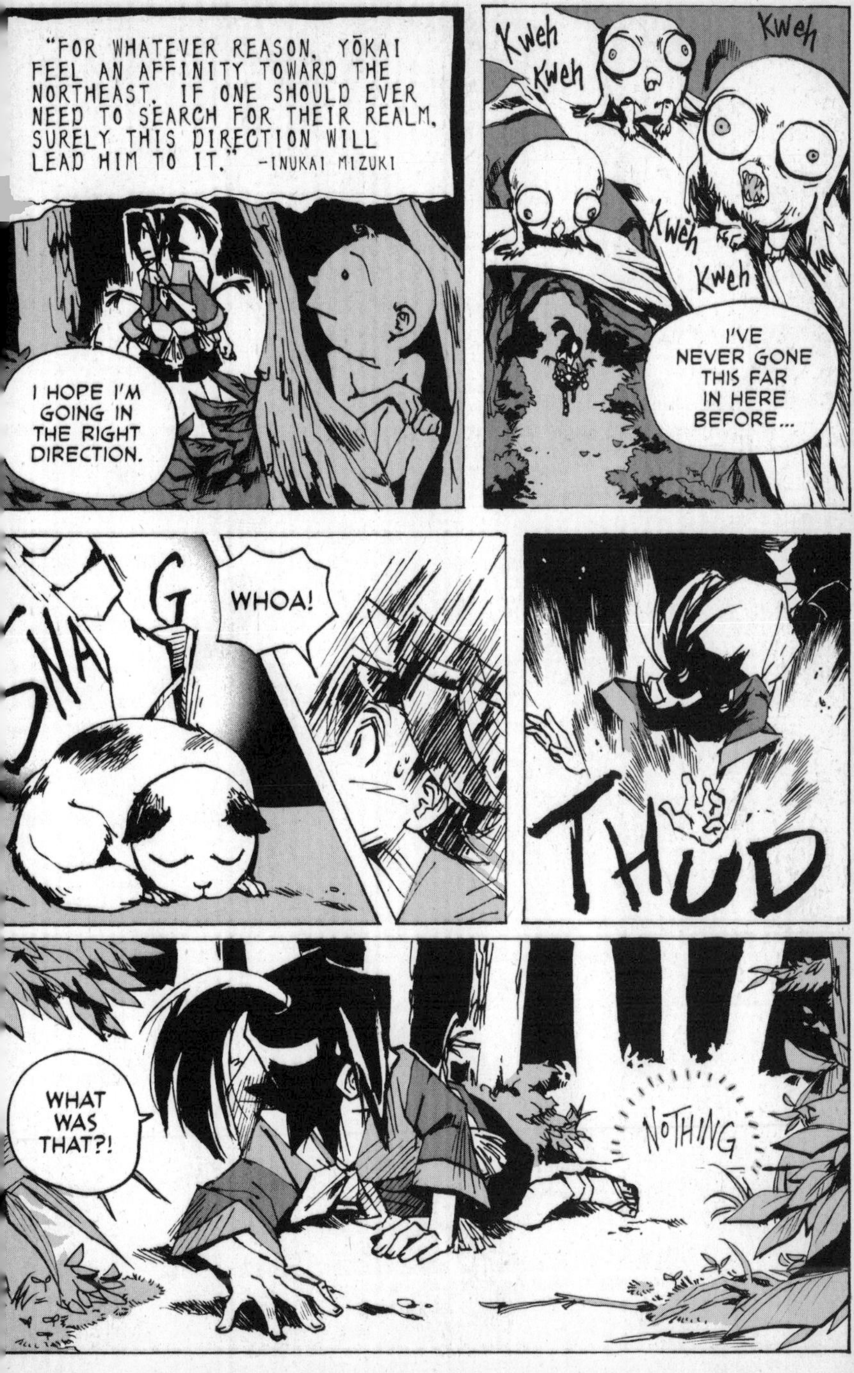
"FOR WHATEVER REASON, YŌKAI FEEL AN AFFINITY TOWARD THE NORTHEAST. IF ONE SHOULD EVER NEED TO SEARCH FOR THEIR REALM, SURELY THIS DIRECTION WILL LEAD HIM TO IT." -INUKAI MIZUKI
I HOPE I'M GOING IN THE RIGHT DIRECTION.
Kweh
Kweh
Kweh
Kweh
Kweh
I'VE NEVER GONE THIS FAR IN HERE BEFORE...
SNAG
WHOA!
THUD
WHAT WAS THAT?!
NOTHING

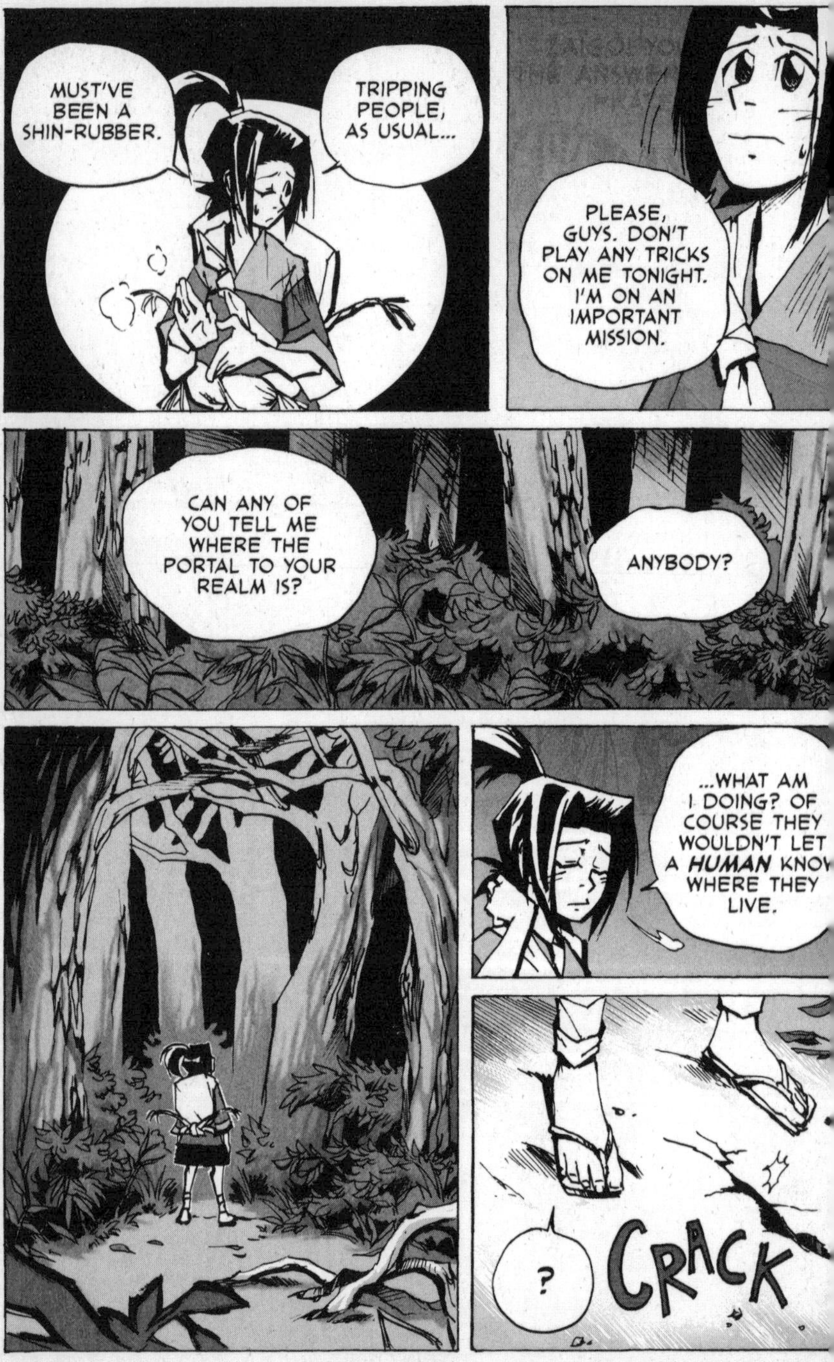
MUST'VE BEEN A SHIN-RUBBER.
TRIPPING PEOPLE, AS USUAL...
PLEASE, GUYS. DON'T PLAY ANY TRICKS ON ME TONIGHT. I'M ON AN IMPORTANT MISSION.
CAN ANY OF YOU TELL ME WHERE THE PORTAL TO YOUR REALM IS?
ANYBODY?
...WHAT AM I DOING? OF COURSE THEY WOULDN'T LET A *HUMAN* KNOW WHERE THEY LIVE.
?
CRACK

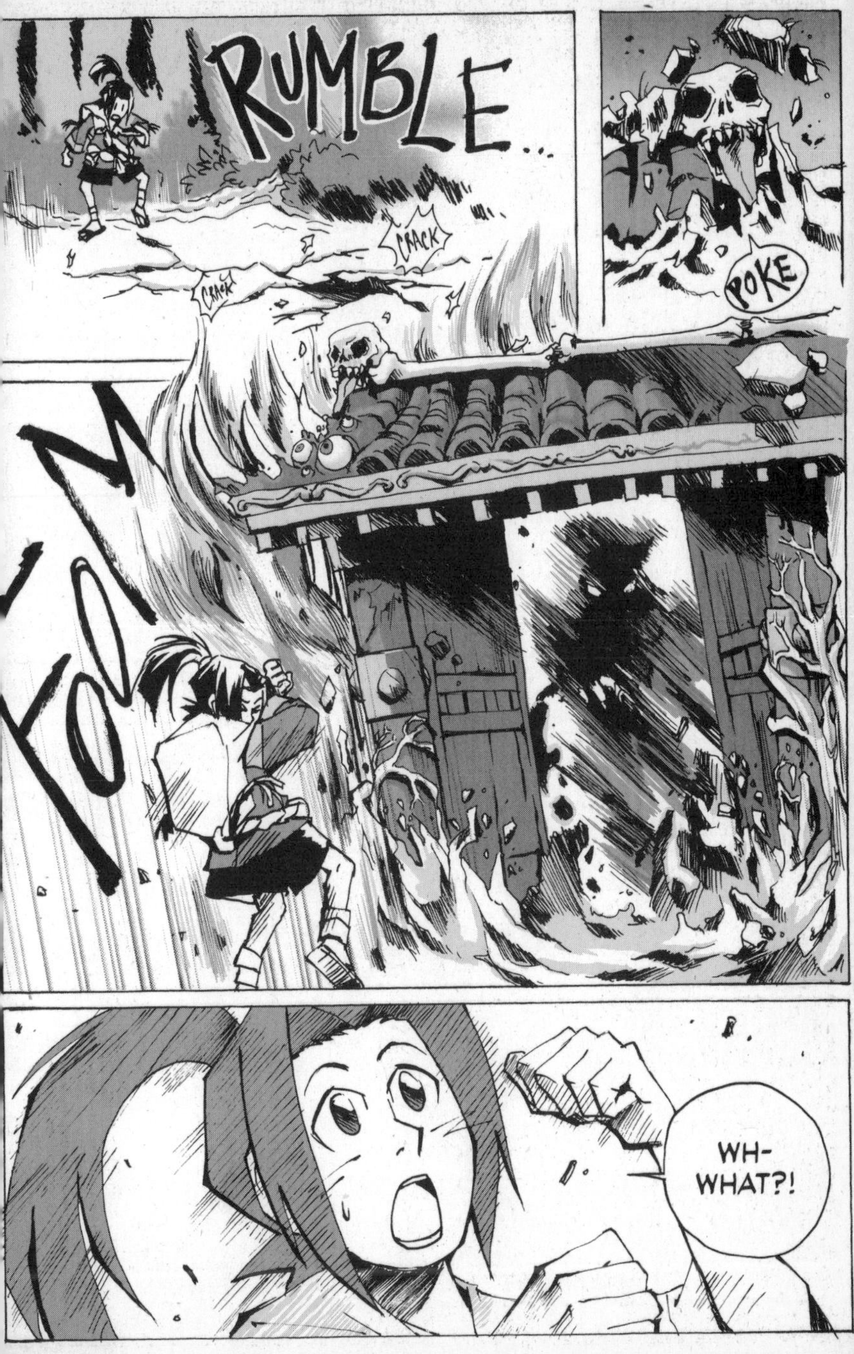
RUMBLE...
CRACK
CRACK
POKE
FOOM
WH-
WHAT?!

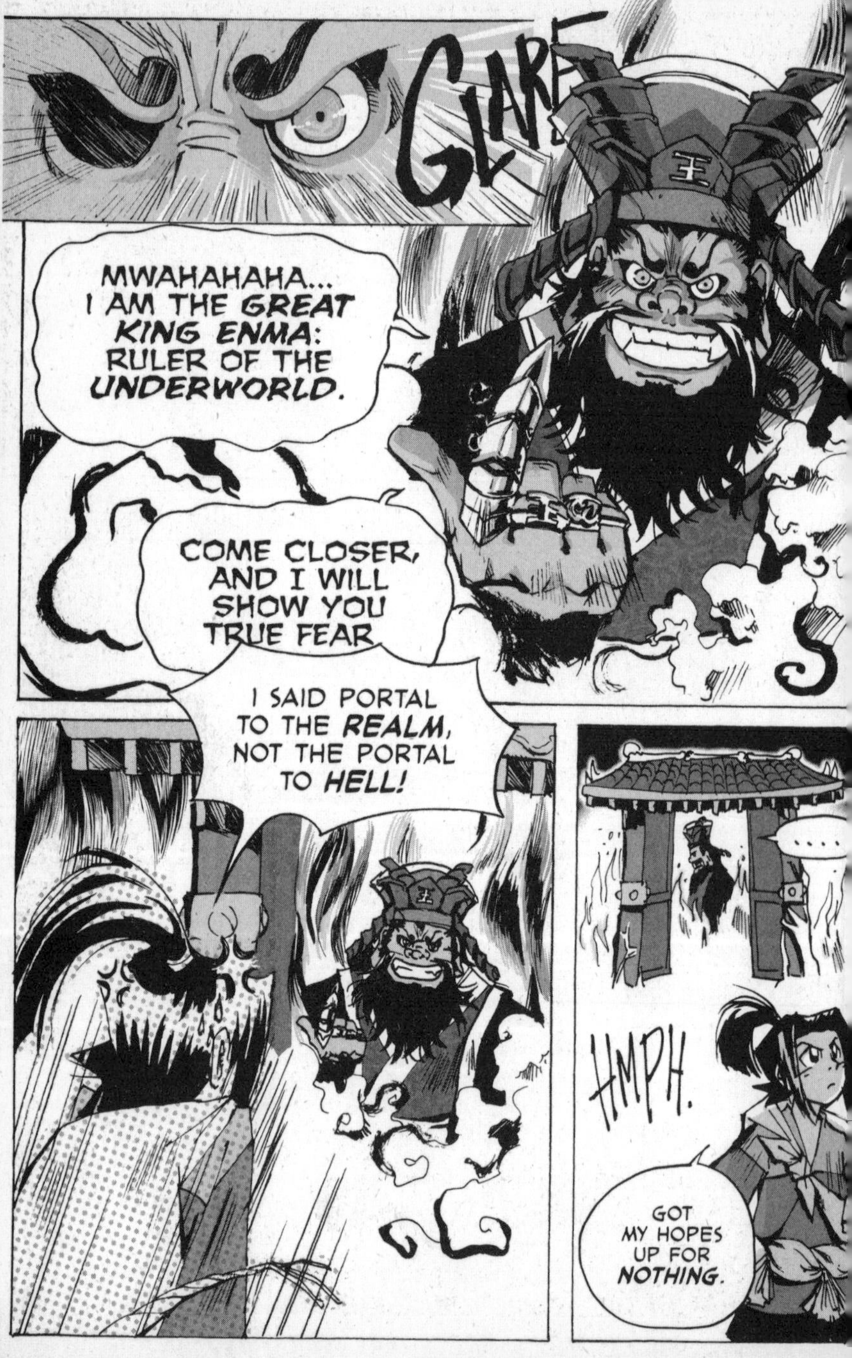
GLARE
MWAHAHAHA... I AM THE GREAT KING ENMA: RULER OF THE UNDERWORLD.
COME CLOSER, AND I WILL SHOW YOU TRUE FEAR
I SAID PORTAL TO THE REALM, NOT THE PORTAL TO HELL!
...
HMPH.
GOT MY HOPES UP FOR NOTHING.

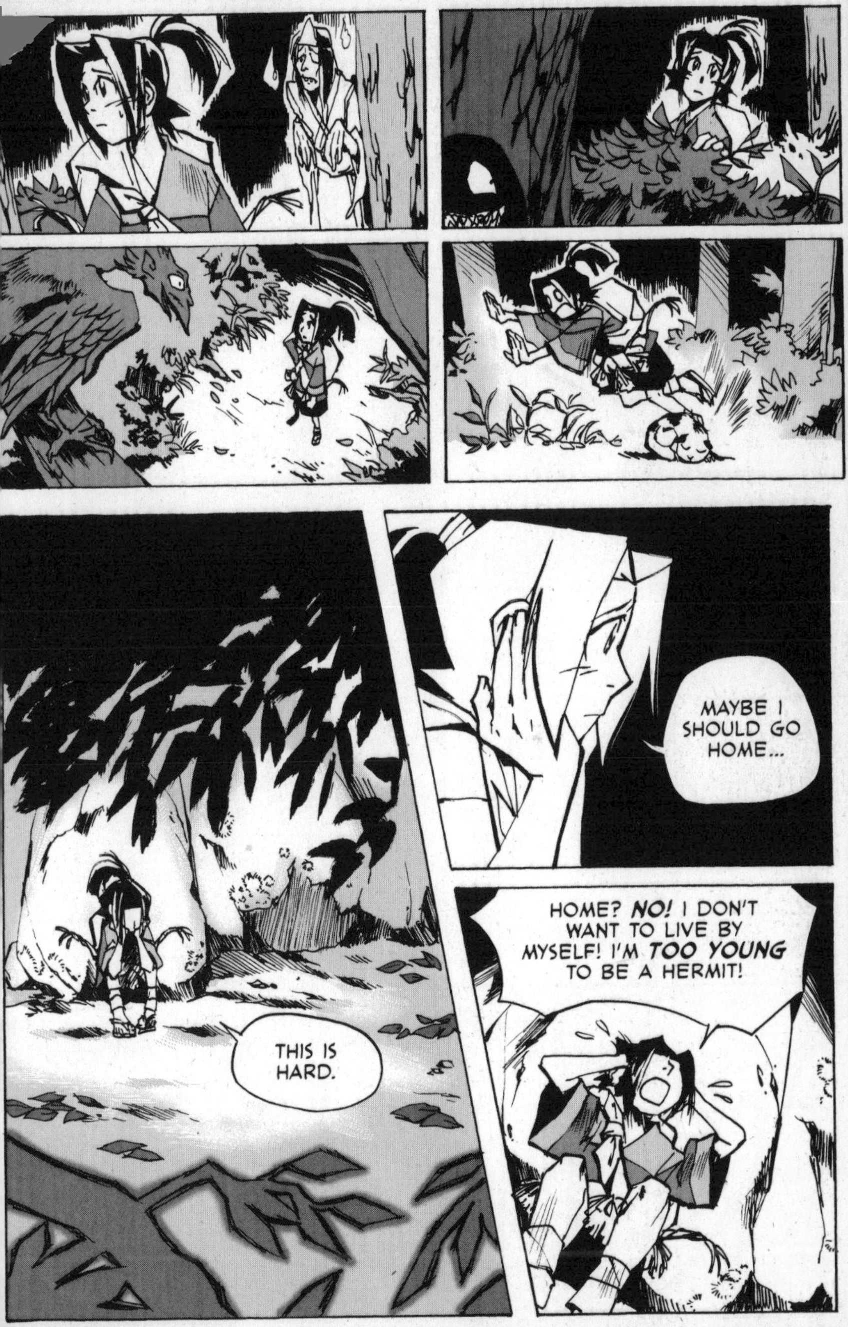

THIS IS HARD.
MAYBE I SHOULD GO HOME...
HOME? ***NO!*** I DON'T WANT TO LIVE BY MYSELF! I'M ***TOO YOUNG*** TO BE A HERMIT!

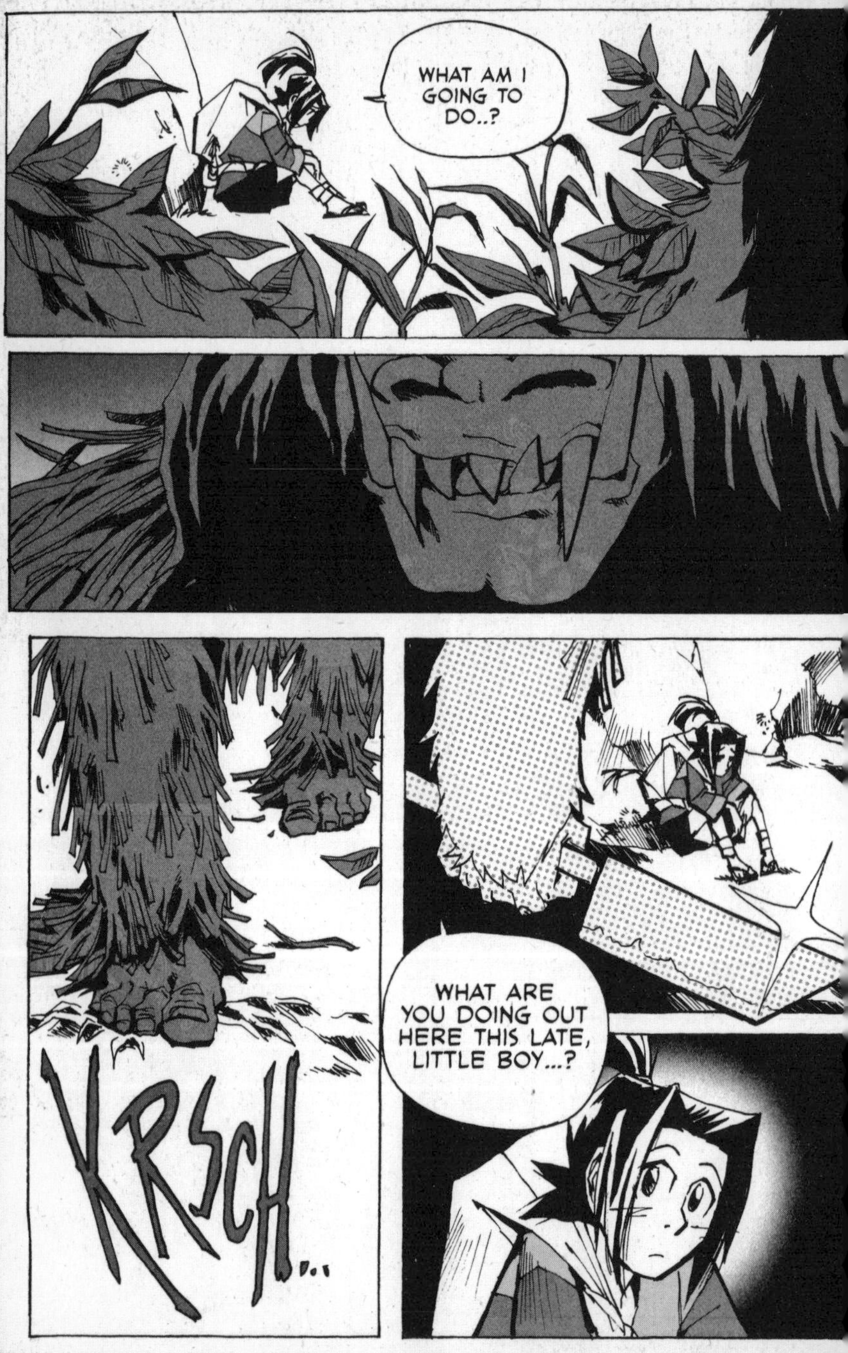
WHAT AM I GOING TO DO..?
KRSCH...
WHAT ARE YOU DOING OUT HERE THIS LATE, LITTLE BOY...?

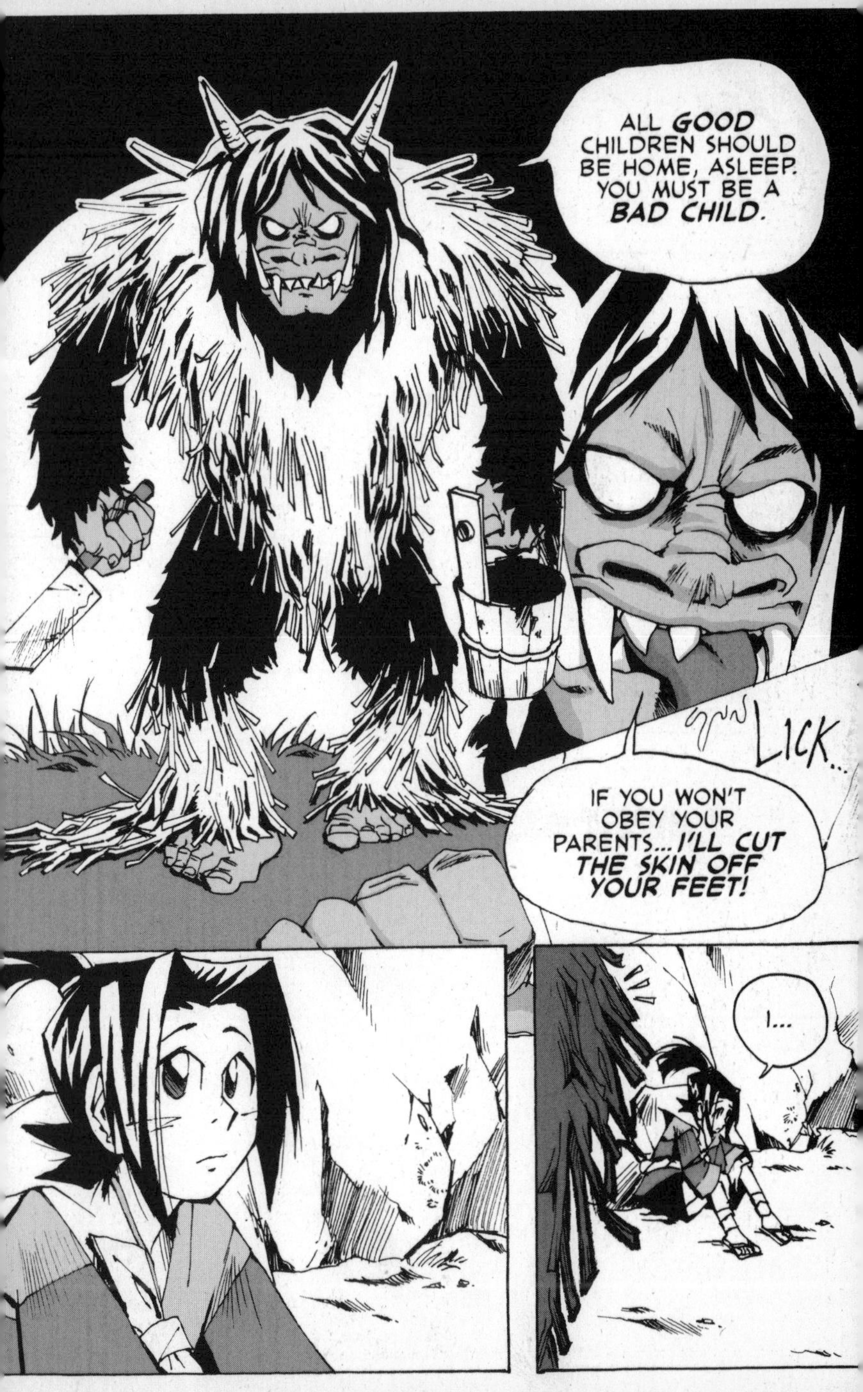

ALL GOOD CHILDREN SHOULD BE HOME, ASLEEP. YOU MUST BE A BAD CHILD.
LICK...
IF YOU WON'T OBEY YOUR PARENTS... I'LL CUT THE SKIN OFF YOUR FEET!
I...

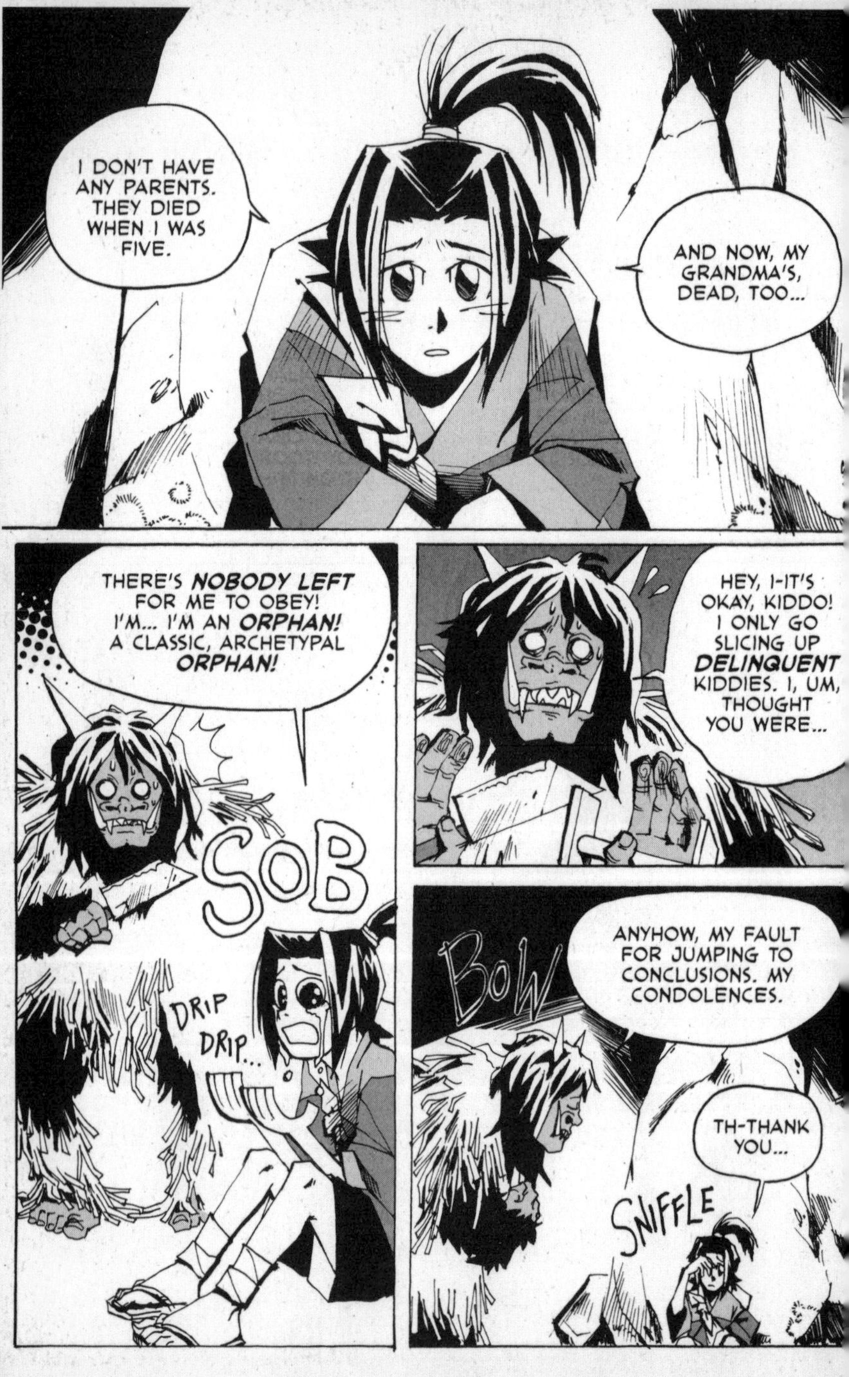
I DON'T HAVE ANY PARENTS. THEY DIED WHEN I WAS FIVE.
AND NOW, MY GRANDMA'S, DEAD, TOO...
THERE'S NOBODY LEFT FOR ME TO OBEY! I'M... I'M AN ORPHAN! A CLASSIC, ARCHETYPAL ORPHAN!
SOB
DRIP DRIP...
HEY, I-IT'S OKAY, KIDDO! I ONLY GO SLICING UP DELINQUENT KIDDIES. I, UM, THOUGHT YOU WERE...
BOW
ANYHOW, MY FAULT FOR JUMPING TO CONCLUSIONS. MY CONDOLENCES.
TH-THANK YOU...
SNIFFLE

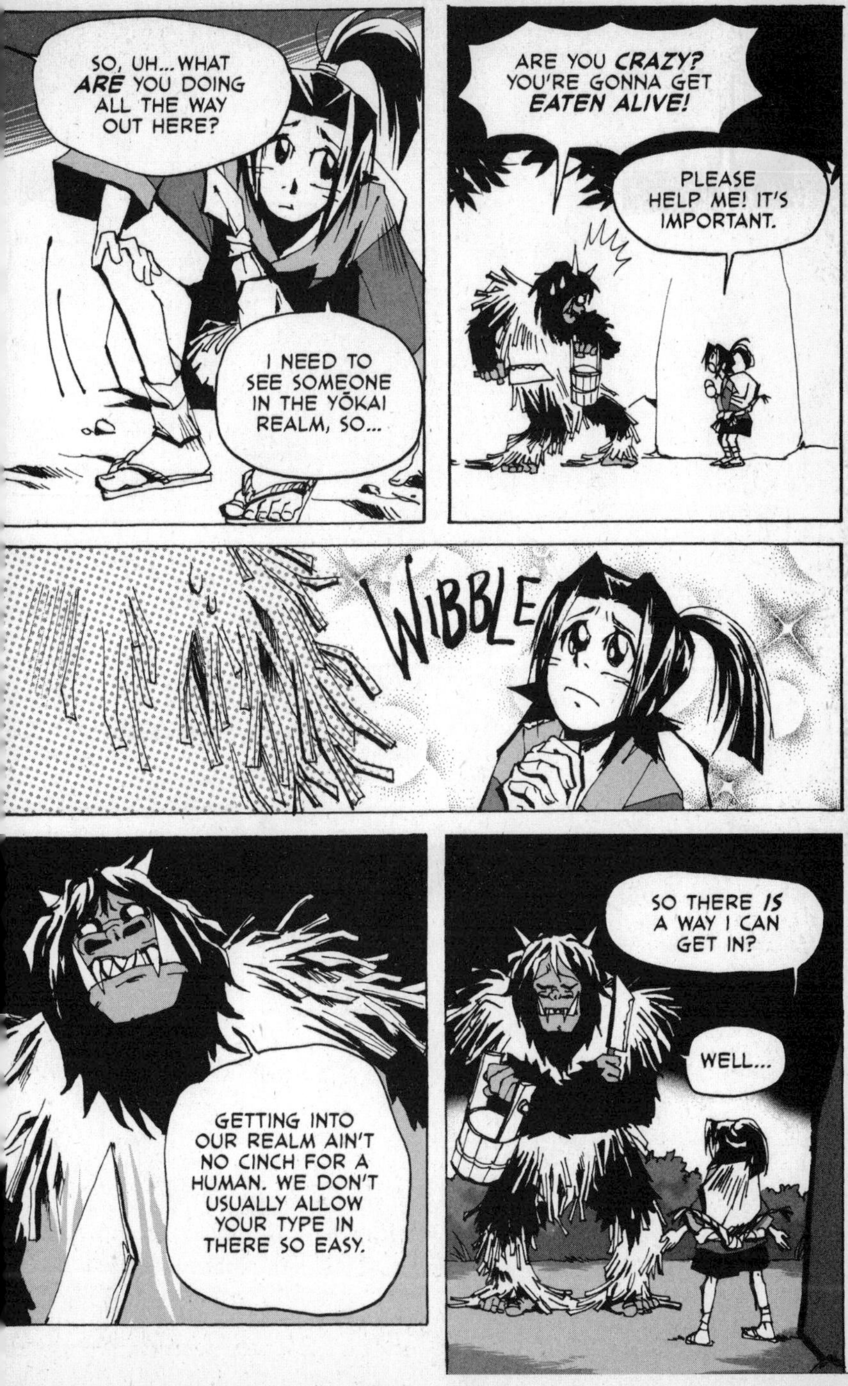
SO, UH...WHAT ARE YOU DOING ALL THE WAY OUT HERE?
I NEED TO SEE SOMEONE IN THE YŌKAI REALM, SO...
ARE YOU CRAZY? YOU'RE GONNA GET EATEN ALIVE!
PLEASE HELP ME! IT'S IMPORTANT.
WIBBLE
GETTING INTO OUR REALM AIN'T NO CINCH FOR A HUMAN. WE DON'T USUALLY ALLOW YOUR TYPE IN THERE SO EASY.
SO THERE IS A WAY I CAN GET IN?
WELL...

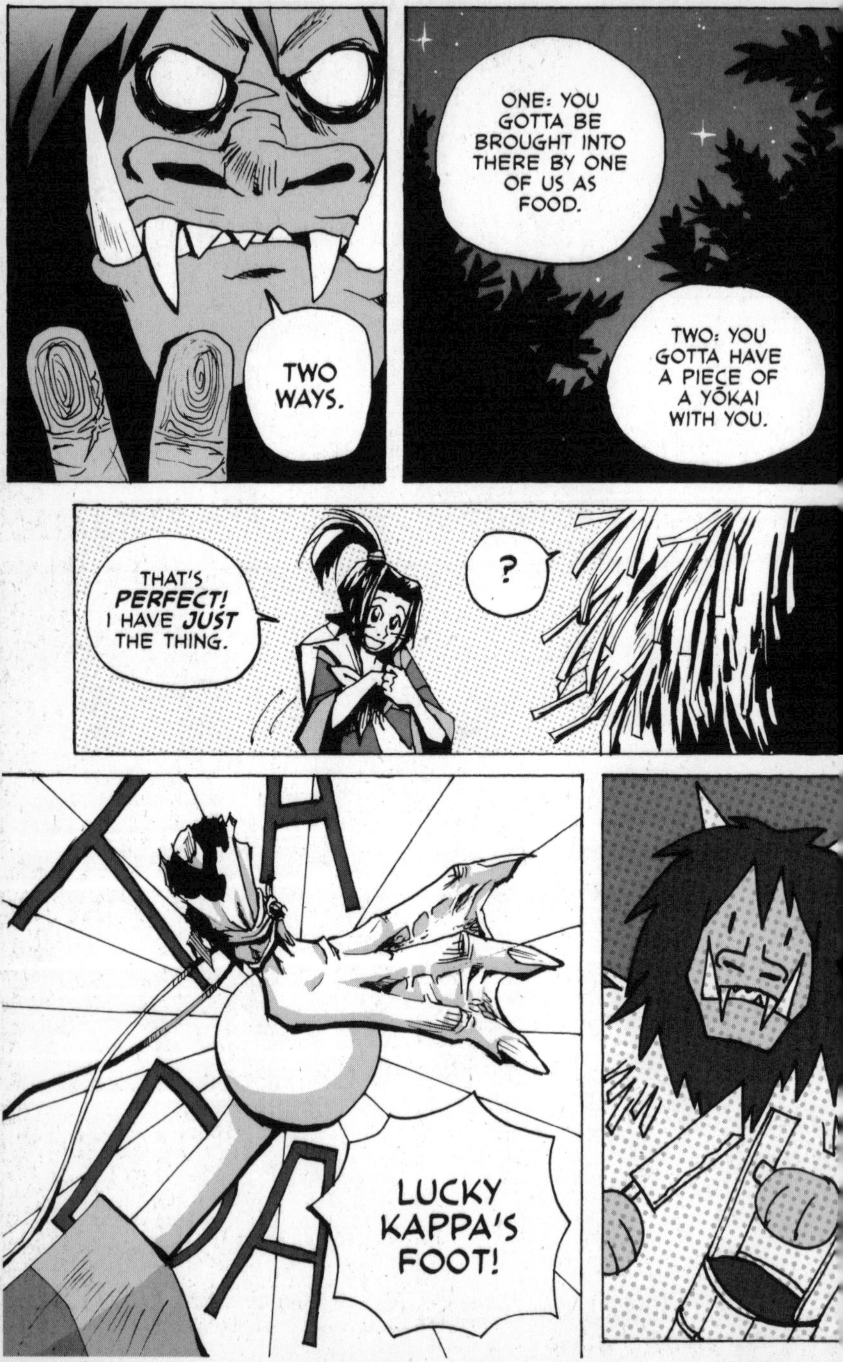
TWO WAYS.
ONE: YOU GOTTA BE BROUGHT INTO THERE BY ONE OF US AS FOOD.
TWO: YOU GOTTA HAVE A PIECE OF A YŌKAI WITH YOU.
THAT'S PERFECT! I HAVE JUST THE THING.
?
LUCKY KAPPA'S FOOT!

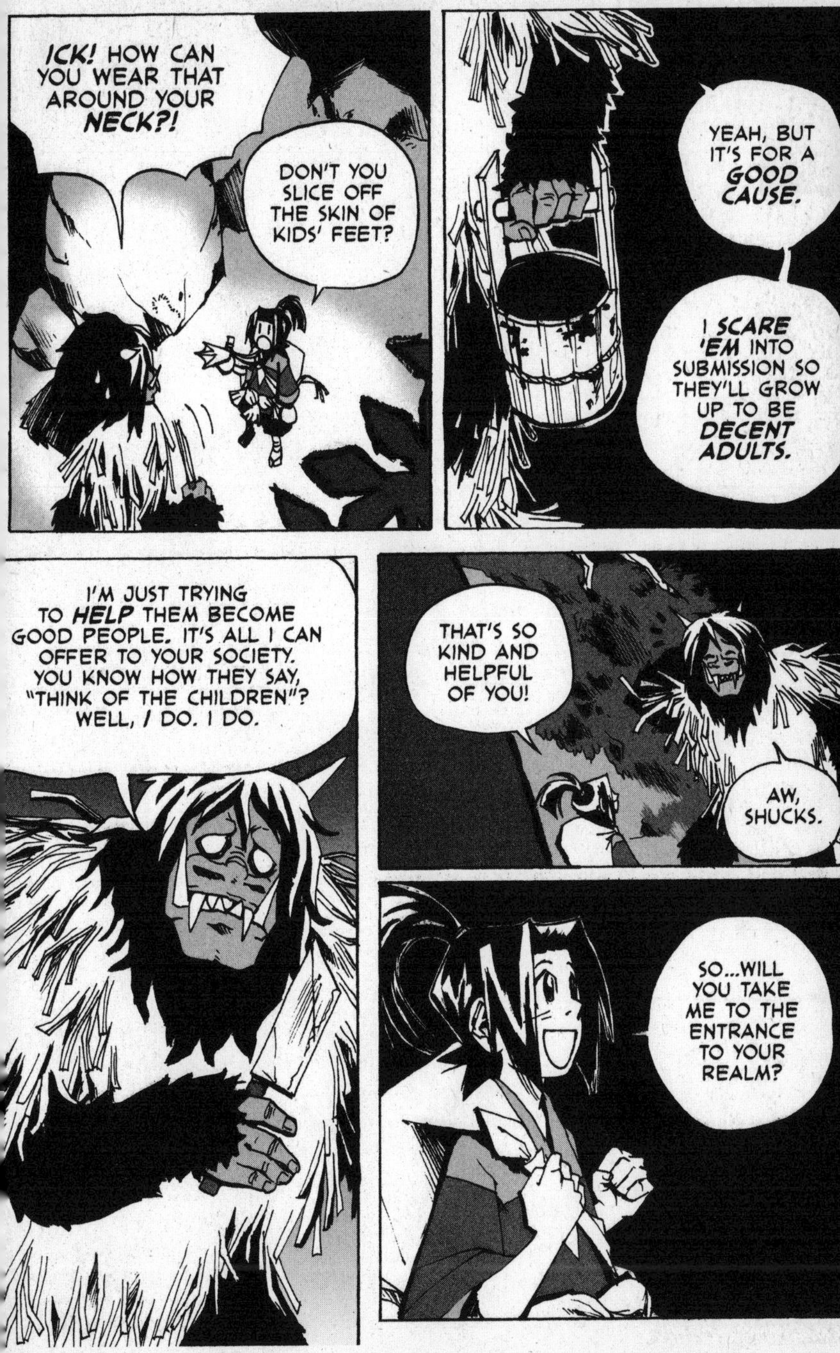
ICK! HOW CAN YOU WEAR THAT AROUND YOUR NECK?!
DON'T YOU SLICE OFF THE SKIN OF KIDS' FEET?
YEAH, BUT IT'S FOR A GOOD CAUSE.
I SCARE 'EM INTO SUBMISSION SO THEY'LL GROW UP TO BE DECENT ADULTS.
I'M JUST TRYING TO HELP THEM BECOME GOOD PEOPLE. IT'S ALL I CAN OFFER TO YOUR SOCIETY. YOU KNOW HOW THEY SAY, "THINK OF THE CHILDREN"? WELL, I DO. I DO.
THAT'S SO KIND AND HELPFUL OF YOU!
AW, SHUCKS.
SO...WILL YOU TAKE ME TO THE ENTRANCE TO YOUR REALM?

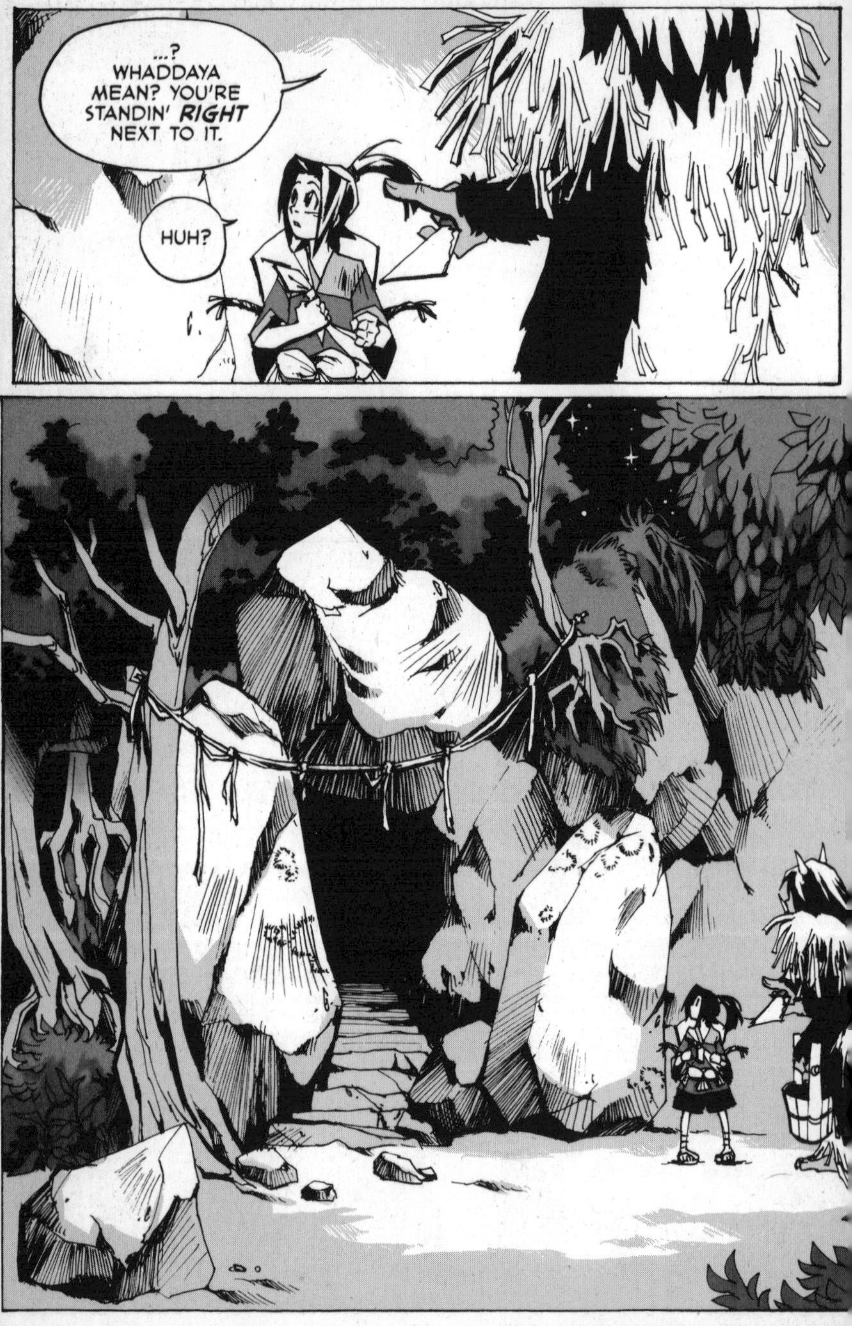
...? WHADDAYA MEAN? YOU'RE STANDIN' RIGHT NEXT TO IT.
HUH?

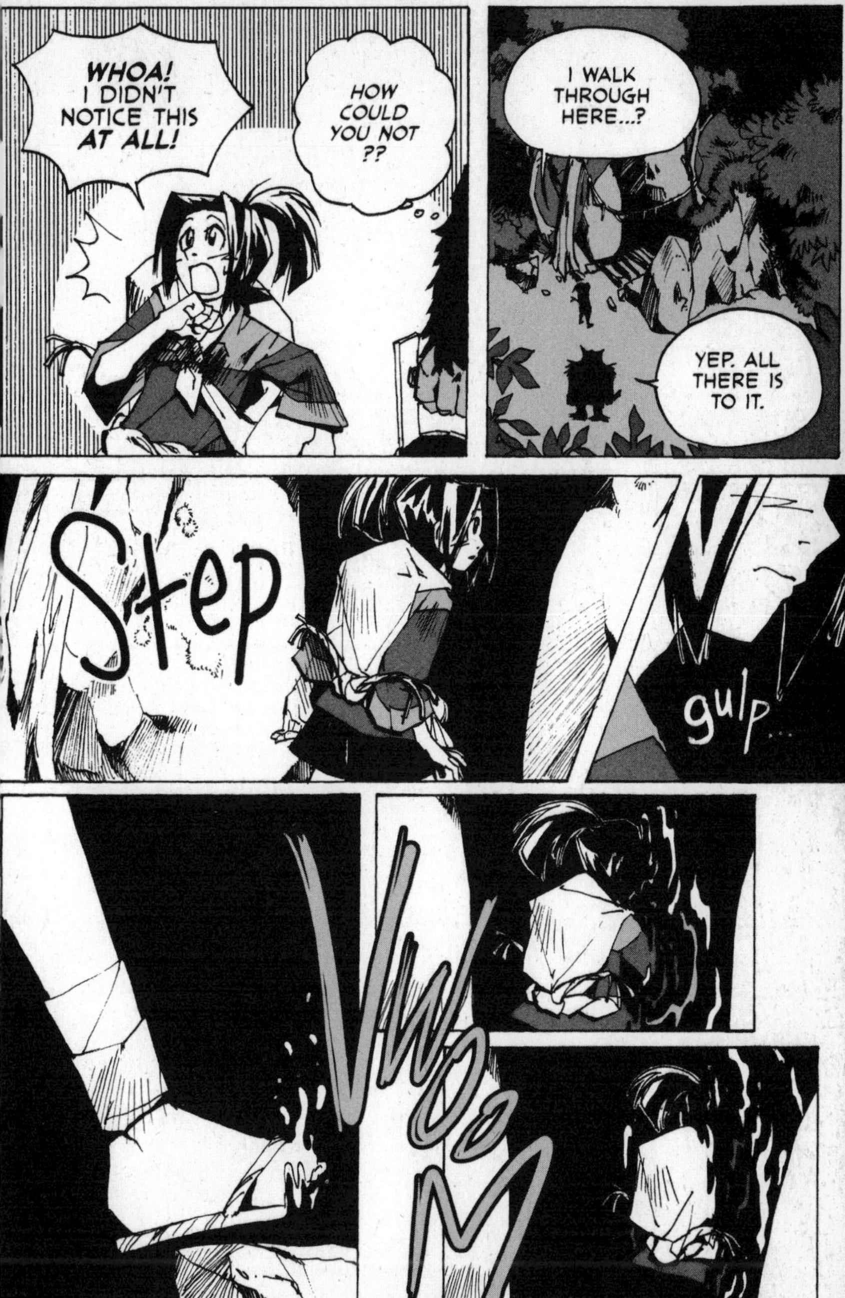
WHOA! I DIDN'T NOTICE THIS AT ALL!
HOW COULD YOU NOT ??
I WALK THROUGH HERE...?
YEP. ALL THERE IS TO IT.
Step
gulp...
VWOOM

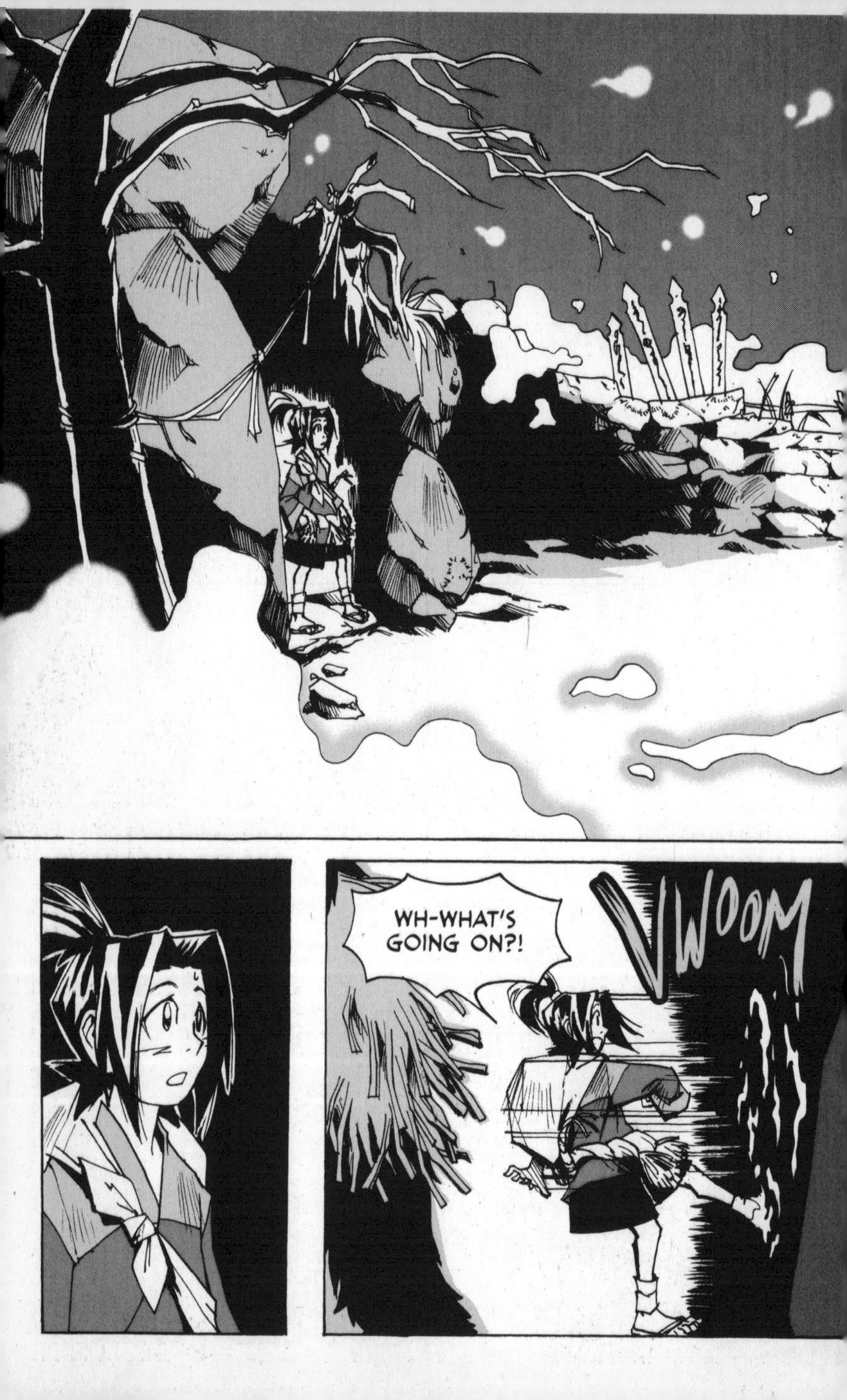
WH-WHAT'S GOING ON?!
VWOOM

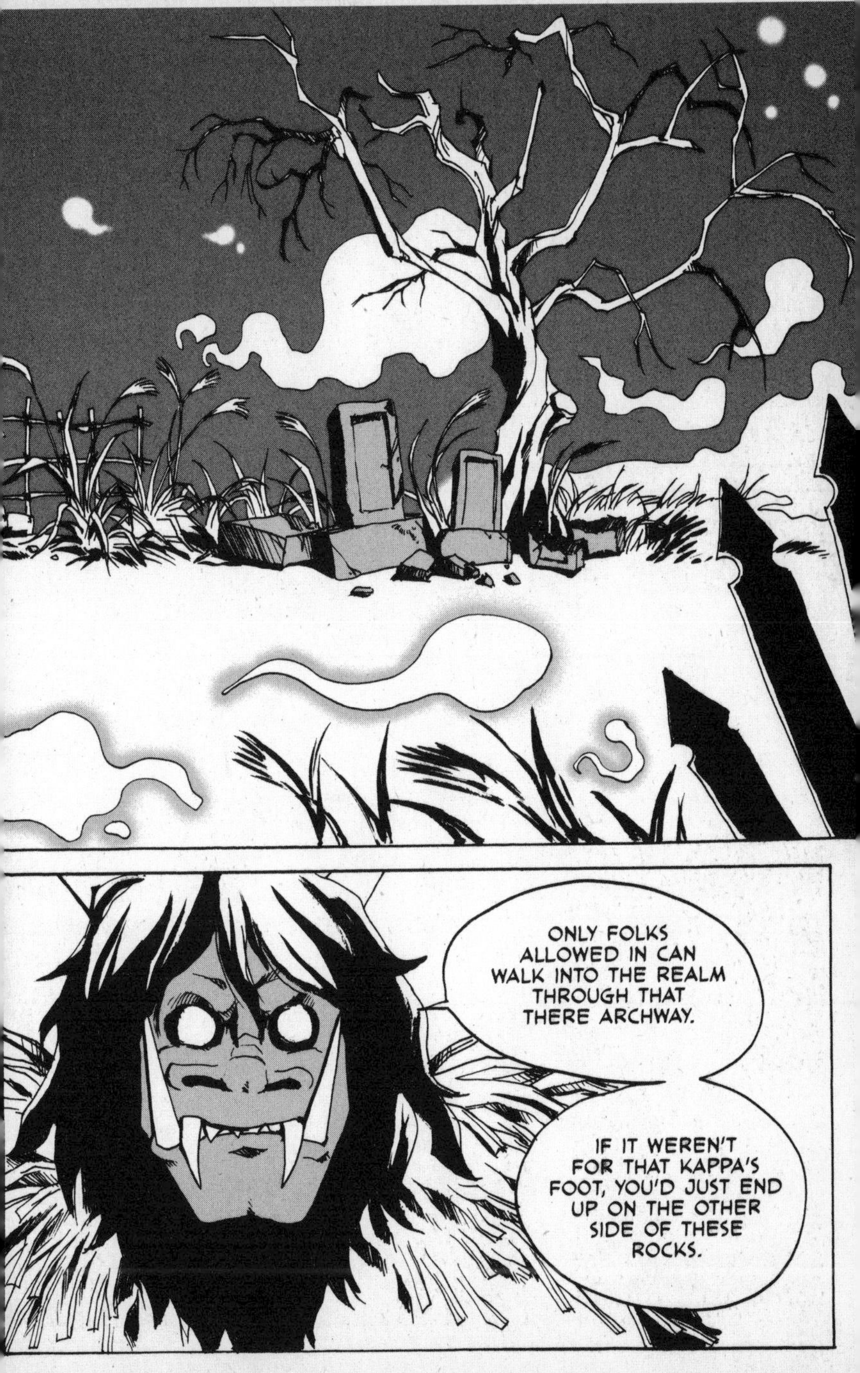
ONLY FOLKS ALLOWED IN CAN WALK INTO THE REALM THROUGH THAT THERE ARCHWAY.
IF IT WEREN'T FOR THAT KAPPA'S FOOT, YOU'D JUST END UP ON THE OTHER SIDE OF THESE ROCKS.

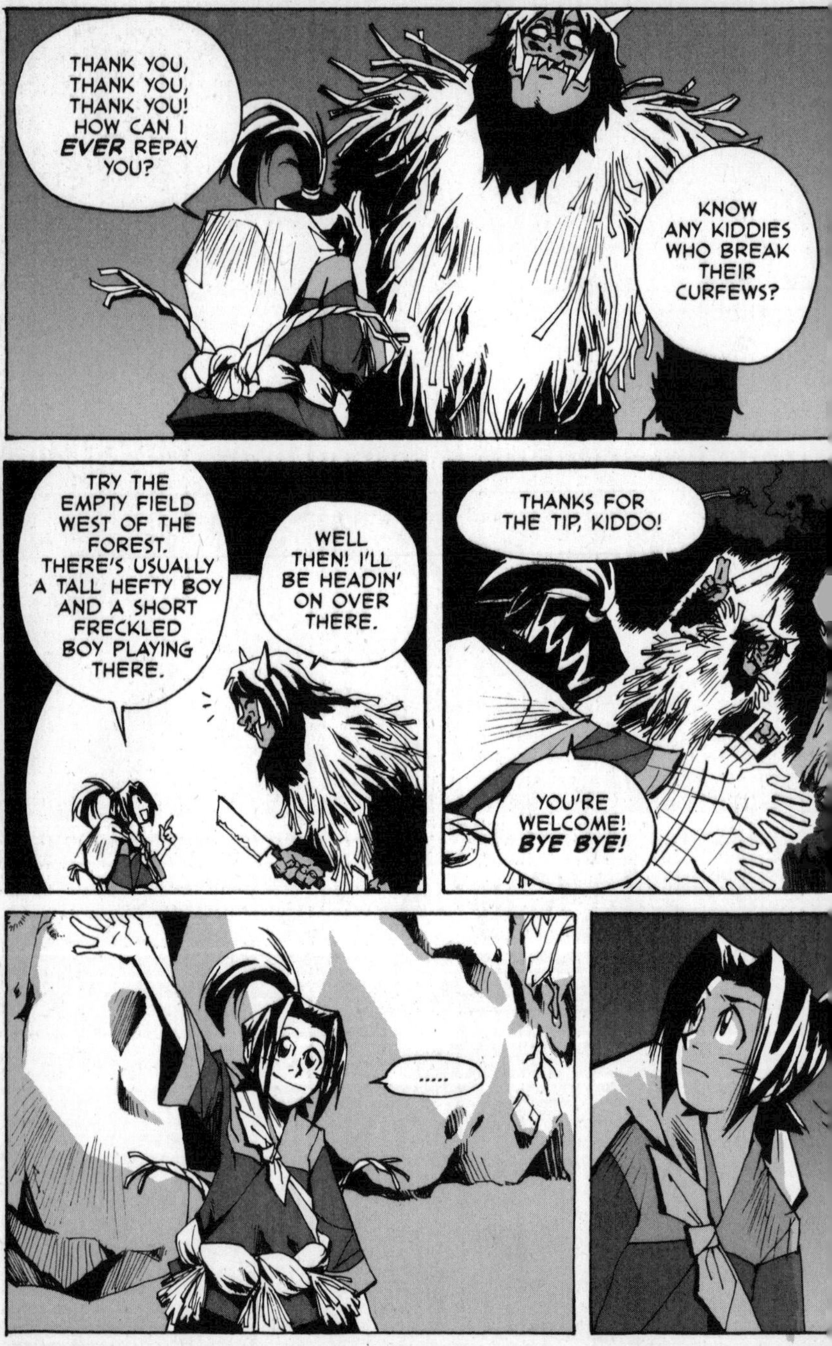
THANK YOU, THANK YOU, THANK YOU! HOW CAN I *EVER* REPAY YOU?
KNOW ANY KIDDIES WHO BREAK THEIR CURFEWS?
TRY THE EMPTY FIELD WEST OF THE FOREST. THERE'S USUALLY A TALL HEFTY BOY AND A SHORT FRECKLED BOY PLAYING THERE.
WELL THEN! I'LL BE HEADIN' ON OVER THERE.
THANKS FOR THE TIP, KIDDO!
YOU'RE WELCOME! *BYE BYE!*
......

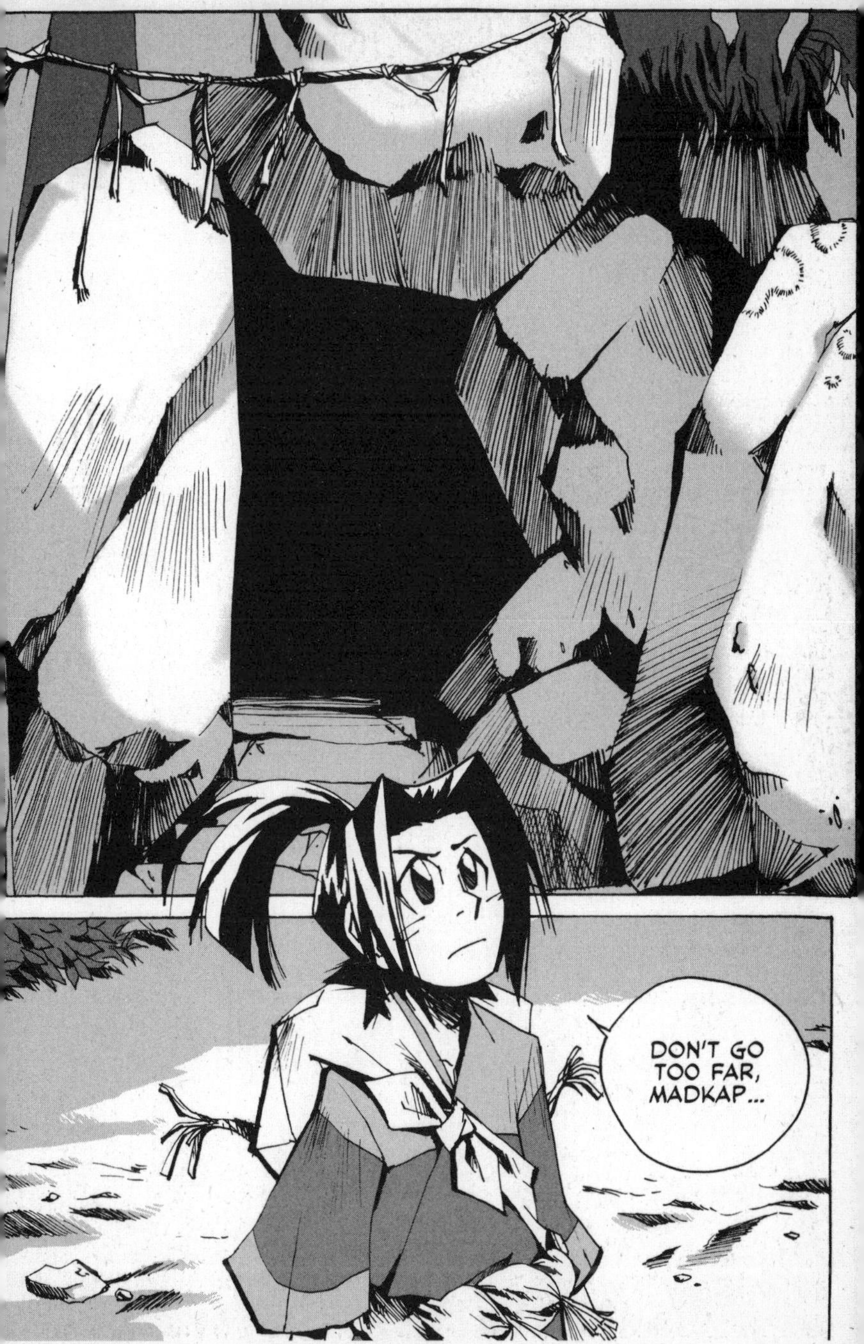
DON'T GO TOO FAR, MADKAP...

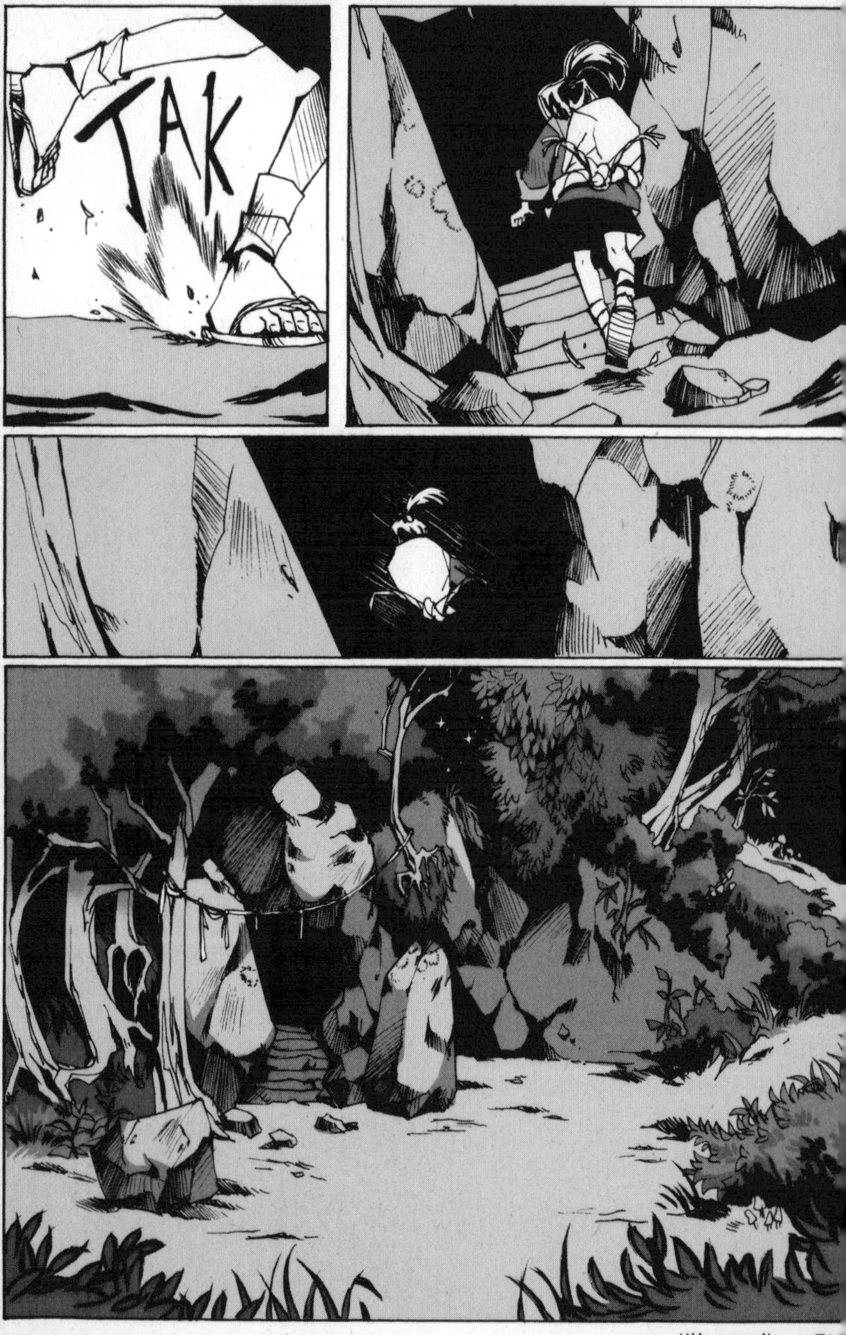
TAK

4th candle - EN

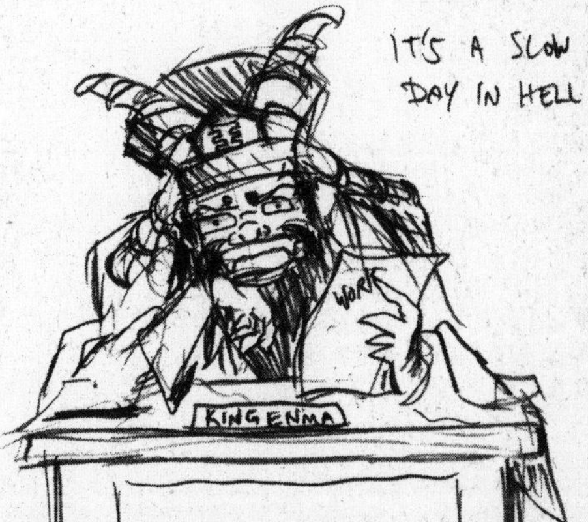
IT'S A SLOW DAY IN HELL
WORK
KINGENMA

Inukai Mizuki's FIELD GUIDE to YŌKAI

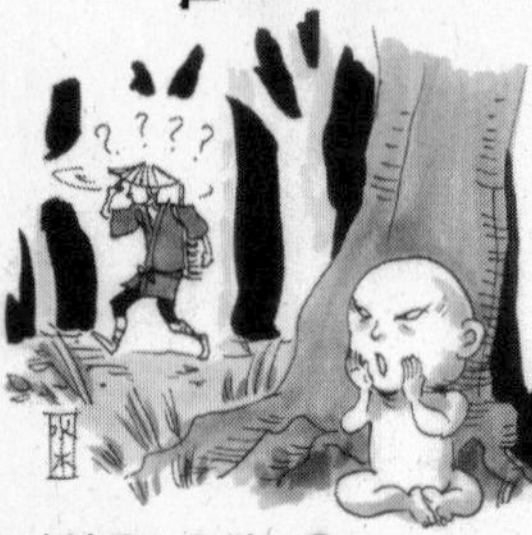

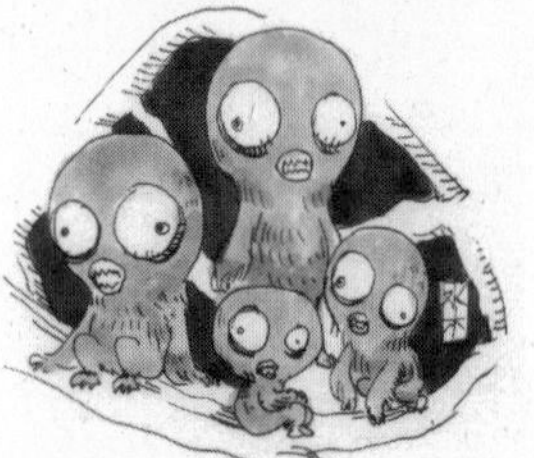

MOUNTAIN BOY
(a.k.a. yamanbo) ヤマンボ

It spends most of its time hiding, waiting for men who are lost from their group. If a lost man calls out, "Hey!" it may answer, "Hey!" in return, thereby confusing and causing him to become more lost.

KIJIMUNAA
キジムナー

Red, furry, beaked creatures. They play many tricks on people, such as blowing out their lamps at night, pressing down on their chests as they sleep, and putting dirt in their meals.

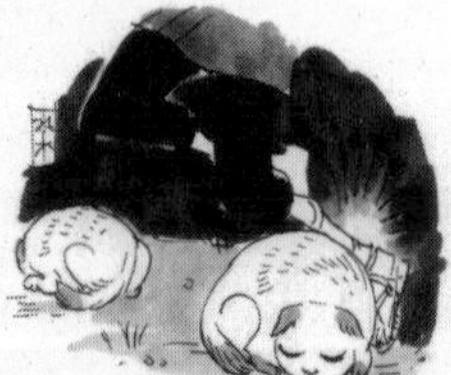

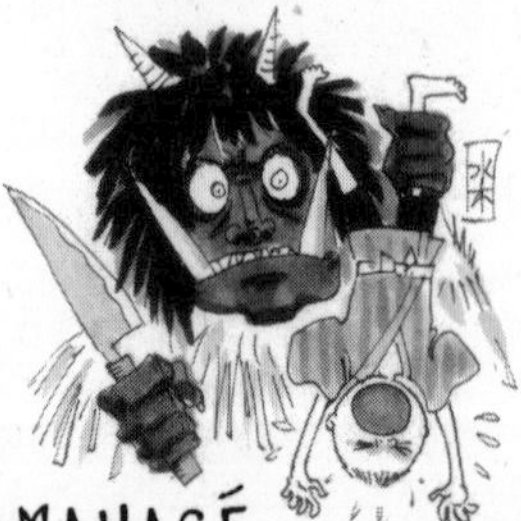

SHIN-RUBBER
(a.k.a sunékosuri) すねこすり

They remain largely unseen. They curl up in the middle of man-made paths at night to deliberately trip anyone passing through.

NAMAHAGÉ
ナマハゲ

These large, straw-clad ogres come out at night to seek children to discipline by crippling them for a few weeks with their knives.

"FRIENDS OF THE FORESTS!"

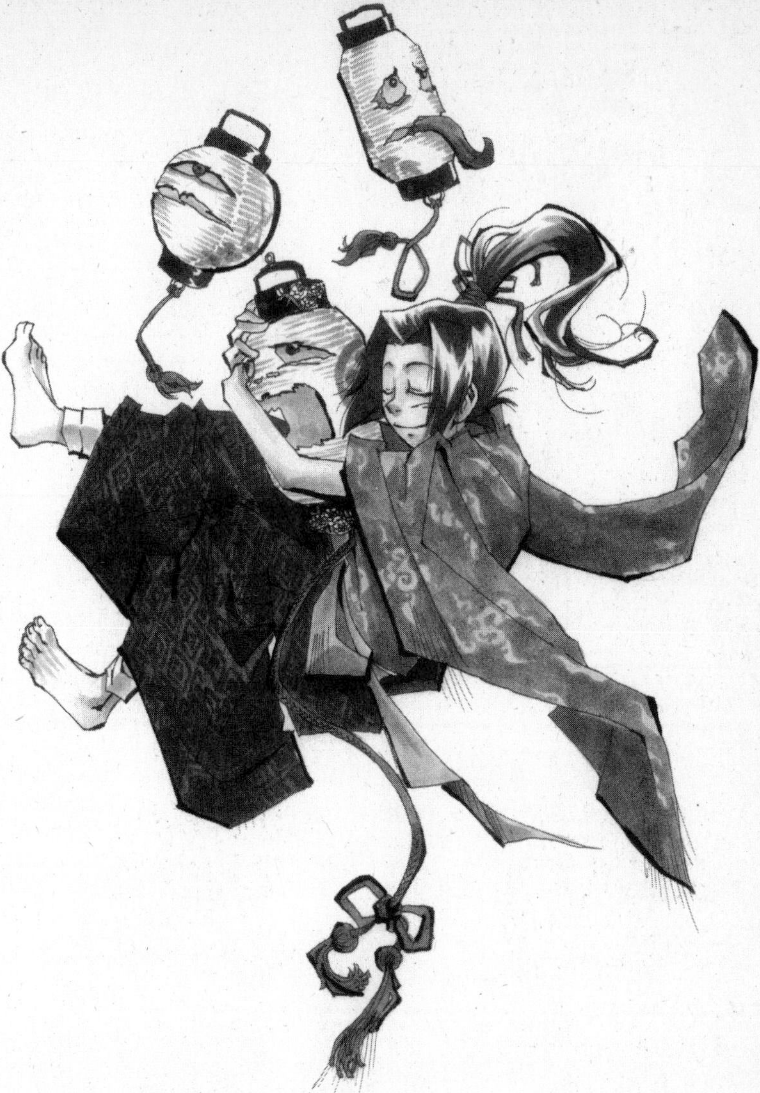

5th candle

The Lantern Is Not French

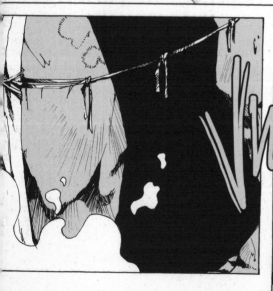

VWOOM

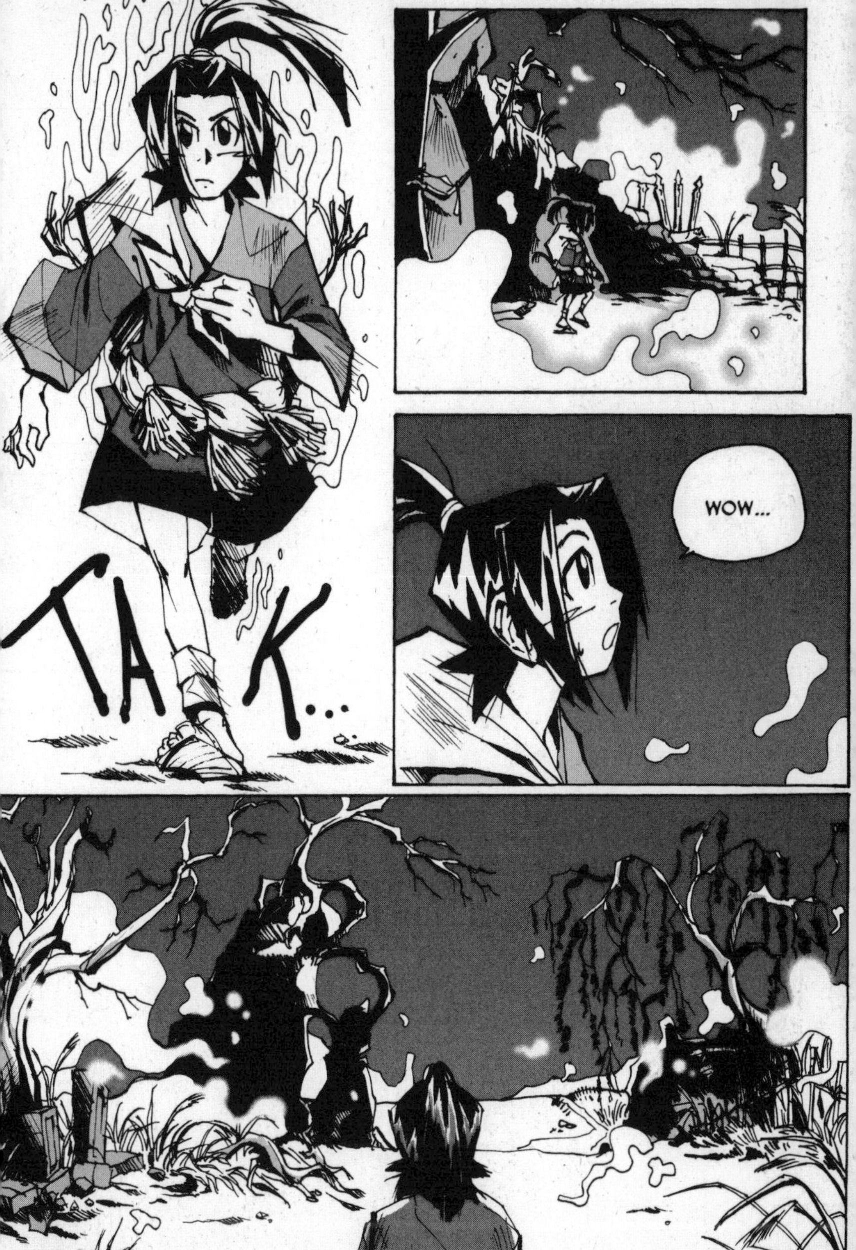
TAK...
WOW...

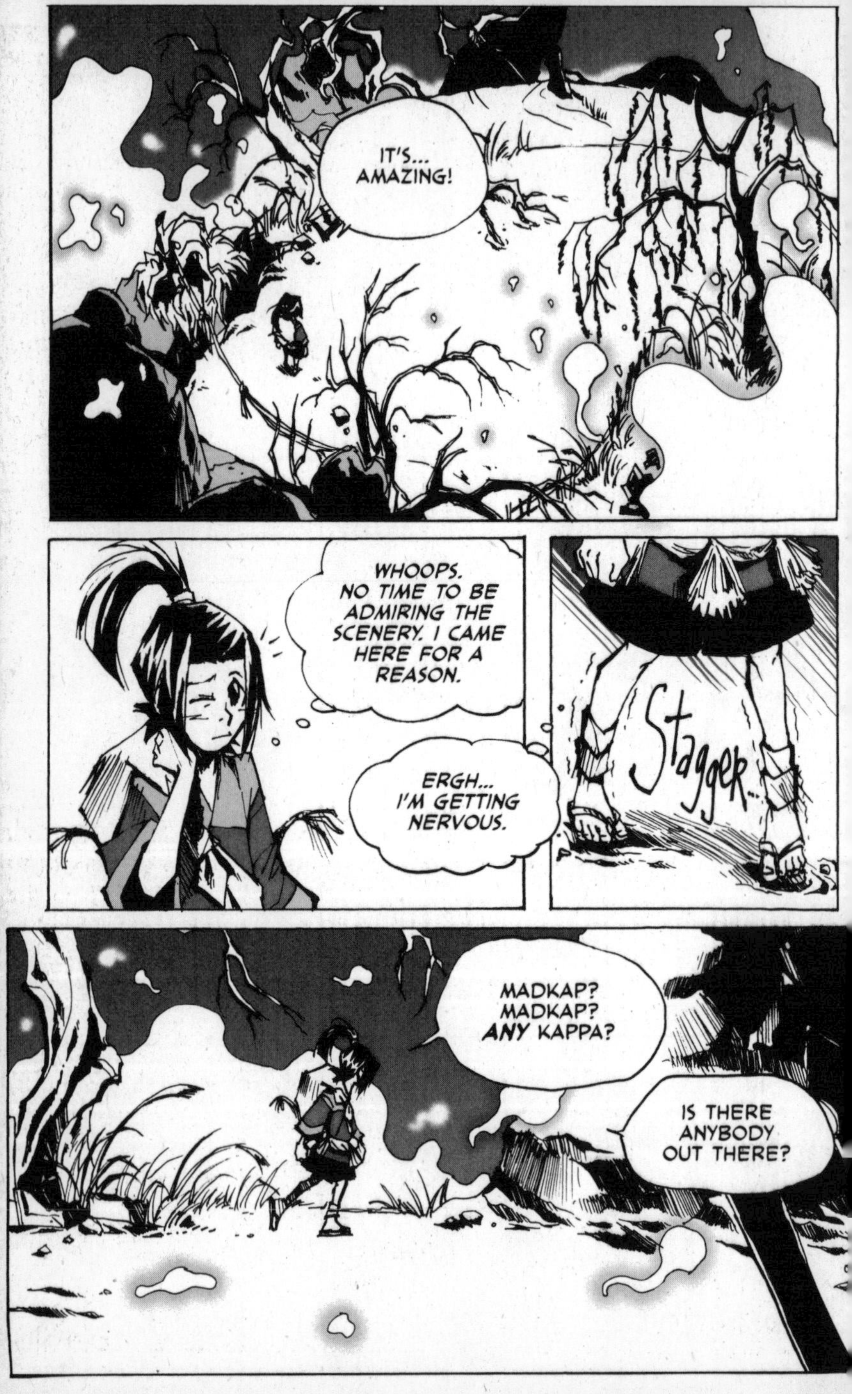
IT'S... AMAZING!
WHOOPS. NO TIME TO BE ADMIRING THE SCENERY. I CAME HERE FOR A REASON.
ERGH... I'M GETTING NERVOUS.
Stagger...
MADKAP? MADKAP? ANY KAPPA?
IS THERE ANYBODY OUT THERE?

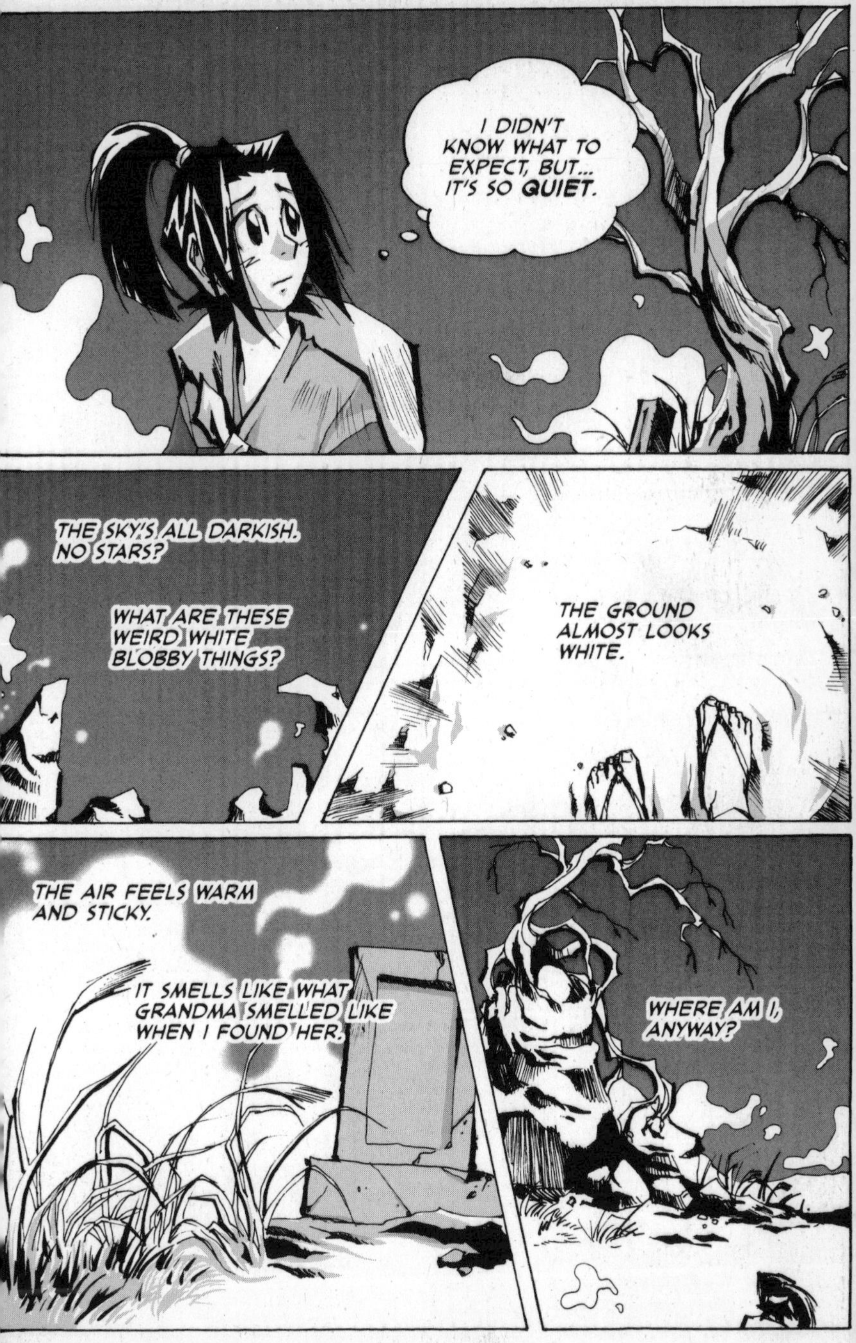
I DIDN'T KNOW WHAT TO EXPECT, BUT... IT'S SO **QUIET**.
THE SKY'S ALL DARKISH. NO STARS?
WHAT ARE THESE WEIRD WHITE BLOBBY THINGS?
THE GROUND ALMOST LOOKS WHITE.
THE AIR FEELS WARM AND STICKY.
IT SMELLS LIKE WHAT GRANDMA SMELLED LIKE WHEN I FOUND HER.
WHERE AM I, ANYWAY?

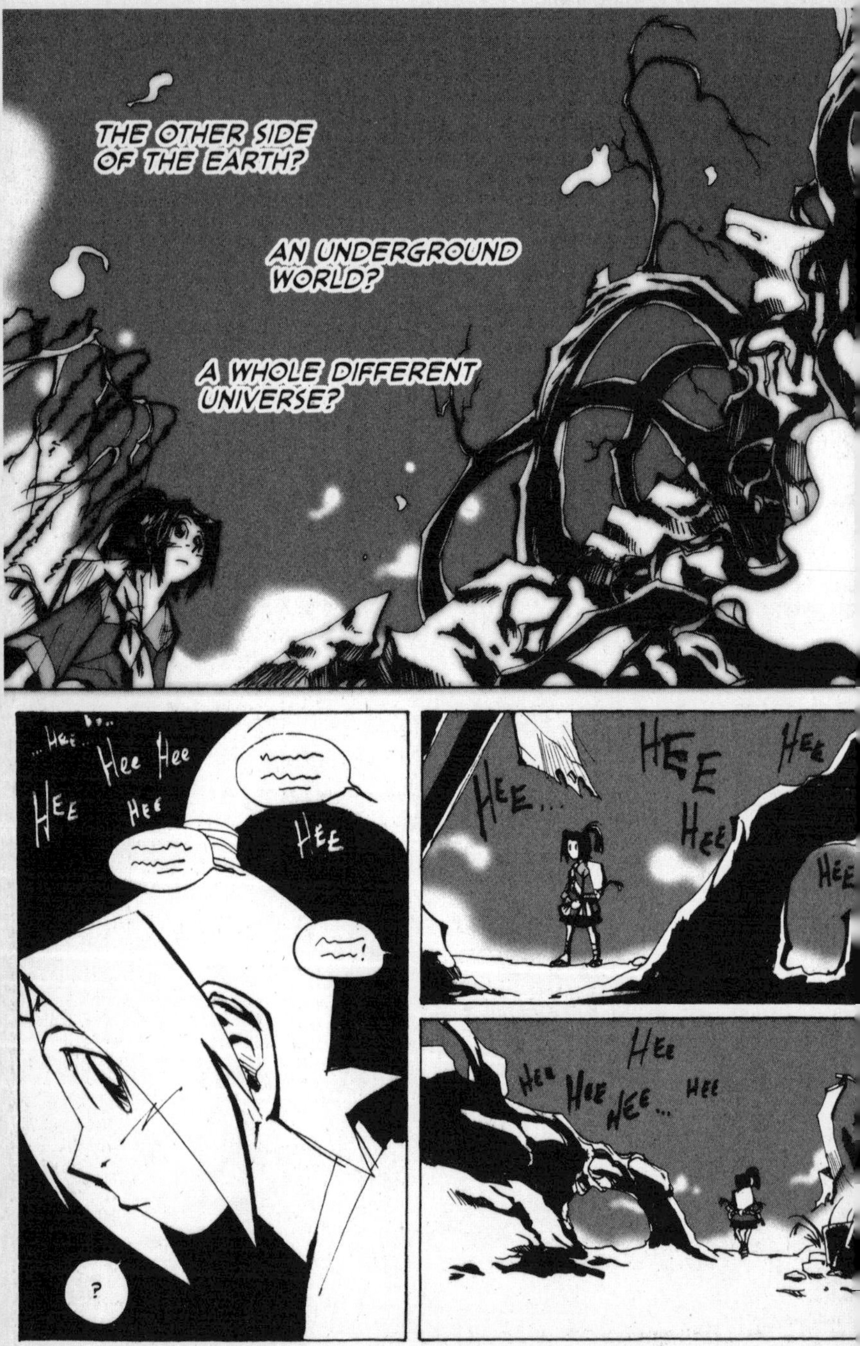
THE OTHER SIDE OF THE EARTH?
AN UNDERGROUND WORLD?
A WHOLE DIFFERENT UNIVERSE?
HEE... HEE HEE HEE
HEE HEE
HEE...
HEE HEE
HEE
HEE HEE...
...HEE... HEE HEE HEE HEE HEE
?

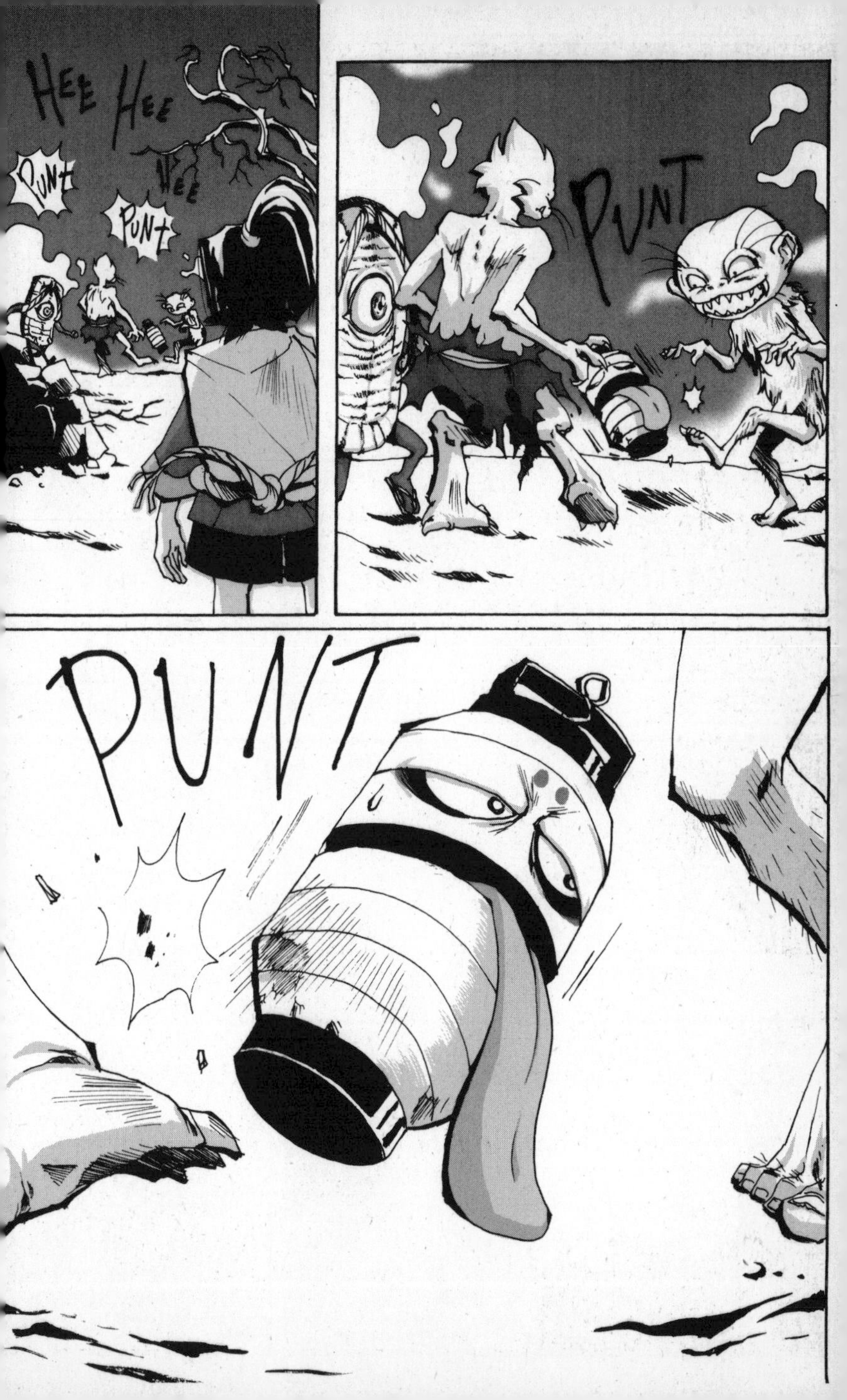
HEE HEE
PUNT
WEE
PUNT
PUNT
PUNT

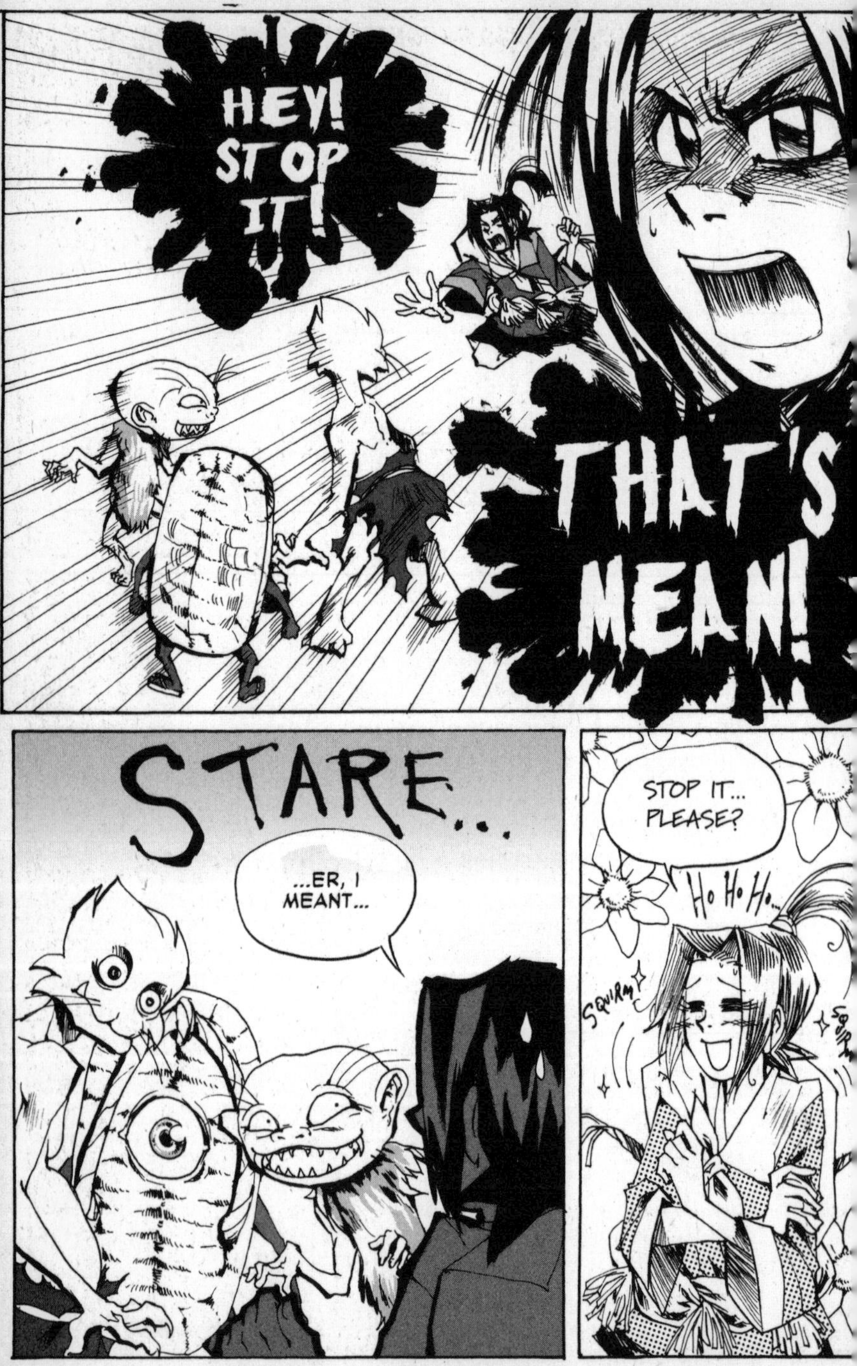

HEY! STOP IT!
THAT'S MEAN!
STARE...
...ER, I MEANT...
STOP IT... PLEASE?
HO HO HO...
SQUIRM

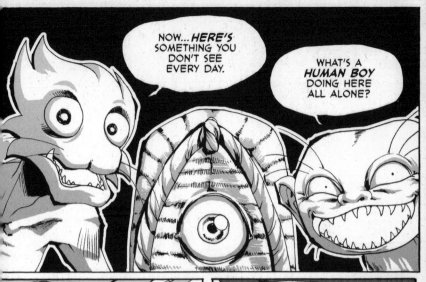

NOW... *HERE'S* SOMETHING YOU DON'T SEE EVERY DAY.

WHAT'S A *HUMAN BOY* DOING HERE ALL ALONE?

I DON'T KNOW, BUT HE'S GOT A LOT OF NERVE COMING IN HERE AND TELLING *US* WHAT TO DO.

E-EXCUSE ME, I... I'M LOOKING FOR A KAPPA.

~TEP!...

SWAGGER...

HE LOOKS MAD ALL THE TIME, AND... *OH!* HE HAS A *PEG LEG.* HAVE YOU SEEN HIM?

A ONE-LEGGED KAPPA?

?

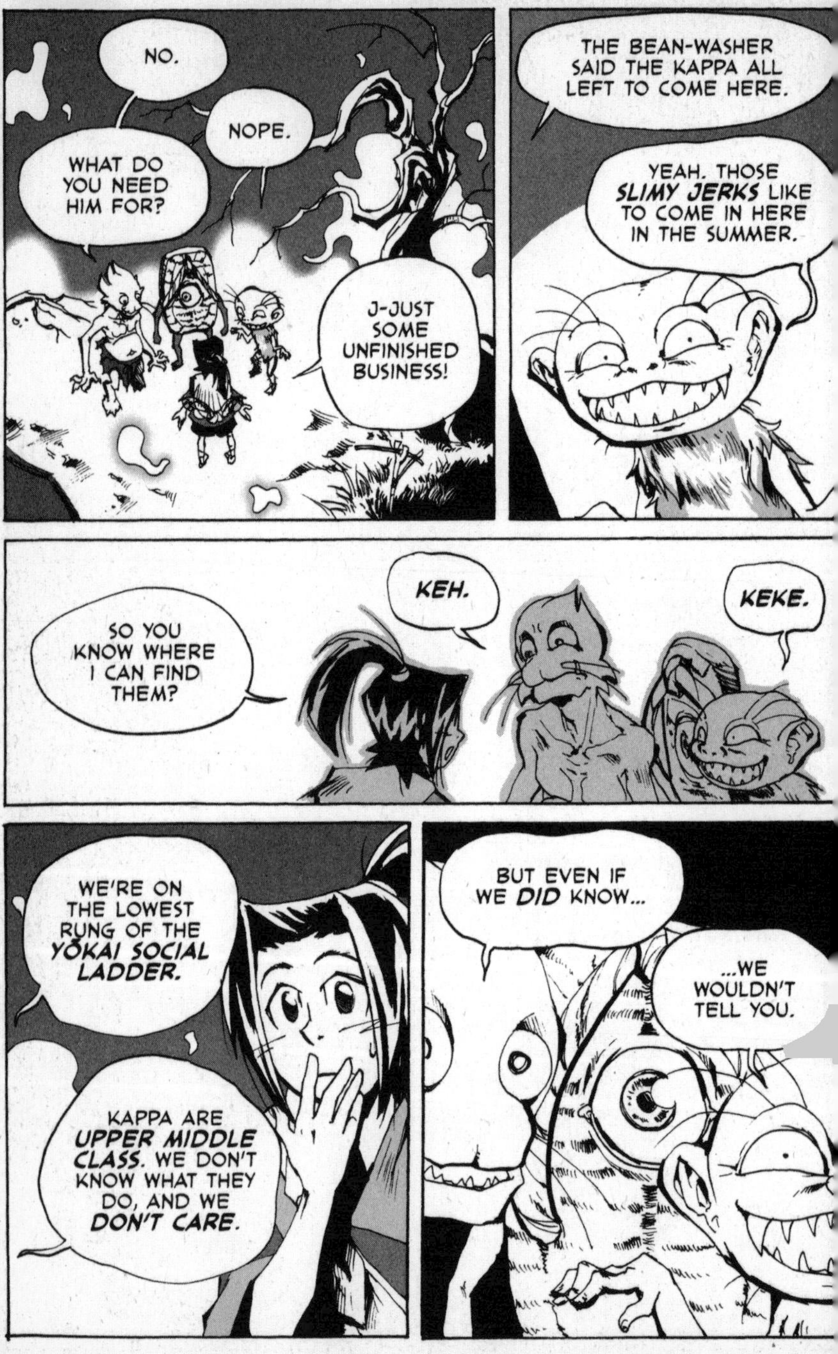
NO.
NOPE.
WHAT DO YOU NEED HIM FOR?
J-JUST SOME UNFINISHED BUSINESS!
THE BEAN-WASHER SAID THE KAPPA ALL LEFT TO COME HERE.
YEAH. THOSE *SLIMY JERKS* LIKE TO COME IN HERE IN THE SUMMER.
SO YOU KNOW WHERE I CAN FIND THEM?
KEH.
KEKE.
WE'RE ON THE LOWEST RUNG OF THE *YŌKAI SOCIAL LADDER.*
KAPPA ARE *UPPER MIDDLE CLASS*. WE DON'T KNOW WHAT THEY DO, AND WE *DON'T CARE*.
BUT EVEN IF WE *DID* KNOW...
...WE WOULDN'T TELL YOU.

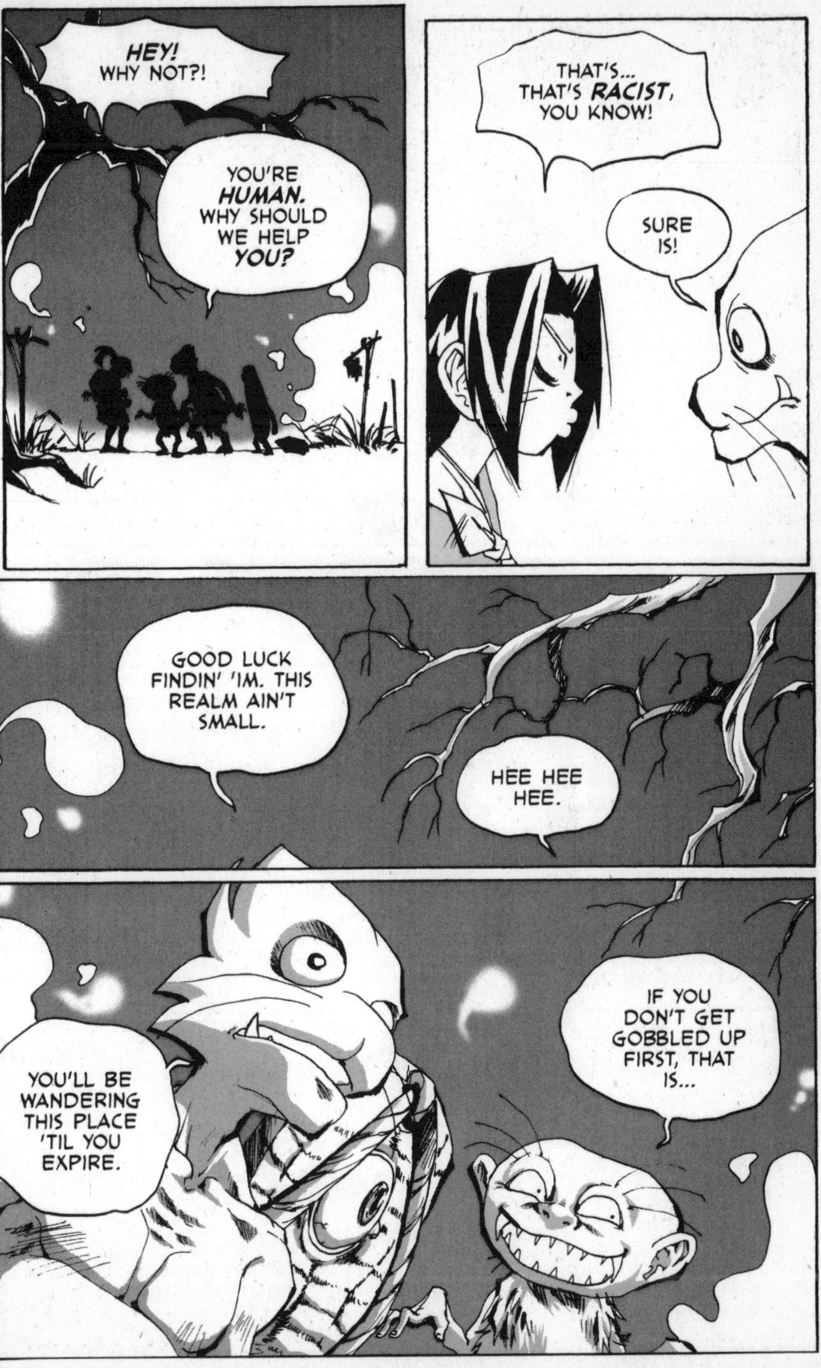
HEY! WHY NOT?!
YOU'RE HUMAN. WHY SHOULD WE HELP YOU?
THAT'S... THAT'S RACIST, YOU KNOW!
SURE IS!
GOOD LUCK FINDIN' 'IM. THIS REALM AIN'T SMALL.
HEE HEE HEE.
YOU'LL BE WANDERING THIS PLACE 'TIL YOU EXPIRE.
IF YOU DON'T GET GOBBLED UP FIRST, THAT IS...

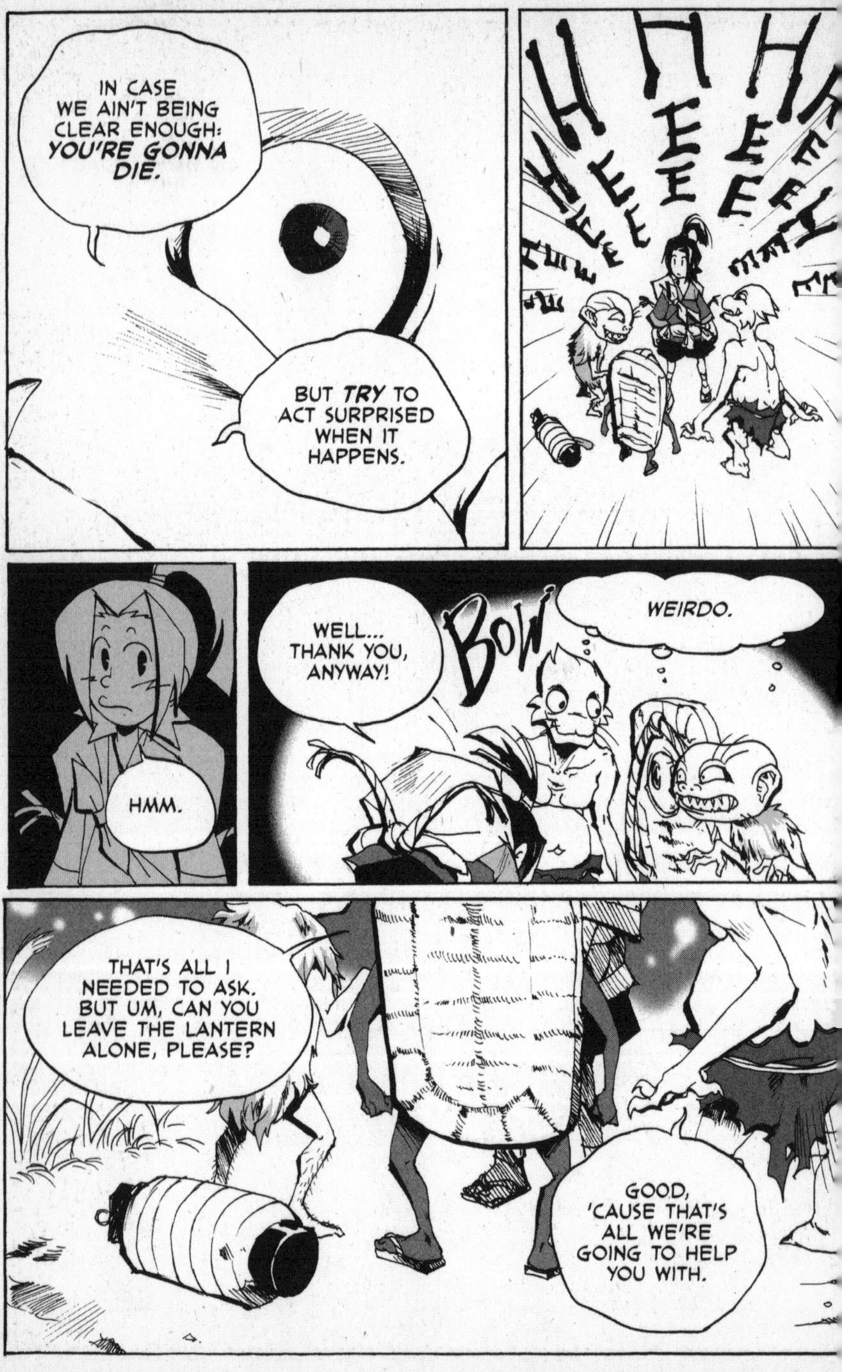
IN CASE WE AIN'T BEING CLEAR ENOUGH: ***YOU'RE GONNA DIE.***
BUT ***TRY*** TO ACT SURPRISED WHEN IT HAPPENS.
HMM.
WELL... THANK YOU, ANYWAY!
BOW
WEIRDO.
THAT'S ALL I NEEDED TO ASK. BUT UM, CAN YOU LEAVE THE LANTERN ALONE, PLEASE?
GOOD, 'CAUSE THAT'S ALL WE'RE GOING TO HELP YOU WITH.

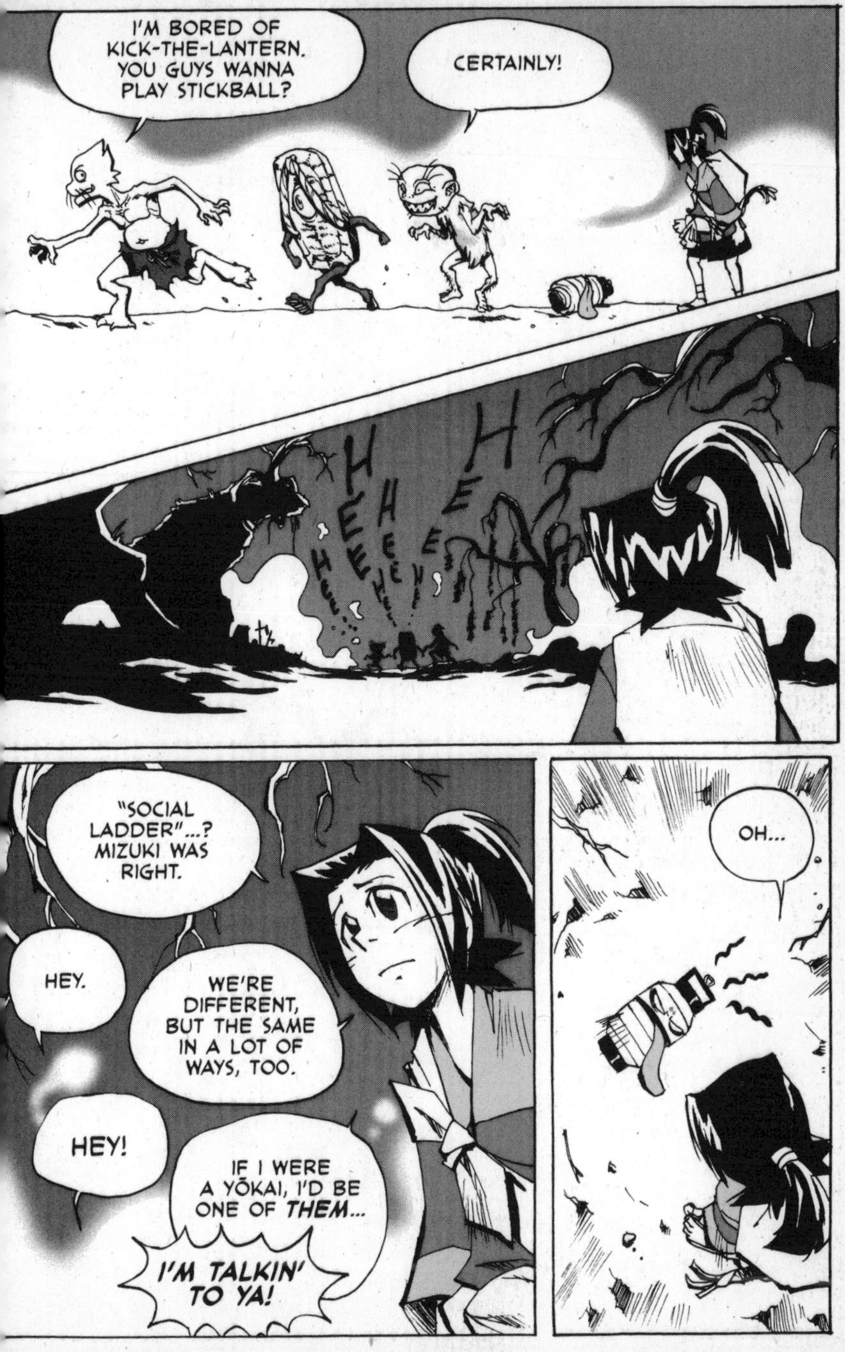
I'M BORED OF KICK-THE-LANTERN. YOU GUYS WANNA PLAY STICKBALL?
CERTAINLY!
HEHEHEHEHE...
"SOCIAL LADDER"...? MIZUKI WAS RIGHT.
HEY.
WE'RE DIFFERENT, BUT THE SAME IN A LOT OF WAYS, TOO.
HEY!
IF I WERE A YŌKAI, I'D BE ONE OF *THEM*...
I'M TALKIN' TO YA!
OH...

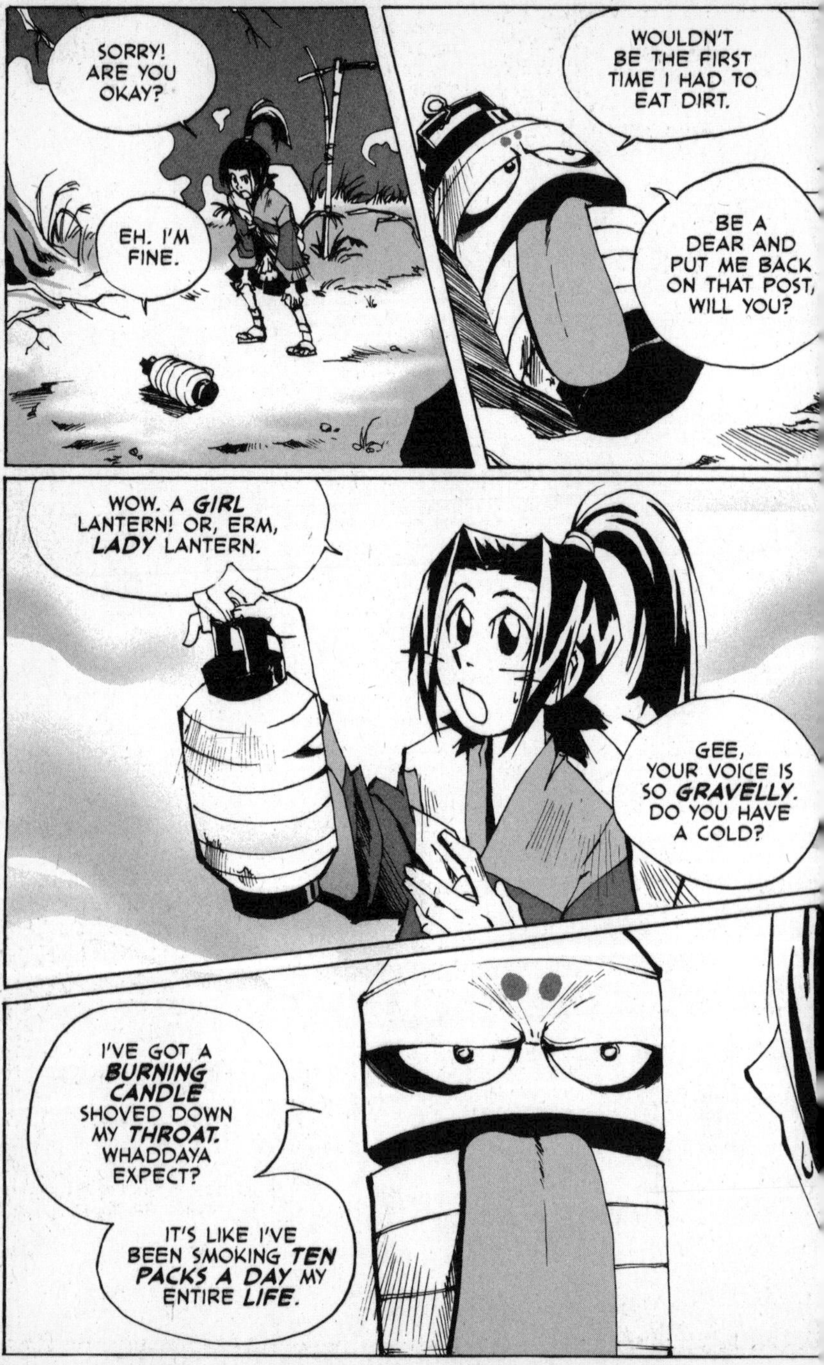
SORRY! ARE YOU OKAY?
EH. I'M FINE.
WOULDN'T BE THE FIRST TIME I HAD TO EAT DIRT.
BE A DEAR AND PUT ME BACK ON THAT POST, WILL YOU?
WOW. A GIRL LANTERN! OR, ERM, LADY LANTERN.
GEE, YOUR VOICE IS SO GRAVELLY. DO YOU HAVE A COLD?
I'VE GOT A BURNING CANDLE SHOVED DOWN MY THROAT. WHADDAYA EXPECT?
IT'S LIKE I'VE BEEN SMOKING TEN PACKS A DAY MY ENTIRE LIFE.

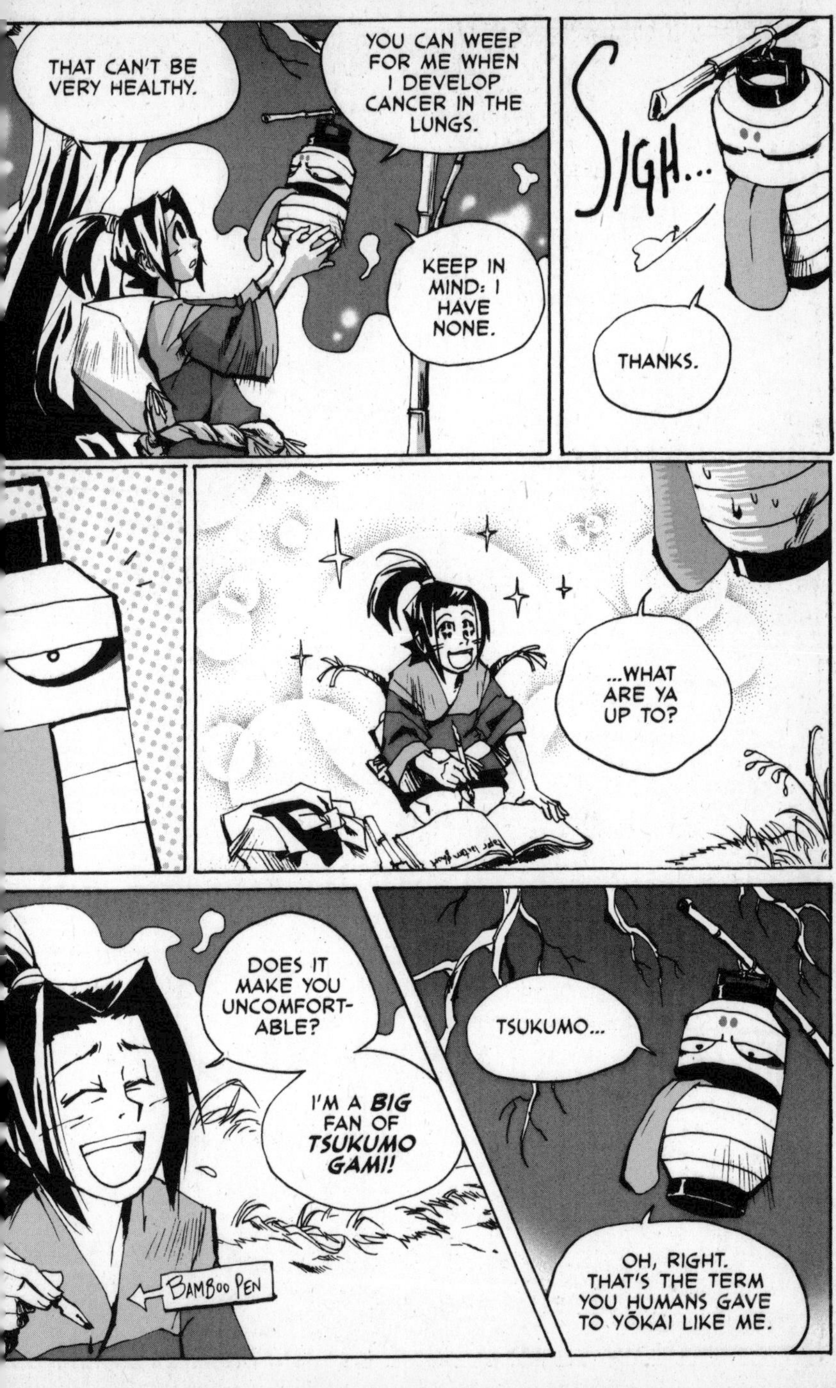
THAT CAN'T BE VERY HEALTHY.
YOU CAN WEEP FOR ME WHEN I DEVELOP CANCER IN THE LUNGS.
KEEP IN MIND: I HAVE NONE.
SIGH...
THANKS.
THANKS.
...WHAT ARE YA UP TO?
DOES IT MAKE YOU UNCOMFORT-ABLE?
I'M A **BIG** FAN OF ***TSUKUMO GAMI!***
BAMBOO PEN
TSUKUMO...
OH, RIGHT. THAT'S THE TERM YOU HUMANS GAVE TO YŌKAI LIKE ME.

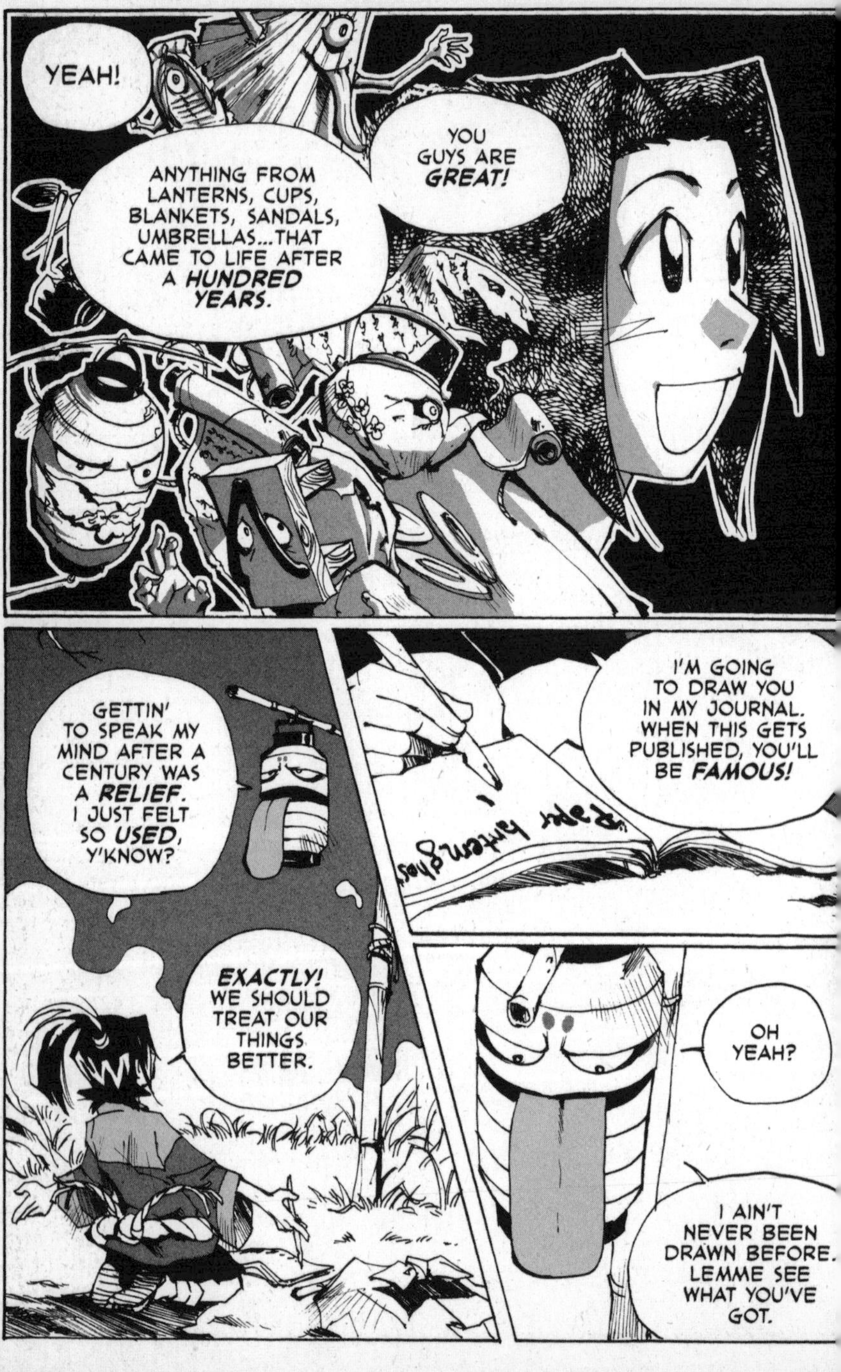
YOU GUYS ARE GREAT!
YEAH!
ANYTHING FROM LANTERNS, CUPS, BLANKETS, SANDALS, UMBRELLAS...THAT CAME TO LIFE AFTER A HUNDRED YEARS.
GETTIN' TO SPEAK MY MIND AFTER A CENTURY WAS A RELIEF. I JUST FELT SO USED, Y'KNOW?
EXACTLY! WE SHOULD TREAT OUR THINGS BETTER.
I'M GOING TO DRAW YOU IN MY JOURNAL. WHEN THIS GETS PUBLISHED, YOU'LL BE FAMOUS!
OH YEAH?
I AIN'T NEVER BEEN DRAWN BEFORE. LEMME SEE WHAT YOU'VE GOT.

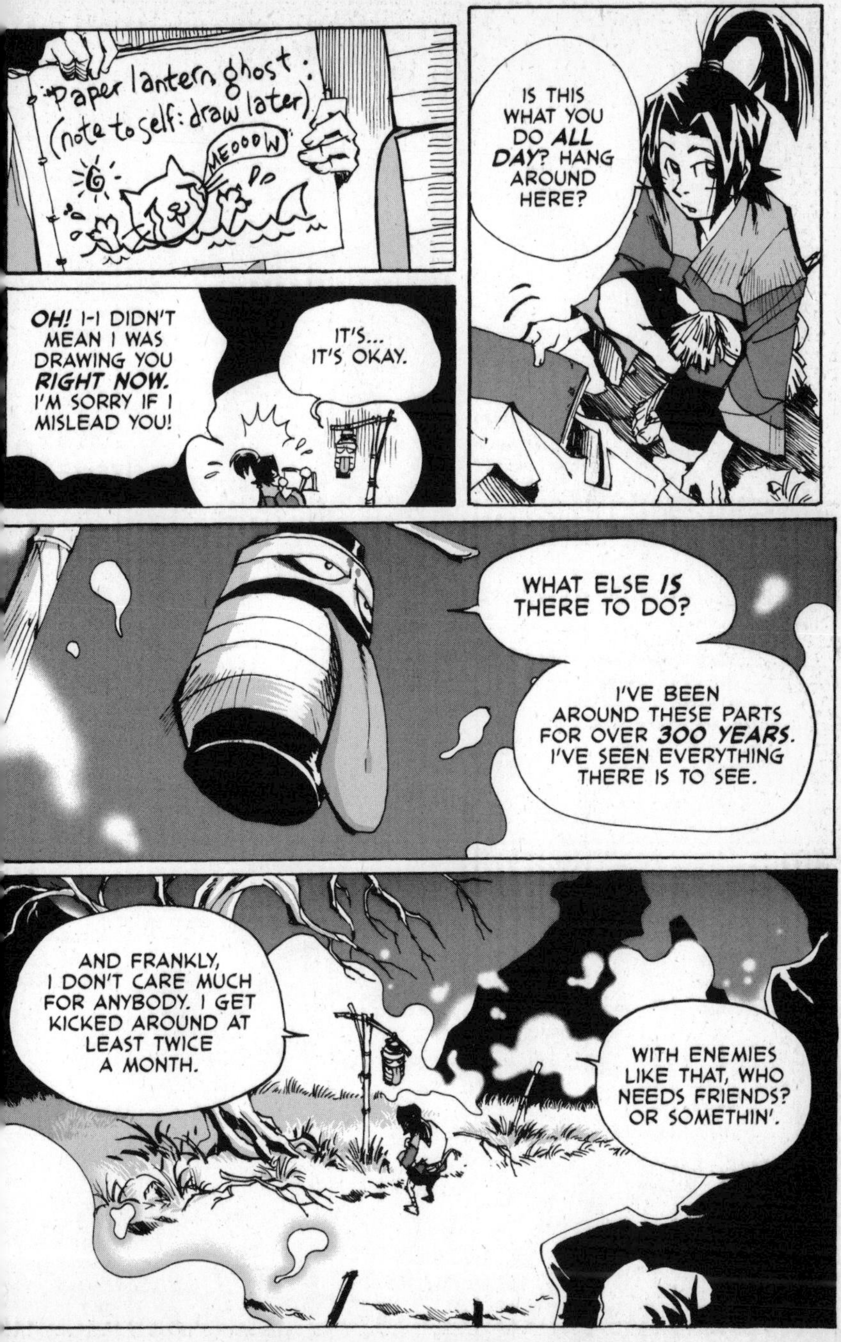
Paper lantern ghost:
(note to self: draw later)
MEOOOW
IS THIS WHAT YOU DO ALL DAY? HANG AROUND HERE?
OH! I-I DIDN'T MEAN I WAS DRAWING YOU RIGHT NOW. I'M SORRY IF I MISLEAD YOU!
IT'S... IT'S OKAY.
WHAT ELSE IS THERE TO DO?
I'VE BEEN AROUND THESE PARTS FOR OVER 300 YEARS. I'VE SEEN EVERYTHING THERE IS TO SEE.
AND FRANKLY, I DON'T CARE MUCH FOR ANYBODY. I GET KICKED AROUND AT LEAST TWICE A MONTH.
WITH ENEMIES LIKE THAT, WHO NEEDS FRIENDS? OR SOMETHIN'.

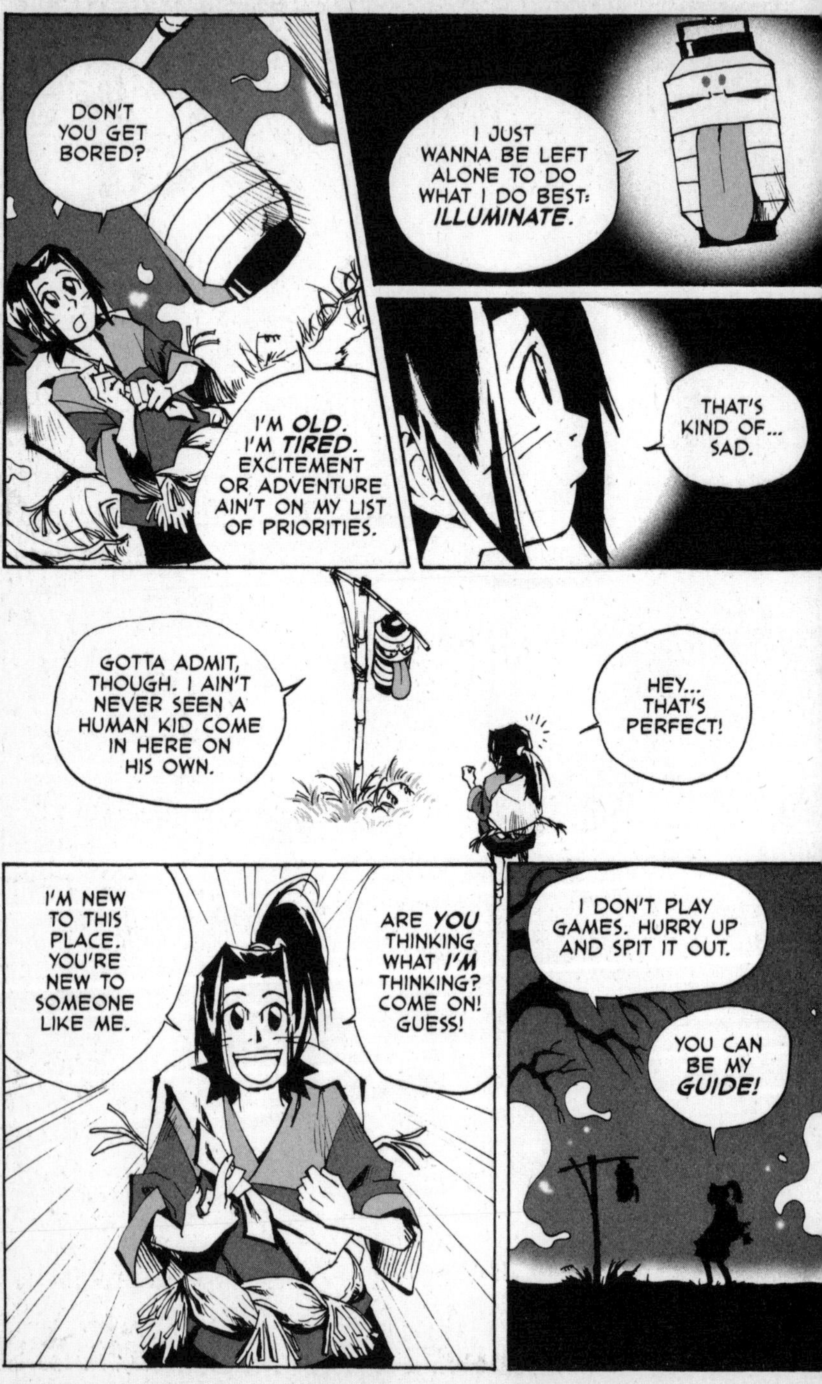
DON'T YOU GET BORED?
I JUST WANNA BE LEFT ALONE TO DO WHAT I DO BEST: *ILLUMINATE*.
I'M *OLD*. I'M *TIRED*. EXCITEMENT OR ADVENTURE AIN'T ON MY LIST OF PRIORITIES.
THAT'S KIND OF... SAD.
GOTTA ADMIT, THOUGH. I AIN'T NEVER SEEN A HUMAN KID COME IN HERE ON HIS OWN.
HEY... THAT'S PERFECT!
I'M NEW TO THIS PLACE. YOU'RE NEW TO SOMEONE LIKE ME.
ARE *YOU* THINKING WHAT *I'M* THINKING? COME ON! GUESS!
I DON'T PLAY GAMES. HURRY UP AND SPIT IT OUT.
YOU CAN BE MY *GUIDE*!

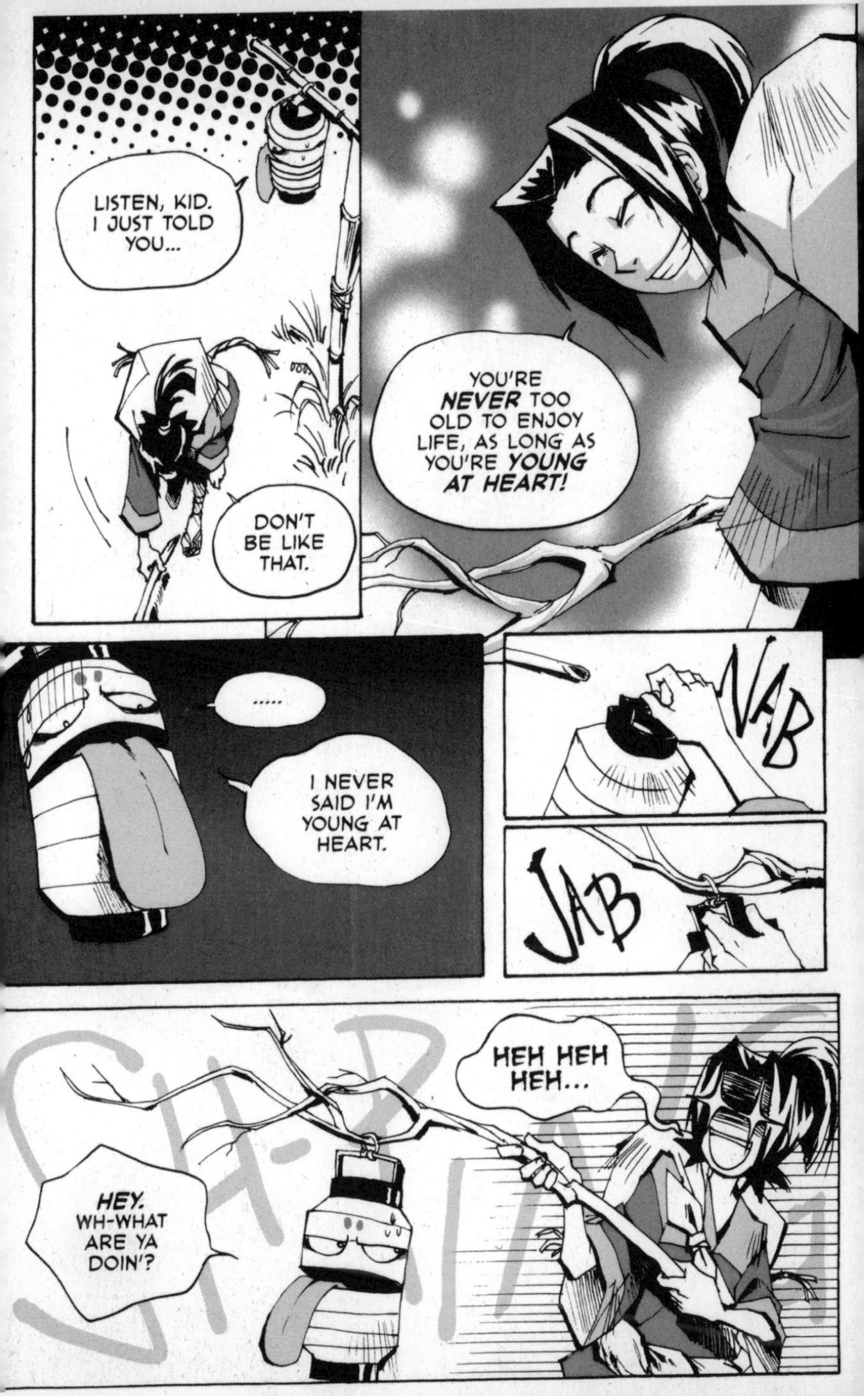
LISTEN, KID. I JUST TOLD YOU...
DON'T BE LIKE THAT.
YOU'RE NEVER TOO OLD TO ENJOY LIFE, AS LONG AS YOU'RE YOUNG AT HEART!
.....
I NEVER SAID I'M YOUNG AT HEART.
NAB
JAB
HEY. WH-WHAT ARE YA DOIN'?
HEH HEH HEH...

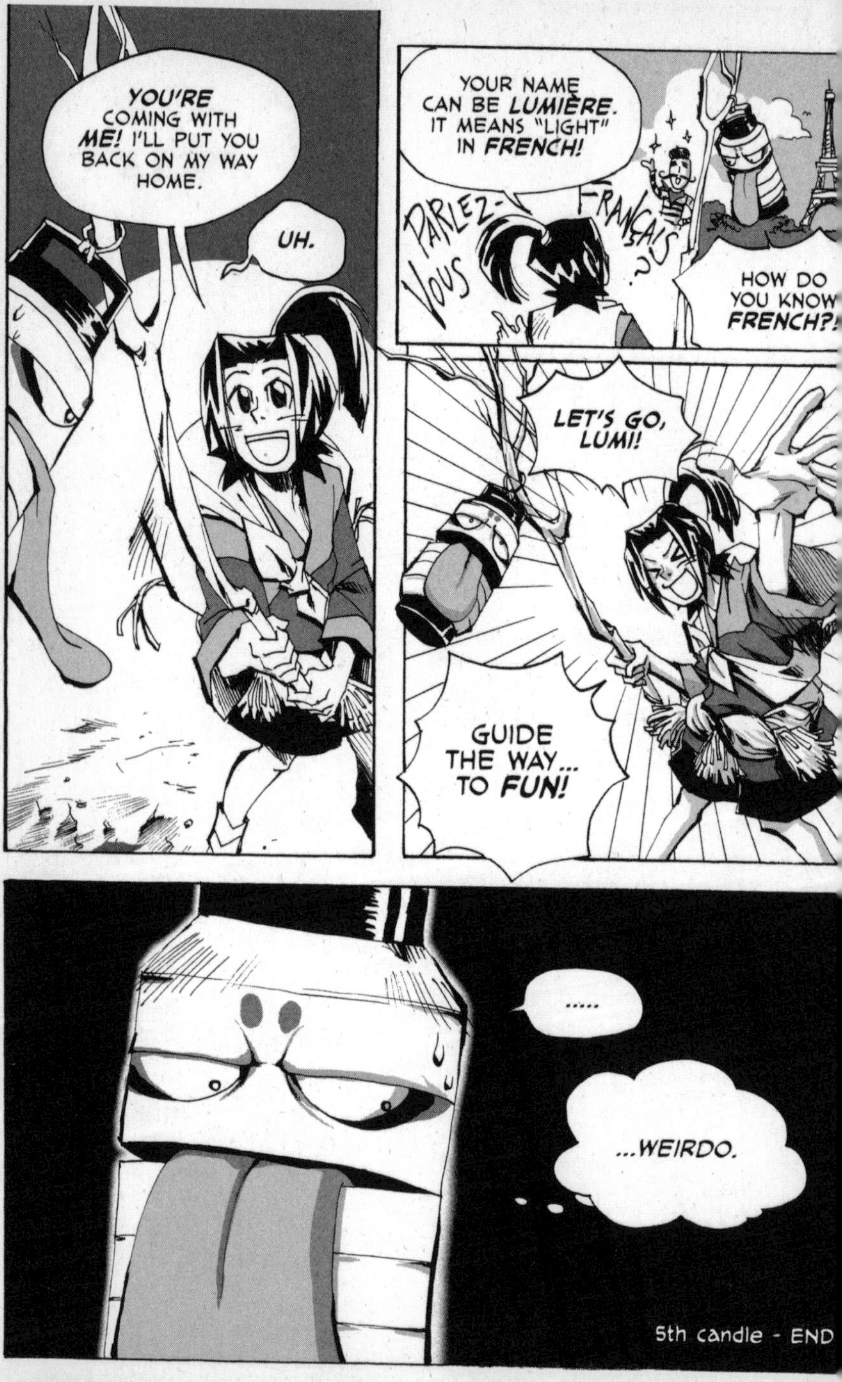
YOU'RE COMING WITH ME! I'LL PUT YOU BACK ON MY WAY HOME.
UH.
YOUR NAME CAN BE LUMIÈRE. IT MEANS "LIGHT" IN FRENCH!
PARLEZ-VOUS FRANÇAIS?
HOW DO YOU KNOW FRENCH?!
LET'S GO, LUMI!
GUIDE THE WAY... TO FUN!
......
...WEIRDO.
5th candle - END

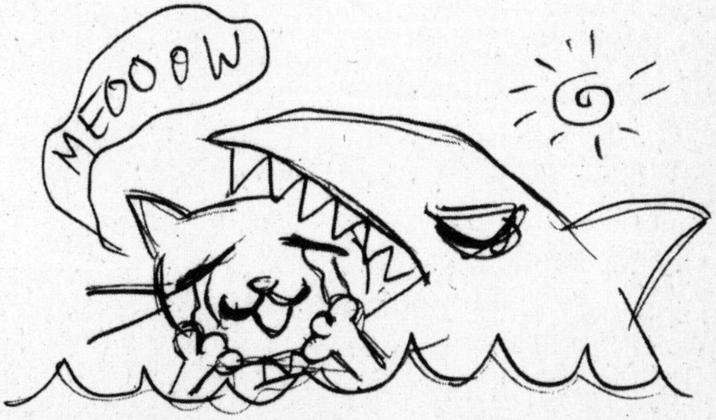
MEOOOW

HAMACHI'S JOURNAL

Paper lantern ghost
(a.k.a. chōchin-obaké)

 "THEY'RE OLD PAPER LANTERNS WITH TWO EYES AND A MOUTH. THEY HAVE BIG TONGUES THAT HANG OUT, TOO. THEY SOMETIMES EVEN HAVE HAIR. THEY ARE NICE AND NEVER HURT ANYONE."

 "...THAT AIN'T ME. THAT'S AN OCTOPUS HAVING TEA AND SUSHI WITH A CAT."

 "I'LL DRAW YOU LATER, OKAY?"

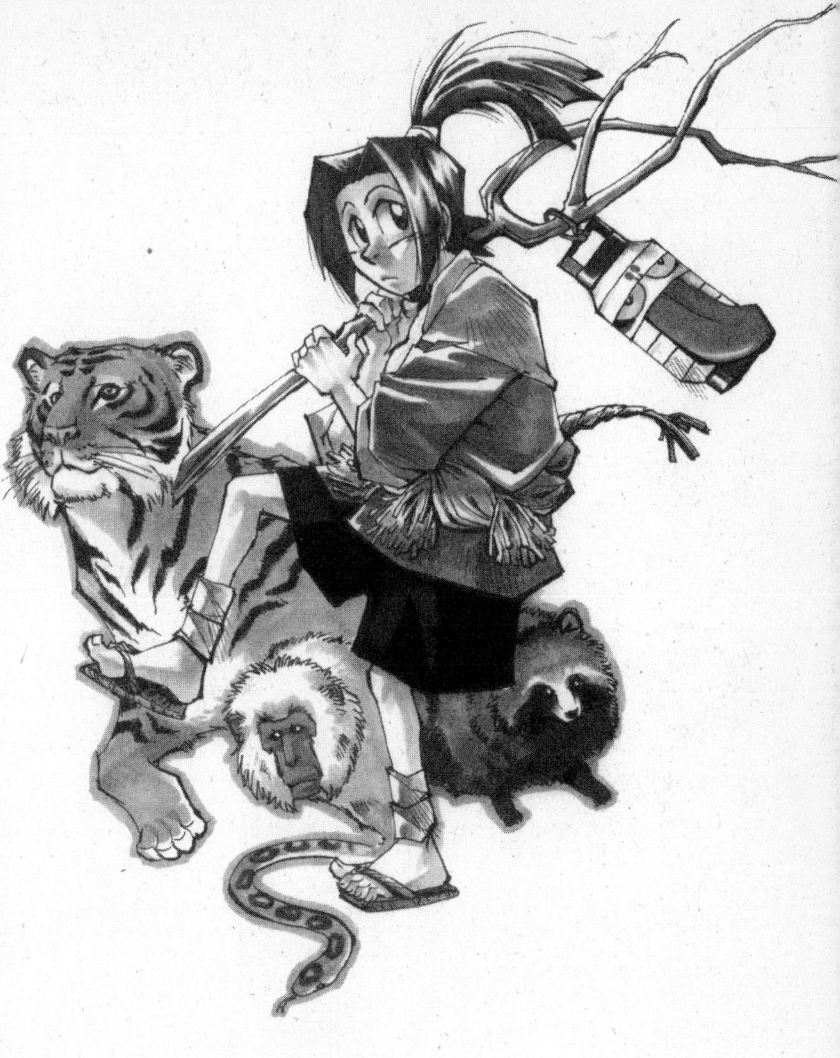

6th candle

Chimera

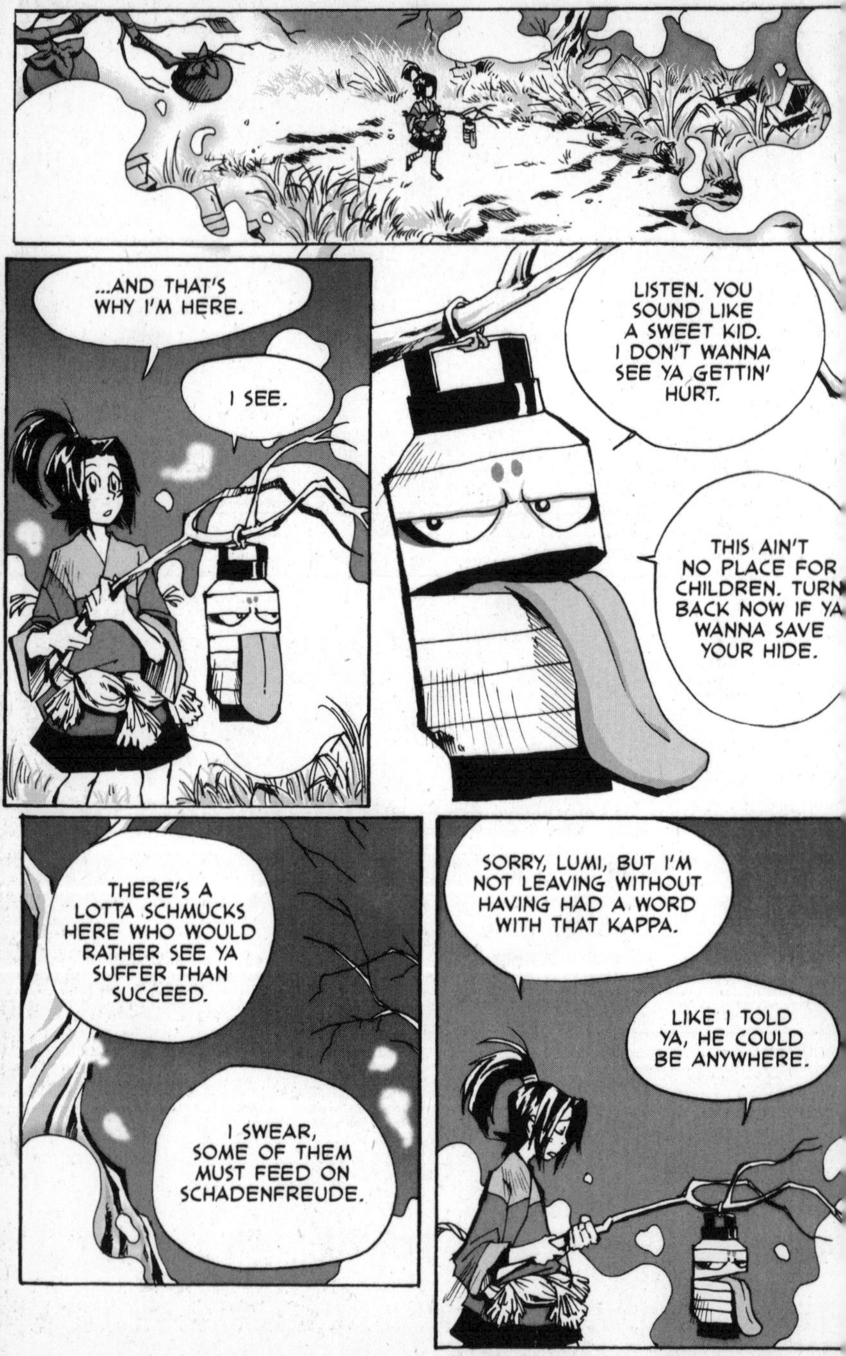
...AND THAT'S WHY I'M HERE.
I SEE.
LISTEN. YOU SOUND LIKE A SWEET KID. I DON'T WANNA SEE YA GETTIN' HURT.
THIS AIN'T NO PLACE FOR CHILDREN. TURN BACK NOW IF YA WANNA SAVE YOUR HIDE.
THERE'S A LOTTA SCHMUCKS HERE WHO WOULD RATHER SEE YA SUFFER THAN SUCCEED.
I SWEAR, SOME OF THEM MUST FEED ON SCHADENFREUDE.
SORRY, LUMI, BUT I'M NOT LEAVING WITHOUT HAVING HAD A WORD WITH THAT KAPPA.
LIKE I TOLD YA, HE COULD BE ANYWHERE.

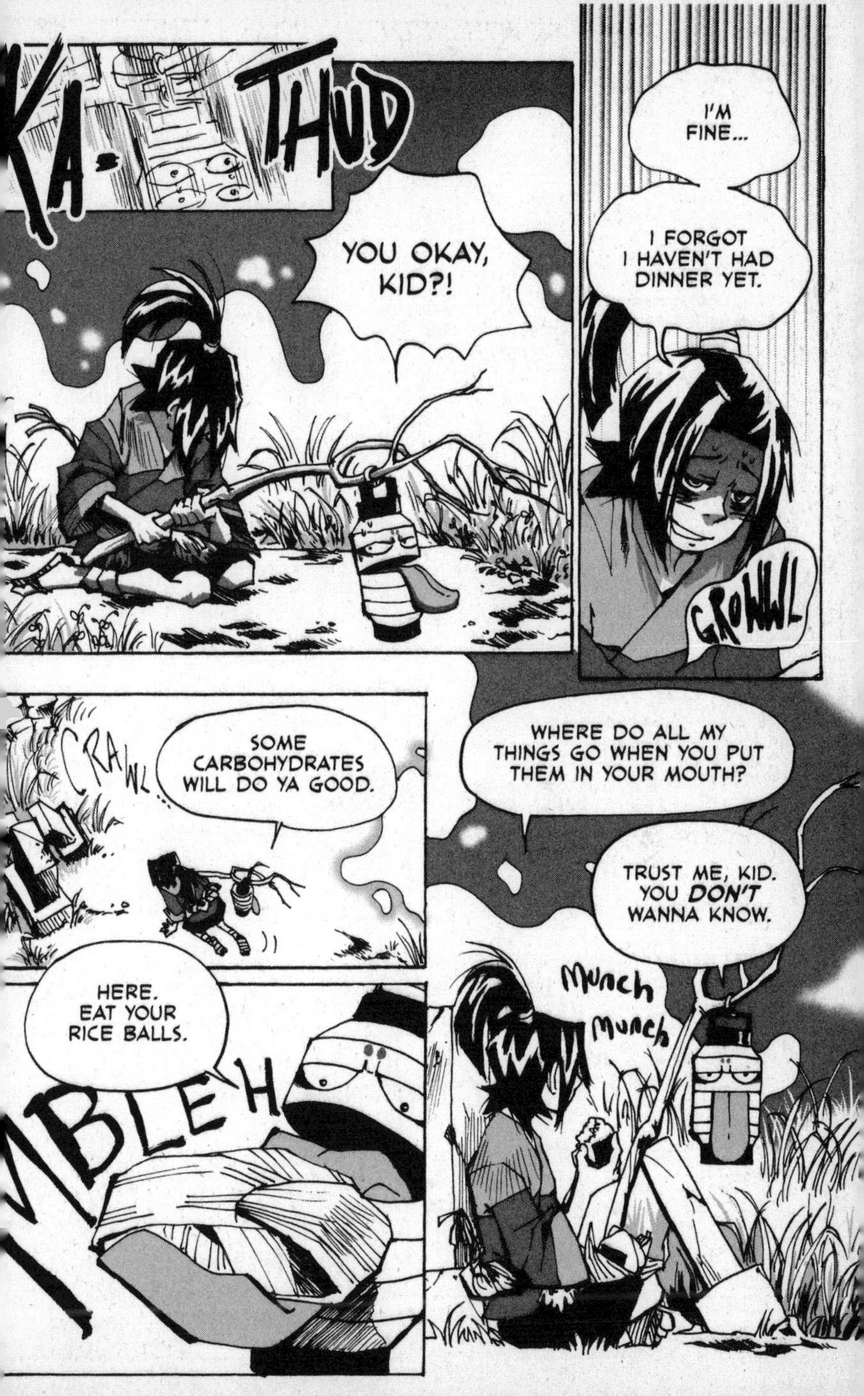

KA-THUD
YOU OKAY, KID?!
I'M FINE...
I FORGOT I HAVEN'T HAD DINNER YET.
GROWWL
CRAWL
SOME CARBOHYDRATES WILL DO YA GOOD.
WHERE DO ALL MY THINGS GO WHEN YOU PUT THEM IN YOUR MOUTH?
TRUST ME, KID. YOU *DON'T* WANNA KNOW.
HERE. EAT YOUR RICE BALLS.
BLEH
munch munch

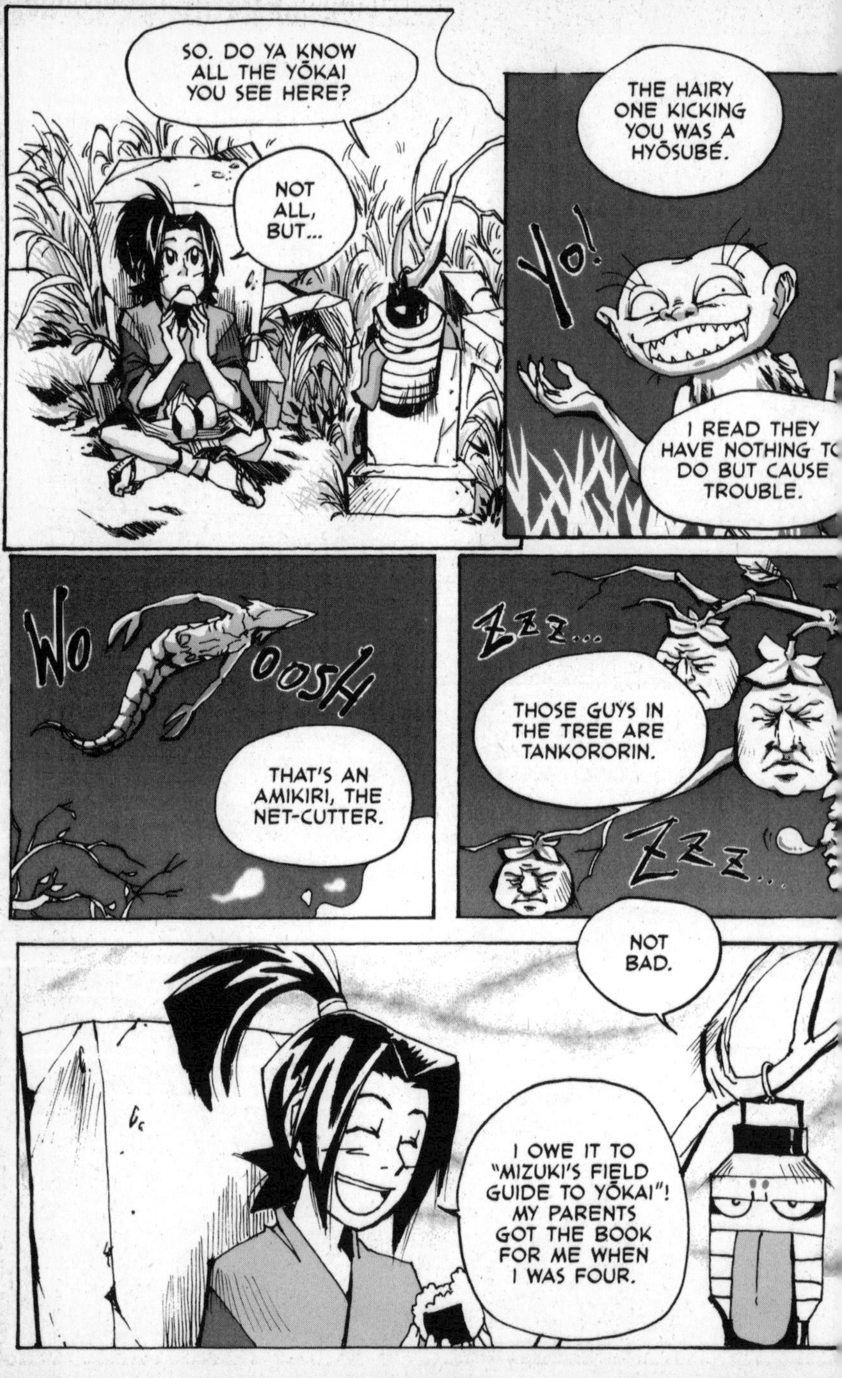
SO. DO YA KNOW ALL THE YŌKAI YOU SEE HERE?
NOT ALL, BUT...
THE HAIRY ONE KICKING YOU WAS A HYŌSUBÉ.
YO!
I READ THEY HAVE NOTHING TO DO BUT CAUSE TROUBLE.
WOOOSH
THAT'S AN AMIKIRI, THE NET-CUTTER.
ZZZ...
THOSE GUYS IN THE TREE ARE TANKORORIN.
ZZZ...
NOT BAD.
I OWE IT TO "MIZUKI'S FIELD GUIDE TO YŌKAI"! MY PARENTS GOT THE BOOK FOR ME WHEN I WAS FOUR.

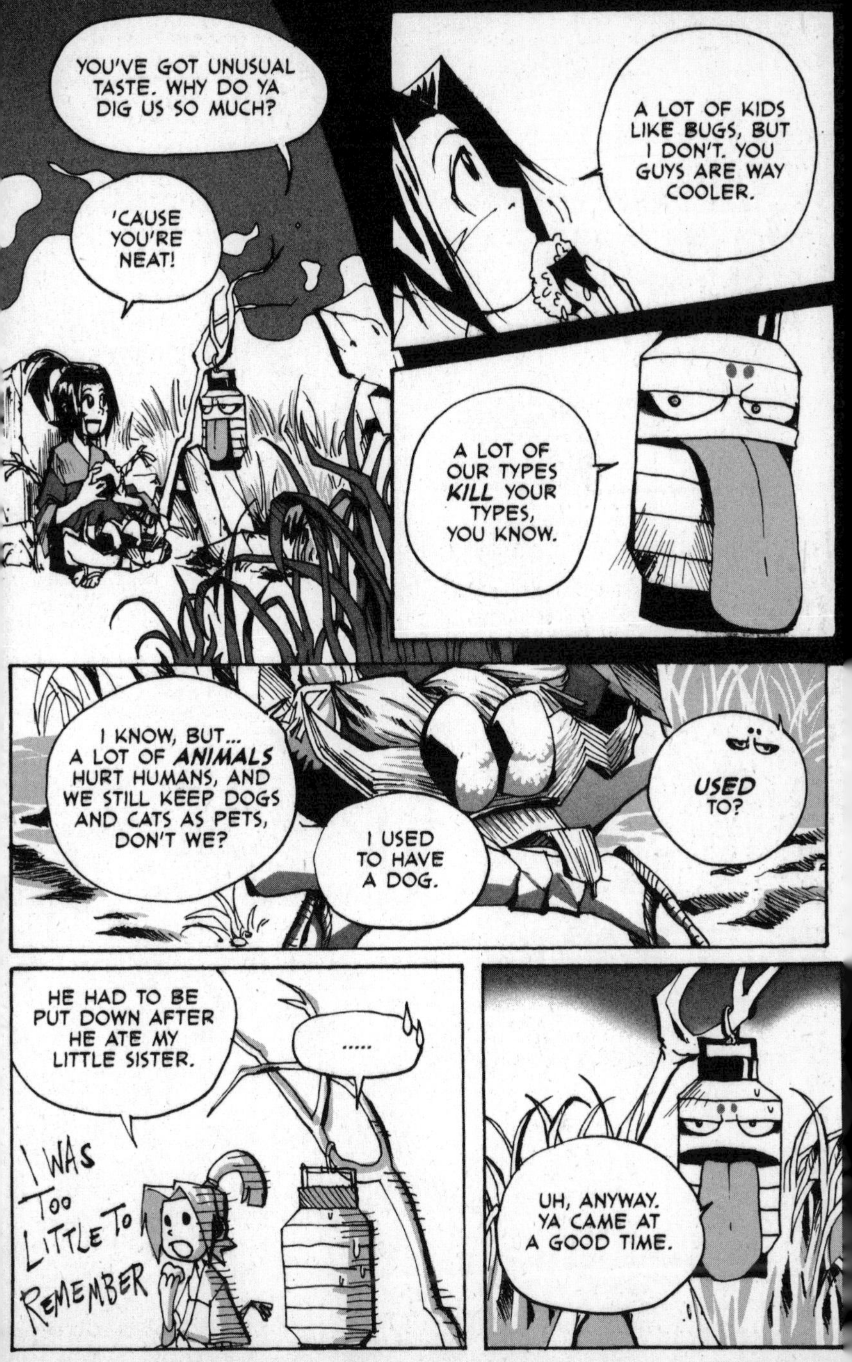
YOU'VE GOT UNUSUAL TASTE. WHY DO YA DIG US SO MUCH?
'CAUSE YOU'RE NEAT!
A LOT OF KIDS LIKE BUGS, BUT I DON'T. YOU GUYS ARE WAY COOLER.
A LOT OF OUR TYPES *KILL* YOUR TYPES, YOU KNOW.
I KNOW, BUT... A LOT OF *ANIMALS* HURT HUMANS, AND WE STILL KEEP DOGS AND CATS AS PETS, DON'T WE?
I USED TO HAVE A DOG.
USED TO?
HE HAD TO BE PUT DOWN AFTER HE ATE MY LITTLE SISTER.
......
I WAS TOO LITTLE TO REMEMBER
UH, ANYWAY. YA CAME AT A GOOD TIME.

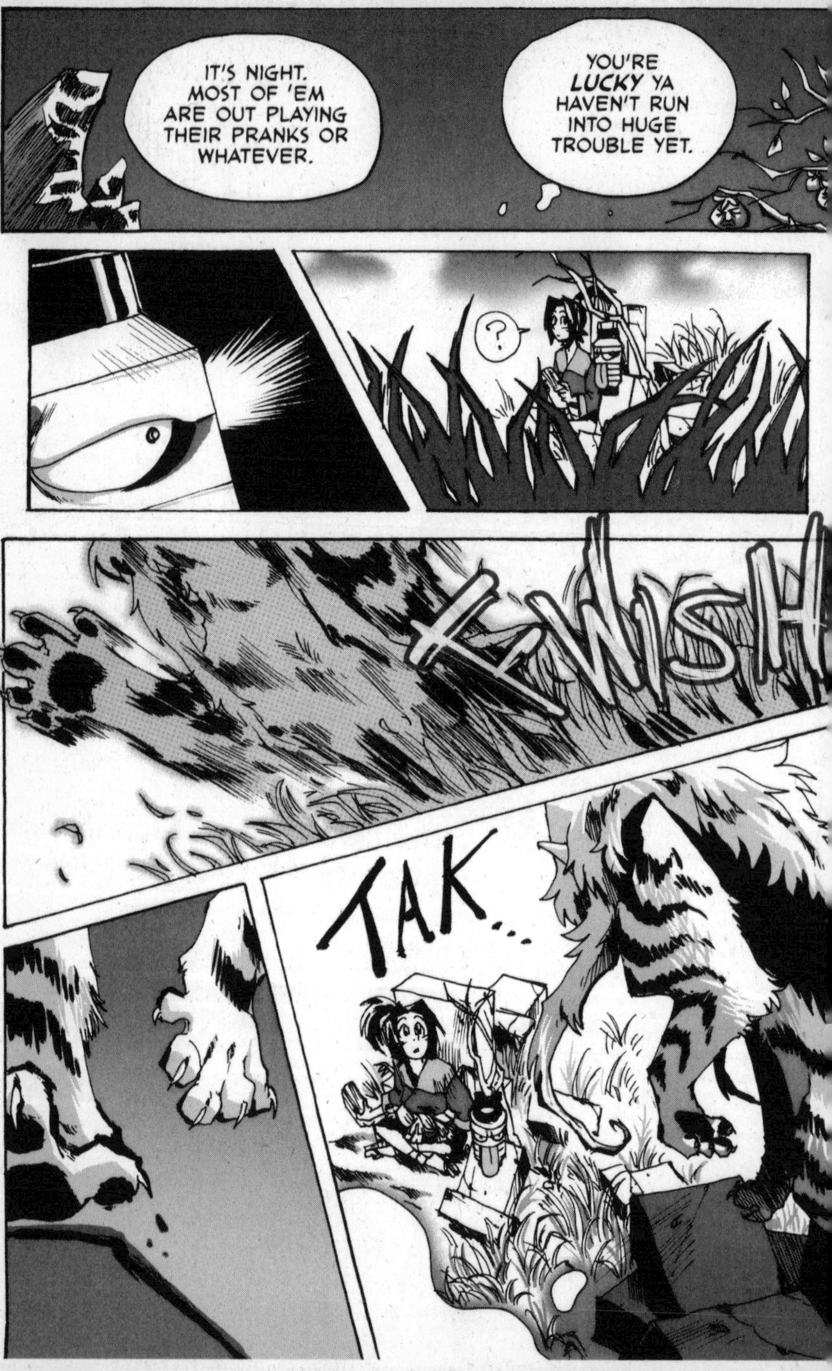
IT'S NIGHT. MOST OF 'EM ARE OUT PLAYING THEIR PRANKS OR WHATEVER.
YOU'RE LUCKY YA HAVEN'T RUN INTO HUGE TROUBLE YET.
?
FWISH
TAK...

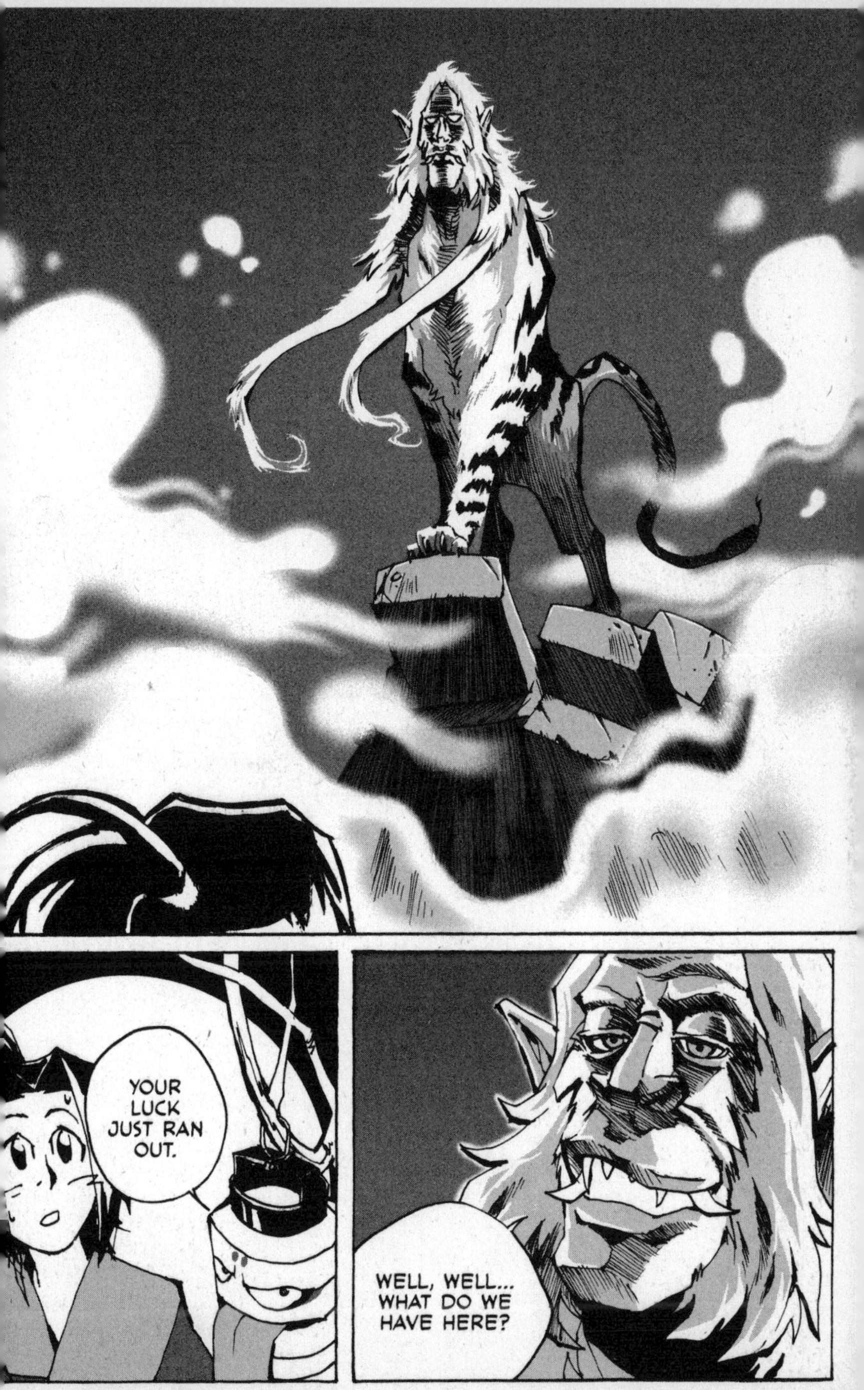
YOUR LUCK JUST RAN OUT.
WELL, WELL... WHAT DO WE HAVE HERE?

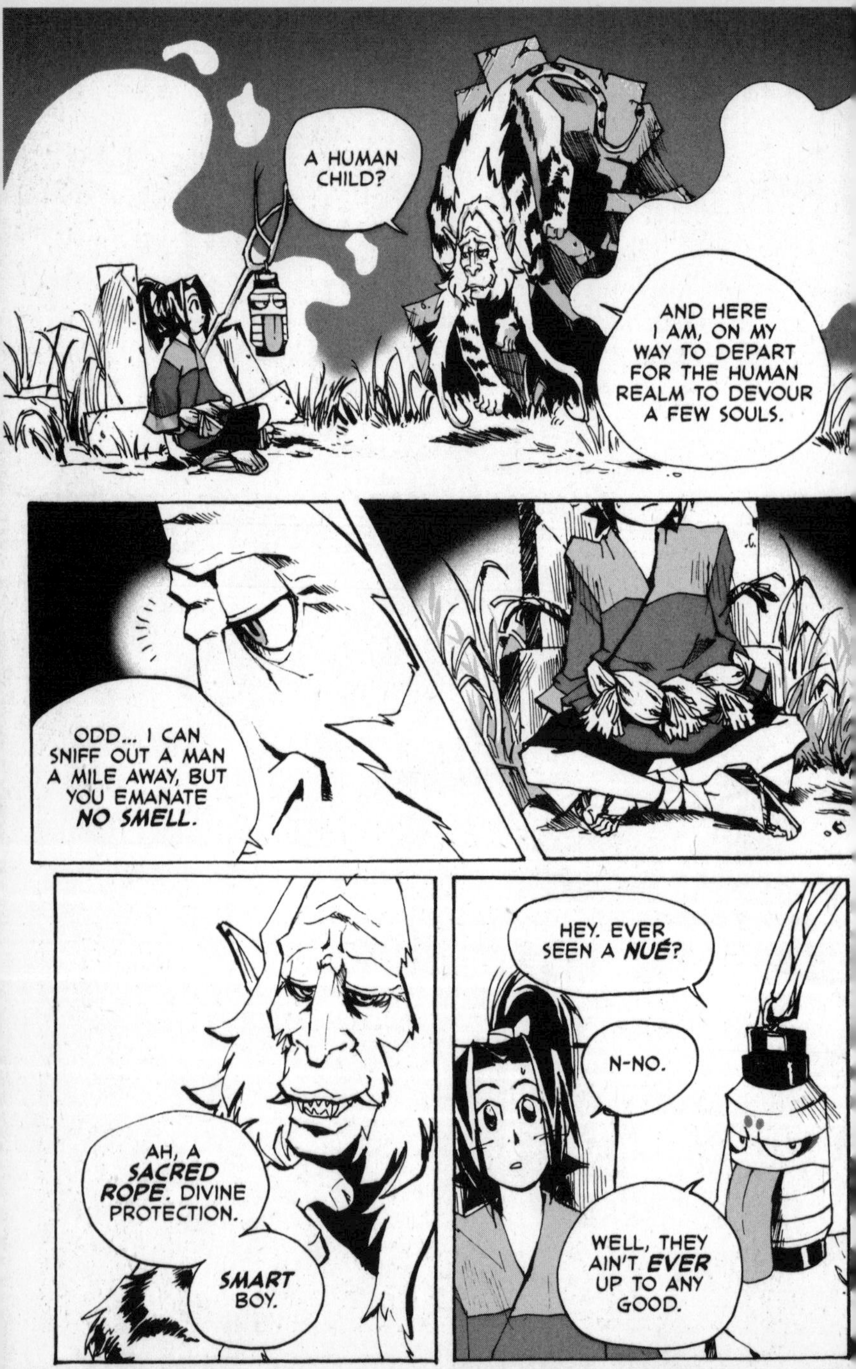
A HUMAN CHILD?
AND HERE I AM, ON MY WAY TO DEPART FOR THE HUMAN REALM TO DEVOUR A FEW SOULS.
ODD... I CAN SNIFF OUT A MAN A MILE AWAY, BUT YOU EMANATE NO SMELL.
AH, A SACRED ROPE. DIVINE PROTECTION.
SMART BOY.
HEY. EVER SEEN A NUÉ?
N-NO.
WELL, THEY AIN'T EVER UP TO ANY GOOD.

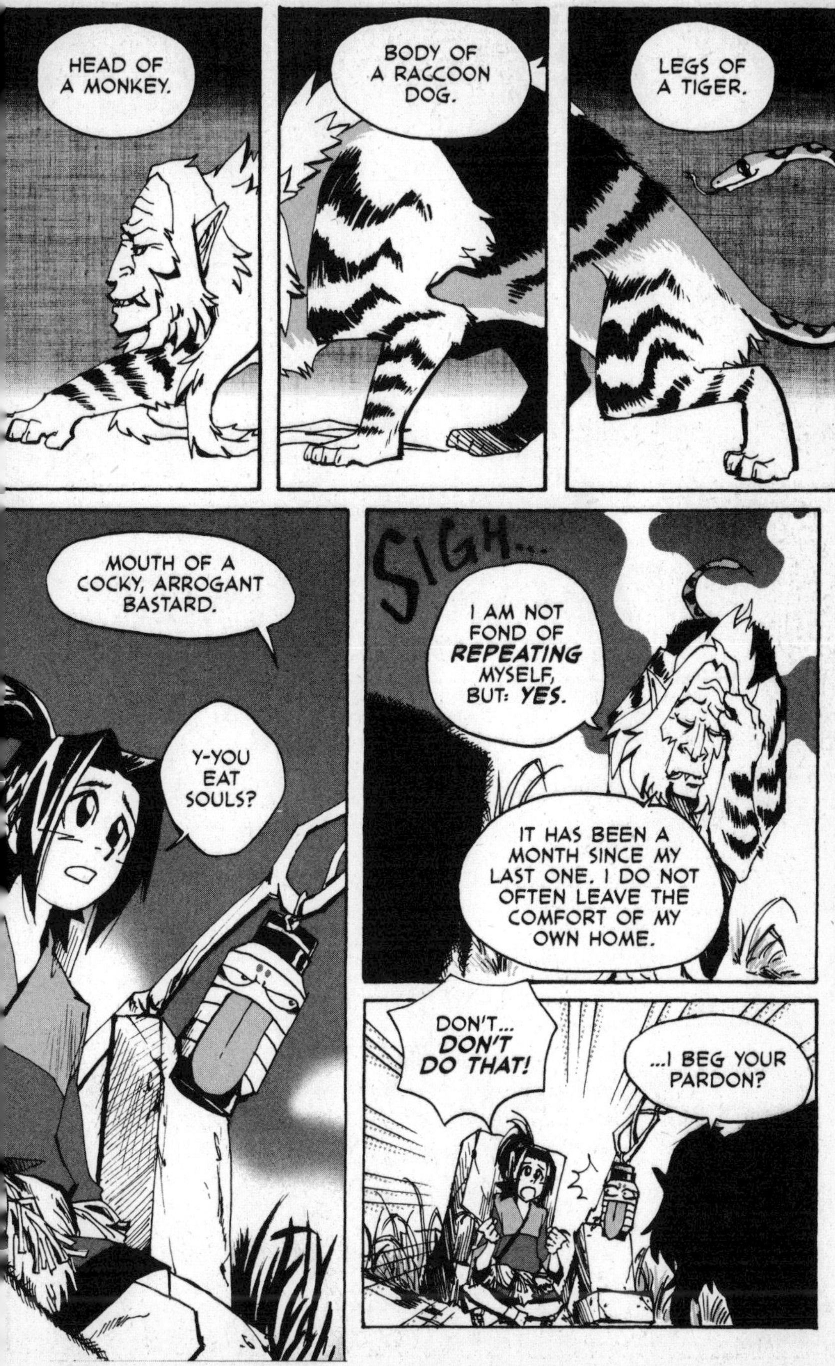
HEAD OF A MONKEY.
BODY OF A RACCOON DOG.
LEGS OF A TIGER.
MOUTH OF A COCKY, ARROGANT BASTARD.
Y-YOU EAT SOULS?
SIGH...
I AM NOT FOND OF REPEATING MYSELF, BUT: YES.
IT HAS BEEN A MONTH SINCE MY LAST ONE. I DO NOT OFTEN LEAVE THE COMFORT OF MY OWN HOME.
DON'T... DON'T DO THAT!
...I BEG YOUR PARDON?

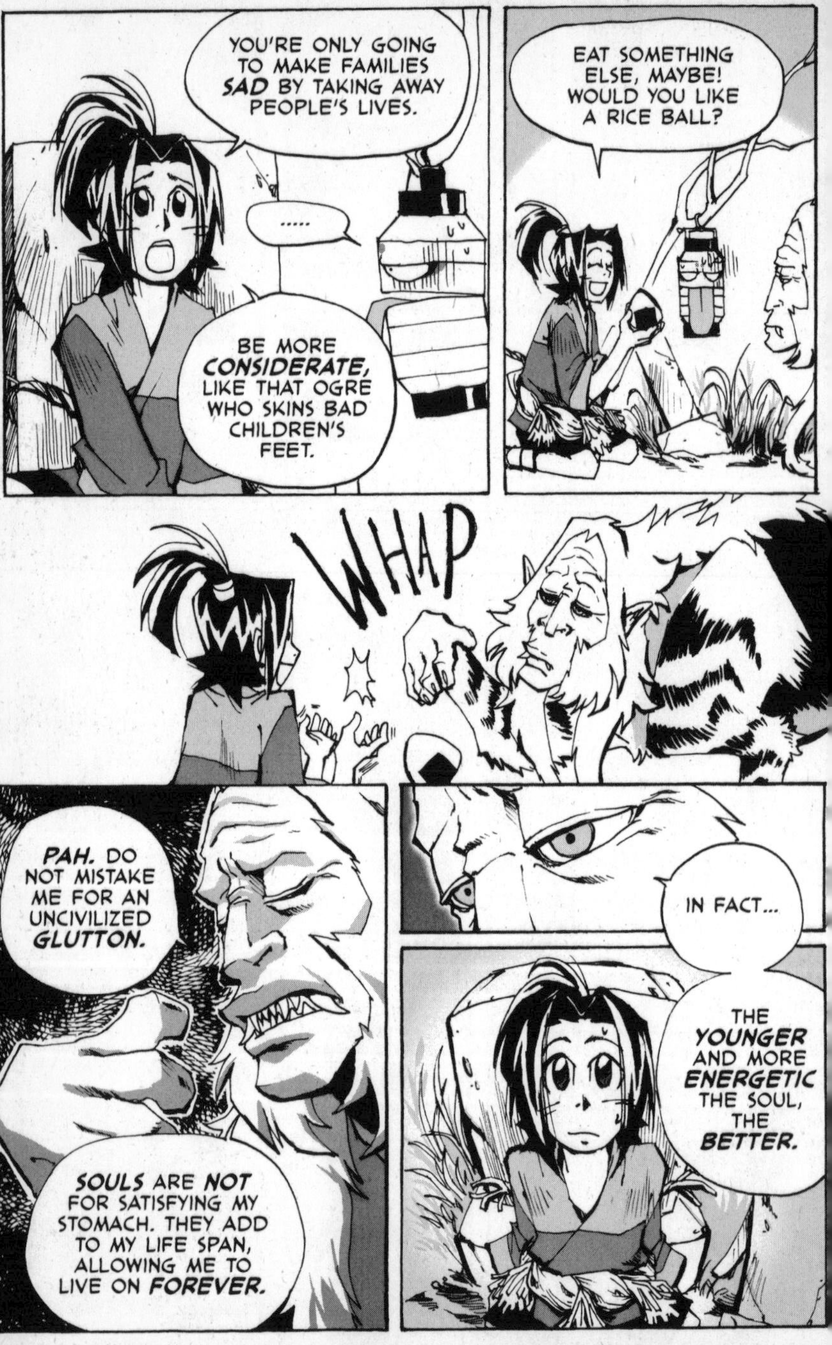
YOU'RE ONLY GOING TO MAKE FAMILIES *SAD* BY TAKING AWAY PEOPLE'S LIVES.
......
BE MORE *CONSIDERATE,* LIKE THAT OGRE WHO SKINS BAD CHILDREN'S FEET.
EAT SOMETHING ELSE, MAYBE! WOULD YOU LIKE A RICE BALL?
WHAP
PAH. DO NOT MISTAKE ME FOR AN UNCIVILIZED *GLUTTON.*
SOULS ARE *NOT* FOR SATISFYING MY STOMACH. THEY ADD TO MY LIFE SPAN, ALLOWING ME TO LIVE ON *FOREVER.*
IN FACT...
THE *YOUNGER* AND MORE *ENERGETIC* THE SOUL, THE *BETTER.*

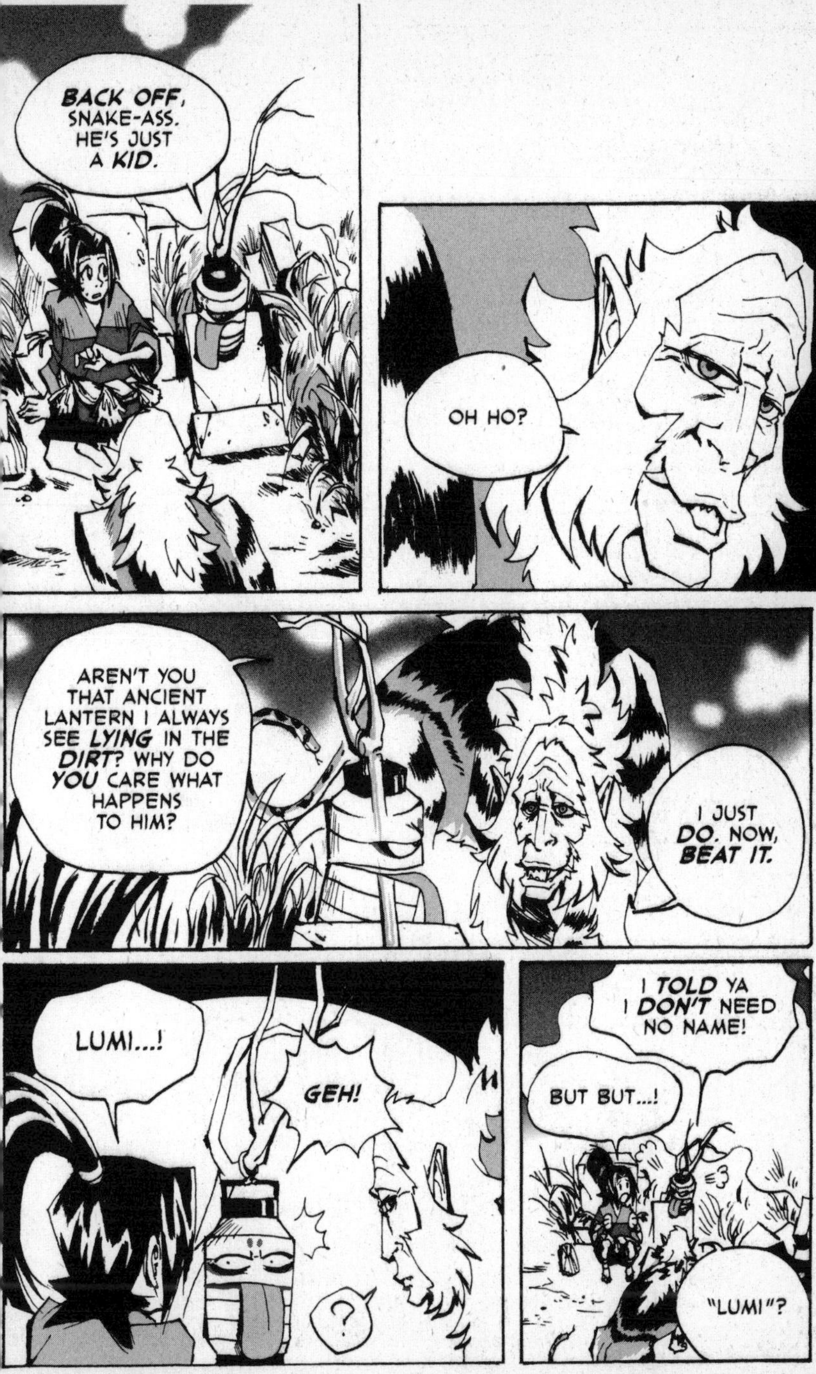
BACK OFF, SNAKE-ASS. HE'S JUST A KID.
OH HO?
AREN'T YOU THAT ANCIENT LANTERN I ALWAYS SEE LYING IN THE DIRT? WHY DO YOU CARE WHAT HAPPENS TO HIM?
I JUST DO. NOW, BEAT IT.
LUMI...!
GEH!
?
I TOLD YA I DON'T NEED NO NAME!
BUT BUT...!
"LUMI"?

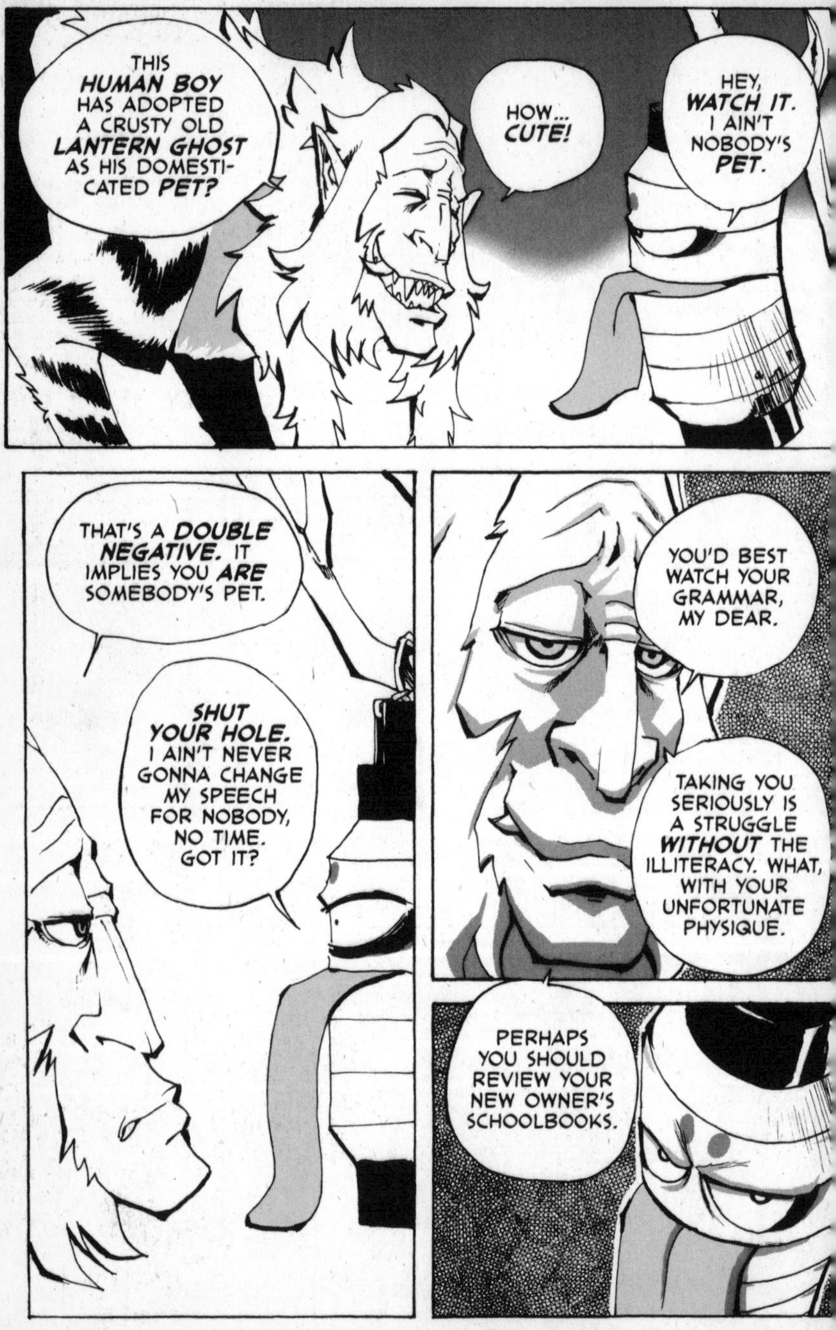
THIS HUMAN BOY HAS ADOPTED A CRUSTY OLD LANTERN GHOST AS HIS DOMESTICATED PET?
HOW... CUTE!
HEY, WATCH IT. I AIN'T NOBODY'S PET.
THAT'S A DOUBLE NEGATIVE. IT IMPLIES YOU ARE SOMEBODY'S PET.
SHUT YOUR HOLE. I AIN'T NEVER GONNA CHANGE MY SPEECH FOR NOBODY, NO TIME. GOT IT?
YOU'D BEST WATCH YOUR GRAMMAR, MY DEAR.
TAKING YOU SERIOUSLY IS A STRUGGLE WITHOUT THE ILLITERACY. WHAT, WITH YOUR UNFORTUNATE PHYSIQUE.
PERHAPS YOU SHOULD REVIEW YOUR NEW OWNER'S SCHOOLBOOKS.

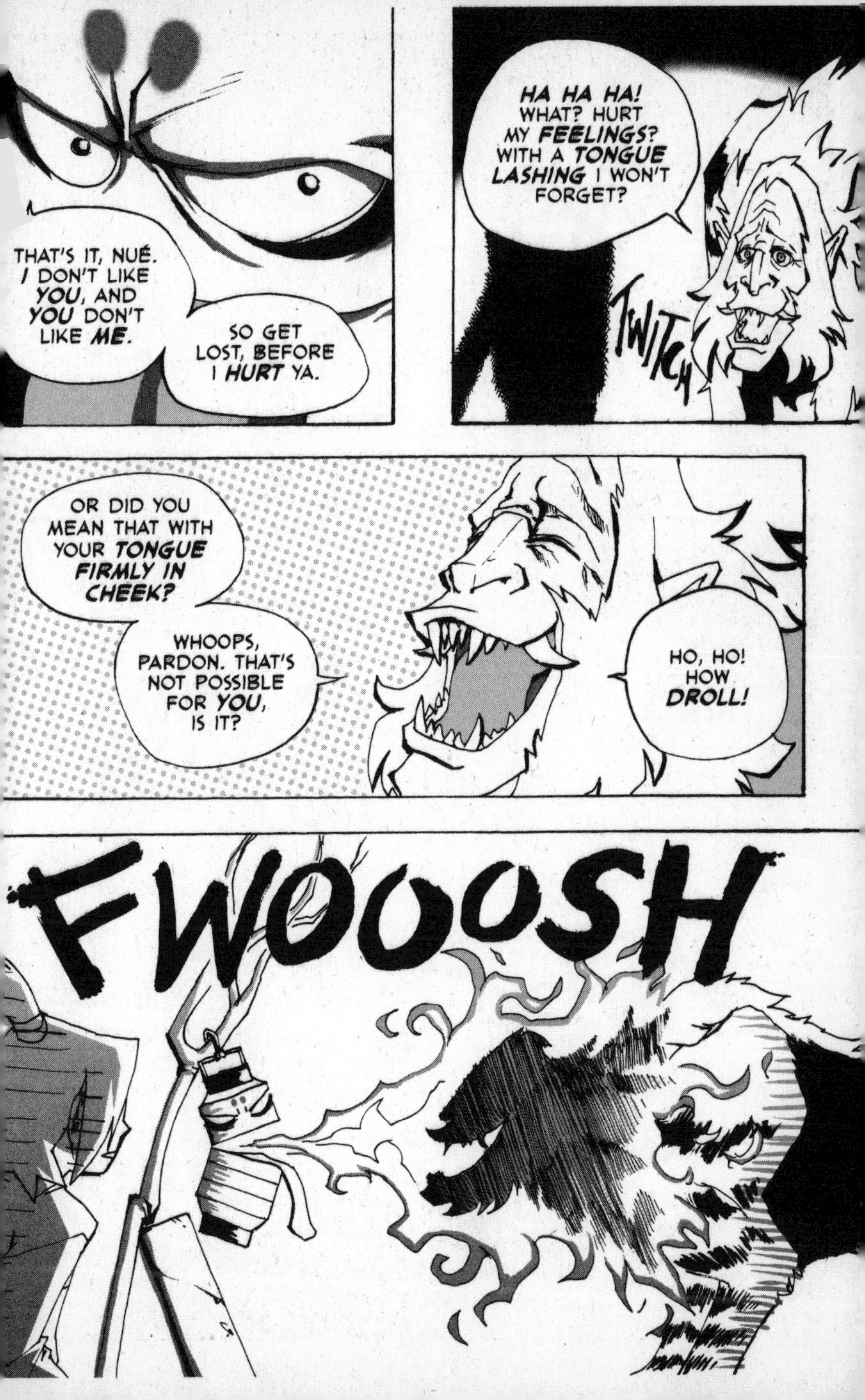
THAT'S IT, NUÉ. I DON'T LIKE YOU, AND YOU DON'T LIKE ME.
SO GET LOST, BEFORE I HURT YA.
HA HA HA! WHAT? HURT MY FEELINGS? WITH A TONGUE LASHING I WON'T FORGET?
TWITCH
OR DID YOU MEAN THAT WITH YOUR TONGUE FIRMLY IN CHEEK?
WHOOPS, PARDON. THAT'S NOT POSSIBLE FOR YOU, IS IT?
HO, HO! HOW DROLL!
FWOOOSH

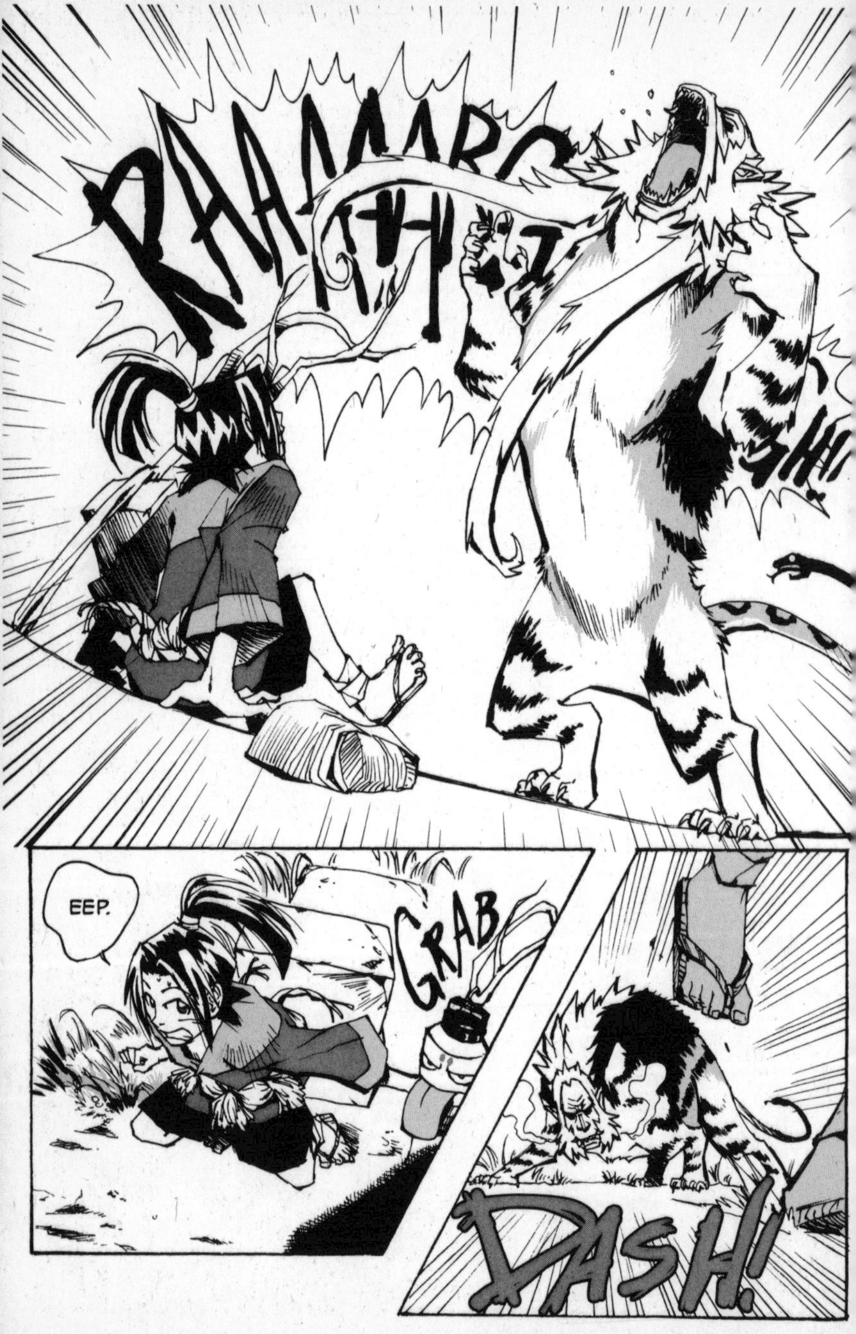
EEP.
GRAB
DASH!

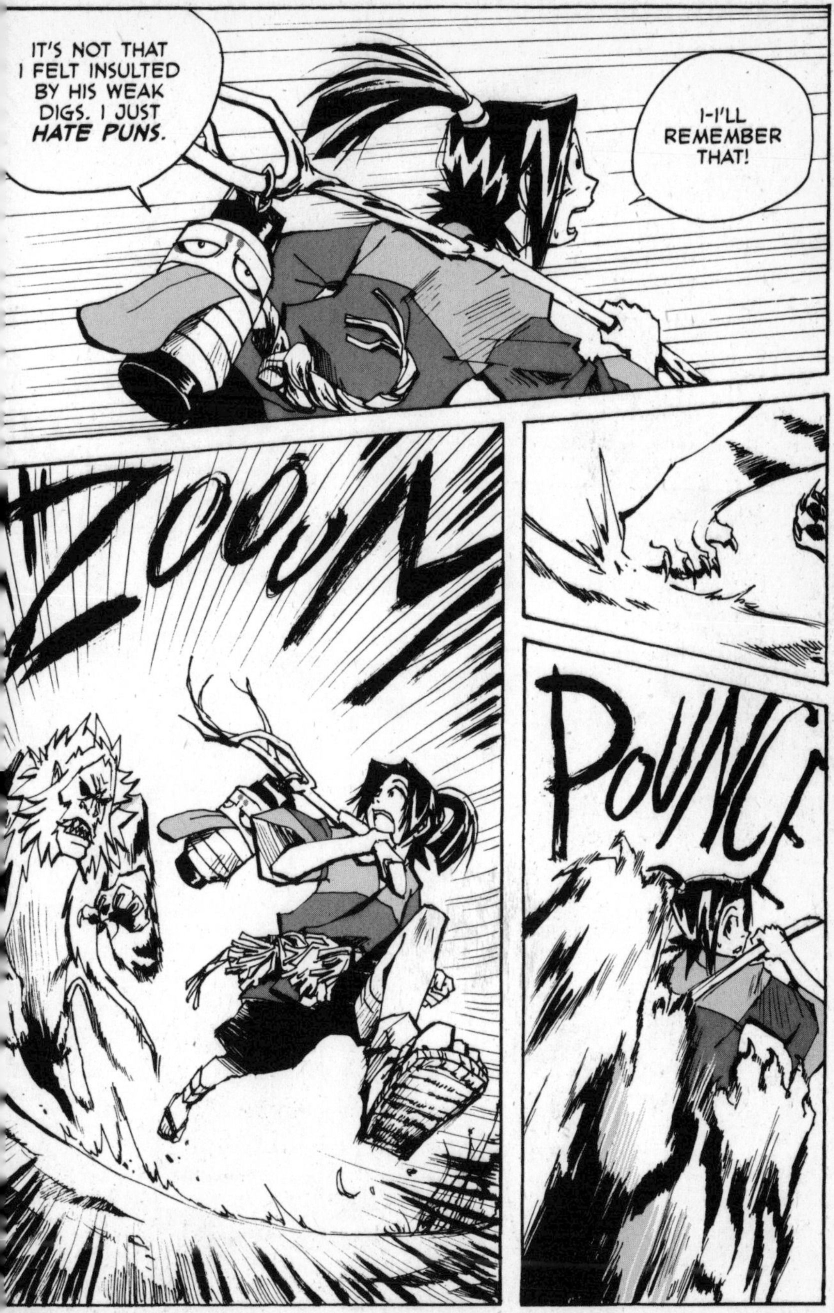

IT'S NOT THAT I FELT INSULTED BY HIS WEAK DIGS. I JUST *HATE PUNS.*
I-I'LL REMEMBER THAT!
ZOOOM
POUNCE

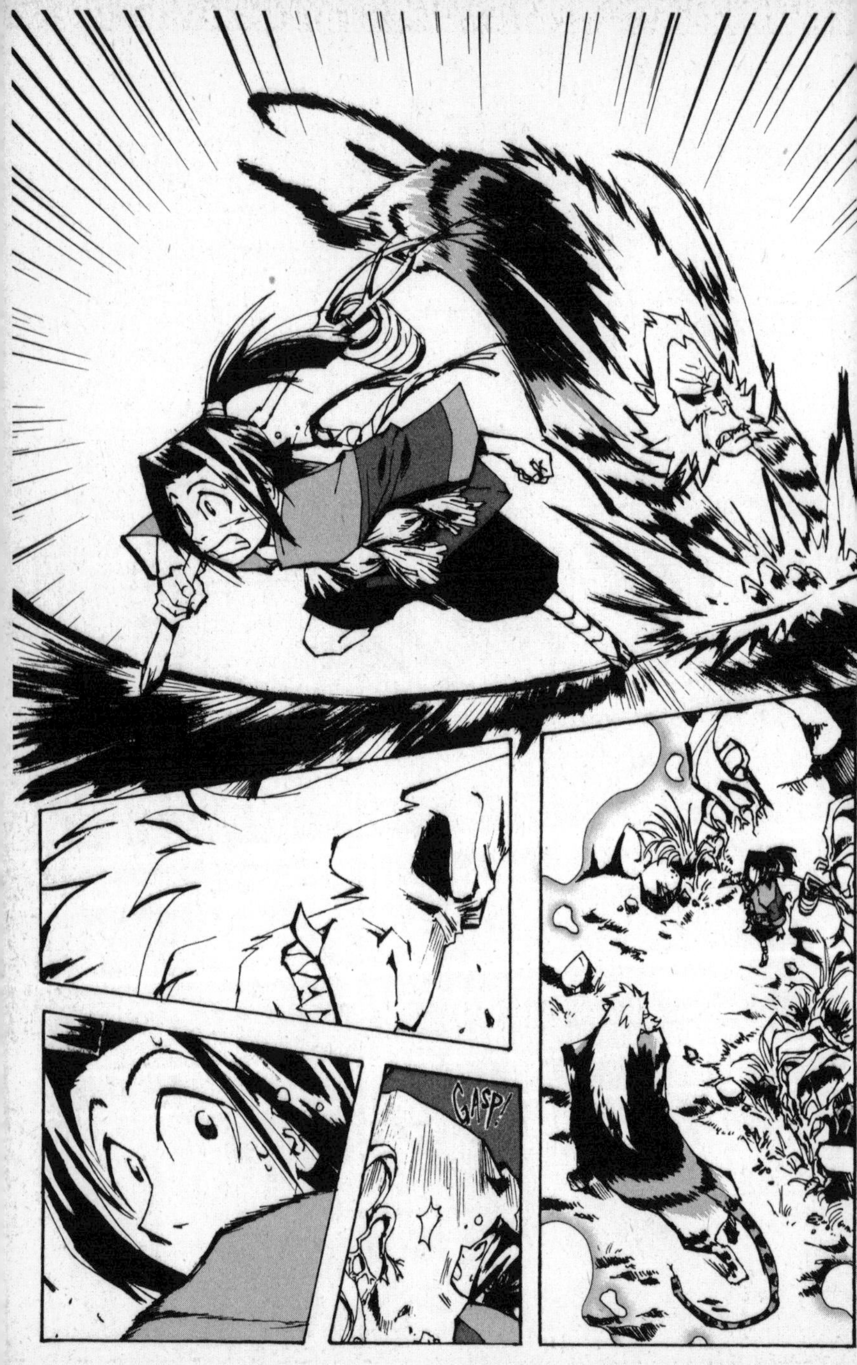
GASP!

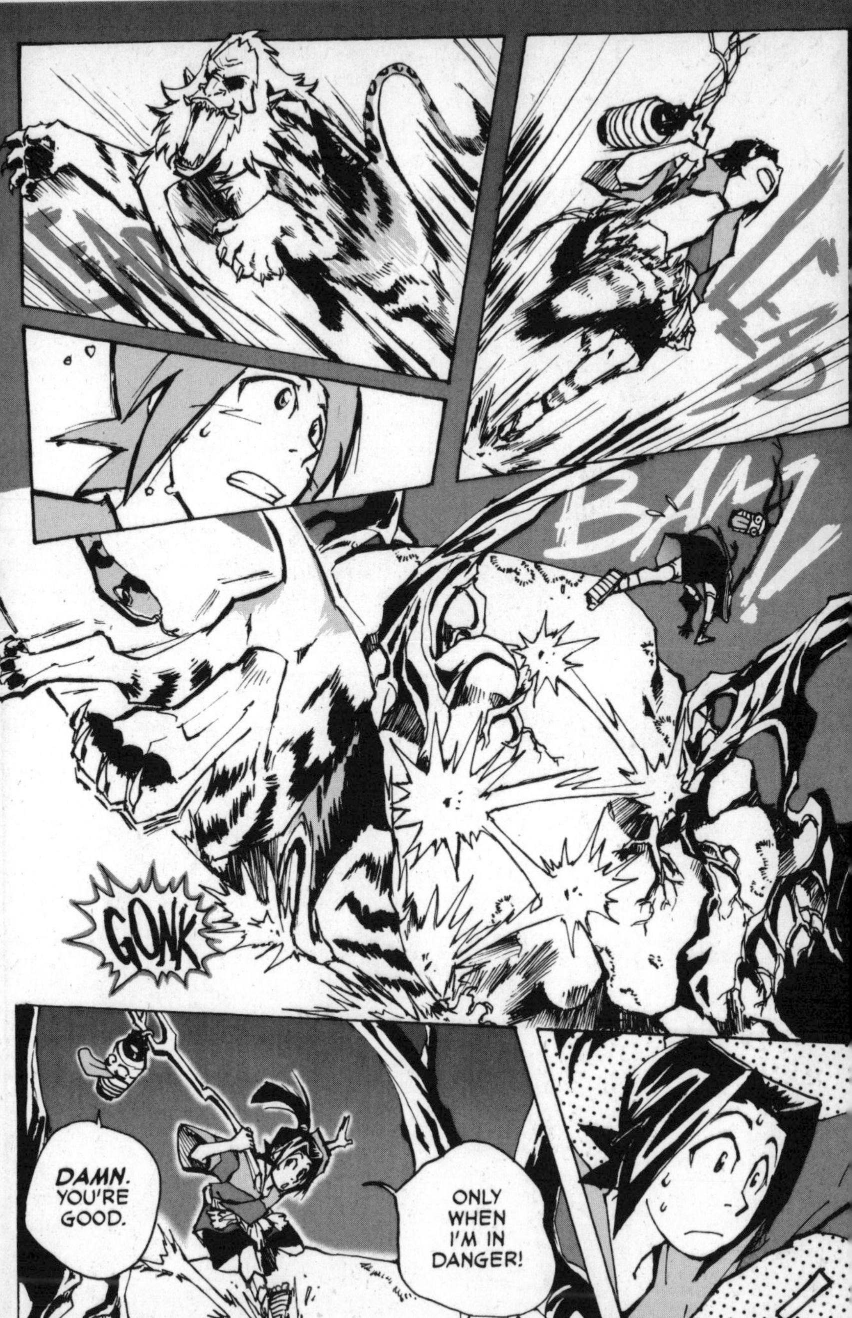
FAP
BAM!!
GONK
DAMN. YOU'RE GOOD.
ONLY WHEN I'M IN DANGER!
!

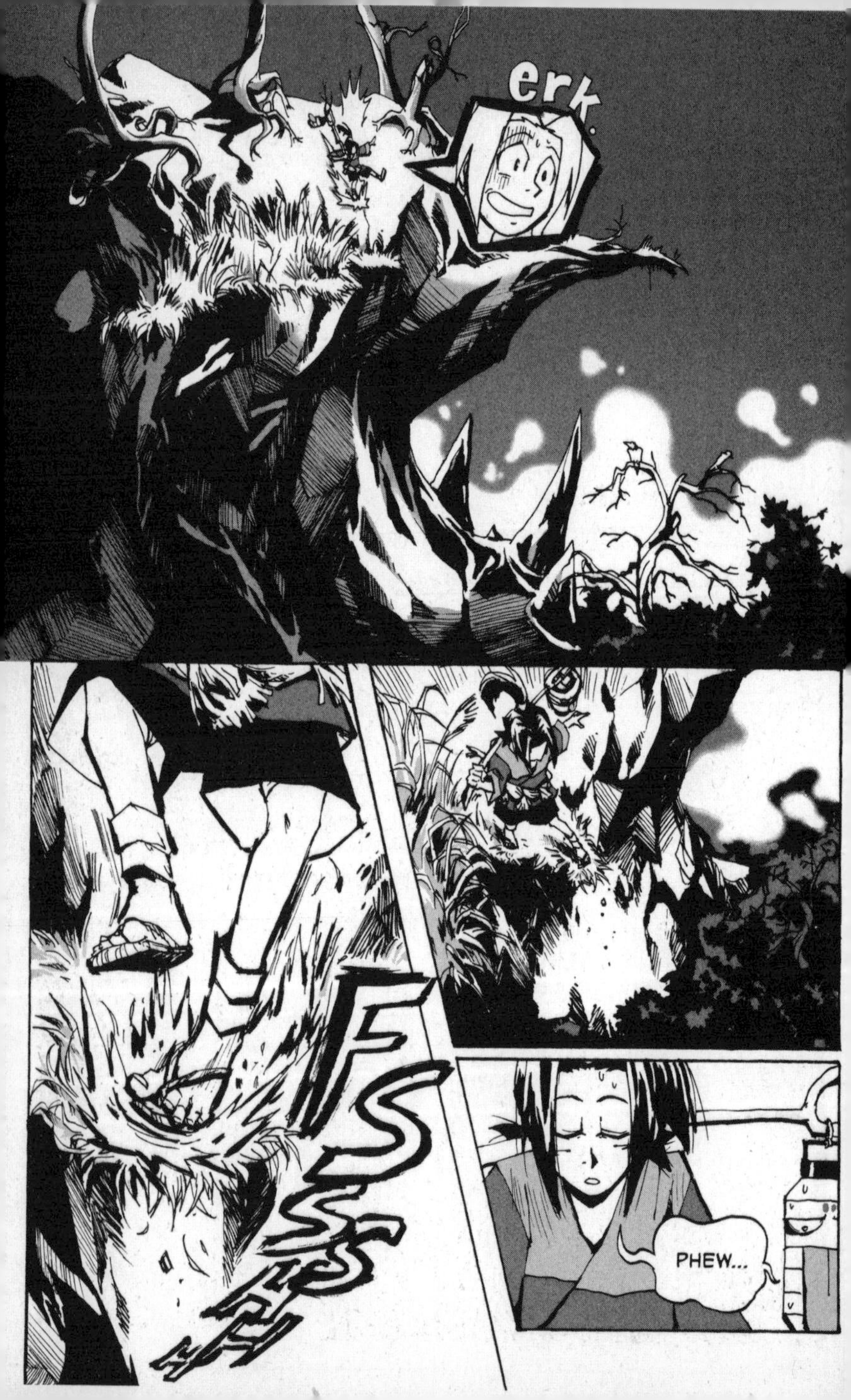
erk.
FSSSHH
PHEW...

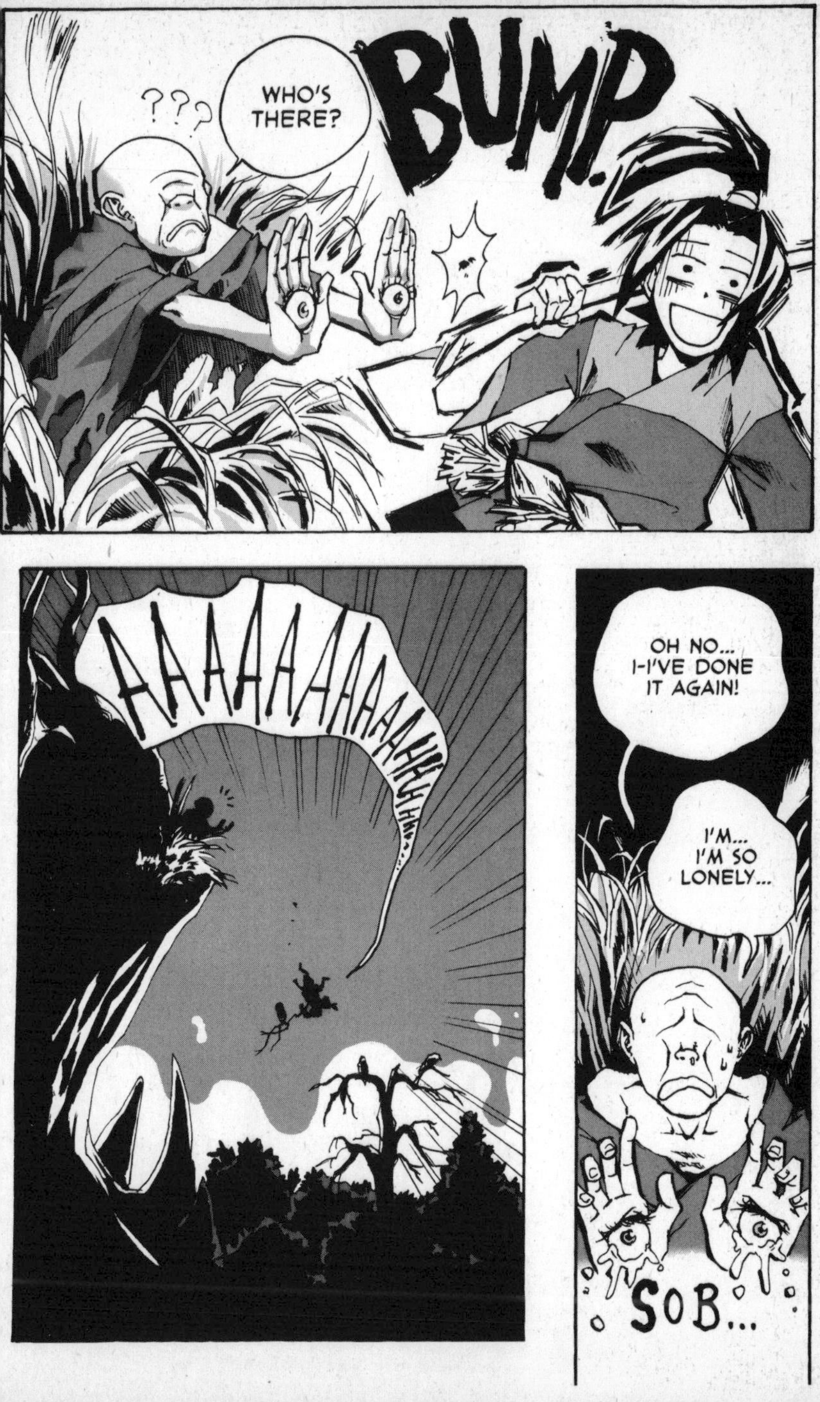
???
WHO'S THERE?
BUMP
AAAAAAAAAAAHH...
OH NO... I-I'VE DONE IT AGAIN!
I'M... I'M SO LONELY...
SOB...

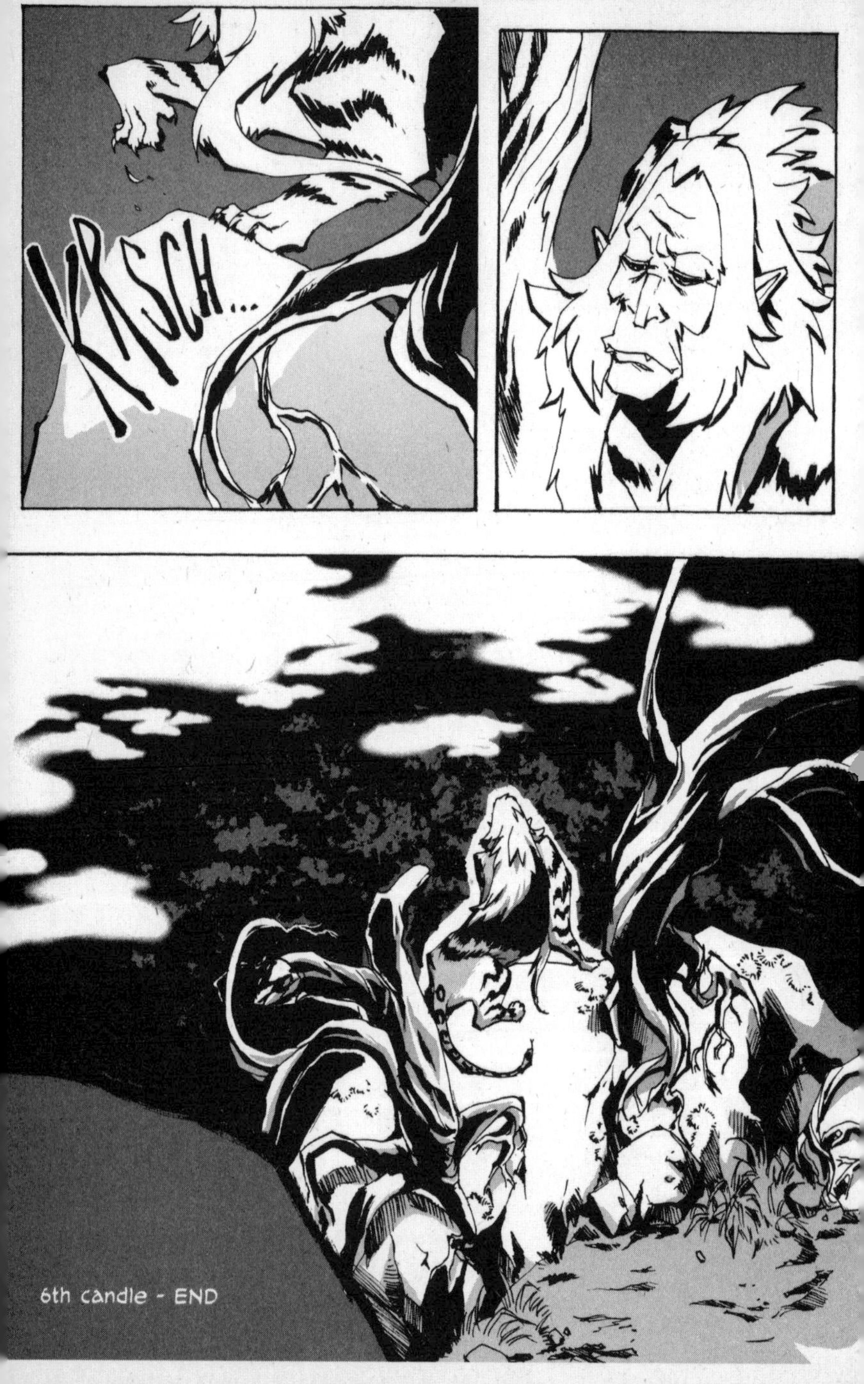
KRSCH...
6th candle - END

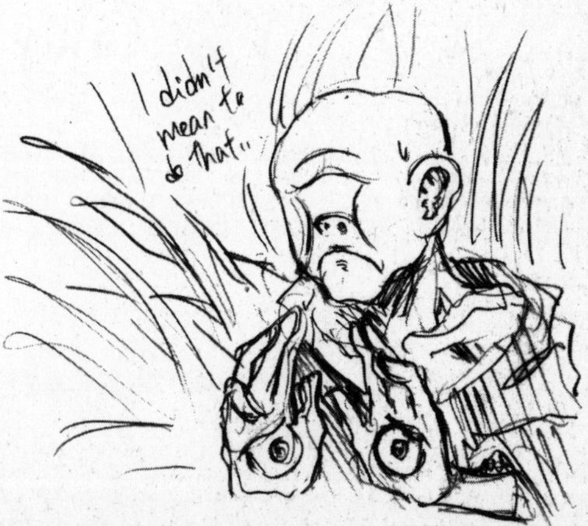
I didn't mean to do that..

HAMACHI'S JOURNAL

 "NOTE TO SELF: SCRATCH THAT PART ABOUT LANTERN GHOSTS NEVER HURTING ANYONE."

NUÉ

 "HE IS FOUR ANIMALS STUCK TOGETHER AS ONE. HE IS BIG AND FAST, AND TALKS MORE GROWN-UP THAN OTHER GROWN-UPS. I.E., HE SAYS 'PERHAPS' INSTEAD OF 'MAYBE.' I DON'T KNOW IF THAT MEANS HE'S SMARTER THAN EVERYONE ELSE."

HAND-EYES
(a.k.a. té-no-mé)

 "A POOR MAN WHO WAS KILLED BY THIEVES AND LEFT IN THE GRASS AND GREW EYES ON THE PALM OF HIS HANDS SO HE COULD LOOK FOR HIS KILLERS BETTER. I DON'T KNOW WHY, BUT THE EYES ON HIS FACE DIDN'T STAY. YŌKAI BIOLOGY IS WEIRD AND MEAN."

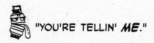 "YOU'RE TELLIN' *ME*."

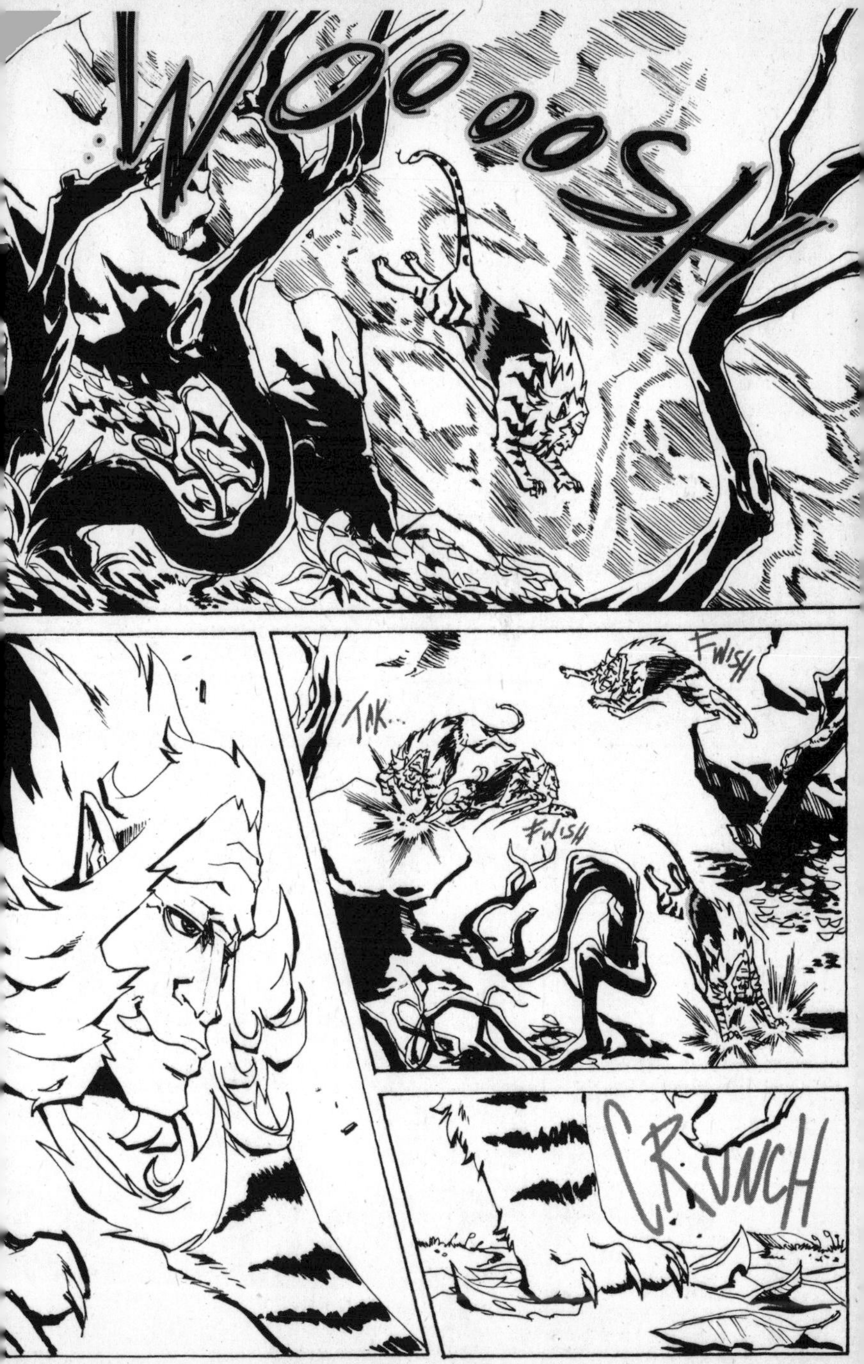
WOOOOOSH
TAK...
FWISH
FWISH
CRUNCH

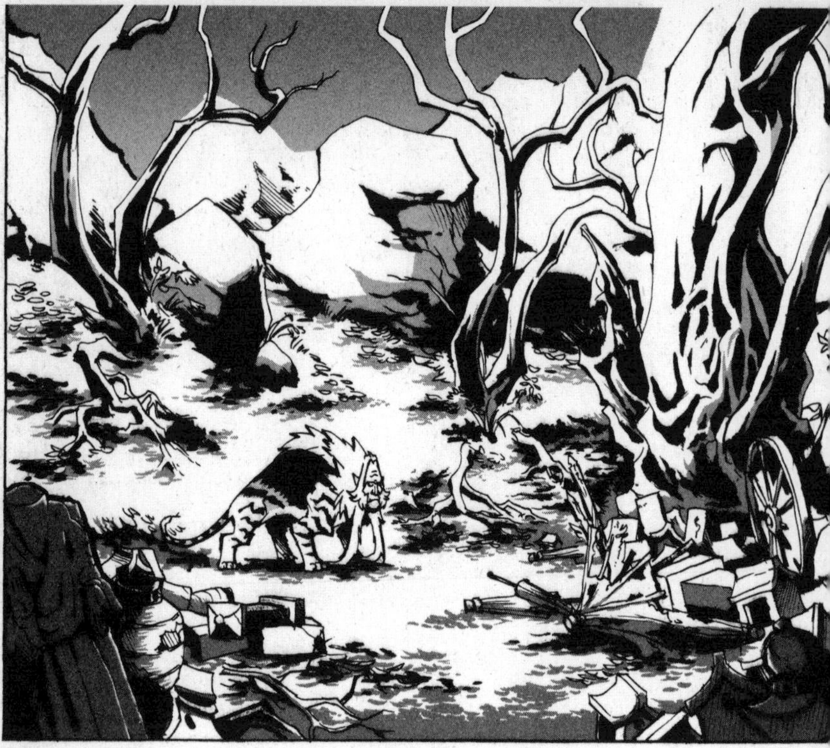

7th candle

One Man's Trash

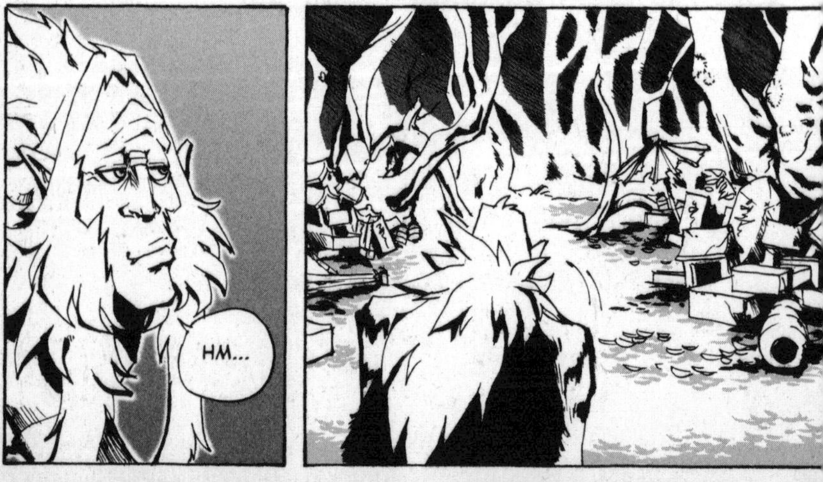
HM...

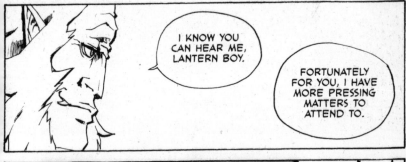

I KNOW YOU CAN HEAR ME, LANTERN BOY.

FORTUNATELY FOR YOU, I HAVE MORE PRESSING MATTERS TO ATTEND TO.

I KNOW NOT HOW YOU GOT IN HERE OR WHAT THE PURPOSE OF YOUR TRIP IS, BUT, NO MATTER.

I ENJOYED THE BRIEF TIME WE SPENT TOGETHER.

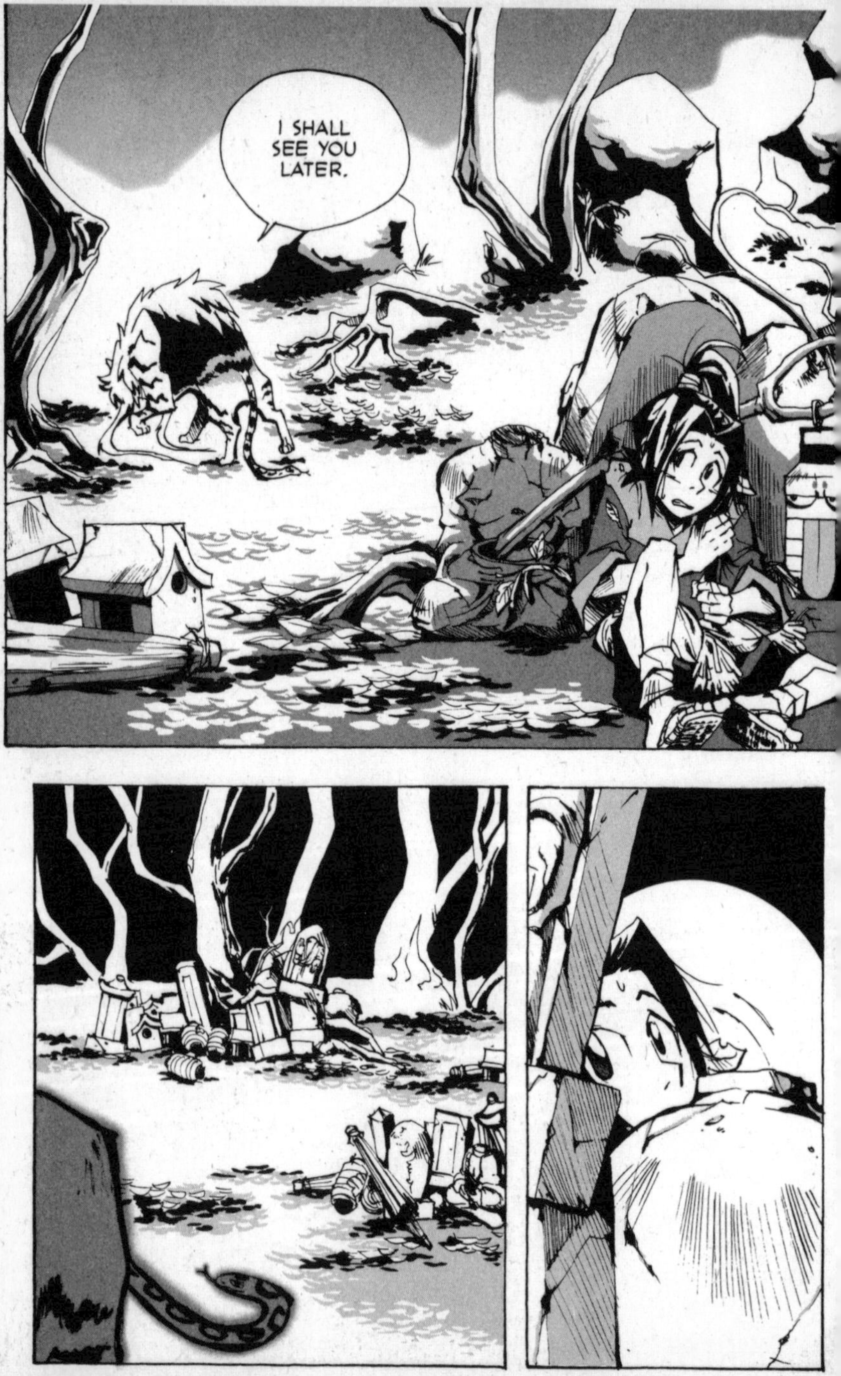
I SHALL SEE YOU LATER.

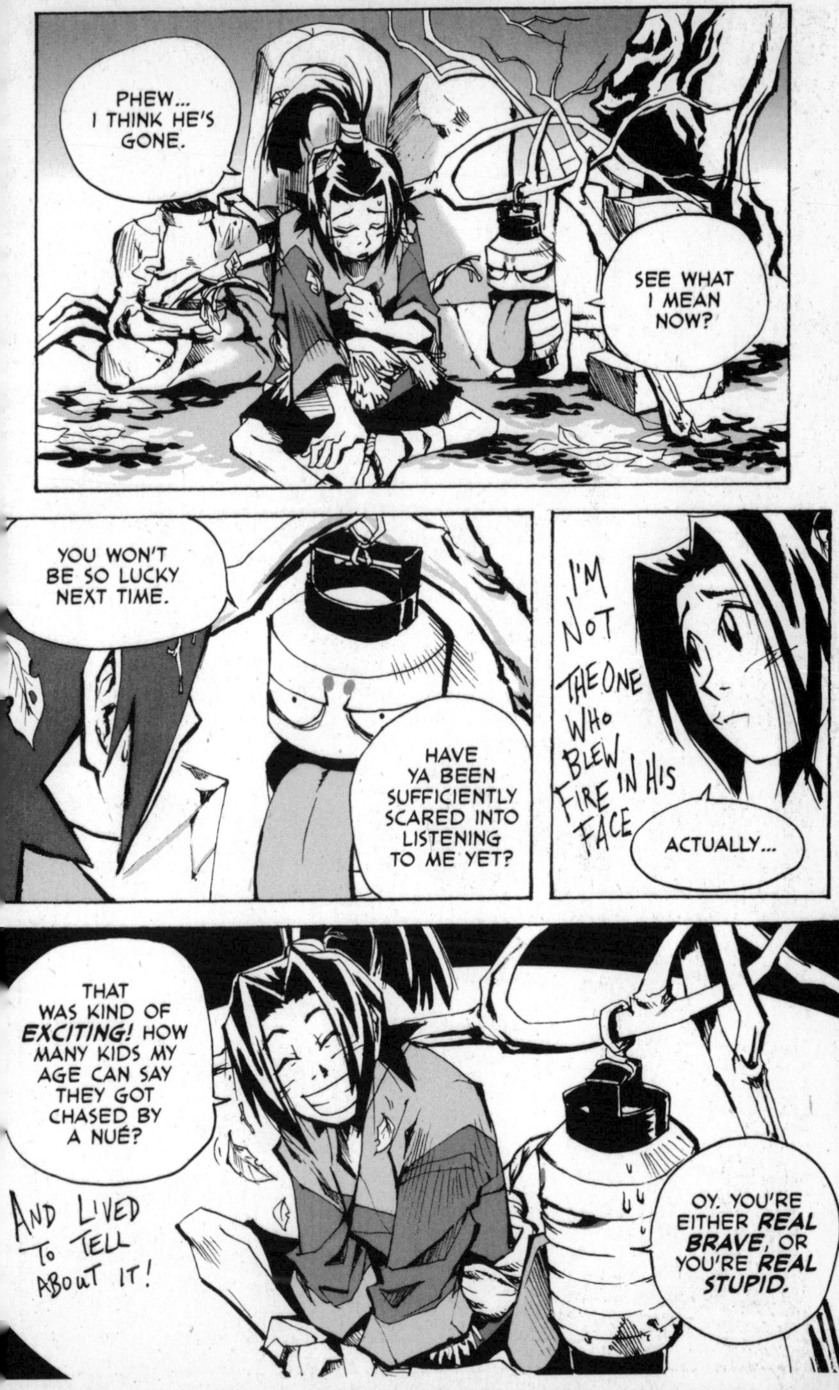
PHEW... I THINK HE'S GONE.
SEE WHAT I MEAN NOW?
YOU WON'T BE SO LUCKY NEXT TIME.
HAVE YA BEEN SUFFICIENTLY SCARED INTO LISTENING TO ME YET?
I'M NOT THE ONE WHO BLEW FIRE IN HIS FACE
ACTUALLY...
THAT WAS KIND OF EXCITING! HOW MANY KIDS MY AGE CAN SAY THEY GOT CHASED BY A NUÉ?
AND LIVED TO TELL ABOUT IT!
OY. YOU'RE EITHER REAL BRAVE, OR YOU'RE REAL STUPID.

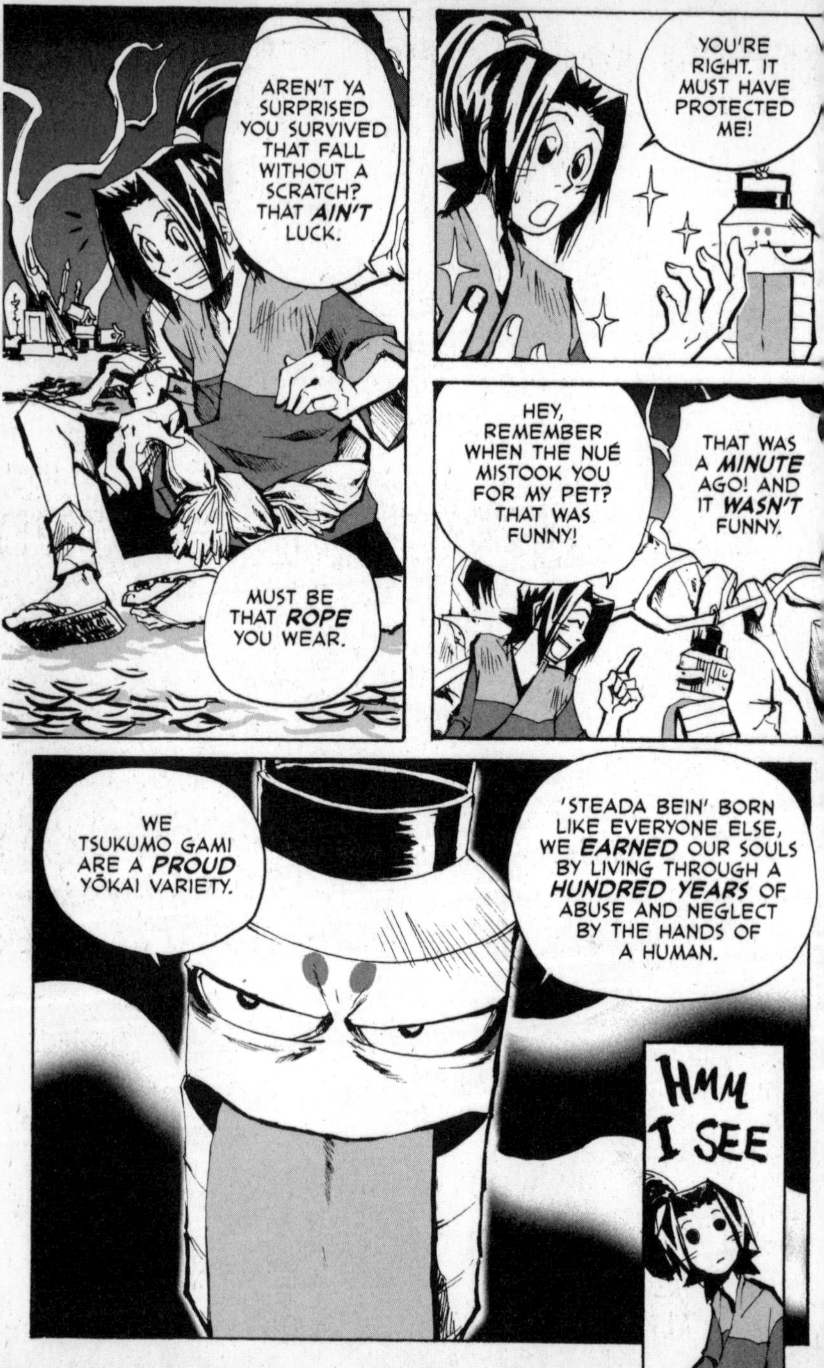
AREN'T YA SURPRISED YOU SURVIVED THAT FALL WITHOUT A SCRATCH? THAT AIN'T LUCK.
MUST BE THAT ROPE YOU WEAR.
YOU'RE RIGHT. IT MUST HAVE PROTECTED ME!
HEY, REMEMBER WHEN THE NUÉ MISTOOK YOU FOR MY PET? THAT WAS FUNNY!
THAT WAS A MINUTE AGO! AND IT WASN'T FUNNY.
WE TSUKUMO GAMI ARE A PROUD YŌKAI VARIETY.
'STEADA BEIN' BORN LIKE EVERYONE ELSE, WE EARNED OUR SOULS BY LIVING THROUGH A HUNDRED YEARS OF ABUSE AND NEGLECT BY THE HANDS OF A HUMAN.
HMM I SEE

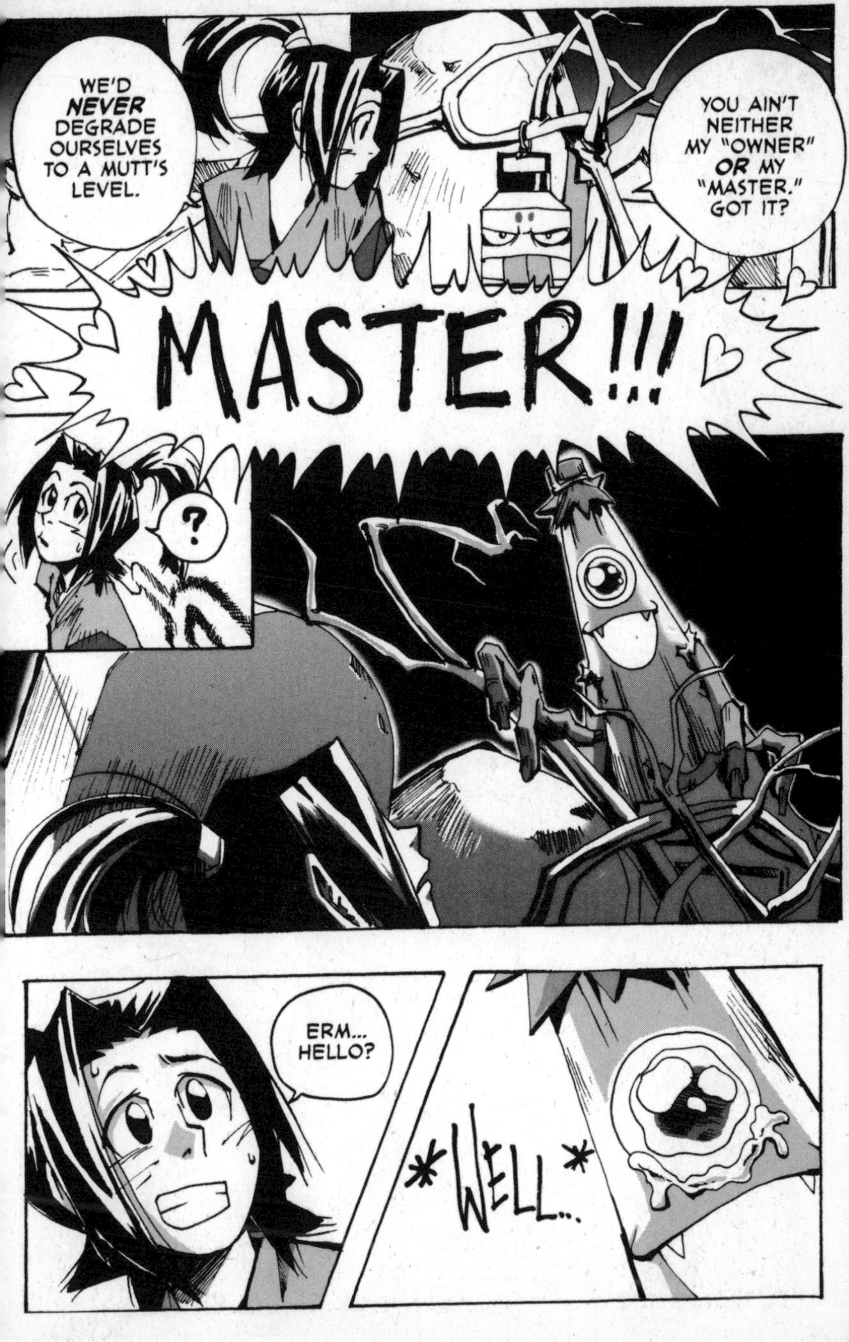
WE'D NEVER DEGRADE OURSELVES TO A MUTT'S LEVEL.
YOU AIN'T NEITHER MY "OWNER" OR MY "MASTER." GOT IT?
MASTER!!!
?
ERM... HELLO?
WELL...

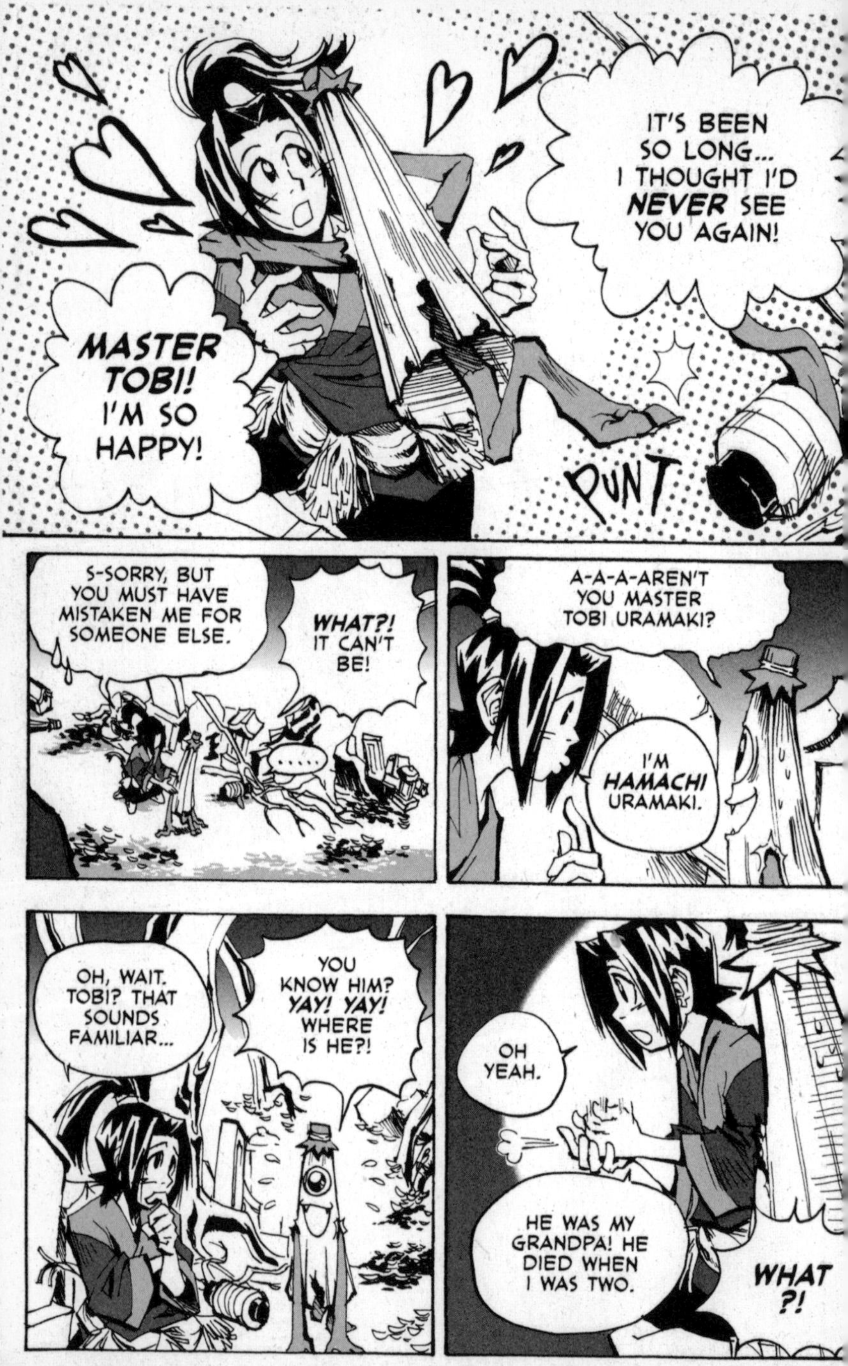
MASTER TOBI! I'M SO HAPPY!
IT'S BEEN SO LONG... I THOUGHT I'D NEVER SEE YOU AGAIN!
PUNT
S-SORRY, BUT YOU MUST HAVE MISTAKEN ME FOR SOMEONE ELSE.
WHAT?! IT CAN'T BE!
.....
A-A-A-AREN'T YOU MASTER TOBI URAMAKI?
I'M HAMACHI URAMAKI.
OH, WAIT. TOBI? THAT SOUNDS FAMILIAR...
YOU KNOW HIM? YAY! YAY! WHERE IS HE?!
OH YEAH.
HE WAS MY GRANDPA! HE DIED WHEN I WAS TWO.
WHAT?!

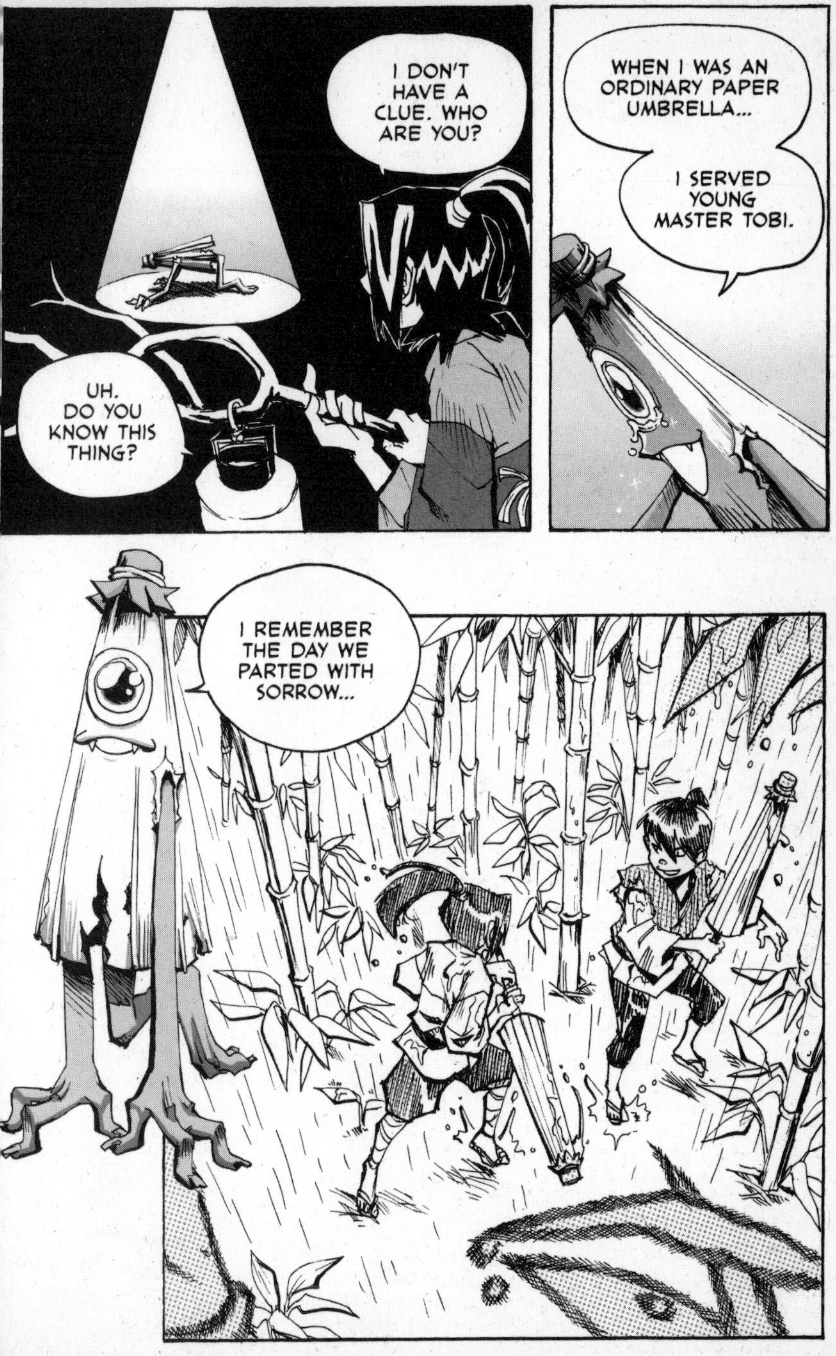
UH. DO YOU KNOW THIS THING?
I DON'T HAVE A CLUE. WHO ARE YOU?
WHEN I WAS AN ORDINARY PAPER UMBRELLA...
I SERVED YOUNG MASTER TOBI.
I REMEMBER THE DAY WE PARTED WITH SORROW...

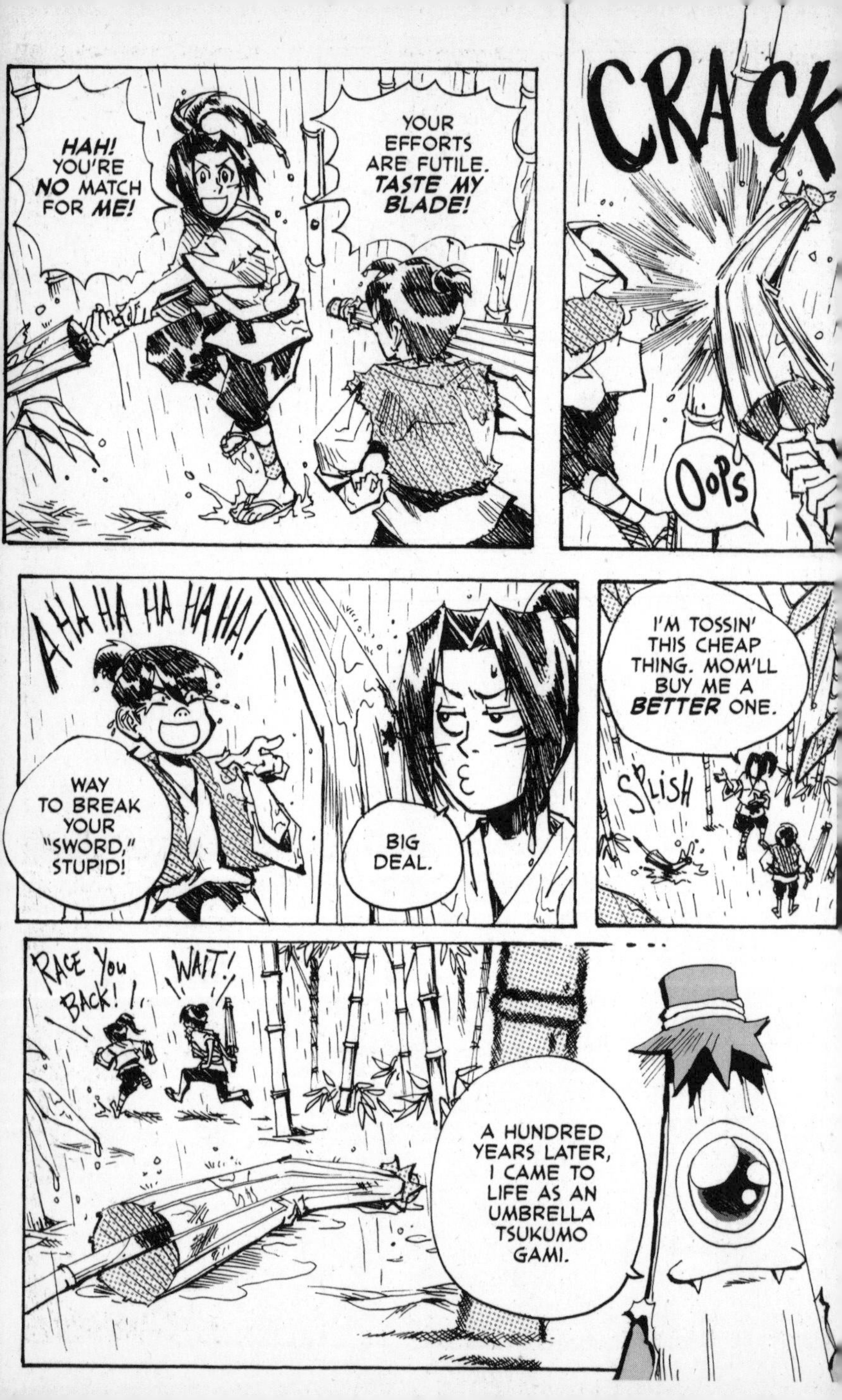
HAH! YOU'RE NO MATCH FOR ME!
YOUR EFFORTS ARE FUTILE. TASTE MY BLADE!
CRACK
OOPS
AHA HA HA HAHA!
WAY TO BREAK YOUR "SWORD," STUPID!
BIG DEAL.
I'M TOSSIN' THIS CHEAP THING. MOM'LL BUY ME A BETTER ONE.
SPLISH
RACE YOU BACK!
WAIT!
A HUNDRED YEARS LATER, I CAME TO LIFE AS AN UMBRELLA TSUKUMO GAMI.

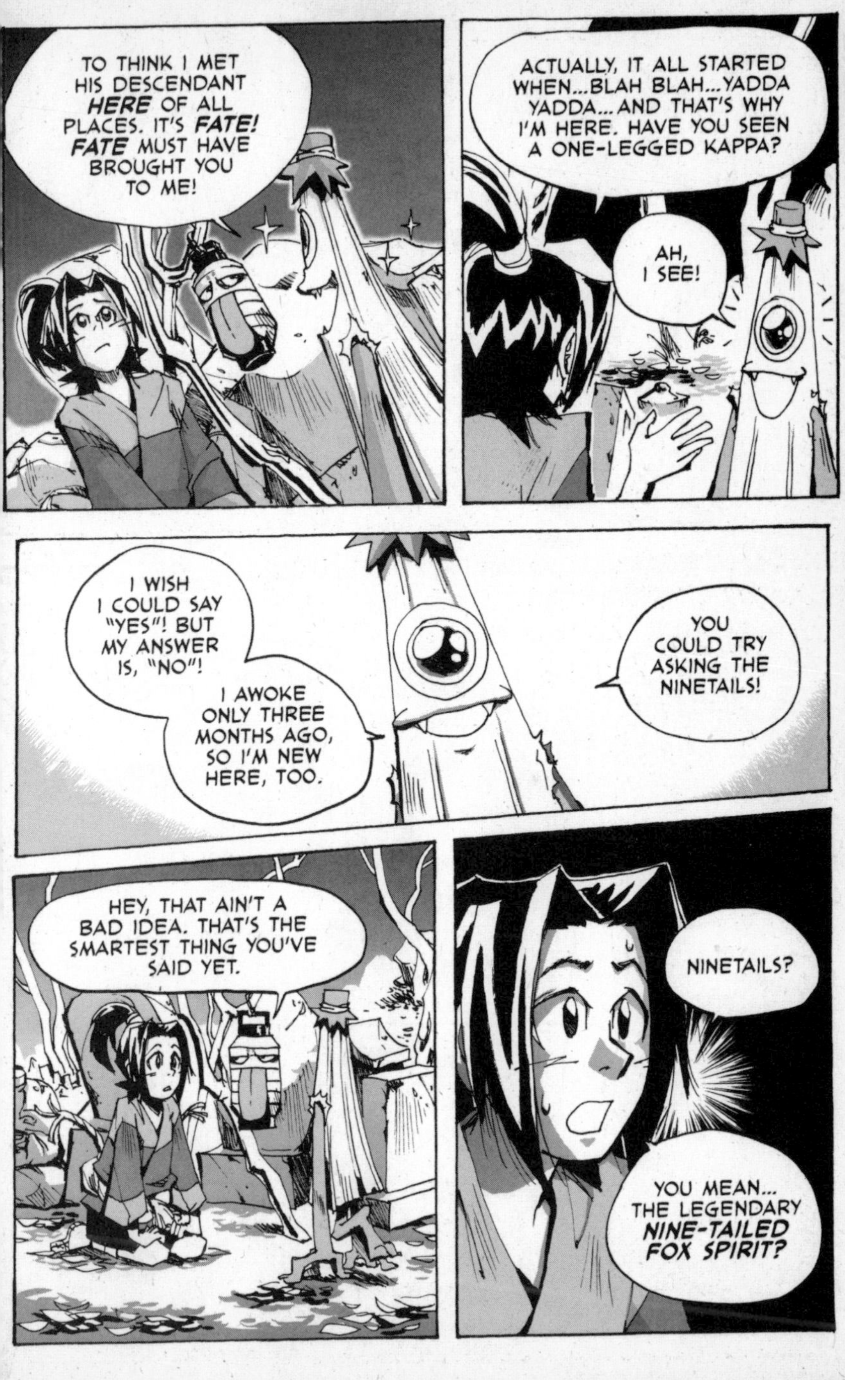
TO THINK I MET HIS DESCENDANT HERE OF ALL PLACES. IT'S FATE! FATE MUST HAVE BROUGHT YOU TO ME!
ACTUALLY, IT ALL STARTED WHEN...BLAH BLAH...YADDA YADDA...AND THAT'S WHY I'M HERE. HAVE YOU SEEN A ONE-LEGGED KAPPA?
AH, I SEE!
I WISH I COULD SAY "YES"! BUT MY ANSWER IS, "NO"!
I AWOKE ONLY THREE MONTHS AGO, SO I'M NEW HERE, TOO.
YOU COULD TRY ASKING THE NINETAILS!
HEY, THAT AIN'T A BAD IDEA. THAT'S THE SMARTEST THING YOU'VE SAID YET.
NINETAILS?
YOU MEAN... THE LEGENDARY NINE-TAILED FOX SPIRIT?

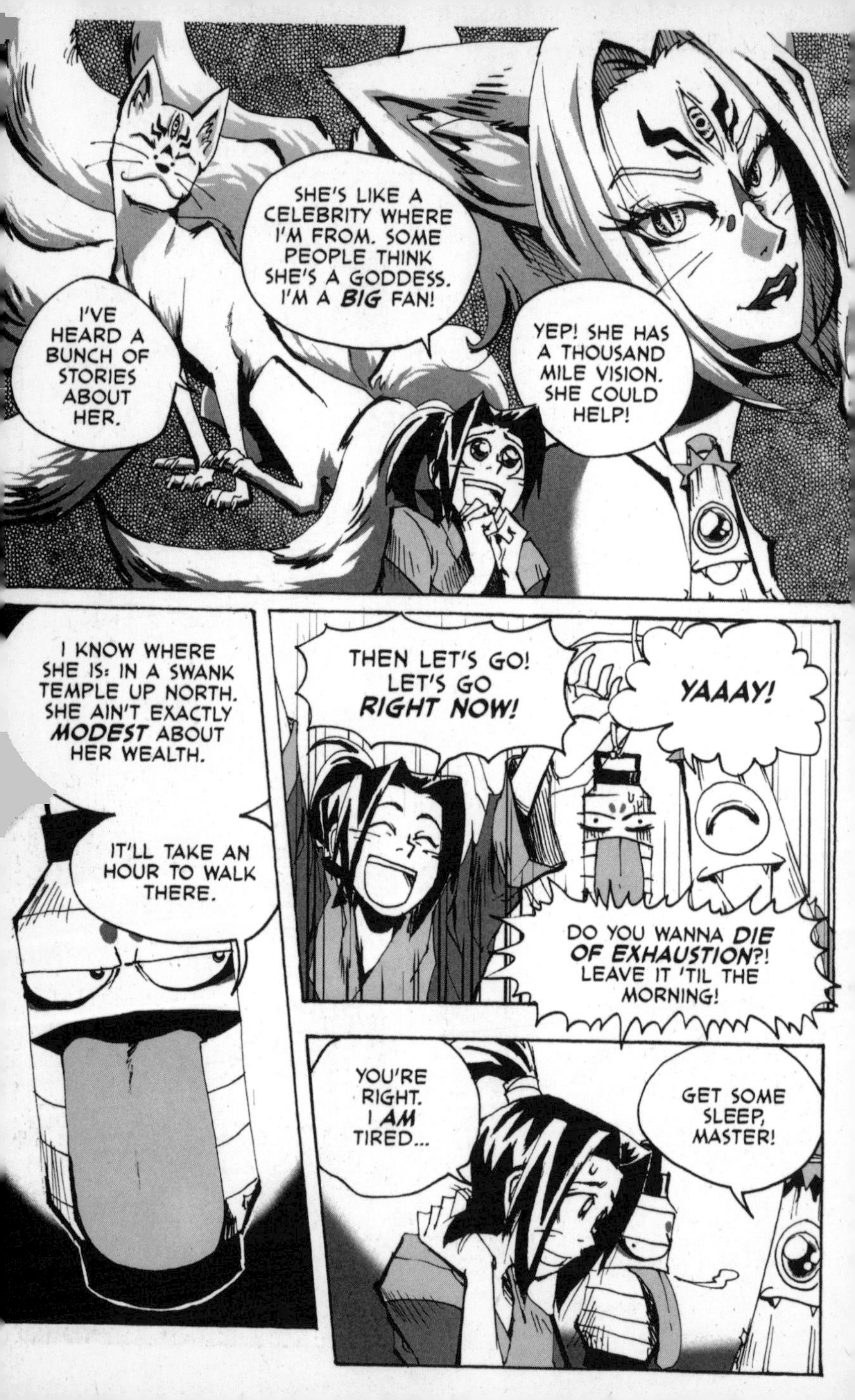
SHE'S LIKE A CELEBRITY WHERE I'M FROM. SOME PEOPLE THINK SHE'S A GODDESS. I'M A BIG FAN!
I'VE HEARD A BUNCH OF STORIES ABOUT HER.
YEP! SHE HAS A THOUSAND MILE VISION. SHE COULD HELP!
I KNOW WHERE SHE IS: IN A SWANK TEMPLE UP NORTH. SHE AIN'T EXACTLY MODEST ABOUT HER WEALTH.
IT'LL TAKE AN HOUR TO WALK THERE.
THEN LET'S GO! LET'S GO RIGHT NOW!
YAAAY!
DO YOU WANNA DIE OF EXHAUSTION?! LEAVE IT 'TIL THE MORNING!
YOU'RE RIGHT. I AM TIRED...
GET SOME SLEEP, MASTER!

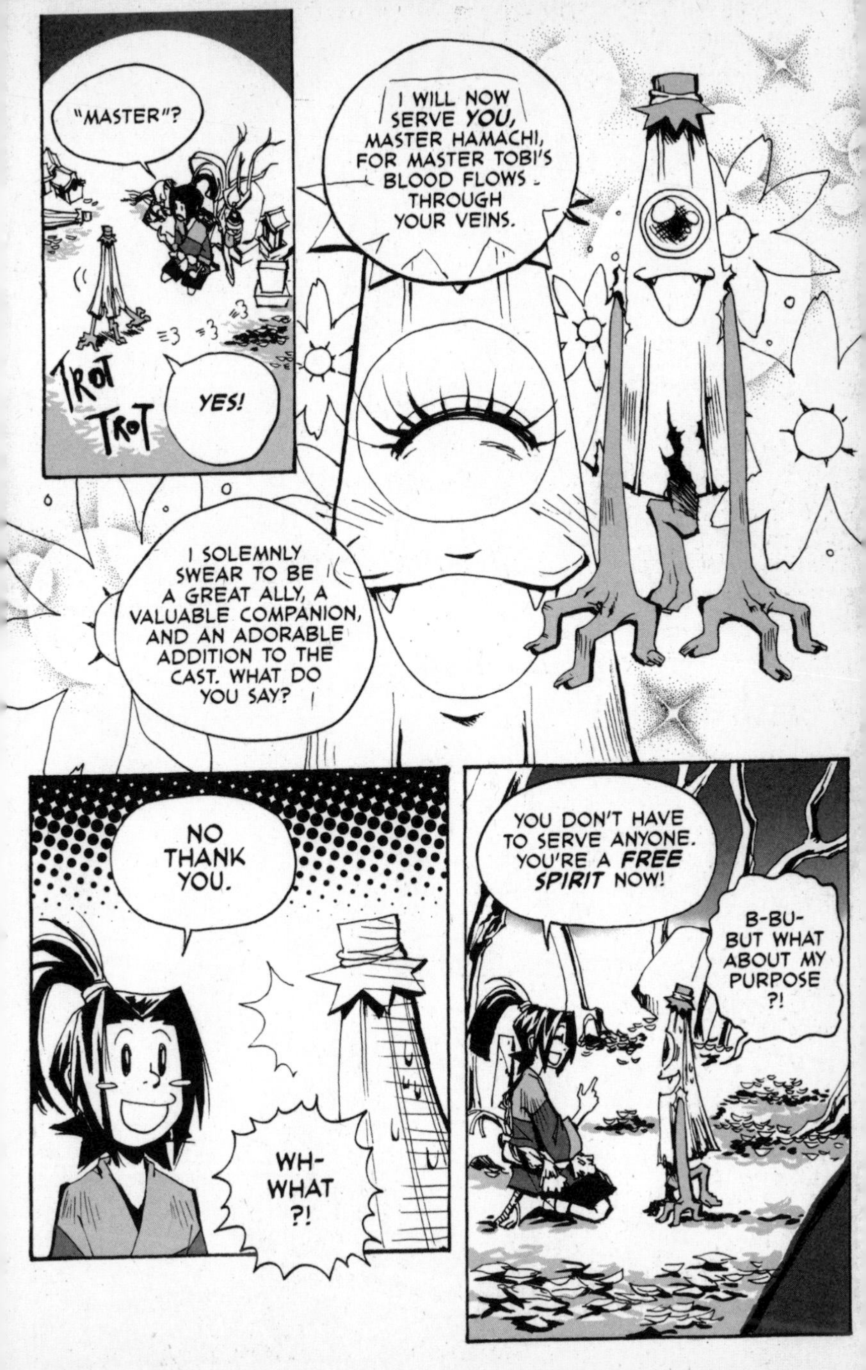
"MASTER"?
TROT TROT
YES!
I WILL NOW SERVE *YOU,* MASTER HAMACHI, FOR MASTER TOBI'S BLOOD FLOWS THROUGH YOUR VEINS.
I SOLEMNLY SWEAR TO BE A GREAT ALLY, A VALUABLE COMPANION, AND AN ADORABLE ADDITION TO THE CAST. WHAT DO YOU SAY?
NO THANK YOU.
WH- WHAT ?!
YOU DON'T HAVE TO SERVE ANYONE. YOU'RE A *FREE SPIRIT* NOW!
B-BU- BUT WHAT ABOUT MY PURPOSE ?!

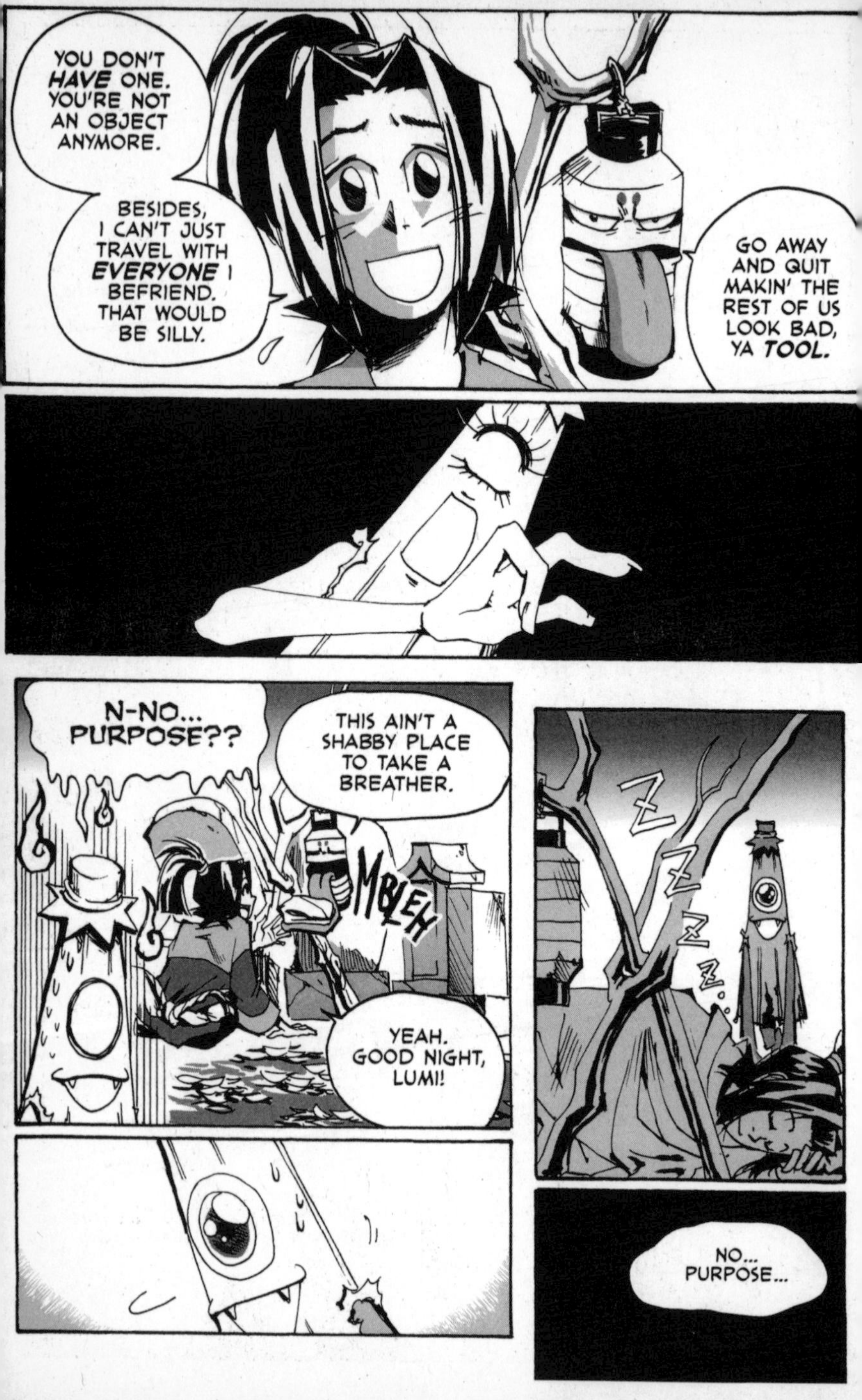
YOU DON'T *HAVE* ONE. YOU'RE NOT AN OBJECT ANYMORE.
BESIDES, I CAN'T JUST TRAVEL WITH *EVERYONE* I BEFRIEND. THAT WOULD BE SILLY.
GO AWAY AND QUIT MAKIN' THE REST OF US LOOK BAD, YA *TOOL.*
N-NO... PURPOSE??
THIS AIN'T A SHABBY PLACE TO TAKE A BREATHER.
MBLEH
YEAH. GOOD NIGHT, LUMI!
Z Z Z Z
NO... PURPOSE...

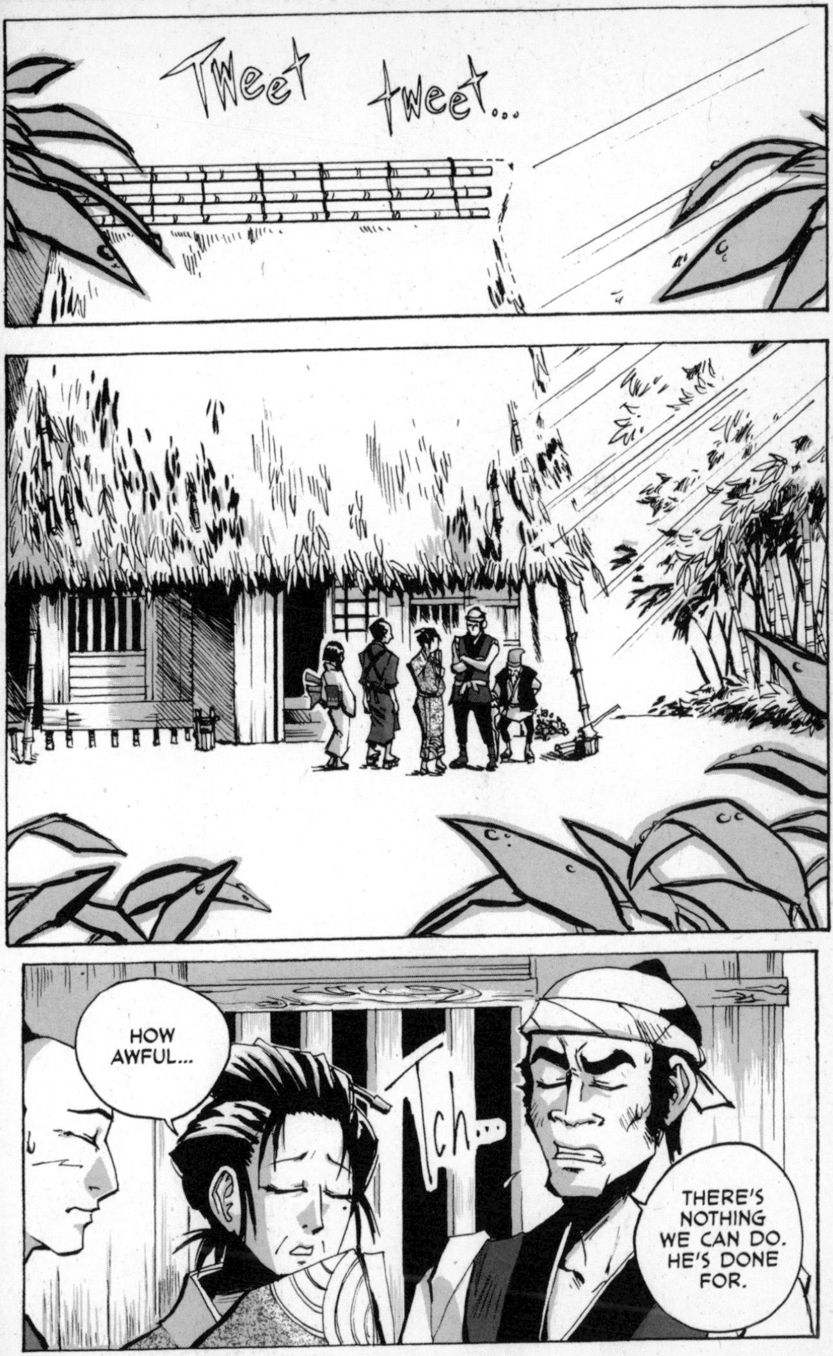
Tweet tweet...
HOW AWFUL...
Tch...
THERE'S NOTHING WE CAN DO. HE'S DONE FOR.

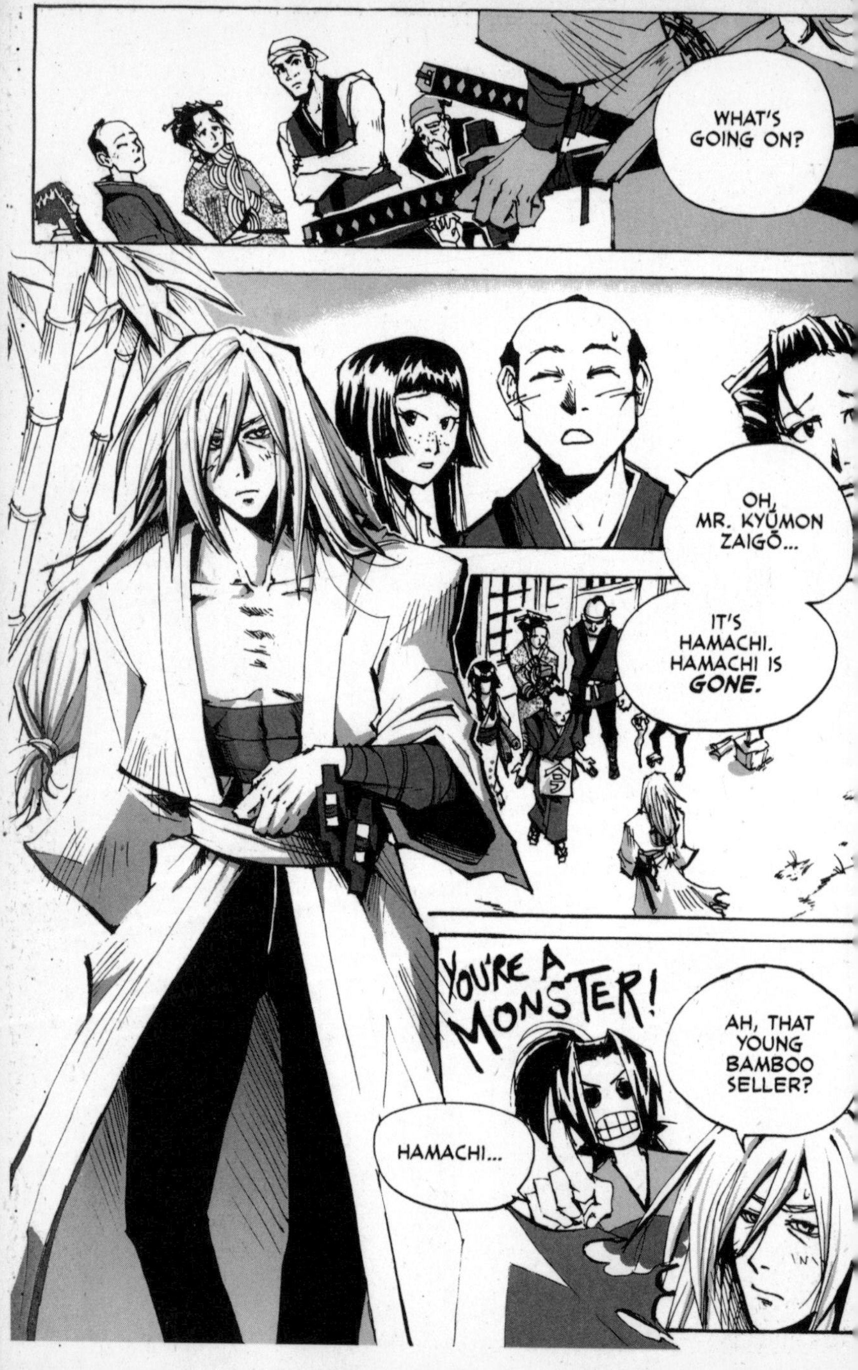
WHAT'S GOING ON?
OH, MR. KYŪMON ZAIGŌ...
IT'S HAMACHI. HAMACHI IS *GONE.*
AH, THAT YOUNG BAMBOO SELLER?
YOU'RE A MONSTER!
HAMACHI...

I WAS PASSING BY HERE, AND I WANTED TO SAY HELLO TO HIS GRANDMOTHER. SO, I LOOKED INSIDE...

...AND FOUND HER DEAD ON THE FLOOR... OH, HOW I'LL MISS HER BOISTEROUS YELLING.

WHAT? WHERE IS THE REST OF HIS FAMILY?

SHE WAS ALL HE HAD...

HE LEFT BEHIND THIS NOTE.

......

To whom it may concern,
I have gone to the yōkai realm to avenge grandma.
Be right back!
Hamachi♡

TWITCH...

これを読む人へ
おばーちゃんを
かいを殺した
妖怪世界へ行き
になりました
もどり
すぐにハマチより

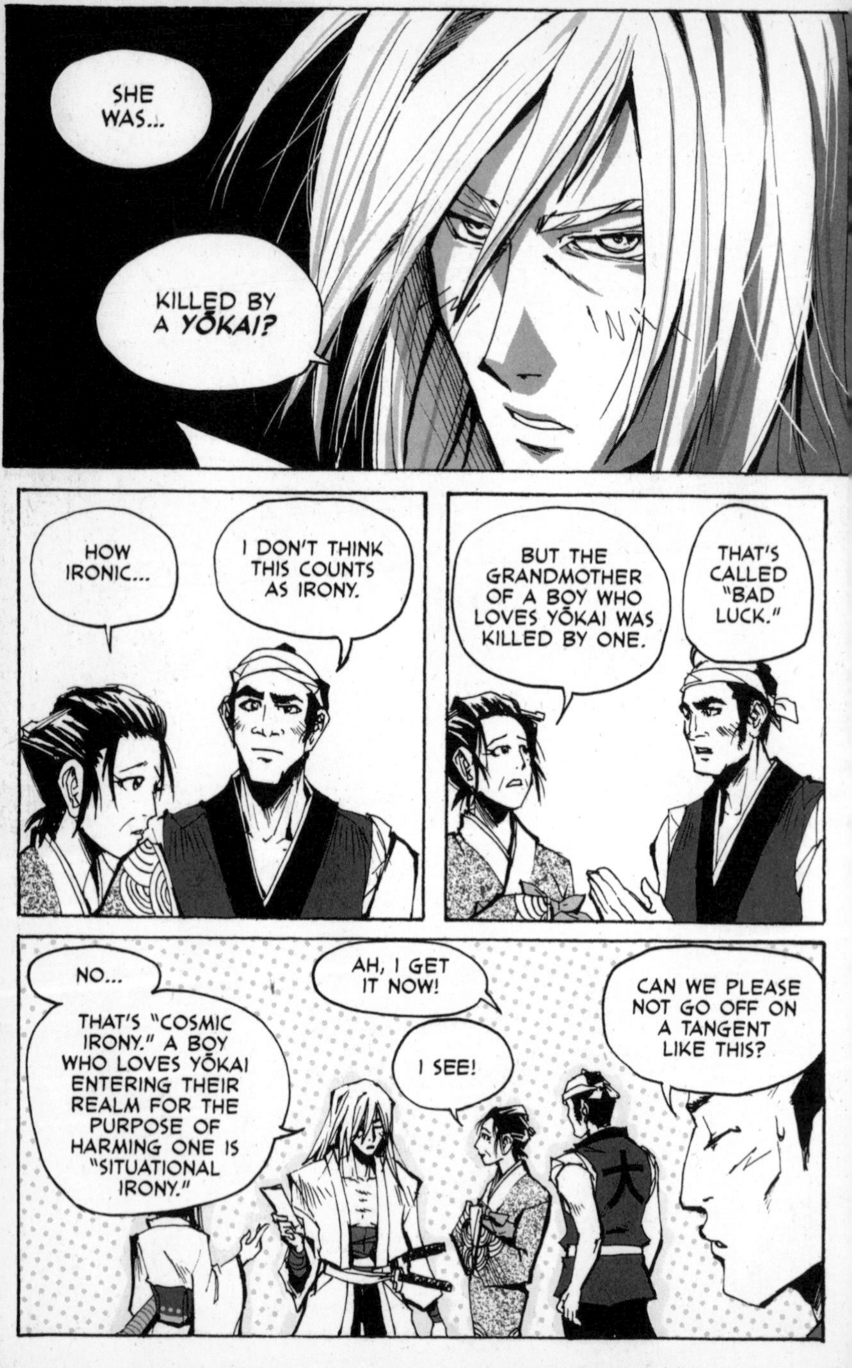
SHE WAS...
KILLED BY A *YŌKAI?*
HOW IRONIC...
I DON'T THINK THIS COUNTS AS IRONY.
BUT THE GRANDMOTHER OF A BOY WHO LOVES YŌKAI WAS KILLED BY ONE.
THAT'S CALLED "BAD LUCK."
NO...
THAT'S "COSMIC IRONY." A BOY WHO LOVES YŌKAI ENTERING THEIR REALM FOR THE PURPOSE OF HARMING ONE IS "SITUATIONAL IRONY."
AH, I GET IT NOW!
I SEE!
CAN WE PLEASE NOT GO OFF ON A TANGENT LIKE THIS?
大

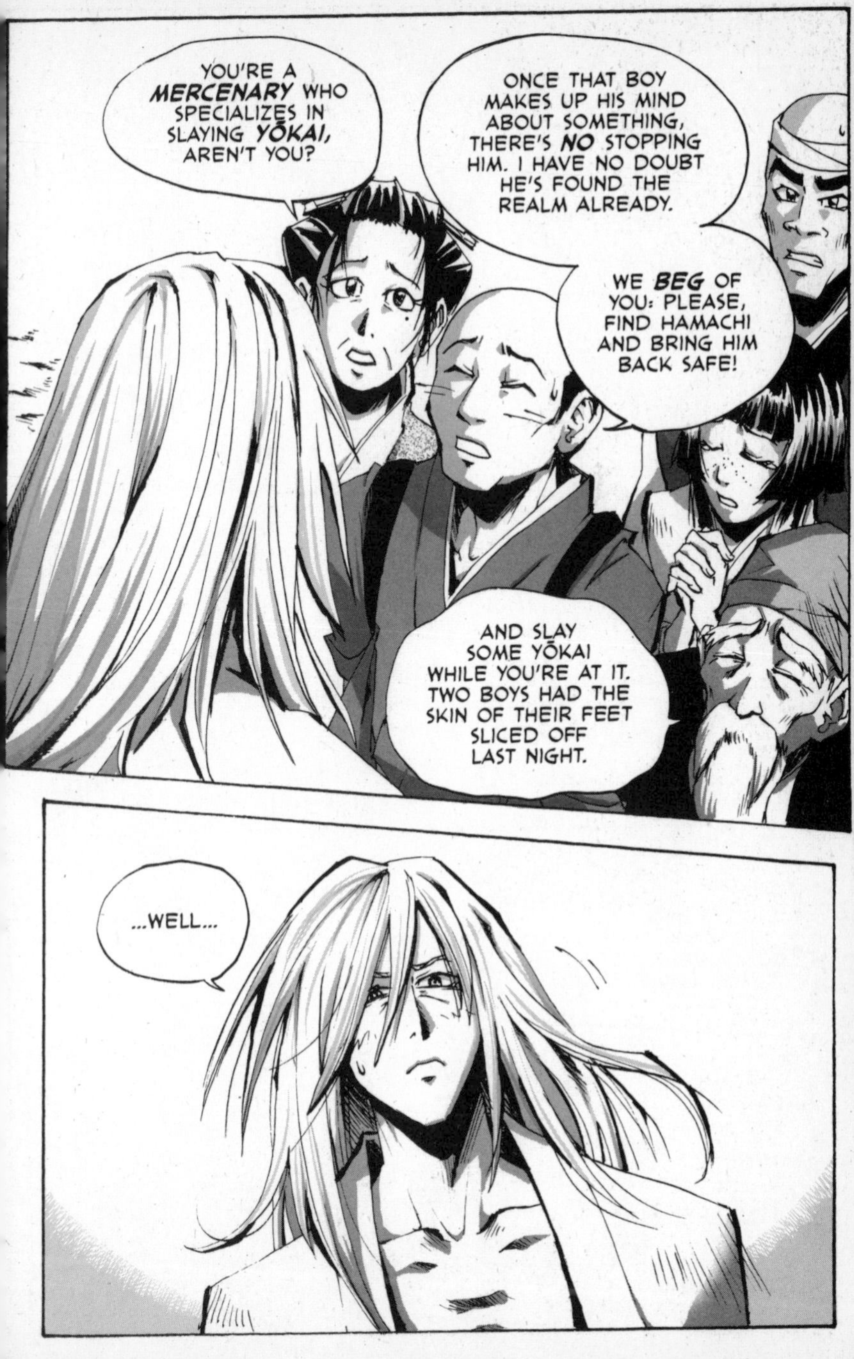
YOU'RE A MERCENARY WHO SPECIALIZES IN SLAYING YŌKAI, AREN'T YOU?
ONCE THAT BOY MAKES UP HIS MIND ABOUT SOMETHING, THERE'S NO STOPPING HIM. I HAVE NO DOUBT HE'S FOUND THE REALM ALREADY.
WE BEG OF YOU: PLEASE, FIND HAMACHI AND BRING HIM BACK SAFE!
AND SLAY SOME YŌKAI WHILE YOU'RE AT IT. TWO BOYS HAD THE SKIN OF THEIR FEET SLICED OFF LAST NIGHT.
...WELL...

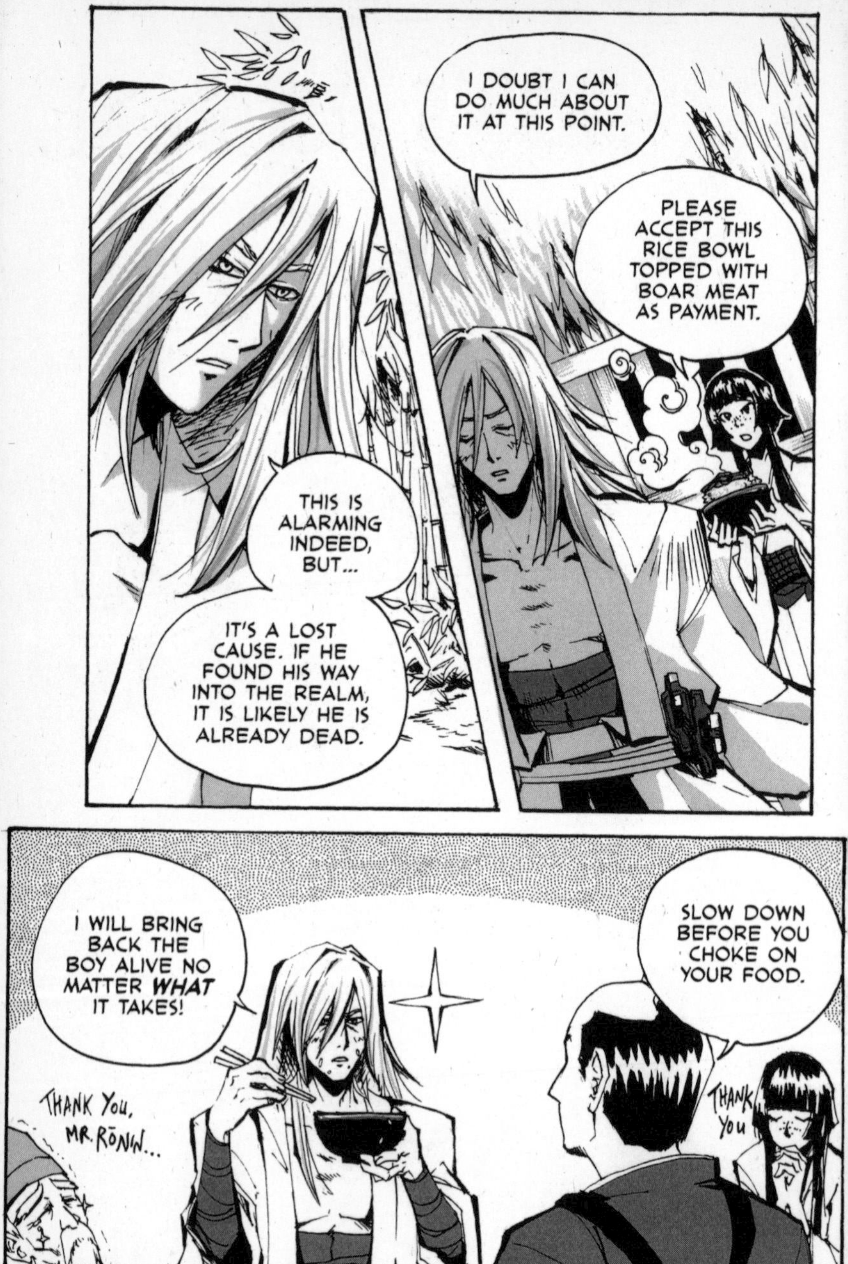
THIS IS ALARMING INDEED, BUT...
IT'S A LOST CAUSE. IF HE FOUND HIS WAY INTO THE REALM, IT IS LIKELY HE IS ALREADY DEAD.
I DOUBT I CAN DO MUCH ABOUT IT AT THIS POINT.
PLEASE ACCEPT THIS RICE BOWL TOPPED WITH BOAR MEAT AS PAYMENT.
I WILL BRING BACK THE BOY ALIVE NO MATTER *WHAT* IT TAKES!
SLOW DOWN BEFORE YOU CHOKE ON YOUR FOOD.
THANK YOU, MR. RŌNIN...
THANK YOU

7th candle - END

To be continued...

HAMACHI'S JOURNAL

Paper Umbrella Ghost
(a.k.a. Karakasa-obaké)

Normal → Weird! → Lumi! →

 "OLD UMBRELLAS WITH ONE BIG EYE, ONE BIG MOUTH, ONE BIG FOOT, AND TWO ARMS. THEY USUALLY HOP AROUND ON THEIR FOOT AND WEAR A WOODEN SANDAL, BUT THE ONE I SAW WAS BAREFOOT AND WALKED ON HIS HANDS!"

"WAIT, WHY AM *I* IN THIS PICTURE? I DON'T WANNA BE GROUPED IN WITH THAT THING. UGH."

"I TOLD YOU I'D DRAW YOU LATER!"

"I-I'M *WEIRD*?"

INTRODUCING the LOCALS OF SHAMOJI VILLAGE

KIMURA (tall) and TATSUTA (short)

Hamachi's fair-weather friends. They pay attention to him whenever they're dying of boredom. Kimura is, in fact, the local bully; Tatsuta befriended him and acts as his "right-hand man" because he fears him. The two are currently recovering from epidermal loss.

MR. IMADA

Owner of Kokonoka, a drinking establishment in the Shamoji Village marketplace. Charmed by Hamachi's passion for yōkai. Self-conscious about his squinty eyes and tries to draw less attention to them by smiling as often as possible.

FRECKLED GIRL

The local tailor's middle child. Very reserved and always busy helping at her family's shop. Self-conscious about her freckles and tries to draw less attention to them by smiling as little as possible.

GOSSIP LADY

Always seen carrying a mysterious box covered by a wrapping cloth. Rumours say the box contains a yōkai that attaches itself to her and compels her to gossip. The truth is there is nothing of significance inside and she started these rumours herself to make herself appear more interesting.

CARPENTER

Notoriously pessimistic. Not very reliable, as he gives up easily. A single wrong measurement or missing hammer when working on a structure is enough to throw his spirit into a pit.

OLD OLD MAN

The oldest man in the village. Admired the youthful energy Hamachi's grandmother always displayed. He would stop by her house nearly every morning to say hello, forgetting every single time that she dislikes people.

Yōkai Bites

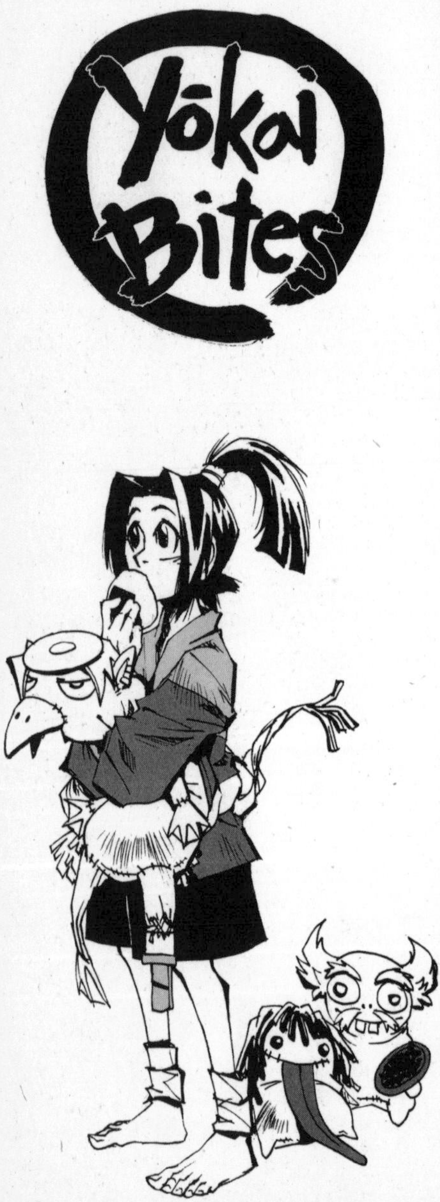

FOOL ME ONCE

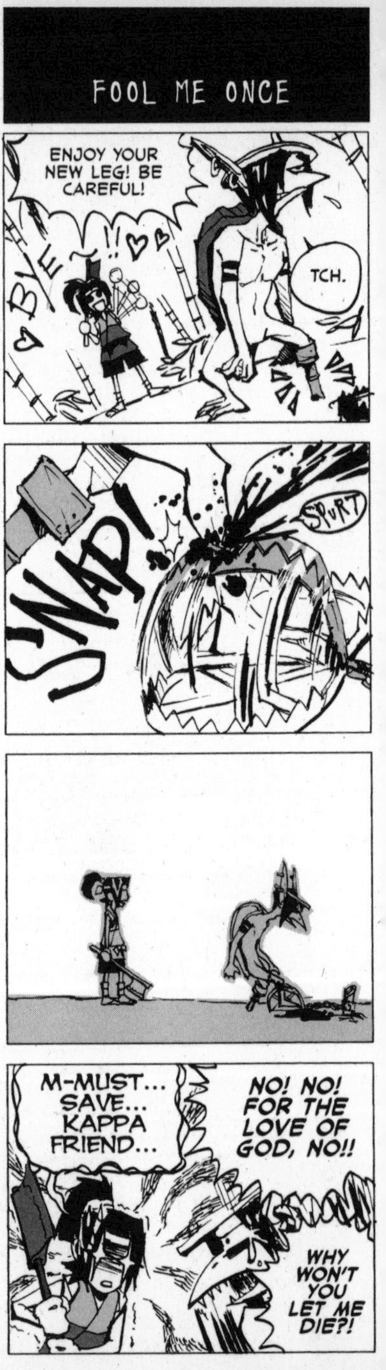
ENJOY YOUR NEW LEG! BE CAREFUL!
BYE~!!
TCH.
SNAP!
SPURT
M-MUST... SAVE... KAPPA FRIEND...
NO! NO! FOR THE LOVE OF GOD, NO!!
WHY WON'T YOU LET ME DIE?!

I SEE

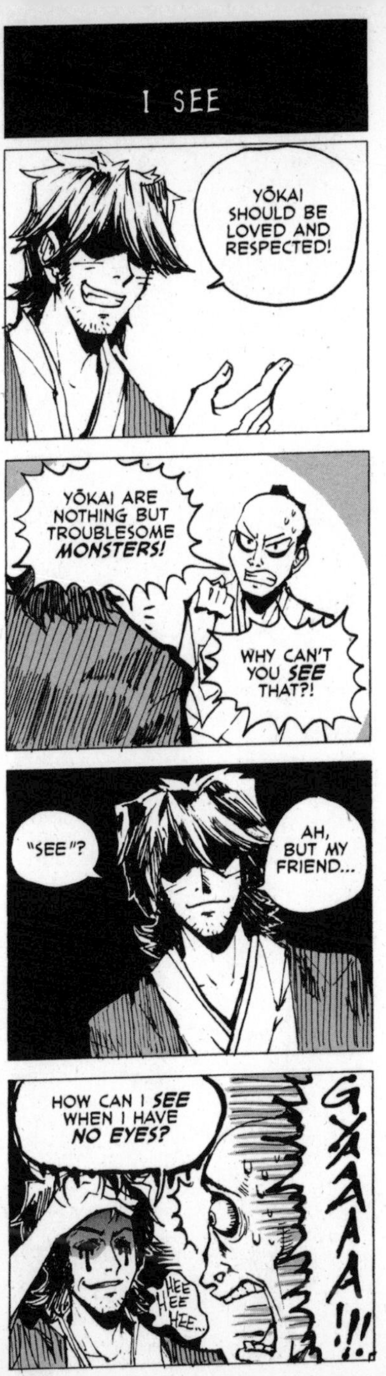
YŌKAI SHOULD BE LOVED AND RESPECTED!
YŌKAI ARE NOTHING BUT TROUBLESOME *MONSTERS!*
WHY CAN'T YOU *SEE* THAT?!
AH, BUT MY FRIEND...
"SEE"?
HOW CAN I *SEE* WHEN I HAVE *NO EYES?*
HEE HEE HEE...
GYAAAA!!!

DISTURBING TRUTH

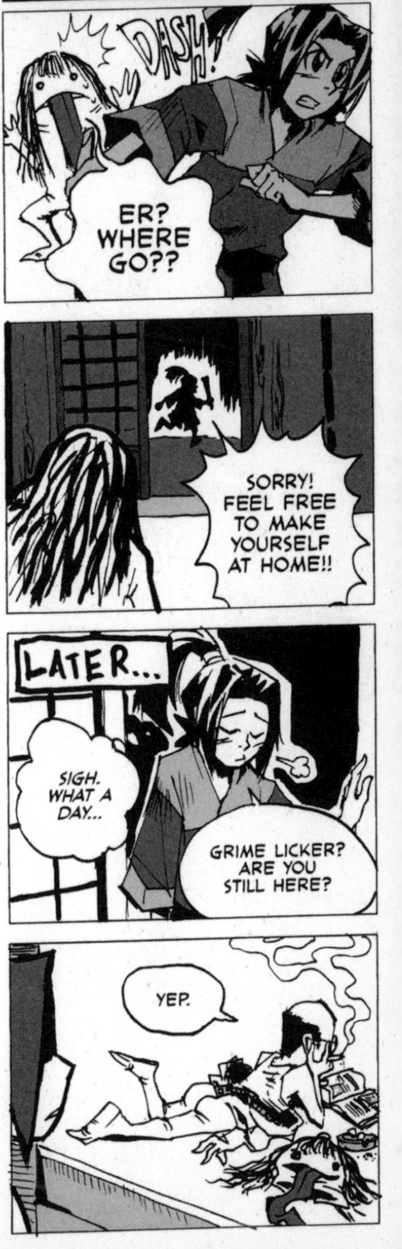
DASH!
ER? WHERE GO??
SORRY! FEEL FREE TO MAKE YOURSELF AT HOME!!
LATER...
SIGH. WHAT A DAY...
GRIME LICKER? ARE YOU STILL HERE?
YEP.

MAGIC TRICK

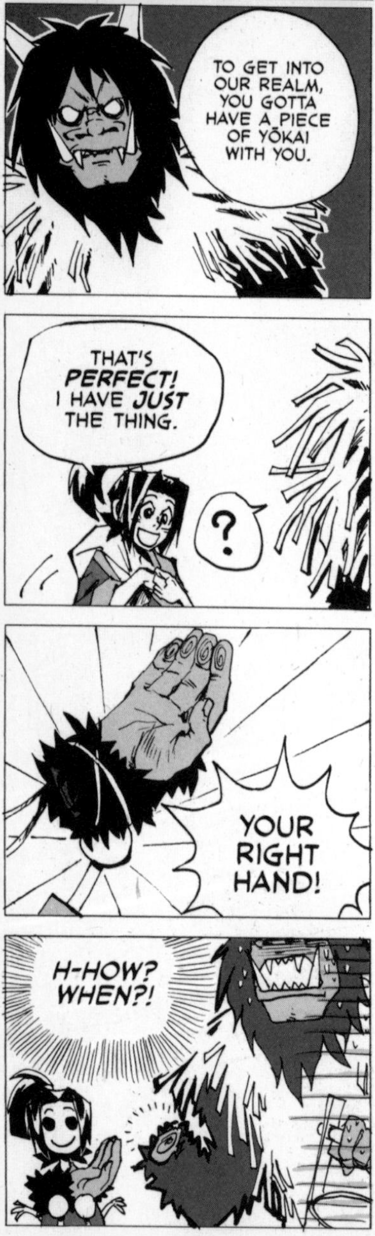
TO GET INTO OUR REALM, YOU GOTTA HAVE A PIECE OF YŌKAI WITH YOU.
THAT'S *PERFECT!* I HAVE *JUST* THE THING.
?
YOUR RIGHT HAND!
H-HOW? WHEN?!

CELEBRITY CHIMERA

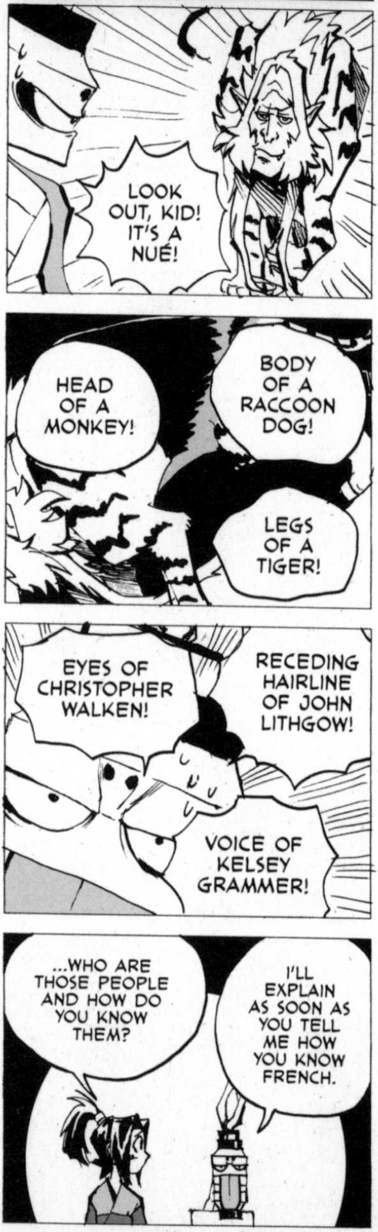
LOOK OUT, KID! IT'S A NUÉ!
HEAD OF A MONKEY!
BODY OF A RACCOON DOG!
LEGS OF A TIGER!
EYES OF CHRISTOPHER WALKEN!
RECEDING HAIRLINE OF JOHN LITHGOW!
VOICE OF KELSEY GRAMMER!
...WHO ARE THOSE PEOPLE AND HOW DO YOU KNOW THEM?
I'LL EXPLAIN AS SOON AS YOU TELL ME HOW YOU KNOW FRENCH.

SIDETRACKED

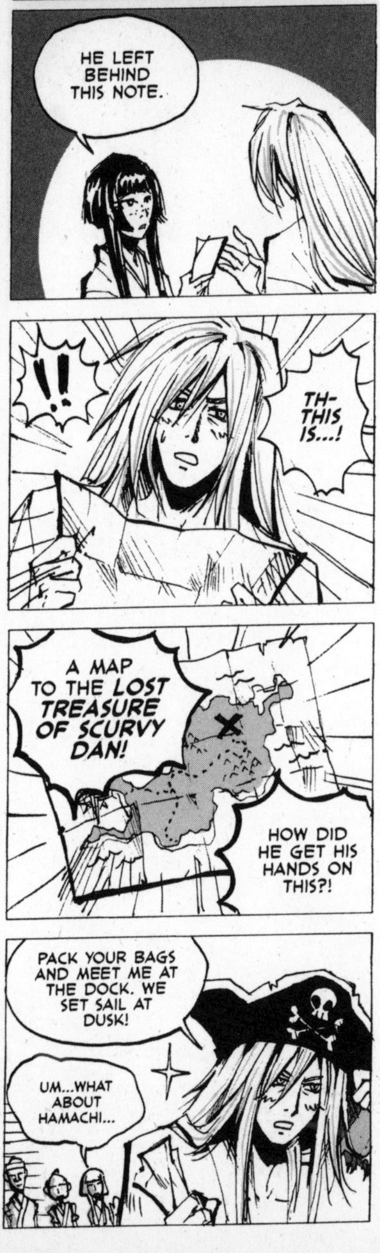
HE LEFT BEHIND THIS NOTE.
!!
TH-THIS IS...!
A MAP TO THE LOST TREASURE OF SCURVY DAN!
HOW DID HE GET HIS HANDS ON THIS?!
PACK YOUR BAGS AND MEET ME AT THE DOCK. WE SET SAIL AT DUSK!
UM...WHAT ABOUT HAMACHI...

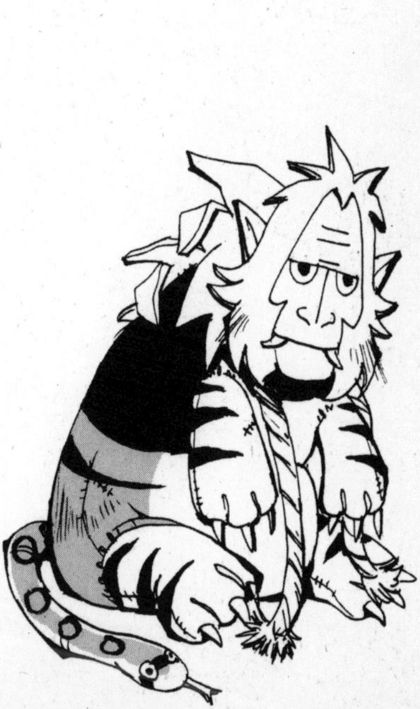

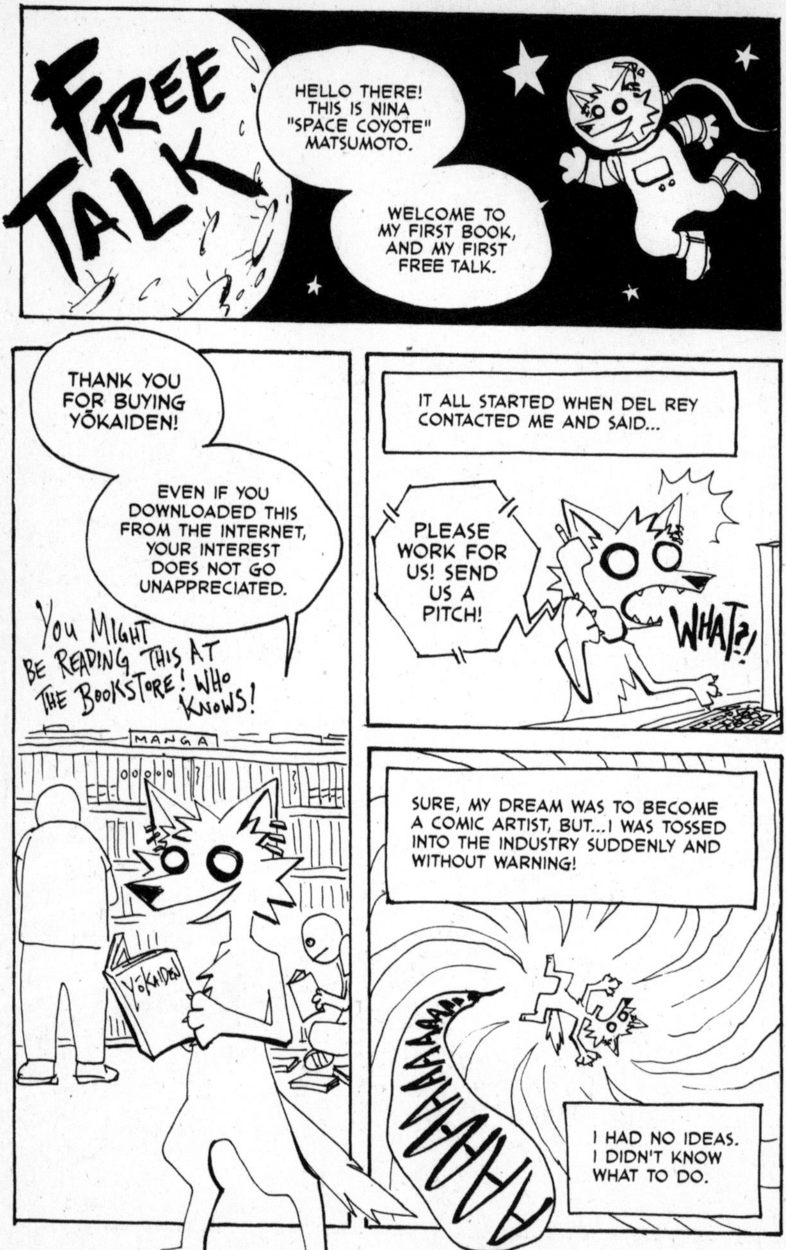
FREE TALK
HELLO THERE! THIS IS NINA "SPACE COYOTE" MATSUMOTO.
WELCOME TO MY FIRST BOOK, AND MY FIRST FREE TALK.
THANK YOU FOR BUYING YŌKAIDEN!
EVEN IF YOU DOWNLOADED THIS FROM THE INTERNET, YOUR INTEREST DOES NOT GO UNAPPRECIATED.
YOU MIGHT BE READING THIS AT THE BOOKSTORE! WHO KNOWS!
MANGA
YŌKAIDEN
IT ALL STARTED WHEN DEL REY CONTACTED ME AND SAID...
PLEASE WORK FOR US! SEND US A PITCH!
WHAT?!
SURE, MY DREAM WAS TO BECOME A COMIC ARTIST, BUT...I WAS TOSSED INTO THE INDUSTRY SUDDENLY AND WITHOUT WARNING!
AAAAAAAAAAAAAAAH
I HAD NO IDEAS. I DIDN'T KNOW WHAT TO DO.

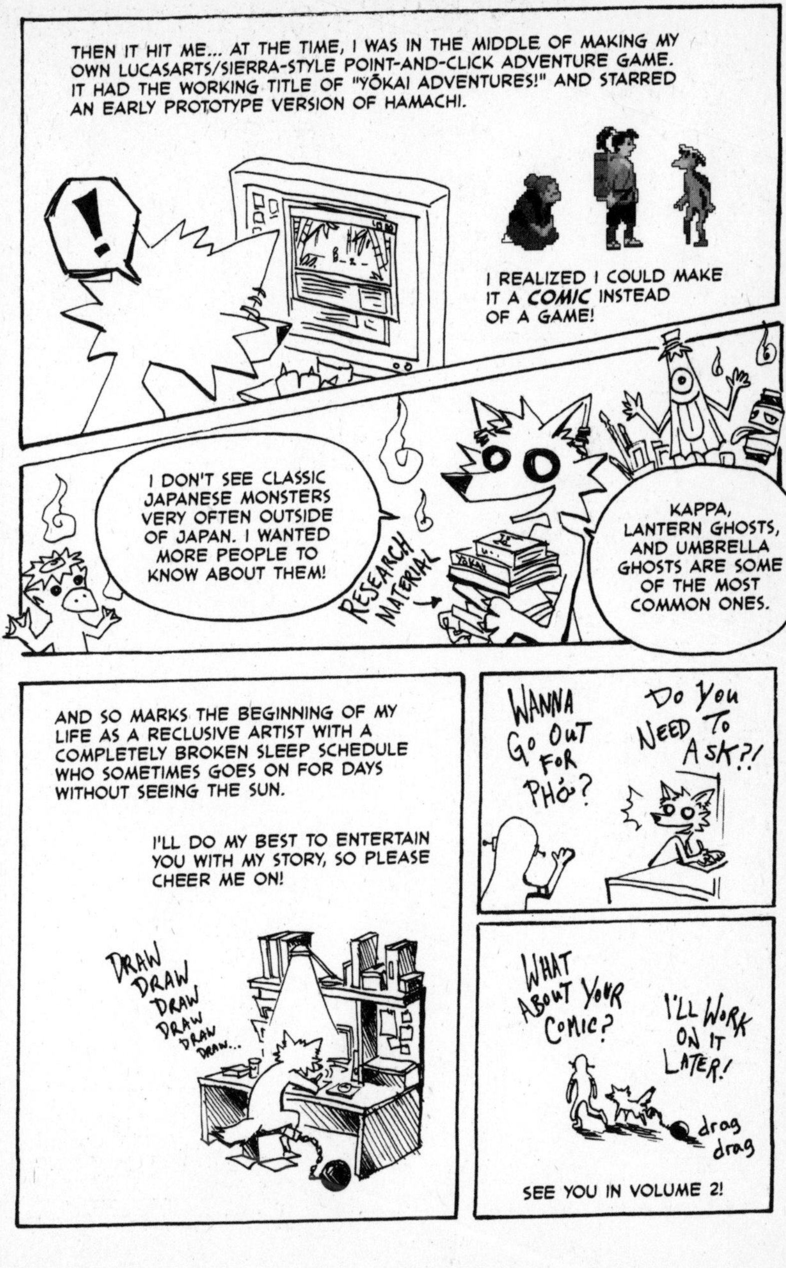
THEN IT HIT ME... AT THE TIME, I WAS IN THE MIDDLE OF MAKING MY OWN LUCASARTS/SIERRA-STYLE POINT-AND-CLICK ADVENTURE GAME. IT HAD THE WORKING TITLE OF "YŌKAI ADVENTURES!" AND STARRED AN EARLY PROTOTYPE VERSION OF HAMACHI.
!
I REALIZED I COULD MAKE IT A *COMIC* INSTEAD OF A GAME!
I DON'T SEE CLASSIC JAPANESE MONSTERS VERY OFTEN OUTSIDE OF JAPAN. I WANTED MORE PEOPLE TO KNOW ABOUT THEM!
RESEARCH MATERIAL
YŌKAI
KAPPA, LANTERN GHOSTS, AND UMBRELLA GHOSTS ARE SOME OF THE MOST COMMON ONES.
AND SO MARKS THE BEGINNING OF MY LIFE AS A RECLUSIVE ARTIST WITH A COMPLETELY BROKEN SLEEP SCHEDULE WHO SOMETIMES GOES ON FOR DAYS WITHOUT SEEING THE SUN.
I'LL DO MY BEST TO ENTERTAIN YOU WITH MY STORY, SO PLEASE CHEER ME ON!
DRAW DRAW DRAW DRAW DRAW DRAW...
WANNA GO OUT FOR PHỞ?
DO YOU NEED TO ASK?!
WHAT ABOUT YOUR COMIC?
I'LL WORK ON IT LATER!
drag drag
SEE YOU IN VOLUME 2!

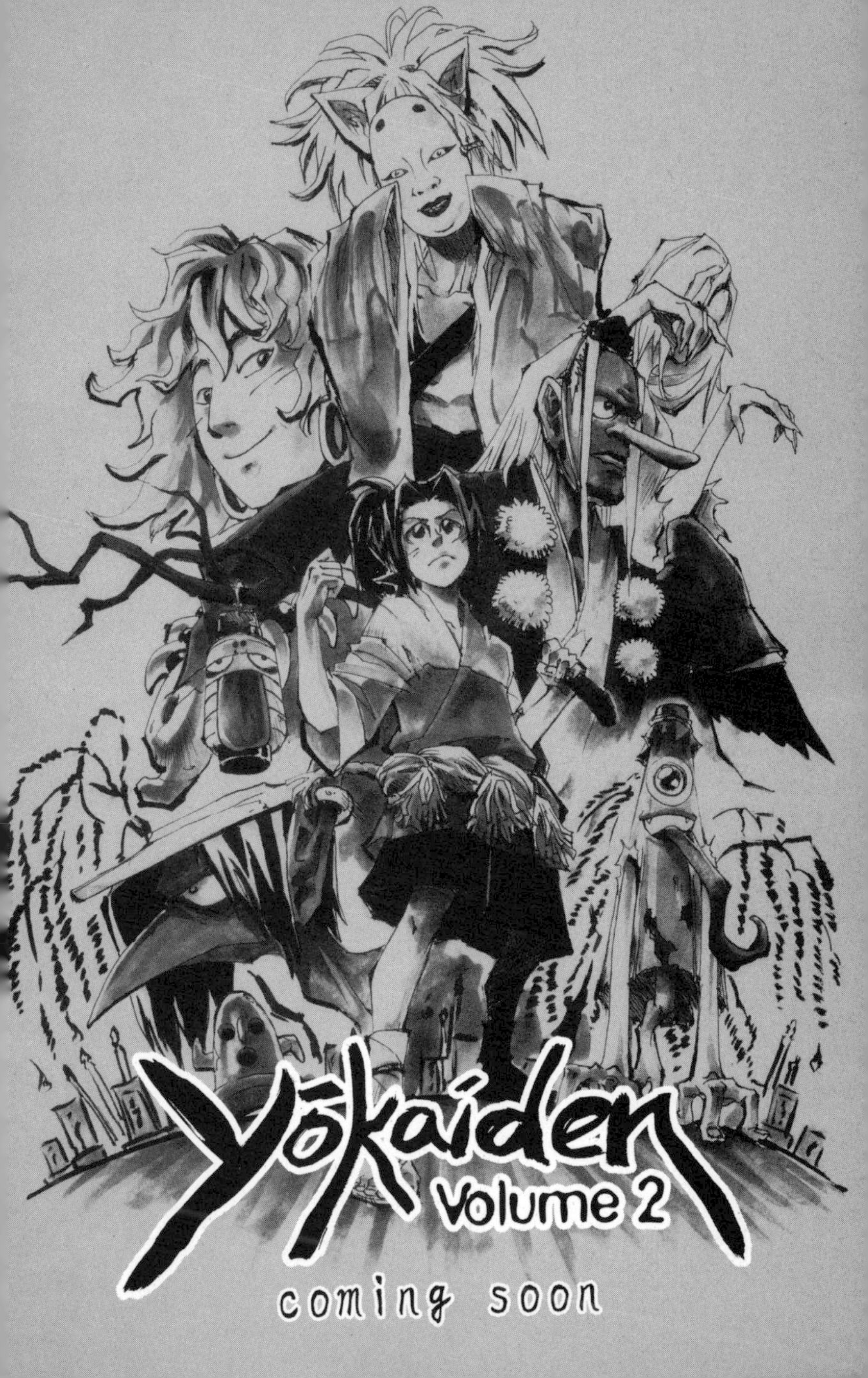
Yōkaiden
Volume 2
coming soon

KASUMI

かすみ

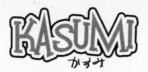

Story by Surt Lim
Art by Hirofumi Sugimoto

A DEL REY MANGA ORIGINAL

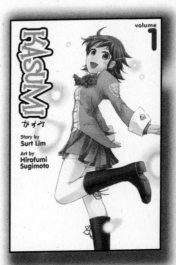

Exploring the woods, young Kasumi encounters an ancient tree god, who bestows upon her the power of invisibility. Together with classmates who have had similar experiences, Kasumi forms the Magic Play Club, dedicated to using their powers for good while avoiding sinister forces that would exploit them.

volume
1
KASUMI
かすみ
Story by
Surt Lim
Art by
Hirofumi
Sugimoto

Special extras in each volume! Read them all!

VISIT WWW.DELREYMANGA.COM TO:

- Read sample pages
- View release date calendars for upcoming volumes
- Sign up for Del Rey's free manga e-newsletter
- Find out the latest about new Del Rey Manga series

RATING T AGES 13+

DEL REY MANGA デルレイ

The Otaku's Choice™

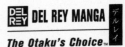

FROM HIRO MASHIMA, CREATOR OF *RAVE MASTER*

FAIRY TAIL

FAIRY TAIL 1
Hiro Mashima Creator of Rave Master

FAIRY TAIL 2
Hiro Mashima Creator of Rave Master

Lucy has always dreamed of joining the Fairy Tail, a club for the most powerful sorcerers in the land. But once she becomes a member, the fun really starts!

Special extras in each volume! Read them all!

VISIT WWW.DELREYMANGA.COM TO:

- Read sample pages
- View release date calendars for upcoming volumes
- Sign up for Del Rey's free manga e-newsletter
- Find out the latest about new Del Rey Manga series

RATING T AGES 13+

DEL REY MANGA デルレイ

The Otaku's Choice™

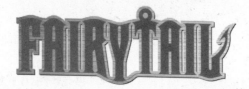

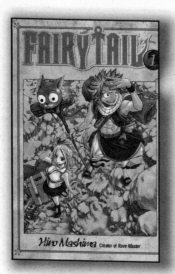

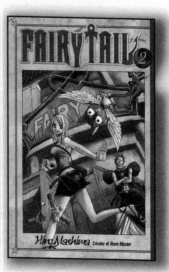

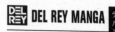

NEGIMA!™

BY KEN AKAMATSU

Negi Springfield is a ten-year-old wizard teaching English at an all-girls Japanese school. He dreams of becoming a master wizard like his legendary father, the Thousand Master. At first his biggest concern was concealing his magic powers, because if he's ever caught using them publicly, he thinks he'll be turned into an ermine! But in a world that gets stranger every day, it turns out that the strangest people of all are Negi's students! From a librarian with a magic book to a centuries-old vampire, from a robot to a ninja, Negi will risk his own life to protect the girls in his care!

Ages: 16+

Special extras in each volume! Read them all!

VISIT WWW.DELREYMANGA.COM TO:
• View release date calendars for upcoming volumes
• Sign up for Del Rey's free manga e-newsletter
• Find out the latest about new Del Rey Manga series

MY HEAVENLY HOCKEY CLUB

BY AI MORINAGA

WHERE THE BOYS ARE!

Hana Suzuki loves only two things in life: eating and sleeping. So when handsome classmate Izumi Oda asks Hana—his major crush—to join the school hockey club, convincing her proves to be a difficult task. True, the Grand Hockey Club is full of boys—and all the boys are super-cute—but, given a choice, Hana prefers a sizzling steak to a hot date. Then Izumi mentions the field trips to fancy resorts. Now Hana can't wait for the first away game, with its promise of delicious food and luxurious linens. Of course there's the getting up early, working hard, and playing well with others. How will Hana survive?

Special extras in each volume! Read them all!

VISIT WWW.DELREYMANGA.COM TO:
• Read sample pages
• View release date calendars for upcoming volumes
• Sign up for Del Rey's free manga e-newsletter
• Find out the latest about new Del Rey Manga series

RATING   AGES T 13+

DEL REY MANGA デルレイ

The Otaku's Choice.™